Hope you enjoy reading my book + the Sa 6 to follow

Follow me on my Thangadlenyk.com

Please Leave comments

Day Dreamer

Thanya Olenyk

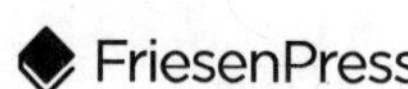

One Printers Way
Altona, MB R0G 0B0
Canada

www.friesenpress.com

First Edition — 2022

ISBN
978-1-03-911692-4 (Hardcover)
978-1-03-911691-7 (Paperback)
978-1-03-911693-1 (eBook)

1. YOUNG ADULT FICTION

Distributed to the trade by The Ingram Book Company

TABLE OF CONTENTS

The Daydream

Today was another summer day; one seemed to flow into the other. I was simply lying on the beach, minding my own business, taking in some rays. The beach was always great for people watching. I like to people watch, and I tend to drift off into my own fantasies a lot, which sometimes gets me into trouble.

Speaking of trouble, as I sat up to look at the marvels of all the nearly naked bodies around me, I caught a glimpse of a magnificent creature coming out of the water. Don't get me wrong, there was more than one on this large beach of half-naked people, but this one took hold of my eyes, which is very hard to do. I am hard on everyone, including myself, being a very opinionated artist. The human body is my toughest subject.

This specimen was a masterpiece; her wet hair must have been blonde, but I couldn't tell what shade, and it was just past her shoulders. I was about thirty feet away and could tell her eyes were beautiful, though I couldn't make out the color, and they were the most predominant feature on her face. I'm just being nice right now, because the hair and the eyes are not what I first saw. This impressive being had curves and the right-sized bumps, if you know what I mean—right where they should be. Remember, I am just speaking from my artistic point of view. Who is kidding who? This woman was everyone's dream, man, *or* woman.

This admiration of a woman is not meant to be demeaning in any way, just the opposite. Perhaps beauty strikes me differently, being an artist, especially in the human-body form. She was coming out of the water ever so slowly, wringing it from her hair. I could see her muscles in her lean, slender arms; she was in great shape, not too muscular, just well-toned. Her bright-orange bikini helped highlight her shape as her tanned, sculpted body emerged from the water. She had an hourglass figure that could be spotted from a mile away, and perfect-sized breasts to go with the small waist and the curves of her hips, like a *Playboy* body. Oh! She had great legs too. To give you an approximation of her measurements, I would have to say 36" by 26" by 38," and perhaps a "C" cup. Now you can put that all together and imagine it for yourselves. Everything flowed very well from top to bottom. If she turned around, I could only imagine that she would have a perfect heart-shaped butt to boot!

I could go on about this incredible being before me, but I'd better get back to the real story at hand. If you haven't guessed already, this was only a daydream to invite you into what lies ahead in this story.

CHAPTER ONE

WOW! It was mindboggling how high school and four years of summer work was over, just like that. It had gone by in what seemed like a blink of an eye. I stopped in the park, took my T-shirt off, and put my legs up on my John Deere tractor. Come on now. I did have a tank on under my T-shirt, though a bra isn't too different from a bikini top, is it?

The girls and I always met up at the park for our breaks and grabbed some rays, weather permitting, of course. I sucked back a large mouthful of Slurpee, which I probably shouldn't have done, as I am prone to getting a head-rush or brain freeze. Two hours to go before Miller time! Today was my last day of work before the first day of college. I'd decided to take a week off before entering the next phase of my life.

No one knew what was in store for me in the near future...

I had been working for the city for the past four years. I'd started working earlier than most, because my mother had worked for the city for about fifteen years, and she'd pulled a few strings to get me in there. I'd started at minimum wage, not even the city's starting wage, as my mother insisted that I learn the value of hard work and money. I had been given whipper-snipper duty for the whole summer, which wouldn't have been my first pick as a job. Watering truck, lawn tractor, or even self-propelled push mower would have been nice. I worked hard and saved most of the money I made, and eventually, bought my Jeep. My parents had agreed to match what

I had to spend on a car when I was ready, and if my grades were good of course. I wanted to have a new car, though nothing fancy, if I could afford one. I was not an "A" student; I was a B or B+ student. If I had gotten better grades, my father would have paid for the entire thing. I was accused of cheating at a young age and had decided to stop studying for tests. I just took them and went with the grade I got. I did my assignments and got 70–80s on tests, and that was good enough. My father was never ecstatic about my grades, but he dealt with them.

The hours seemed long. I started early, at seven a.m., on what was supposed to have been my holidays, which seemed quite harsh, but I was never late, and I never missed a day in four years. After the first summer, I had it easy; I had proved myself. So, for the next three summers, I was given lead in the ride-on lawnmower division. My new role brought a good raise in pay, so I got away from minimum wage.

My life was great. It was easy driving around all day on a John Deere mower, overseeing a crew of about sixteen. Even though my crew worked on the ride-on mowers, sometimes I oversaw the whipper snippers and the push-mower crew. My workday was done at three p.m., and I had all my weekends off and paid long weekends off too. Sweet job, right? I was only sixteen when I was given crew chief, but I'd earned it and proved myself even to the guys on my crew.

A few of my school friends worked with me; they were not my party buds, though on occasions we would go to the pub near the shop. In some ways, they were better than my high school party buds, who were the rich snotty kids in school and were older than me. They pretty much used me for protection because I never took crap from no one. I even got into provoked altercations because of their need to run their mouths off, but I was usually able to talk my way out of the situations. So, really, they were not true friends. My work friends were the closest thing I had to good friends. I was acquaintances with everyone in high school, even the "geeks." I actually stood up for them when my so-called "popular, rich party friends" were putting them down or talking down at them. Thinking back, I'm not sure why I'd tried so hard to be part of their clique. They went to lots of parties, and I thought that was what I wanted to do, but that only lasted for grade nine and ten. I was young and foolish then, even though it was only a few years ago. I had done a lot of growing up since then. They caused me more harm than good. Senior year, I was pretty much a loner but had many so-called friends.

Kelsie and Jenn approached on their mowers. They were already in their tank tops and short shorts; they were always less conservative than me. I was shy and extremely hard on myself, as I had often been told. I tended not to wear short shorts or shirts that showed cleavage.

"Hey, Angel! The guys want to know if we are still on for tonight!" Kelsie said loudly as they approached.

I waited till they parked beside me to give them an answer. "Well, I'm up for it if you ladies are. By the way, where did you run into the guys? Are they on their way here?"

"No! Are you kidding me? When are they ever done as fast as we are? They told us they were behind schedule and couldn't meet us at the park; they will meet us back at the shop," Jenn replied.

Sometimes Jenn spoke about the guys harshly, but she was always right. They did tend to take too many breaks and yap a lot, but if they finished their area by the end of the day, I didn't say much. I was responsible for their productivity, but they knew not to push my buttons too much.

"Well, let's finish and meet at the shop. It's one o'clock, and I have about an hour of work to do. I will see you a little later."

Jenn and Kelsie had about an hour or so left too. I was usually done first, but I had some paperwork to do when I got to the shop. I finished up and headed back, and on my way to the shop, I started thinking about how lucky I was having parents that were paying for my first year of general studies. I had been fairly good with saving my money these past four years, though I did pay for half my car.

I still wasn't sure what I was going to major in. I liked creative writing, but I also liked drawing and painting and other forms of art. My parents were not pressuring me; they would be happy with whatever I chose. My father also said he would pay half for as many years as I needed, *if* I got good grades.

I liked to be creative, but being a "starving artist," as they say, kind of scared me. I'd always liked writing. I'd taken a poetry class, and I quite enjoyed it. I wasn't sure if it was the course as much as it could have been the teacher. Yeah! Mr. Richardson was smoking HOT! Still was—I had seen him not too long ago, and he hadn't changed much. He didn't teach many classes; he spent most his time with the football team as a special-teams coach.

I had many great daydreams about him. He used to be a football player, and let's put it this way: He'd maintained his physique. I don't think he went any further than college ball, but wow! He was offense, not defense, which makes a difference in the physique, of course. You could tell he liked to hit the gym lots. He helped the football coach with the weight-training programs for the team. He must be in his late thirties, but his body said he was in his late twenties. Mr. Richardson had that V-shape every guy dreams of having; some can pull off the top portion, but most cannot pull off the bottom too. Some men work so hard on their upper body and forget about their lower parts, which complete the package, I think. The abs, or should I say, the eight pack, the bottom set of stomach muscles leading to the forbidden zone, were the best muscles. When developed right, just the sight of them sent shivers down my spine and gave me goosebumps.

I had seen him one day in the training room, all sweaty, and that never really escaped my mind. Mr. Richardson was the ideal kind of guy I would like to end up with, but that's only wishful thinking. I was far from being perfect myself, so how could I possibly land me one like that? I had caught a glimpse of his body before at a preseason fundraiser they held for the football team. They had the cheerleaders and the football guys washing cars one weekend, and Mr. Richardson was there helping. He wore a tight white T-shirt, which got soaked, of course, and it came off. I tried not to stare and drool too much, but I could never get that image out of my head either. There was probably a puddle left behind where I was standing.

Don't get me wrong; I like all forms of art—the woman's body can be looked at artistically and taken for what it is too. Women are a little bit different, as art forms. They are more beautiful to look at, and come in all shapes and sizes, which appeal to everyone in different ways. I think like most men do: If they were given the choice or opportunity, they'd usually take the good with the bad. Women and men, in my opinion, should have a tight body, which does not mean they have to be muscular. Toned or healthy is good and toned and a little thicker is good too. I think an hourglass figure is the best shape. We are what we are, though. No one is perfect, and we should make the most of what was given to us.

Back to Mr. Richardson. Every time I saw him after that, I found myself remembering his dripping-wet see-through shirt, and the amazing pecs underneath it. He had the right amount of hair on his chest: not bushy, well-dispersed, and not too dark. A man should have some hair on his chest. Very few can pull off no hair and still look manly unless they are in great shape. Some men should really keep their shirts on, in my opinion.

My record with hot guys was next to none. They wanted ditsy "yes girls." An opinionated, headstrong girl scared the best of them. I also had the tendency to punch guys I liked in the stomach, because I was too shy to strike up a conversation. I'd had a boyfriend, and he broke my heart, but that's a conversation some other time.

Enough reminiscing of the past.

As I approached the shop, I saw that my Jeep had been toilet-papered and shrink-wrapped. I had always wanted a jeep, mostly to ride with no top in the summer, but I had also purchased a hard top for the winter. That was the only way my father would let me get the Jeep.

I stormed into the shop to see who I could catch. I was an hour early, so maybe the culprit or culprits were still lurking around. No one was around, so I went to my boss's office. He was on the computer. I knocked on the door, and he looked up and smiled.

"Hi, Evangeline. I don't know who got your car, but it happened before lunch, because I saw it when I went out."

"That's okay," I replied. "I was expecting something; everything I need to finish up before I leave has been done."

"I know," he said. "I've never had any problems in the three years since I put you in charge of your area. You know, if you want to come back during your college summers, you are more than welcome. Just give me a call, and your job will be there. Just let me know a week in advance. Let your friends know the same."

"Thanks. I will take you up on that for sure, and I'll ask the others if they're interested," I said. "Are you coming tonight?"

"Sure! I'll be there," he said with a big smile.

Kelsie and Jenn walked in with Tom and Jim. They all had smiles on their faces from ear to ear. They threw their arms in the air and said they'd had nothing to do with messing up my Jeep. It was okay; it would come out one day who had done it, and even then, who cared? It was all in the name of fun. It just meant that someone was going to miss me. "It's all good," I said.

Everyone was back and saying they would be at the pub to buy me a farewell drink. I went home to change. When I got home, my parents asked me who was driving tonight. They knew I didn't drink very often, but given the occasion, I might. They wanted to know if I needed a ride later. I reassured them that Tom was the designated driver tonight, and they smiled.

"Just checking," they said together, giving me the "*we know you are responsible*" look. I went upstairs to have a shower, and as I passed the mirror in the hallway, I reflected on my life for a moment. I remembered my short hair and when I'd finally grown it out. Now I actually looked like a girl instead of a boy with added features. It was always hard for me to grow my hair; I was a swimmer, which meant I spent most of my time in chlorinated water, training or competing. Even at the age of fifteen, when I chose to end my swimming career, it took two years for my hair to start growing and be healthy. I quit swimming because I started to have an interest in boys. I started wearing make-up, curling my hair, and wearing dress clothes every day to school.

I'd had a few boyfriends in high school, but I really crushed out on one, my "first love," you could say. Story short, he ended up with my ex best friend. That's probably why I never believed in best friends after that. My record with people being true friends and not using me was not good, so I settled for just having acquaintances. From then on, boyfriends were nothing too serious, as I was afraid to get hurt.

By the time I hit grade twelve, I'd decided I would dress down and relax a bit, having pretty much had it with guys. I looked younger and more natural with less make-up and fewer chemicals in my hair. I was known for being stubborn, rough around the edges, and keeping to myself. As I got older, my patience got a bit better. I was more approachable, though I still had problems talking to those I didn't know. If I knew you well, though, you couldn't shut me up!

Tom was picking me up last. It was my day, so I got to ride shotgun. When they got to my house, Jim got out and jumped into the back. Everyone from work was meeting at the pub beside the shop. The whole group was pretty tight for birthdays and other special occasions. We got along at work, almost like a large family, but we didn't hang out outside of work much.

We got to the bar, called "Jimmy's," which was just a regular little pub with a restaurant on one side. They held special events, like karaoke, comedy showcases, and theme parties for New Year's, Valentine's Day, St. Patrick's Day, Canada Day, Halloween, and others. It was a fairly popular little place, and everyone got along. There was the occasional spat maybe but nothing out of control.

Everyone I had worked with was there, and even some I knew through my mother, and all had come either to congratulate me for moving on to college or just to have an excuse to drink. My boss bought a round for everyone, and the other area supervisors bought rounds too. I decided to have a couple. We were not heavy drinkers. In school, the others were known as nerds or geeks, and I was just me. There were probably those that called me a geek too, or worse, though I wasn't as smart as the other four. Tom and Jim had perfect grade point averages and were going to be doctors of some sort. Jenn had a 95 percent grade point average and was going to be a veterinarian. Kelsie and I had grade point averages around 70 to 80 percent. Kelsie was going to college to be a hairdresser, and I still wasn't sure what I wanted to major in.

I made my way around the pub and thanked those who'd worked under me and made being a department manager easier. It was always easier to stick with the same job for years when everyone you oversaw worked well together and did their job well. I think for the most part everyone liked me as their manager; I treated everyone very well if they did a great job. I let them leave early if they had somewhere important to go, like family events, medical appointments, and such.

I finished my second beer, and Kelsie, Jenn, Tom, and Jim had already finished theirs. Sometimes they got carried away but not often. Drinking and I didn't really go together; I could get out of control when I passed a certain point. I have been told by some that I'm very unpleasant to be around when I overdo it. We decided to call it a night because the following night could be a doozy…

The next night, Saturday, Tom, and Jim drove over, and we picked the girls up at Kelsie's, since they lived practically next door to each other. The work gang had agreed to have one more night together before the "real" work began. I was driving and had convinced everyone to come out with me to Hay City, the most popular bar in the town where I was going to college. I knew it had lots of cowboys; someone I knew had gone there and told me it was a redneck bar but had a great atmosphere, nevertheless. I wanted to see what the nightlife was like in my little college town, though I wasn't planning on seeing much nightlife, as I was supposed to be going to school to increase my knowledge and decide what I wanted to do with the rest of my life.

That was the plan, but it wouldn't really work out that way. College *was* going to change my life forever, but at this point, I'd had no clue how much change that would entail.

The bar was about a half hour north, on Highway 2, in a farming community. It was nine o'clock when we got there, and the parking lot was already more than half full. Tom and Jim were well dressed but kind of preppy. They wore collared short-sleeved shirts and long golf shorts. The bouncers gave them a funny look as they carded them. Kelsie was well-endowed and always used her cleavage to her advantage. This night, she wore a tight, short-sleeved shirt with a tank under it. Most of the time, Kelsie wore what I call "cleavage shirts" or see-through shirts, so by her standards, she was well covered. The bouncers took one look at her blonde hair, blue eyes, and her rack and smiled for her to go ahead. Jenn was a little bit on the heavier side, and so she tended to dress more conservatively in a bar atmosphere. She wore golf shorts and a dressy blouse, open a little with a tank underneath it. They gave her the quick once over and let her in.

I went in last. I wore my usual tight jeans and a T-shirt. I never wore shorts to a bar, or anywhere besides work. I was very hard on myself appearance-wise. I had more of a sporty look: not tiny or petite, but more square-shouldered, with a medium build and muscular structure. I did have an hourglass figure, though, and was always told I had a great ass. That probably had a lot to do with me liking to wear tight jeans, as showing off my best asset, as they say, took the eyes off the rest. I had always played sports, run, and weight trained.

The bouncers looked at me and asked for my ID. I also wore a ponytail, which made me look younger, and I wore very little make-up. We all made it in. Over half the people in there were cowboys, and there were lots of different types of girls eager for their attention. Cowboys seemed to have that effect on most girls—well, especially around here, being a hick college town.

When you first walked in, there were stairs that led up to a second level where you could play pool, while the main bar was to the left and straight ahead. That area was full. They didn't seem like a friendly bunch, although they did look at Kelsie. Surprise, surprise! There was a huge dance floor with another bar on the other side that had a variety of different people, just not cowboys, and it was not as busy on that side, so we headed over there.

On the way, Kelsie and Jenn were asked to dance, but they said to come find them again in a while, after we were settled in and got drinks. Tom and Jim were ahead of us and had grabbed us seats and drinks. Kelsie and Jenn always drank slimes, and I drank Corona with no lime. The guys drank Budweiser or rye and Coke. Just as we sat down, a couple of guys came to grab Kelsie and Jenn. They were rather good dancers; I have rarely ever seen real cowboys dance, but they seemed to know what they were doing. They either knew it and did it well or didn't ever step foot on the dance floor. Cowboys are quite a proud bunch and never like to look bad. The guys asked if it was okay to leave me alone for a bit, as they wanted to go check out the pool tables and see if they could get in on a game.

"Sure," I said. What did I care? The bartender came over and asked me if my friends had abandoned me. I told him I was used to it. It's not that I wasn't sociable, but I may have come across that way because I was shy or liked to keep to myself. I was once told that I show too much self-confidence and tend to scare guys away. I have never been one to accept a drink from a guy or engage in a conversation that began with a cheesy pick-up line. I can't be bothered with crap like that; if you can strike up a good conversation or show some intelligence, I may choose to talk to you, or not. I never went home with anyone, and only ever dated guys I knew through school or who were friends of friends.

They had been gone for at least an hour, and I was already starting on my third drink. The bartender had kept me amused with his stories, but I decided to occupy myself by taking a casual glance around the room without being too obvious that I was checking everyone out. I could see Tom and Jim were still playing pool; they seemed to be having a good time. They had even found a couple girls to share the table with. I looked at the dance floor to find the girls. They weren't there, so I turned my head to find them at a table by the other bar, which had been full when we came in. They were still with the same guys who had taken them to the dance floor, and they were smiling and laughing. Kelsie seemed taken with the guy she was talking to.

In the far left-hand corner, I noticed a group of four guys and a girl who were wearing black clothing and had pale faces. At a quick glance, I would have to say they were goth. I didn't mind gothic followers. They also tended to stick to their own kind. They did stand out in a cowboy bar, though, and I couldn't help but be very curious. We'd had a large group of them in high school, and I had gotten to know a few because we were partnered to do projects from time to time.

I looked towards the goths, thinking I might know someone in the bar after all. I didn't want to stare too much, and they were far away, but I happened to catch a glance of what seemed to be a nice-looking guy. Don't get me wrong, there was more than one good-looking guy in this bar, but when I say nice-looking, I mean hotter than hot. This also meant I shouldn't waste my time, because he wouldn't look twice at someone like me. When I quickly turned around to chance another peek, he was gone; maybe he really wasn't there in the first place. I turned back to the bartender to get another drink and got pushed hard into the bar. I turned around to give someone shit, but it was him.

"I'm really sorry," he said. "I got shoved and fell into you. Can I buy you drink for your inconvenience?" He smiled and my heart melted.

"Watch it!" I shoved him back, giving him the stink eye and quickly turned around. Oh my god! It was the guy! Good thing I'd turned back and hadn't stared into those eyes any longer. I could feel myself drooling. He was hotter than I imagined any male could possibly be. His eyes were crystal blue, his hair was dirty-blond and just to his shoulders, and he had beautiful, luscious lips. He was wearing a long black jacket and black clothing. Oh, but the best thing if all that wasn't enough, was his smell. He smelled sweet, and it made me want to get in close and give his neck a quick sniff … better yet, a nibble, maybe even a small bite. I didn't know where that thought had come from, but I'd had an overwhelming sensation as our eyes briefly met. It had seemed like time stood still, and what may have been a split second had seemed like minutes.

My mystery man probably thought I was a real bitch, but I was afraid he would see right through me, which could have been worse than being a bitch. Why would a girl like me have those intentions with a guy like him? I was so beneath him; he could have just laughed in my face. I didn't even know if I saw what I thought I saw or if I'd made up what I wanted him to look like; I had only turned towards him briefly after all. If my imagination wasn't playing a part in what I had seen, he was ultimately the guy of my dreams and definitely out of my league anyway.

Our split-second touch lingered in my head for the rest of the evening. One o'clock came, and Kelsie and Jenn made their way back to the bar.

"What time is it?" I asked in a daze.

"What's with you?" they asked simultaneously.

"Nothing!" I answered.

"Right, who is kidding who?" said Jenn—she was always so direct. "Looks like you saw a ghost."

"I saw this guy," I told them, "There are no words to explain him. Well, I'm still not sure if he was real or I made him up."

"How many drinks did you have, Angel?" Jenn asked.

"I barely got halfway through my fourth beer." I looked at the bartender as he put up his hands to signal five beer and two shots. "Oh, I'm on my fifth beer, apparently. I had my first three beers and a few shots probably in the first two hours, and I don't think I really finished the fourth. It got warm, and I asked for another. I have been all wrapped up and consumed by my emotions. See how confused this crystal-blue-eyed man has made me?"

"He must have been something," Kelsie said.

"Let's go," I insisted.

"Are you okay to drive?" asked Kelsie.

"Probably not." I replied.

We went towards the pool tables and grabbed the guys. I nudged Tom as I walked by and snuck my keys into his hand, signifying that I shouldn't be driving.

"Are you good to drive?" I asked.

"Yes, I was too busy playing pool and chatting up the ladies to actually drink. I may have finished two, so I am good." Tom smiled.

We stopped at 7-Eleven and got Slurpee's and snacks for the ride home. Tom dropped the girls off at Kelsie's house, and I don't even remember the drive from Kelsie's to my house, which was approximately three blocks. Good thing I didn't drive. I thanked Tom for driving us back and thanked them both for coming out. The guys left and all I thought about for the next hour was my mystery guy. I had a shower, put on my pajamas, brushed my hair, and got into bed without remembering doing so. I don't think my lapse in time had anything to do with my drinking; I think I was simply dazed by the incredible guy I might have imagined. But he seemed very real. I don't know when I fell asleep, but I replayed the encounter over and over as I slept.

I woke up smiling ear to ear. My mother asked how my evening went, and I told her there wasn't much to tell, that I didn't remember most of it.

"Did you drink and drive?"

"No, I gave my keys to Tom, and he drove back." I didn't want to explain my mystery guy, especially when he could have been a figment of my imagination. I was supposed to go have a late breakfast or brunch with the girls, so I called them and moved it to a lunch date and went back to bed till ten. I really didn't sleep. I kept thinking of him.

I picked the girls up at noon, and we went to the food court at the mall. I had to do some school shopping for books, pens, markers, and stuff. I also wanted a couple pairs of jeans, colored tees, new runners, a ball cap, a watch, and a new fall jacket. The girls picked up similar items.

The shopping trip took most of the afternoon, and when we got to my house, we found out we were having a BBQ, so the girls stayed over for dinner. My mother and father tried to get information about the night before, but we were all quiet. I drove the girl's home after we ate, and I told them we should hang at Jen's in the pool tomorrow. I decided to dodge my parents and just go upstairs to my room.

The next morning, Monday, there was no dodging my mother. I knew as soon as our eyes met that I would be done for. "It's nothing," I told her. "I saw this guy, I think. I'm not sure if he was real, but if he was, he is the hottest thing since sliced bread."

"Sliced bread, eh! Did he smell good too?" She giggled.

"Well, as a matter a fact, if he was real, he smelled good enough to eat, or at least lick up and down. Sorry, that shouldn't have come out that way." I quickly caught myself.

"Well, if some young man got that much of your undivided attention, I guess he must be something. I would like to have a glance at him myself." She winked at me.

"I haven't been able to get my mind away from the image I saw. I was rude to him. He apologized for bumping into me, and I freaked out and shoved him back and turned around as quick as I could. I really hope I didn't imagine him and that I can see him again to apologize for my rude behavior," I said, kind of freaking out.

"Well," my mother replied, "why don't you go back to the bar and see if he is there next weekend? If he is, let him know you are sorry for your behavior during your last run-in. Then you can kill two birds with one stone, face to face, apologizing *and* seeing if he really is all that."

"Nice, Mom." I smirked. "I don't think I can even look at him, let alone apologize without breaking down or freaking out, or whatever that was."

"It can't hurt to go and try, right?"

"Yeah, yeah. I will talk to the girls," I mumbled as I left the room.

I decided to call Kelsie to ask if we were still on for lounging by the pool, and she told me she would be right home after work and to come over whenever. So, I had time to waste, as it was only one p.m. I should have gone to work for a few more days instead of taking a whole week off; it never took me that long to get ready for anything.

At three, the girls were off work. I left right away, as I needed to get everything out and clear my mind. Maybe I could deal with the situation and get on with my life (So dramatic, right?) if I talked through my thoughts with the girls. I hadn't been sleeping. I had just been thinking ever since I saw him. When I got to Kelsie's, Jenn was already there, and drinks and snacks were already served.

Kelsie smiled. "I figured you had to do some serious talking; I could sense it in your voice. So different, you needing to have us help you; it's always the other way around, isn't it?"

I agreed, then started talking about the mystery guy and how confused I was about it all. Then I told them what my mother had said and that I needed to find a way to deal with my emotions about him.

"I'll go with you Friday night," Kelsie said, "and if you can't approach him, I will talk to him for you."

We dropped the subject then and talked about things we still had to do before next weekend and the things we were dreading and looking forward to.

I went home for supper and my mom and dad didn't bring up the subject, which made me very happy. My mom must have told my dad what was going on.

The week was full of running around for final things I needed for school, and I got all my papers in order and started planning a grocery list and a menu plan. As I said, I am well-organized and studious. I organized all my binders and notebooks, and I made sure I re-checked the list of items suggested for each class and color-coded everything to make it easier to keep each subject organized. I'm a little OCD when it comes to everything being in order and having its rightful place. I'm the type of person whose cupboards should contain all the same products aligned and in the same row. Even glasses should be laid out the same, based on size, type, and so on. Items that are by themselves all get put off to the side, together, like baking goods or special sauces. Things you need on occasion but don't use often tend to wreck the pattern and cleanliness of the rest of the cupboard. I'm a little obsessed, I know. I have heard that once or twice before. My mom deals with my excessiveness well. She likes things well organized, but not to my extent. I can just imagine how crazy organized my own house will be when I get one.

Chapter Two

I talked to the girls a few times this past week, but that was it. When they worked, they didn't get out much, plus they had their own things to get ready before they started their courses. Friday came fast, and all day my heart was pounding, anticipating the night at the bar. I'd thought about my mystery guy all week. What would I say? Why was I so wrapped up with the entire situation? Should I ask Kelsie to talk to him? Did he even really exist or was I going crazy?

I got ready early and tried to relax on my bed, which didn't work, as I ended up still thinking about him. The phone rang, startling me. It was Kelsie. She told me she would drive, because I might need a few drinks to be able to talk to my mystery guy if he showed or was even real. Kelsie showed up at nine o'clock, and my girl actually wore a regular T-shirt and jeans, with no cleavage. I also wore a T-shirt and jeans. Even though I might find my mystery guy, I still wanted to be me, which meant very casual.

We got to the bar just before ten o'clock, and the parking lot was full already. Kelsie parked in the parking lot across the street, and when we walked in, the bouncers looked at her—they must have remembered her—and smiled. As we entered, we got some stares. There were a lot of cowboys and girls everywhere, and it seemed to be quite busy, even though we were there a bit earlier than the previous weekend. Perhaps everyone was planning on letting loose this weekend before concentrating on school next week. Ha ha! How many people buckle down with the studying right from the start? Or at all, for that matter, in the first months of college, right? Only the geeks like me went to school to study.

The place was packed, and we decided to go to the second bar, where we had gone the weekend before. It took about ten minutes to get to that section of the bar, and the first thing we did was get drinks. I got the usual, a Corona, and Kelsie decided to get a Budweiser, which was very unusual for her. It was hard to make out everyone standing around the bar like packed sardines. Kelsie suggested that we walk around, moving to where I had seen the mystery guy the previous weekend.

There were goths there. As we got closer, I could see his hair and the side of his face. I looked at Kelsie and said, "He's here." My heart started to pound so hard that I thought it would jump from my chest. I stopped breathing momentarily.

"Breathe." Kelsie hit my back pretty hard. "He's just a guy. If he accepts your apology great, if not, who cares?" She shook her head at me. "It all will work itself out, so relax." She tried to be understanding.

"Thanks, man, but I don't think I can do this, never mind getting even one inch closer to him." I was shaking.

"I'm going to grab you some more liquid courage." Kelsie smiled. "You just make sure your mystery guy doesn't go anywhere, okay?"

She returned with two sambuca shooters and another Corona to chase them with. She knew from my younger drinking days that I could only do sambuca shots if I chased each shot with half a beer. The only problem with that liquid courage is that it had sometimes led me to fighting. I haven't mentioned that yet here because it's not something I am proud of. I had a tendency in my early teens to occasionally get into disagreements, to put it lightly. Anyway, the shots with the chaser went down well. About five minutes later, I was feeling a buzz. I decided to walk up to him and apologize for being ignorant to him the last time we'd run into each other.

When I approached him, it was obvious he didn't recognize me or remember the previous encounter, but why would he? My mystery guy was even more beautiful than I had remembered. I paused and looked back at Kelsie, and she signaled me to go ahead, mouthing the word "*WOW!*" So, I proceeded towards where he was engaged in conversation with a guy and two girls.

When he seemed to take a brief pause in the conversation, I said, "Hi, I know you probably don't remember me, but I—"

"Yeah!" he said, interrupting me. "You're the girl I fell into last weekend. I am deeply sorry; you didn't seem to believe me when I apologized." He was very soft spoken.

I froze and didn't know what to say. I needed to get back to the original reason I had come to the bar. I wanted to tell him that I did believe him and that I really wasn't a bitch. "I just wanted to say that I'm sorry about not accepting your nice apology and pushing you back. It was extremely rude of me, and I don't normally behave that way. I hope you can except my apology. I'm not usually that inconsiderate. I just wanted to let you know that I felt bad about my behavior." I was shaking.

"Why are you apologizing? It's often a natural reaction to push back when pushed. There's no need. I was the one in the wrong. I do not think badly of you in any way." As my mystery man spoke, he gently touched my arm, and look me in the eyes with genuine sincerity.

I was nervous and had nothing to say, or at least, nothing would come out of my mouth, so I smiled at him and turned around to walk away.

"Hey! Are we good?" he asked, grabbing my hand gently.

"Sure," I said, turning to look at him again. "Everything is good!" I walked away then and didn't look back. I grabbed Kelsie as I walked past her, signaling to her that it was time to go.

She handed me a drink. "Hey! It looked like the discussion went okay! There was even a little bit of contact, and you don't even know each other's names. Just so we are clear, and you are clear, this guy is hotter than hot. I would even go as far as give him an eleven out of ten. I think there is some sort of connection between the two of you. I just can't put my finger on it."

"My mystery man is hot; I *knew* I hadn't imagined what I had seen. I was trembling the entire time I stood in front of him. When he touched me, I felt something, maybe a sense of energy. I couldn't sort through anything I was feeling, especially when he was touching me." I was dazed.

"Do you want another drink before we go?" Kelsie handed me another with a smile.

It was about midnight when we left. I hadn't had the opportunity to run into the mystery guy again, but I'd always had my eye on him, and when he was out of sight, I would make sure to discreetly find him again. Oh, how I wanted so bad to be the one he was talking to. Instead, he was always surrounded by beautiful girls. I didn't know why I was feeling jealous and even angry; this was only the second time I'd run into him. I didn't know if I even existed to him, as I definitely wasn't as pretty as the girls he was hanging with.

The discussion on the ride home was next to nil. Kelsie did ask if I intended to find out where my feelings lay, if given the chance to see him again. She knew quite a bit about my past and that I was not trusting when it came to guys. At this point, I was in awe; there was something there—something weird and very different. I'd felt something when he touched my arm, but when he'd grabbed my hand, it was tenfold. I remembered too that his hand was quite cold. And his smell … he smelled so good, almost exotic.

I replied, "Kelsie, I don't know his name. I don't know if he lives in town, if he goes to school, or if he is even around my age. I can't allow myself to have feelings about someone I may never see again."

"Angel, just because you had a traumatic experience once, that doesn't mean you should never allow yourself to move forward from that experience and perhaps pursue the feeling you have for this individual. Keep an open mind—maybe you'll see him again, maybe sooner than you think, and if not, then there are others." She leaned over from the driver's seat and gave me a comforting hug.

She dropped me off, and I told her to call me when she got up. I was moving to my dorm tomorrow, and Kelsie, Jenn, and the guys, Tom, and Jim, were going to help me. They didn't start school till mid-week, so they had plenty of time to help me, as their families were going to help them, and my parents had to work.

Morning took forever to come; I couldn't fall asleep. Surprise, surprise! I may have gotten two hours … maybe. I thought of the mystery man dressed in black. His eyes were a cobalt blue, so bright that they had to be contacts. The locks of long, dirty-blond hair looked so soft, healthy, and chemical free. I wanted to run my fingers through it. I would guess he was about 5'10" and 185 pounds. The weight was hard to measure though, as he was covered from head to toe in black, with a black overcoat to top it all off. He had full, luscious lips, probably soft and sweet to kiss. I wondered if he was muscular, and well proportioned—you know, the ideal guy I'd always dreamed about who was nonexistent. I don't know how someone's physical appearance deserved to be judged by the likes of me anyway though. I was most definitely not perfect by any means.

I lay in bed till Kelsie called, which was around ten a.m. We agreed we would use all the vehicles in our group to help me move and that we would meet at noon at my house. She would spread the word. I was staying at the college. They arrived on time, and I had made cream of mushroom soup and grilled ham and cheese sandwiches. After lunch, we filled all the cars with my stuff. I had a 30" TV and a ghetto blaster, my free weights, my step-up blocks, my recumbent bike, and my treadmill. We put the big stuff in Jim's truck and the rest wherever if fit. I had decided to have my dad pick me up a small deep freeze, about two cubic feet, a few weeks earlier. I thought it could come in handy. I had about six boxes of clothes, one box of toiletries, and two heavy kitchen boxes with pots and pans, dishes, and cups/glasses and utensils.

We were done loading the vehicles in about an hour and were off to my new residence. It took roughly thirty-five minutes to get to the dorms. It took less time to unload the stuff; we just dropped everything in the living room. I'd have time that night or the next to place things where I wanted them. One of my roommates had arrived before me: the lady with the large room beside mine. I introduced myself and my friends to her. Her name was Amy, and she told me she had moved here from China about a year ago and had done one semester and that her friend would be there later to have supper, if that was alright. I told her to do as she pleased. She spoke great English for just having moved here.

My friends and I decided to look around the college. By this time, it was three in the afternoon, and we figured there was probably no one around anyway. I had a map. It was about a five-minute hike across the field to get to the main entrance. We entered through the main corridor and the cafeteria was straight ahead. There were a few people in it, but nothing interesting seemed to be happening. There was loud noise and screaming coming from beside the cafeteria, and it sounded like an indoor pool party, so we decided to go check it out. Down the hall there were two large doors, which seemed to be where the noise was coming from. It was a gymnasium, and there was a girls' basketball game going on.

"Hey, let's go watch for a bit." Tom smiled.

"Yeah! There are a couple hot chicks, or they look good from here anyway. Let's get a closer look." Jim's tongue was dragging on the ground as he spoke.

Kelsie and Jenn both commented at the same time. "Typical guys, with one thing on their brains."

I gave in. "Let's go in, but only for a few minutes, and then we need to get back to the dorms."

My parents were going to take us out for a steak dinner, and they were treating my friends as well because they'd helped me move when they couldn't be there. I had great parents. Everyone in town knew them; they were the kind of parents who had block parties and BBQs, even though they weren't heavy drinkers themselves. They always gave thanks to those who helped them out.

Dinner was great. We all had steak except my mother, as she tended to eat more chicken than red meat—a digestive problem, I think. The dessert was cheesecake, and we all indulged in some. I tend not to eat that kind of stuff, and Kelsie watches that figure of hers. After supper, my father decided we should have a drink to toast the new beginning in our lives. He ordered Irish coffees for all of us!

My parents dropped us off at the dorms and everyone left. It was late, and they were tired and full. It was only eight thirty, but they had a bit of a drive, and the guys had had a late night the night before.

My parents sighed. "We'll be back around ten to help you organize things and go grocery shopping."

We were all a little teary-eyed as they each gave me a hug. "Let's stop this," I said. "It's not like I'm going out of the country to school. I'm just around the corner, and you'll probably be seeing me just as much as before. Okay, maybe a little less."

We all wiped our eyes and agreed that it was a little silly. My parents left, and I started to put things away. Kelsie was going to also stop by, after she finished her last-minute shopping with her mom, and maybe stay the night. She was not starting till Tuesday, but she was going to be staying with her aunt. Her hairdressing course was at community college fifteen minutes from me, and only four days a week, and she was planning on going home on weekends or coming to stay with me sometimes. I would have to see how my roommates were with that idea first.

Jenn and the guys were leaving first thing Tuesday morning. They started university on Wednesday, whereas I started Monday. They had small U-Haul trailers to move with, and they had a longer distance to go. Their school was about an hour in the opposite direction from Kelsie and me.

When I got to my dorm, my other two roommates were in the kitchen with Amy and her friend. Amy introduced me to Wesley, her boyfriend's best friend, and her protector, I think. My other two roommates were Kim and Karen, and they were both art majors, one a first year like me and the other a second year. Amy, whose room was beside mine, was a science major, and I thought she and I would get along well. The others seemed nice and quiet, and everyone seemed to be okay with the divided areas we came up with. I tended to keep to myself anyways, so I figured all should be well.

I didn't stay in the kitchen for too long. I wanted to get some stuff unpacked before I went to sleep and clear my room enough to be able to do so. I put the towels away, hung up my clothes, put my socks and underwear in baskets, and placed them in the closet on two shelves. Then I went downstairs to put my toiletries in my bathroom. I had hoped that no one else wanted to use that bathroom, but that would have to be a discussion for another day. I went back upstairs to bed.

I had a pretty good sleep; the mattress was comfortable. I have never been one to get homesick, and I knew my parents were just a call away. It was about eight when I woke-up, and I went downstairs to shower and get ready. My mother would be here at about ten, and Kelsie said she would be here probably after lunch sometime, depending on how her own shopping went. When my mother arrived, I was ready and had put almost all my kitchen stuff away. My roommates had already divided the cupboards up and put names on them. I wasn't worried about not being involved; I had done enough of ruling the roost in high school, and I wanted college to be a new start, involving peace and quiet if possible. So, until (or unless) I stopped feeling okay with the decisions being made, I was willing to go with the flow. We all had three large cupboards and one smaller one, and a drawer for our utensils. I found everything in the house was well designed to accommodate four individuals.

I gave my mother a tour of the townhouse. My father hadn't come, as he'd had been called into the office. He worked for a small oil company as an accountant and financial advisor and sometimes had emergencies to tend to, they were trying to expand, double their size int the next year. It was okay. We were just going grocery shopping anyway. Kelsie got there at twelve thirty, and we decided to grab some lunch before heading to the grocery store. We went to Dairy Queen for a burger and a Blizzard.

I like to grocery shop. I hate any other kind of shopping unless it's for stationery of some sort. At the grocery store, my mother asked me what I wanted, and I said I wanted healthy food.

"Do you not want any junk food? Granola bars, maybe?" asked Kelsie.

"No, I intend on working out and getting into the best shape I can. I want this to be a total new start." I smiled convincingly.

When we got back to the dorms, we put the groceries away and filled my deep freeze; I also let my roommates know they could use the deep freeze. I needed it for veggies, bread, and a little meat, so there was plenty of room for other stuff. My mother made a batch of vegetable and chicken soup and left around three o'clock. Kelsie decided not to stay the night, saying that I needed some time to settle in, and she would let me know about next Friday during the week. She left shortly after my mum did, and I finished setting up the rest of my stuff and got my books and other stuff ready for the next day.

I pulled out my school map. The school was pretty easy to figure out—all my classes were down on the main hallway. I just needed to find the easiest way to get to the building across the way for my art classes. I had already seen the cafeteria and the gymnasium, so I didn't need to know anything else right now, I would figure it out when time came.

My roommates were all downstairs in the kitchen, so I made my way down there. We discussed the bathroom situation and kitchen division again to make sure, and everyone seemed okay with what was decided. I got my own bathroom. Excellent.

Everyone went their own ways, and I went to my room, turned my TV on, and then Amy knocked on my door.

"Yes?" I answered.

"Hi, do you want to try some Cantonese dessert?"

"Sure," I replied and took a spoonful from the bowl she handed me. "Wow, this is pretty good. What is it?"

"It's a type of bean we have to which we add sweet spice to create a dessert," Amy explained. "Maybe when Wesley comes over every night, you might come down, if you're home, and try some of our food. We always make plenty."

"Sure, why not? I'm not one to pass up food." I was impressed at how friendly Amy was; I felt at ease around her as soon as we'd shaken hands. Maybe it was the energy she gave off, which flowed with mine. We left things at that, as it was getting late, and I wanted to get a good night's sleep. I attempted to sleep and tried to avoid thinking about my mystery guy. It worked quite well; I hadn't thought about him all weekend until now! I finally fell asleep and dreamed that he was in one of my classes. He sat at the back of the room and saw there was a spot behind me and came closer.

"Hello. Remember me? I am truly sorry and hope you really do forgive me. Can I treat you to lunch today?" said my dreamy mystery guy.

Of course, I said I did forgive him and that I would be delighted to have lunch with him. As we got up at the end of the class, he put his hand on the small of my back, and I woke up.

Wow, what a dream! It seemed real, and I was covered in perspiration. I was breathing intensely and had to give my head a couple of shakes. Too bad I'd woken up so soon.

CHAPTER THREE

It was the first day of college! I know I'm a geek, but I always liked the first day of school, the new stationery, the clean smell in the air everywhere. When I was a child, I'd especially liked the new clothes and two pair of shoes I would get, one indoor and one outdoor. My family had an okay amount of money, but my parents believed in having more of what we needed, not what we wanted. This allowed us to have at least one yearly vacation, usually to somewhere warm, and my parents' saved money for my schooling and their retirement, although I don't think my parents will stop working at a very early age—too much time in the day, they both say.

Sorry. Rambling about nothing again. I had set my alarm for seven and woke up at six thirty. I always woke up earlier than my alarm. I took my time getting ready. I wanted to dress comfortably my first day, so I wore black cargo-looking shorts and a black and orange writing sweatshirt, my sporty sandals, and my hair in a ponytail. I decided to bring only one book till I knew exactly what I needed for each class, and my map, just in case I forgot which classes were in which building.

My roommates were also up early, and we all had our first classes at eight, so we all went in together. Kim had English with me. She was a first year, and English was mandatory. Karen had English in the room next door, which was also my lecture room. Amy had all her classes in another area, as she was a second-year science major. She must had taken some classes back home that could be used here. Perhaps a topic for conversation later. We all parted and went to our classes.

Our English class was down the main corridor on the left. Kim had friends from her hometown there, so she went and sat with them. I just chose an empty seat in the middle and sat by myself. It was about ten minutes till the class was to begin, so I scanned the classroom without being too obvious. I looked to my left, and there was a group of about six guys and four girls, maybe jocks. They all wore sport shorts, running shoes, and T-shirts. At the front left, there was a group of three guys and three girls who seemed to be well prepared for class and were awaiting the teacher patiently. They must be the studious bunch, the brains, or geeks of the bunch I should say. The front right-hand side of the room had a group of about six girls and three guys. They were very well dressed; they wore preppy clothes, collared pastel shirts with cardigan sweaters on their shoulders with the arms tied in front to hold them on. The rich bunch. They were hard miss; everything they had looked very costly, and they look like they could not be bothered to be there.

At the back of the room were a group of goths. They too were hard not to notice, as they were all dressed in black and pale skinned. There were two girls and four guys in their group. The rest of the kids didn't seem to know anyone in this class, so they sat in the middle, quite spread out, like me.

I'd chosen to go to school where none of my high school "friends" or acquaintances were planning on going, I had hoped anyway. I'd wanted a clean slate, a new start. I hadn't enjoyed my high school years. I had created tension with some older kids when I was in grade school; I wasn't always the well-behaved young lady I pretended to be. In school, I was studious and never got in trouble—or never got caught,

I should say. The weekend was another story. My party buds were all from an older crowd. I would go to parties and sometimes get into fights or disagreements with others because of my friends' big mouths. I tended to have older boyfriends too, which created problems, overstepping my boundaries with the older girls.

When I'd entered high school, rumors had been started that were not true. Rumors created by the jealous girls, who were assuming the worst. I was always around guys; they were easier than dealing with nattering girls. I have always had problems with girls, as they were jealous of me; the guys were just my buds. No one ever believed that I could be friends with all of them with "nothing asked in return." Anyways, no need to talk anymore about this stuff; it just angers me.

The teacher entered the classroom, or should I say the theater classroom, which could probably hold five hundred people at its full capacity. She introduced herself as Mrs. Mathews and went about handing out the class outline and going through it with us. She seemed okay, implying we should follow the rules to get good grades.

English class was let out fifteen minutes early, which gave me time to grab a drink in the cafeteria. As everyone was exiting the theater, I decided to file out behind the goth group, maybe to catch a glimpse of my mystery guy. I had no idea, if he even went to college there at all; I could only wish. Well, no such luck, there was no mystery guy to be seen in the cafeteria. I headed back to the main corridor I had just come from, as my next class was next door to the previous one.

The second classroom was the same size with the same groups of people: the jocks, the geeks, the preps, the goths, and those with no one dispersed through the middle. A man entered the theatre class and introduced himself as Mr. Vladimir, the literature teacher.

Wow! He was a great-looking man and well built, looking like he took good care of himself. Mr. Vladimir had short (but not too short) light-brown, feathered hair, and he dressed well. I couldn't see the color of his eyes or make out his features clearly though, because he was too far away to catch the details.

Mr. Vladimir handed out his outline; this must be the way they do things in college, giving us outlines in all the classes. I guess it was a good idea, so nothing assigned came as a shock, and we knew the grading system. He went through the outline and explained the breakdown of marks and assignments, as had the previous teacher. Mr. Vladimir let us out one hour early, with a word of advice on being ready for Wednesday's class.

I went back to the dorm and ate some chicken and rice with broccoli—leftovers my mom had brought yesterday. Everyone was home today; I guess we all had short classes. I decided to go up to my room after I ate and rest before my next class. I lay on my bed and began to think about my mystery guy. I wondered if I would ever see him again, and if I did, if he would remember me. I thought that, if a few weeks went by and I hadn't seen him in or around the college, I might have to get Kelsie to come with me back to Hay City.

His hair had looked so soft… Would I ever be able to run my fingers through it? Who was kidding who? I was probably never going to see him ever again. I gave my head a shake once more.

I must have been tired, considering I hadn't slept well the night before, and took an unexpected catnap. When I woke up, I looked at the clock—it was twelve thirty, and my class started at one. I'd wanted to leave early to find out if I could take a shortcut through the corridor where my other classes were, but there was no time now. My next class was in the next building, across the way from my previous classes. I brushed my hair and teeth, and headed out, not seeing anyone in my dorm along the way. They must have had classes at one also. I entered the college and turned down the corridor where my other classes were. I peeked into my English class to see if I could catch my teacher or even a student to ask about the exit door at the end of the hallway. Mrs. Mathews was in the room.

"Excuse me, Mrs. Mathews; I was wondering if the exit door can be used to go to the building across the way?"

"Sure, that door is not alarmed. Hey, are you in my first-period class? Did you sit in the middle section?"

"Yes," I said, surprised. "How could you have seen me from so far away?"

"I always pay attention to those who sit by themselves; I concern myself, sometimes too much, with how being alone may affect individuals," she replied.

"It's nice of you to be concerned, but I'm always good. A little alone time helps my focus; it won't take me to long to make friends." I smiled.

"If you ever need anything, please do not hesitate to ask." She placed her hand on my shoulder.

"Thanks," I said and left the room.

I went down the corridor and took the exit door across the way to the arts building. The next class I had was drawing. I entered the main door and checked my map; my class was the second door on the right. As I passed the first door, I kind of stretched my neck and peeked in the window. I saw a classroom of desks circling what seemed to be a naked guy standing in the middle of the room. I didn't stop to take a second look, but from my quick glance I noticed that the guy had shoulder length dirty-blond hair and nice back muscles.

I shook my head and wondered if I was going to be drawing naked guys also. I entered my classroom, but there was no one there yet; it was still ten minutes till the class was scheduled to start. It was great living in the dorms, which were next door, as it only took about five minutes to walk to the school. This room was an average classroom, not a theater. The desks were set up in a circle, so I could only assume we were also drawing an object or person that would be in the center. Getting different perspectives on what you were drawing was great, and if we were drawing a person, that would be something new for me. I could draw anything else, even paint and sculpt, but people were hard for me. I'd signed up for this class to hopefully broaden my skills, so nudes would be good and very different.

I thought of the naked guy I had just seen through the window. Was he fully naked? Was he wearing a towel or underwear? I hadn't seen that far down. Maybe he was just naked to his mid to lower back. He'd had beautiful hair, dirty blond, almost shoulder length, and wavy. Wow! I started to think of my mystery guy; he had dirty-blond wavy hair and gorgeous cobalt-blue eyes. Maybe that was the mystery guy in the other room. Well, if it was him, there was no way he could ever be interested in someone like me. The guy I'd just seen looked super-hot, completely out of my league. Without seeing his face, I was assuming too much, maybe. Great body, though.

The door opened and a few girls came in, and then the room filled up quickly. A lady entered with many portfolios, and I assumed she was my teacher. I was right.

"Alright, class, settle down. We have lots to go through today, and I'll try to let you out early if you let me go through everything I need to," she expressed in a raised tone.

The room went quiet, and she thanked us and introduced herself as Mrs. Tanner. She handed out an outline of the semester; her marking system was much different than the two previous teachers, with 40 percent of the grade for attendance and punctuality and 60 percent for two projects. Wow! I couldn't believe that attendance and punctuality were worth so much.

"Obviously, it's very important for you to attend this class; the marks are easy to achieve, so please don't let me or yourself down," she said. She then started to explain the classwork:

"You will be drawing some still lives, but mainly nudes. If you have any problems with this, then I think this is not the class for you, and you may be excused and enroll in another class." Well, she was straight to the point! No one got up to leave, so they were all intending on staying, or maybe they would leave later and not come back to avoid embarrassment.

"Another thing I need to add," Mrs. Tanner said. "There is not to be any pointing or laughing, and everything needs to be drawn to scale as best as possible on your drawings. It's hard enough for someone to get up there to model, let alone having to put up with disrespectful students. If this happens, you will be excused, and you will not return to my classroom."

Mrs. Tanner gave us a list of supplies we would need. She said that, if we didn't come prepared, she would give us one chance, with a good reason, and after that we would be excused and not allowed to return. She was a profoundly serious woman—a force to be reckoned with.

"I can provide you with media and medium for the rest of this week if you are waiting to get all your class supplies at once. The one chance starts Monday, so by Tuesday, no excuses. I may sound a little harsh, but college and the rest of your life is on you; we professors are here to teach, not babysit, and it's on your dime, so to speak." Mrs. Tanner gave a little grimace.

Wow! She was an interesting teacher. Well, we were adults, and we did pay them to teach us; she was right. If we didn't want to be there, then why pay for the class? Take another or do not attend post-secondary institution.

On my way back down the hall after class, I copped a look to see if the naked guy was still there. There was no one in the room, so I went home. My roommates were all home doing their own things. I went to my room and put my track suit on, then went downstairs to grab some water. Amy asked me where I was going. I told her, and my other roommates, that I would be taking a run around the track every day and that I had brought weight and cardio equipment, which were downstairs, and they could feel free to use it anytime. Amy smiled. The others were busy and didn't notice as I left.

I went to the track where there were a few others running. I ran about ten kilometers and then went back home. When I got in, no one was in the kitchen. I made myself a protein shake and went to shower. Then I made myself some pasta with ground beef in it, mixed with cream of mushroom soup and corn. I made a big batch, so I'd have leftovers for lunch or supper tomorrow. Then I cleaned up and headed upstairs just as Amy and Wesley came home and went to the kitchen to make their own supper.

I went to sleep at nine, just in case I couldn't fall asleep quickly, like the night before. I started to think about my mystery guy, so I got up and got my headphones and went to sleep to music. I was hoping to pass through the night without dreaming of him, but I ended up dreaming of him and me dancing. I'm not sure where we were, but I remembered looking into his eyes, and they were so dreamy. We danced so close, and I remembered wanting to kiss him. He looked into my eyes. We sank into one another, and I felt like he was leaning to kiss me. I held my breath, our lips were about to touch, and then I woke up.

Chapter Four

I was soaking wet, from top to bottom. I got up from my bed, tore my sheets off, ran them downstairs, and started the washing machine. I went back to my room and noticed it was six in the morning. No one was up yet, so no one had seen my spaz-out episode with the sheets. I remade my bed and went to have a shower, then jumped back into bed at six thirty and got back up an hour later. Everyone must have had early classes because no one was home when I got up. I left at a 7:45 and headed to my class.

Mrs. Mathews decided to do roll call once again, and everyone was there. We went through the structure of a story. Our English assignment for Wednesday's class was to create an outline and a beginning to a story, which we would go through as a class, deconstructing everything.

After class, I saw a bunch of students with long black coats up ahead, going towards the cafeteria, so I quickly caught up to them to see if my mystery guy was there. I tried not to be obvious, so I bought a pop and went to my classroom. I was insane; the only thing on my brain was the guy in the long black coat. Why did I like him? I knew nothing about him … he might have a girlfriend or just not be a nice guy. Who was kidding who? He had been very polite with me at the bar, both times, and he had to be a nice guy all the time. All I know was that I needed to see him again, to get some answers or have a bad encounter with him, so I could forget about him.

I got to my art history class, and there were no preps or geek groups. There were just two groups this time, the creative students, or artsy individuals on my left and the goths on my right, with the loners like me in the middle section again.

My literature teacher, Mr. Vladimir, entered the room. He had someone hand out the outlines and told the class his name and that this was art history. He gave us a breakdown of the quizzes and projects and marks. It didn't take a genius to see that all my classes had high marks for attendance and punctuality, therefore if I was on time, and never missed a day and even just passed my tests, assignments, and quizzes, I could have a decent mark. I could probably get a 75 percent in each class, no problem, without trying too hard. The teacher let us out at ten and asked us to be prepared to start on the first topic, which would be art and artists in the early 1800s.

As I was leaving, I took a glance down the hallway, like I always did, and I stopped at the water fountain for a few seconds. I stood up and looked around again just in case I saw my mystery guy. I know. I was clearly going crazy, but it was automatic now. Well, I couldn't believe my eyes. I saw a guy who (from far away) looked like he could be my mystery guy entering the classroom where I'd had my literature class the previous day. I was sure—the hair, the height, the smile—but it was pretty far away and from a side view. I quickly went towards the classroom. I looked in and saw Mr. Vladimir talking to the guy in gothic attire, whose back was towards me, and they seemed to be in a very intense conversation. It seemed like they knew each other more than I'd expect for just a teacher-student relationship.

It must have been a figment of my imagination … Mr. Vladimir had just been in my art history class down the hall and across the way, so how could he be here so quickly? Maybe I'd been at the fountain longer than I thought, and maybe he'd left first without me seeing him leave. Anyway, I didn't want to stick around to ask questions. I also didn't want to be caught listening in while I waited to see if this was my mystery guy. I turned around and left but knew it would be on my mind all day long.

I went back home for lunch. I had a typography class in the afternoon, and I had an early day. I was finished at three on Tuesdays and Thursdays. I wasn't very hungry, so I grabbed a couple pieces of bologna, cheese, and some crackers. I headed back to the school at 12:40, which gave me a few minutes to look for you-know-who. My class started at one. When I walked in, the hallway was quiet, so I decided to go grab a pop from the cafeteria. I'd thought I would be early for class but had gotten lost, as this class was in the second building across the way; so, I grabbed a seat at the front in the middle and hoped she wouldn't say anything. This was an ordinary classroom, not a theater class, and there weren't many people—no students that weren't art majors.

"Good afternoon class," she started. "My name is Mrs. Reilly, and I will be your typography teacher. In case you are not familiar with the term "typography" or letter setting, let me familiarize you a little. Typography or letter setting is the distancing used when writing, the spacing. Each set of letters has a set distancing when placed beside another letter. This is a very technical class, and I do not put up with misbehaving or the missing of classes."

Mrs. Reilly gave us the breakdown on the marking system and gave us a list of books we needed for next class. Class finished at two today. All the classes these past two days had just been introductory, with no real work or assignments, except English class.

After my class, I went back to the dorm and decided I needed a good workout to get my mind back into focus. I was by myself once again—having roommates wasn't so bad when they were never home. I did about forty minutes of cardio and thirty minutes of weights, and I worked on my back, shoulders, and triceps. When I had finished, I walked back upstairs and went into the kitchen. Everyone was home now. I said hi and grabbed a glass of water, then went to take a shower. I was drenched in sweat, and probably smelled bad too. It was still early, so I should have probably gone for a run, but I thought maybe I could go for a long walk and see what was within walking distance. After showering and getting ready, I went back into the kitchen and had leftovers. Amy was in the kitchen and asked me how my workout was.

"I needed a good workout today; my mind is not focused," I replied. "I saw this guy a few weekends ago at the bar, and I seem to be very obsessed with him."

"Who is he?" Amy asked.

"That's the problem; I don't even know his name. He's just gorgeous." I shook my head.

"Does he go to school here?" Amy questioned.

"I don't even know that. I think I saw him today talking to my literature teacher, but it seemed to be an intense conversation, and I didn't want to get caught there. It could have very well been another figment of my imagination." I shrugged my shoulders.

"What are you going to do about this mystery man?" Amy asked.

"Hopefully forget about him," I replied and started to head upstairs. "I'm going to go up to my room and relax. Thanks for the talk, Amy."

I must have fallen asleep a bit as soon as I had turned the TV on. I don't even remember what I was watching. I woke up at six p.m. when I heard a bang on the wall next door. Amy must have just gotten home or gone into her room. I got up and opened my door to go downstairs.

"Sorry. Did I wake you? The wind caught my door, and I didn't know you were home," Amy said as she opened her door.

"It's okay. I had already slept enough anyway," I replied.

"I am really sorry."

I smiled and headed downstairs, got a drink and an apple, then went back upstairs and got ready to go for a run.

Amy's door was open. "You like to exercise a lot, don't you?" she asked.

"It's how I stay in shape, body and mind," I replied and smiled. "See you in a bit, Amy." I closed my door, left the dorm, and headed towards the track. I only ran about eight kilometers, but I had already worked out earlier and had overdone it on the weights. I was sore and exhausted. I got back to the dorm, and everyone was home. I said hi to be polite and went upstairs to get some clothes and had my third shower of the day. At this rate, I would be a dried-up prune in a month. I went right to my room without supper; I didn't feel like small talk tonight. I turned on my TV.

There was a knock on the door. "Hello?" I spoke. "Come in."

"Hi, it's just me." Amy opened the door and smiled. "I didn't want you to go to sleep without eating. You worked out too hard today not to eat all your meals and more. I brought you some vegetable soup and crackers."

"You didn't have to do that but thanks a lot. I'm hungry, just too lazy to make myself some food." I perked up a little.

"I hope you do not get angry with me, but I probably will offer you food often. Especially if I have leftovers, or if I am making myself a snack."

"Thanks again." I was very appreciative.

I finished the soup, turned off the light, and went to sleep. I briefly remembered the guy I saw that day; I wasn't one hundred percent sure it was the mystery guy. But it had to be him—the hair looked the same color and looked soft and wavy like I remembered from the bar that night. What was I going to do about the model guy? I was very curious. Could my mystery guy and this guy be one and the same? The next time I saw him, or thought I saw him, I had to get close enough to see if it was him. If I thought about him willingly, I thought that, perhaps, I could get a good night's sleep.

His beautiful, naturally wavy, dirty-blond hair … oh, how it shone with health. I remembered how it flowed as he'd turned his head and walked away. The best feature by far had to be his eyes; I didn't take time to stare into them though, as I hadn't wanted anyone to see how attracted I really was to him. Oh, how I want to stand and stare into his eyes, as someone's eyes told everything. You could tell if one was sensitive, caring, and trustworthy, or deceitful. There were very few who could lie and follow through with it and not be found out. Eventually, if you were looking for the truth and were consistent with the follow-through, they would give up their lie somewhere.

My mystery guy had very truthful and sincere eyes; I would maybe even go as far as sensitive. I could read them, even though I'd only stared into them for mere seconds both times. I hoped the naked guy I'd seen was him and that I would somehow run into him. Now I was really going crazy, making up stuff as my thoughts were running wild. If it was him, the naked guy, he had an incredible back, nice and muscular. What was I going to do? I was completely losing my mind … or had lost it. Next time, I would approach him no matter what. It was the only way to resolve all my questions and hopefully my feelings too.

In a way, I hoped I was very wrong about the innocence in his eyes— maybe he would be the biggest prick I had ever met. That way these feelings I had could come to an end. I say that, but I really hoped he was Mr. Right. I didn't even know him, and yet he might break my heart without knowing it. I already had many trust issues from my past; I'd had a boyfriend cheat on me when I was young and another just a year ago. They made you trust in what they said and cut your throat. I needed to leave the past there and move forward. Easier said than done.

CHAPTER FIVE

I woke up at 7:15 a.m. I had set my alarm for seven, but I'd set it for p.m. by mistake, not a.m. good thing the others were up and were making noise, because I may have been late for school otherwise. I quickly went downstairs to my bathroom, showered, and got ready. It only took me about twenty minutes to get ready; I grabbed some cereal and my books and got out of my dorm by 7:50. Today was Wednesday, so I had English at eight and Literature at nine. I didn't have time to grab a Coke in the cafeteria; I went straight to class and arrived with only seconds to spare. I sat in the same seat as I had on Monday, and the class was filling up quickly. Everyone seemed to be claiming the same seats as the previous day.

Mrs. Mathews approached the podium and laid her books down. She took attendance and then there were material lists being handed out. The first novel we were to read was *Gone with the Wind*. I already had this book and had read it a few times. She also mentioned that, if we went to the bookstore and registered before Friday, we would have an additional discount the rest of the year on top of the 25 percent to sign up.

Mrs. Mathews told us a little about herself. She was forty-five and had been teaching college for ten years. She'd also taught grade twelve for ten years before that. She'd needed a change, and so had decided to teach college students.

My next class was literature, next door. I was looking forward to my literature class; well, I was hoping my mystery guy would show up again. I thought it was him. During roll call, I put my arm up and asked Mr. Vladimir to just call me Angel. He handed out the list of books we needed, and I decided I would just go to bookstore at the end of the week when I had been given all the materials needed for all my classes.

I would probably choose something with vampires or werewolves in it. I was a fan of vampires. I had most of the movies that had some sort of vampire or fantasy creature in them and had probably watched them all several times. Almost all the novels I had read in my life had been ones I'd had to read for school, the only real exceptions being *Gone with the Wind* and the *Twilight* series by Stephanie Meyer, which I had chosen to read on my own. I usually read health magazines or books on health and wellness.

Mr. Vladimir told us we would have chapters assigned to read and/or poetry when we got to that part. Mr. Vladimir told us he had been teaching at this college for three years and had taught all over the world. He said he liked change and tended to move every couple of years. He said it gave his son experiences from other cultures and lifelong memories. I thought it might have been hard making and leaving new friends, and that it may not have been as great for his son as he thought. Who knew? Everyone was different; maybe his son did like the experience, but I wouldn't have liked to get uprooted every couple of years for my father's job. Mr. Vladimir also told us that his wife had passed very early in their marriage. He checked his watch and apologized that we'd run a few minutes over time.

I took my time gathering up what little stuff I had and heard some excitement coming from the door. Everyone seemed to be acknowledging someone coming into the room. It was him! My heart started to pound; I swore it was going to jump out of my chest. It seemed like everyone knew him. I turned to the girl passing by me.

"Who is that guy?" I asked with my tongue dragging on the ground.

"Gabriel!" She looked very puzzled.

"The guy everyone is fussing about, the one that just entered the back door of the auditorium, all dressed in black?" I questioned again.

"You mean the guy you're drooling over!" She grinned.

"I'm not drooling," I said defensively.

"You are. He's Mr. Vladimir's son, Gabriel, and he very popular with everyone. Well, all the girl's anyways," she exclaimed. "Unless you are in or have something to do with someone in his click, he probably won't talk to you, he tends to keep to himself."

"You sound like you know him quite well."

"My brother is Gabriel's best friend, so he's over all the time," she answered. It sounded like he annoyed her.

"By the way, my name is Angel," I said.

"Yeah, I heard during roll call. My name is Charlize. Got to go. See ya!" she replied, like she was not impressed with me introducing myself.

I couldn't believe it really was him, my mystery guy, and his name was Gabriel. What a beautiful name, and he was just as beautiful as I remembered or dreamed that he was. Gabriel was one of the popular names in the mystical movies; come to think of it, so was Vladimir. Sounded very vampire-like, doesn't it? I could stare at him now, because he was being accosted by everyone as he walked in. As he made his way down to the stage, I could get away with looking more closely. Gabriel. I could say that name over and over again. Gabriel, Gabriel, Gabriel ... and each time I said it, the sound formed musical notes in my ears. Gabriel's eyes were so blue that they couldn't possibly be real. He had an incredible smile and great teeth—perfect teeth. I was about fifteen feet from him, so I could almost touch him. The classroom emptied, and he started to walk down the aisle. I quickly made my way toward him, so he crossed my path.

"Hi, remember me?" I asked.

"Yes, from the bar, right?" Gabriel questioned.

"Yes. I just wanted to make sure, for the last time, that you accept my apology for my behavior." I looked directly at him this time.

"You didn't do anything wrong from the get-go. It was I that fell into you. Now please, do not worry. I do not feel any ill will towards you!" Gabriel said, like I could not possibly say anything to offend him.

Perhaps he *was* a little uncomfortable in conversation with someone he didn't know, as Charlize had suggested. I froze as I watched him approach Mr. Vladimir. They had no resemblance except for their pale skin tone, but Gabriel wore all black and Mr. Vladimir word regular dress clothes. I just watched him and couldn't move. Even his walk was beautiful. Mr. Vladimir looked over, so I turned to leave, but then he asked, "Evangeline? Do you have a question for me?"

"N-no, sir," I said with a slight stutter as I turned back around to face him. "I was just leaving." I was a little embarrassed and quickly left the theater.

I headed home for lunch and all my roommates were there. Apparently, my smile gave it away.

"Good day?" Amy asked, and I realized that everyone was waiting for my response.

"Can't talk," I replied. "Got to grab my books for next class and go look into something. I will catch up with you later. Bye!"

I went to the cafeteria and grabbed a small turkey and cheese on rye and a Diet Coke. I walked around the grounds. I wasn't sure if I would find Gabriel, and if I did, if I could talk to him for a second time today. I ended up going and sitting in the beautiful garden that was between the buildings.

I figured they must have had gardeners or landscapers that worked for the school system full time. Amongst the flowers, hedges, trees, and ponds were areas for people to relax and admire the scenery. There were seats made of beautiful old logs, and some from large boulders, with a large area with picnic tables in the center. There were ducks in the pond and birds singing in the trees; the atmosphere was to die for. It was so relaxing and inviting. On one side there was a little stream that came from an underground water source and created a pond where the picnic tables were. I got to pass this area every time I went out the main building to go to my art classes. If I could have a request for my own yard—when I had a house and a yard, of course—it would be to have a great garden like this one.

There was also another larger body of water out back behind the art building. It wasn't quite as nice, and it was used for the science majors. They apparently did lots of research from that pond; it was well kept, but there were no flowers or anything, well some wild ones or weeds, I don't really know the difference.

I walked through the gardens on a nice, exposed pathway, making my way back to the doors and to my drawing class. As I walked by the room where I had seen the nude the previous day, I saw him again. This time I saw that the man wasn't completely naked; he had short shorts on. As the guy turned, I noticed that it *was* Gabriel. I couldn't believe it. I quickly left, as I didn't want him to see me looking in.

All through my drawing class, I thought of him. It was hard not to; he was just as hot as I thought he would be. My two brief looks into the classroom had only allowed me to see his back and catch enough of a glimpse to see that it was in fact Gabriel posing as the nude—or almost nude. I didn't get to see the rest of him, but let me tell you, I don't remember much of my drawing class from that day. I was too busy daydreaming of what he might look like from the front. I imagined his chest—I thought I'd seen hair, but I wasn't sure. Nice pec muscles, a V-shape, which I had briefly seen the time before. Perhaps Gabriel had well-developed abs, the last set, the eight -pack that led to a great set of legs. He was still young. What kind of marvelous specimen would he turn out to be? Well, that was what I would like to see and end up with. Wishful thinking.

My god, I certainly had a crazy overactive imagination. He didn't even know I existed. Really, I had put myself in his way each time we'd met. Once was an apology and me being rude, the next was me apologizing for having been rude, and the next was me conveniently stepping out in front of him so he would see me. Gabriel probably thought I was a flake at this point, or just didn't think of me at all. Most guys liked flakes, which might work to my advantage, but what happened when he found out I wasn't one and this is college, not a bar?

Back to drawing class. I was introduced to our nude model, who was a lady six months along in her pregnancy, and we were supposed to be drawing motion or something; the entire class was a blur. Don't really remember much of what the teacher said. I was only thinking of Gabriel. I do remember the teacher talking about having respect for the model and the other classmates, though.

After class, I made my way to where I had seen Gabriel, but he wasn't there. I headed home, and as I walked down the hallway to exit the arts building, I heard Gabriel's name being called out. I froze. I wasn't sure if I wanted to run into him again or exit the building another way. It would have been a huge detour if I didn't go through to the main building, so I decided to keep going. As I got to the door, it opened for me.

"Evangeline," Gabriel said as he held the door for me and then went back into the building.

He knew my name. Well, I guess Mr. Vladimir had said it that morning, but he'd remembered it. Gabriel held the door for me. Was it because he knew I was coming? Or was I just there as he'd needed to get back into the building? Anyway, he did know my name, which counted for something. I think.

I just smiled and nodded my head thanks and kept walking. I was nervous, scared … not sure of anything. I quickly went home to get my running stuff on in the hope that he stuck around the building after classes.

"How was your day?" Amy asked with a big smile, lifting her eyebrow intuitively.

"My day was fine," I replied.

"Just fine? That smile looks like more than a 'just fine' smile. Come to think of it, I have yet to see you smile quite so big," Amy continued. "Even your smile at lunch was pretty big, but no match for this one."

"Really, it was an ordinary day up till the point that Gabriel walked into the classroom just as I was leaving," I replied, delighted.

"You mean the mystery man's name is Gabriel?" Amy asked.

"Yes, his name is Gabriel, and my literature and art history teacher is apparently his father. I ran into him, and I feel much better about the evening at the bar. I saw him three times today, and he addressed me once by my name."

"Gabriel is a very nice name, and he knows your name. I would have to say that is much more than an ordinary day," Amy replied, with a big *"I need more info"* grin on her face.

"I also met a girl that seems to know him quite well; perhaps I can pry more information out of her next class," I said with the biggest smile—so big it must have been ear to ear. "I will have to befriend her better. She didn't seem impressed with my apparent jaw drop when I saw Gabriel."

"I am very happy for you; perhaps now you can sleep better," Amy said sincerely.

I went upstairs. I realized then that my other roommates weren't around too much, and that Amy was going to be a very good roommate to approach for a truthful opinion. I got my track suit on and went for a run. As I was running, I noticed a nice Camaro pull out of the parking lot, and I automatically thought of Gabriel. *A sweet ride for a hot guy*, I thought. I was pretty far away to see clearly. The person had medium-length, maybe light-brown hair, but I could only make that out in the silhouette in the car. I just had a feeling that it was him and his ride; the car suited his name and appearance. My run wasn't all that great, as my mind was on guess who. I went downstairs to work out after, which didn't go too well either. Later, as I was getting ready to go to sleep, Amy knocked on my door.

"Come in!"

"Hi, I noticed that you were working out earlier, and I was wondering if you had eaten," Amy asked, concerned.

"Yes, I ate after my shower."

"Okay, I do have extra food left from my supper. Are you still hungry?" Amy asked. She sounded like she was my mother, needing to make sure I got fed.

"I'm good, Amy. Thanks for asking and being concerned for my wellbeing." I smiled politely.

"By the way, I am very happy you saw Gabriel today and got to talk to him."

"Thanks, I'm very glad I have you as a roommate."

She smiled and left the room.

I found the time and concentration to get my reading done and get started on the English assignment I hadn't gotten done that day. Mrs. Mathews gave us another day to get things started. I went to sleep at about nine; I couldn't believe the day I'd had. My mystery guy was no longer nameless. Gabriel. What a beautiful name. *Gabriel, Gabriel, Gabriel.* I couldn't say it enough. Gabriel. I wondered what his middle name was and if he carried his father's last name, Vladimir. *Gabriel Something Vladimir. Mrs. Evangeline Hope Vladimir.*

I know. I was taking it too far, but he was all I wanted in a guy— perfect. Well, I thought so, anyway. I really didn't know him. I hoped I would get to know him and that he wanted to know me.

I had lost my head. I knew nothing about this guy, but I was ready to be his. Something told me he was the guy for me whenever I saw him or was near him—a flow of energy went right through me. I hoped he didn't have a girlfriend. Why wouldn't he? Gabriel was so hot, hot, hot! No wonder my other roommates thought I was crazy; this mystery guy was all I ever talked about. I was going to have to get control of the situation and quickly. I would keep my thoughts to myself and only mention him with those who knew about him.

Tomorrow I would find the girl I'd talked to and befriend her, and perhaps in time, I could ask her about Gabriel. She did seem a little snooty, but maybe it was just a bad first impression on both our parts. Well, I could and had dealt with snooty before. I just needed to be on my best behavior and seem interested in her.

Chapter Six

I had a great sleep and got up at seven a.m., slowly getting ready and having breakfast with Amy. I just said hello to the other two and left. I had art history today, and I was going to concentrate on finding the girl I'd talked to the previous day. I got to my second class and started to look around, but I didn't see her. She walked in just as the class began. She sat with the jocks; cool, we might have something in common. After class, she walked by me again, and I stopped her.

"Charlize, right? Hope you don't mind me asking, I was just wondering … I don't know anyone except my roommates, and I saw you sit with a group of jocks. Are you all in the Physical Education Program?" I enquired.

"Most of us. Others are taking a general year, but most of us grew up here, so we all hang out. What are you taking? Are you a jock?" Charlize asked.

"Well, I'm taking a general arts program. I'm not really a jock, but I'm known to have played a few sports in my day, and I run and work out quite frequently," I replied. "Are you taking a general year or are you an art major?"

"To answer your question," Charlize said, "I can't even draw a stick man. Some of us just like art and decided to take the class as an extra credit. What about you? Do you live on campus? Where are you from? Do you drive and like to party?"

"Yes, I live on campus. I have a car, and though I only have the odd drink, I will definitely go to a party. I have lived in Airdrie most of my life."

"Why don't you come to my party on Friday night?" Charlize asked. "You don't have to drink lots; have a few and meet some people."

"Sure, you want me to come to your party, where do you live?"

"I won't have invited you," She grabbed a piece of paper from her notebook and said, "Oh! And it's a kegger, first weekend party; my parents are a little bit lenient right now."

"Can I bring a friend from home?" I asked.

"Sure, no problem!" She smiled.

Charlize drew me a map, gave me directions, and even gave me her number. *Well, that went better than I thought it might; she doesn't seem snooty after all.* My first impression of Charlize had not done her justice; she seemed pretty alright after that conversation. I could see us being friends, and she could also help me out with the Gabriel thing.

I went home, ate lunch, and went upstairs to text Kelsie:

Hey Kelsie, I got invited to a kegger tomorrow night. Can you come? I ran into my Mystery Guy; his name is Gabriel. Isn't that a beautiful name? I met a girl. She seems cool. Her name is Charlize, and it's her party.

I asked her to text me back ASAP.

Kelsie texted me back two seconds after I sent mine. I was new at texting, and she had been texting for a couple years now, being more of a social butterfly than me.

Awesome! I'll be at your place at 7:00 p.m.!

After hearing back, I grabbed some cheese and crackers and headed to my typography class. We watched some videos and talked about letter setting, and Mrs. Reilly said we wouldn't start the assignments till Monday, after everyone had their books. Class ended at two thirty. This week was great for finishing early.

I went for a run. I was hoping to see Gabriel today, but I didn't. I worked out, showered, and ate supper. Overall, today had gone well. I did some writing and reading for English, watched a little TV, and then went to sleep. I was excited to go to the kegger, and I was almost sure Gabriel would be there. I closed my eyes, and I could see him like he was in front of me. I reached out to put my hand on his shoulder, and surprise, surprise, he wasn't there.

I woke up as though I had gone for a swim. Soaked to the bone! I didn't remember much of my dream, just that I was running my hands gently down Gabriel's back and getting in close to get a smell of his wonderful scent. There must have been more to it than that because I woke up all hot and bothered. I took in a deep breath and sat up.

It was finally Friday. It had been a very boring week of introductory classes. I only had English and photography on Fridays, so I was finished by noon. I got ready and went downstairs and found that everyone had already left. They must have been in a hurry, maybe because they were going to the bookstore for the discount pricing today. I needed to do that today too. I just wanted to get photography class out of the way. I probably needed lots of supplies for that class. I hoped there were still supplies left at noon.

Photography was in the same building as my drawing class. My teacher was Mrs. Reilly. So, my guess was that this was going to be a serious class. I was happy my teachers each taught several of my classes; it made it easy to remember their names: four teachers and six classes. As usual, there was an outline and a list of materials we needed. Attendance and punctuality were still a big chunk of the marks, and everything else was pretty much the same as the rest of the classes in terms of tests and assignments.

"I know that some of you, or most of you, are in some of my other classes, and rules are still rules, but this is meant to be a little less serious of a class ... maybe even fun," Mrs. Reilly said.

She was a serious lady, and I wasn't quite sure if the word "fun" existed in her vocabulary. I guess we would have to see—time would tell if we had the same meaning for the word.

The class went for a tour of the darkroom and all the components we would be using to develop our film. I was excited to learn photography. I'd always liked black-and-white pictures. Mrs. Reilly let us out early so some of us could go purchase the material we needed. I wasn't prepared for this class, as it was a last-minute decision. I'd had no class scheduled for Friday, except for English, so I'd chosen photography. I know. Why would I schedule something else and not just take the rest of the day off? Well, it would make for a long day if I had nothing to do; I had to get up for English class anyway, so why not take something else? I had always liked to take pictures, so why not learn more about it? It might be useful later in life.

I didn't have a camera, and I had forgotten to talk to my father about buying one. I took out my lists. I had a few books to buy for each class, mostly on the structure used when writing a story or book. I had to buy different types of media, pencils, pastels, and some charcoal, a sketchbook, and a few other special types of paper. Mrs. Tanner did say we would have to frequently buy other types of medium.

I made my way to the camera section, and there was quite the selection. I bought a nice mid-range Canon with large zoom lenses. I used my VISA, but I needed to call my father and tell him I'd spent more money than expected so he could pay it off for me.

I called as soon as I got back to the dorm, as I never brought my phone to school. "Hey, Dad. I enrolled in a photography class and had to buy a camera. It cost me six hundred and forty dollars. I hope you're okay with that. I can pay for half if you want. I got a good deal, 25 percent off saved a hundred and sixty dollars!"

"Well, that's a lot, but cameras are expensive and that was a great deal. Are you sure you will like this class?"

"I've always loved black and white pictures, and I can always use a camera somewhere in my life," I added convincingly.

"That's true. It can end up being a very good investment. I'll pay your VISA on Monday at noon," he replied. "Oh! When are you coming home next?"

"I will come and visit next Friday. I have planned this weekend already," I said.

"Perhaps a party?" my dad asked.

"Yeah! How'd you guess?" I said, surprised.

"I went to college too. There are always tons of parties the first couple months of school. It's probably a kegger, right?"

"Yes, I met a girl, and she's in two of my classes, and it's her party. Charlize, that's her name, asked me if I would like to come, and I'm bringing Kelsie with me." I must have sounded very excited, as I kind of was.

"Well, have fun and don't drink and drive, sweetie. See you next Friday, and enjoy school, and remember, classes are important—not that parties aren't, but you know what I mean."

"Bye, Dad, I love you and thanks." I was glad I had the parents I had; they were very understanding of being a young adult. But they still had the tendency to add a little reminder here and there.

"Your mom and I love you too."

I had nothing but good things to say about my parents. They had always been very supportive of my decisions, probably because I was pretty much a geek and never got caught for any of the mischievous things I had gotten into. They knew I rarely drank and never drank and drive. I was usually the designated driver, but they didn't know of the few really bad times I'd drank too much that had caused me to change.

Especially since I had decided to work out hard, drinking was not something I wanted to add to my life. Drinking and working out were very counterproductive to one another. You could build muscle and see progression in your body, and you can just as easily destroy it with a couple too many drinks, so why put the effort in just to throw away the time and hard work? I know. I know. It was college, and I should be partying like the rest, but I had never been like the rest. I had always been a leader, not a follower, and why change now?

Kelsie got to my place at 6:45, a little early, when I was just finishing my hair. I had gone for my run and had quite the workout, so I was a little bit further behind than I would have liked when she arrived. We left at seven as planned. I drove; the map was quite easy to read. The party was only three blocks from the dorms, so we could have walked. It seemed early to go to a party, but Charlize did say we could come for the BBQ if we wanted, with plenty of burgers, and that the keg would be tapped, so we could stop by any time after six.

Kelsie had already eaten and so had I. I'd needed to after the workout I'd had. We got there and found that there were already quite a few people, probably twenty or maybe even thirty. I was greeted by Charlize at the door. I introduced Kelsie, and Charlize introduced the entire bunch to us. Her mom and dad were there, as well as the jocks I had seen her sitting with at school. Then a few goths came up from downstairs. They were dressed down a little. They were wearing all black, but most of them weren't wearing their long jackets, and there were no real crazy piercings. Charlize introduced them, and finally, Gabriel walked up.

"You have met my brother's best friend, Gabriel, I believe." She smirked at me.

"Hello again, Evangeline!" Gabriel smiled beautifully and kept walking towards the patio door.

"H-hi, Gabriel," I stuttered, taking a few seconds for those words to come out of my mouth. I was stiff. My mouth seemed frozen, dry, but I thought there must have been drool on the ground. I was just not myself when Gabriel was around. It seemed like I froze for a long time, but it was only for a few seconds.

Kelsie grabbed my shoulder. "Dude, pick up your tongue. But WOW! He's hotter than hot, smoking hot! Gabriel is a great name, and it suits him."

I felt a hand on my other shoulder. It was Charlize. "Don't just stand there; let's go out back. Have you eaten? Do you want a beer? We have other liquor too if you don't like beer."

"Kelsie and I have already eaten, but we will both have beers, I think." I turned to Kelsie.

"I'm good with beer," she replied.

The evening went by fast. It was eleven p.m. when I checked my watch again. Everyone was very friendly, and Kelsie and I must have spent time talking to everyone, even Charlize's parents. There were all types of people there; I think the neighbors and some of Charlize's parents' friends were over too. When they decide to have a party, they meant a "party." I had been busy all night and had seen Gabriel a few times but hadn't had the chance to talk to him. Now I tried to find him through the crowd of people, but I couldn't. The yard was quite big and intricate, with lots of pathways, trees, and benches; it was quite beautiful. There was also a two-tier deck and a stone patio that went into the yard a bit, with a very nice fire pit. I would have to ask Charlize's mother about the garden if I were ever asked to come back.

I heard a guy's voice behind me say, "Hey, are you enjoying yourself?" I was by myself, as Kelsie had gone to get herself another drink. I turned around, hoping it was Gabriel, even though it didn't seem like his voice. It was Charlize's brother Caleb, who was also Goth.

"Hi, yeah! It's a great party!" I replied.

"Is it Evangeline?" Caleb asked.

"I prefer Angel, thanks!" I smiled.

"Sorry, I heard Gabriel call you that," he replied.

"It's okay. You have great parents and a very nice place. Where's Gabriel?" I asked.

"Oh! You have your eye out for him, do you?" Caleb said, seeming extremely disappointed.

"I'm sorry, that was rude of me."

"No, I'm very used to being asked about Gabriel, every beautiful girl seems to want him." Caleb was looking for sympathy.

"Does he have a girlfriend?" I asked.

"No, that's the thing. All the girls like him, and Gabriel is very polite with all of them, but he has yet to find one to his liking. He says he's waiting for the right one, that he isn't in a rush, and that he'll know when he finds her. We've been best friend for three years, and he's met many girls, but he claims the right one hasn't been in his presence yet. I think he'll be by himself forever with the attitude he has. There's almost no point in the girls falling for him; it's just not going to happen, so don't waste your time. He already left, anyway. Gabriel had a family gathering tonight." Caleb was negative towards Gabriel's appeal to girls.

I tried to make him feel better, but he said he had to go get a drink and that he would talk to me later. I didn't see him again. Kelsie got back and I filled her in on the conversation, and she told me maybe it wasn't worth my time to get wrapped up with Gabriel just to get disappointed. We left at about one a.m. I only had three drinks the entire night. I said bye to Charlize and thanked her for inviting me, and I also made a point of saying goodbye to her parents. Kelsie was going to stay at my dorm, and when we got back there, everyone was either asleep or still not home. We went right to sleep and didn't even discuss the evening—we were obviously tired.

I woke up, and Kelsie was still asleep, so I went downstairs and made us some instant coffee. I rarely drink coffee, but Kelsie was very much a coffee connoisseur. I wasn't sure if she would like the instant stuff, but it was all I had. All my roommates were up and around, and Amy asked me if I'd had fun last night with a little smirk. I told her quietly as I passed by her that I had seen him. Her smile grew even bigger. When I got back upstairs, Kelsie was just waking up.

I handed her the coffee, and she smiled. "Instant."

"Yes, you know it," I replied. "Hey, let's go shopping in the big city before we hit the university kegger. I will call Jenn and ask if she's up for a little shopping."

I sent Jenn a text, and a few minutes later she replied, saying we should pick her up at two p.m. I texted back saying we would be there. I took Kelsie for some real coffee, stopping at Timmy's to grab a coffee and a bagel for the road. Kelsie wanted to go back home and change first, so we went to her place and then stopped by my parents for lunch. They were glad to see me and invited Kelsie to come over for supper, or a BBQ (weather dependent) next Saturday.

Shopping was great. I found a nice pair of jeans and a top to wear for the kegger. Jenn and Kelsie bought tops and belts. The girls and I loved a good chicken and ribs, so we ate supper at Swiss Chalet. The party was in the next tower over from Jenn's dorm. Tom and Jim called Jenn at seven and let us know they would meet us at the front doors of the tower at eight. We got ready, listened to some tunes, and headed out. Kelsie and Jenn were planning on getting intoxicated, since Kelsie and I were staying at Jenn's for the night. I checked my watch when we arrived at the tower doors. We were on time, and the guys were nowhere to be found. I sent the girls up; the kegger was in the common room on the tenth floor, and I stayed back and waited for the guys. They arrived shortly after the girls went up.

"The girls couldn't wait! I know we're a little late, but it's not like we're an hour late … fifteen minutes. Tops." Tom sneered as he spoke.

"They are out to get totally loaded tonight, so I told them I would wait for you guys," I said calmly.

When the elevator doors opened on the tenth floor, it was as if we were entering a zoo. Some of the individuals were acting like wild animals; they must have started drinking in the early afternoon or were sucking them back like Kool-Aid. Kelsie and Jenn met us at the elevators with drinks for all of us. One minute we were together and the next I was standing all by myself. They got a little friendly after they had a few for "liquid courage." I made my way towards the keg to get myself a beer, and as I was waiting in line, a guy turned toward me and offered me his drink.

"No thanks. I never accept drinks that have been handed to me from someone other than the bartender or my closest friends; it's a safety precaution." I smiled, but I didn't make eye contact or give the guy the time of day, continuing to scan the room.

"That's very smart of you; you never know what one's agenda may be." He smiled. "I respect the confidence you have in saying what's on your mind. You don't know who I am, do you, Evangeline?"

I turned around to see who it was. I look up, straight into the stranger's eyes … I knew the eyes, and I felt a strong feeling, like a force of energy between us. I must have been out of it not to have noticed the voice and the smell, though I had only really spoken to him or heard his voice a few times. In my defense, I hadn't really turned to see who was offering me a drink.

"Gabriel," I said. "What are you doing here?"

"My cousin goes to school here and asked me to stop by and hang for the weekend," Gabriel replied.

"Wow! You look so different not dressed in black, with your hair pulled back. More sophisticated, maybe even older looking. The color brings out your eyes even more than they originally stood out." I was probably creating a puddle at my feet.

"You like my eyes, do you?" he asked inquisitively. "What else do you like on me?"

"Who said I liked your eyes? Or anything else, for that matter? Well, you aren't high on yourself, are you?" I said, a little surprised and kind of snooty.

I went to turn away from him, and he grabbed my arm ever so gently. "Listen, I did not mean to come across as arrogant. I am not really like that. You just make me uncomfortable, and I'm not used to that. I sense that you are quite different than other girls, and I don't know what to say to you. Please give me another chance; I really want to get to know you." Gabriel expressed himself very sincerely.

"Alright, I'm sorry about my reaction to your questions. I'm not myself around you either, not sure why. Apology accepted. You don't seem like the type of guy who would behave like that, anyway. I was surprised that those words came out of your mouth. I can see sincerity in your eyes. You're hot, don't get me wrong, but being hot doesn't give you the right to act like a jerk or think that everyone should get on their knees before you. I don't care if someone is the last man on earth; I don't stand for arrogance. Guys think that women need them, which isn't how it works. There are some, perhaps, that need a man, but this is the twenty-first century, not the nineteenth or twentieth century. Most girls nowadays can fend for themselves, and a man does not even have to enter the picture," I stated, sounding angry.

"Oh, hey! I thought you forgave me?" Gabriel smiled at me.

"Yes, sorry, I don't have the right to treat you like this. I just got carried away. I'm sorry."

"I forgive you, but someone must have done a number on you. I promise I am not here to get in your face or hurt you physically, mentally, or in any other way. I don't believe you should kneel before anyone or take crap from anyone, either. I just want to be your friend. There's something about you that makes you different than other girls. I feel like I could tell you my deepest, darkest secrets, and I barely know you," Gabriel said as he let go of my arm.

"I really would like to be your friend also. I guess you probably have had it pretty hard being so hot." I smiled jokingly. "It must be hard having every girl that sees you want you! Most guys probably wish they could be in your shoes, but it's probably even harder to be in the shoes than just wishing it.

I have been amongst girls nattering about hot guys, and it's like they're just a piece of meat and not a person with feelings of their own. It happens to both sides, and it isn't fair for either." I kept going on and on; he must have been annoyed with me.

"I must go; I am meeting my other cousin downstairs. I will try to come back as soon as I can, and we can continue taking." Gabriel smiled.

"Sorry for rambling; you make me nervous. See you later," I replied.

He left, and I hadn't even asked the questions I wanted to ask him in a real conversation, face to face. I must have totally made a fool out of myself; he might not want to talk to me ever again after rambling on about my beliefs. I thought he was just brushing me off nicely by saying he had to go but would come back. I didn't see him again; I knew I'd blown my shot at even being his friend, not that I would ever have had a chance to be in his life.

I met up with Kelsie and Jenn, and they were hammered. I didn't tell them about Gabriel. Tom and Jim found us and helped carry the girls down and to the other tower; I don't even think it was midnight when we left. I think the guys went back after they dropped us off. Tom and Jim said they would call us in the morning, and we could go for breakfast.

Kelsie and Jenn needed help getting to bed—they'd wanted to get plastered and they had. I put them to bed, brought them each a container of water to drink, and put garbage cans at the side of their beds, just in case. Jenn had thrown up a time or two before. I got ready for bed. I couldn't believe the embarrassing conversation I'd had with Gabriel. What would I do? I didn't even know if he went to college or just worked and visited his father from time to time. If I did see him, what would I say? Or should I even try apologizing for my behavior? There was something between us, I was sure, some sort of energy, a connection of some sort. I tossed and turned all night. I may have blown my only chance to talk to him … I could shoot myself.

In the morning, I didn't mention anything about talking to Gabriel. I just tried to forget it ever happened. The guys called and came to pick us up at eleven. The girls needed lots of sleep; they were in rough shape. After breakfast, or brunch, I should say, they drove us back to the dorm, and Kelsie and I left almost right away.

There was little conversation on the way back. I don't think Kelsie minded the quiet, as she caught up with some sleep she needed. She asked me if I was okay when we got back to my place. I told her I was fine. I knew she knew I was lying, but she didn't feel like listening, and I didn't feel like talking. Kelsie told me she would call me later, before she went to sleep tonight, and apologized for the lack of conversation on the way back. She said she was feeling ill and needed rest, but she'd had a great time.

When I got back home, I went up to my room. No one seemed to be home, which was fine by me, I was kind of down in the dumps anyway. I must have fallen asleep while going over my conversation with Gabriel a million times over. I was an idiot; I'd wanted to see him and spend time with him and possibly make him like me, not make him annoyed with me. What if I never saw him again? Or worse yet, what if I saw him, and he didn't want to have anything to do with me? I needed a reality check; Gabriel was just being nice, striking up a conversation, because he was a nice guy. I was fooling myself in thinking that a guy like him could possibly want to be around little nobody me.

Amy came to my room around suppertime and asked me if I was hungry and if I wanted to talk. I told her I'd had a bad night last night and that I would talk to her tomorrow. She was great. She didn't press the subject, and she went back to her room and didn't pry in my business.

I went to bed early because I knew I wouldn't sleep well. I thought about Gabriel the entire time. I don't think I had four hours of sleep-in total. I knew I'd wrecked whatever could have been, even if it was to only be friends. I really blew it!

Chapter Seven

It was Monday, the day after the worst weekend of my life. I guess I had said that a few times already since the end of summer … since Gabriel had entered my life, or whatever you wanted to call what we had. If my classes weren't graded on a high percentage of attendance and punctuality, I would have stayed home in bed for the entire week. I didn't know if I could handle running into him, but on the same note, I needed to talk to him. I wanted to fix things so I could at least be his friend.

I went to my English class, and Mrs. Mathews started the class by talking about the structure of a short story. I couldn't pay attention and had to ask someone what the assignment was because I'd missed that part of the lecture. I went to my literature class, and we discussed something by Chaucer, but I wasn't not sure what was discussed or if the professor had read the poem in its entirety. My assignment was to read and analyze the meaning of the poem by Friday, when there would be a discussion of the author's meaning.

I quickly left the school and headed home for lunch. Amy was the only one there and asked me what was wrong. We went upstairs and I explained the horrible night I'd had on Saturday. Amy told me it probably wasn't as bad as it seemed and that I should talk to Gabriel and sort things out. I went to my drawing class in the afternoon and passed by the class that Gabriel was modelling for. He turned as I briefly looked in. I'm sure he saw me, but I just kept walking. I went to class. It was cool getting to study and draw a pregnant woman. We were trying to capture motion, and Tara, the model, would change positions every five minutes. The class was about drawing the motion using large circles to show the shapes of the body parts. I was hoping not to run into Gabriel today. I needed some time to figure out how to explain my behavior. Class was over, and I made my way to the doors as fast as I could, getting home without running into him.

I decided I wasn't going for a run or lift weights. I went upstairs and pretty much lay there feeling sorry for myself. I went and grabbed some dry cereal to munch on while watching TV. Amy came to ask me if I was okay, and I just let her know I needed some time to figure out my feelings. She understood and told me she would see me tomorrow, but if I needed anything, she would be studying in her room and not to hesitate to ask.

I turned off the TV and weighed the pros and cons of the situation. I decided I had to find Gabriel and talk to him, or I would never forgive myself for at least not trying to fix things between us. There was no "us," but I wished there was, even if we were to be just friends. I really felt connected to him; there was some sort of energy between us. The energy could be one-sided, but I owed it to myself to find out his feelings and he mine. I recalled Gabriel saying something about energy also, I thought. Everything was a blur when it came to him. I'd never acted like this or had weird behavioral issues around any guy before in my life till now. Was I losing it? He was just a guy. Mind you, an extremely hot one.

The next day, I hoped to catch him, perhaps after my literature class. It would make it much easier on me if he were to talk to his father after class instead of having to ask around to find him. The class finished and Gabriel was nowhere to be found. I found the goth groupies in their usual spot at a picnic table. I walked over to find Gabriel, and he wasn't there. I asked Caleb if he had seen him.

Caleb replied, "He didn't show up yesterday or today; didn't call me either. Gabriel told me he ran into you at the university. What happened between you two? Did you throw yourself at him?"

"I will have you know that I don't throw myself at anyone, no matter how hot he may be, and you don't want to continue the direction of this conversation with me. Do you know where he is?" I snapped.

"Dude, chill out. I don't know where he might be. I did try to find him earlier and had no luck. I left a message on his cell. I'm sure he will get back to me as soon as he can." Caleb was not too impressed with my attitude, I could tell, but I didn't care.

"Can you please let him know that I really need to talk to him if you see him?" I eased up on my tone a little. "Thank you, Caleb."

I left and went in the main building, back to the literature theater, to see if he might be talking with his father now. Gabriel wasn't here, but Mr. Vladimir was at his podium.

"Hi, Angel," he said. "Can I help you with anything?"

"Yes, sorry to bother you. Do you know where Gabriel is?" I asked.

"I do not know where he is. Gabriel should have been at school!" Mr. Vladimir stated. "Why are you looking for him, and how do you know Gabriel?"

"Thanks. He was at school in the morning modelling in a drawing class. I met him a couple weekends ago, and we have run into each other a few times since then. I must go. Just wondered if he'd stopped by and you perhaps knew what he was up to this afternoon," I said and quickly left the theater.

I went home and got changed; I really needed to go for a run. I got to the track and ran about four kilometers, and out of nowhere, Gabriel was sitting on the bleachers. I could have sworn he wasn't there when I'd gone around the track the previous times, and I hadn't seen him approach the area at all. Weird. Could I really be this unperceptive of my surroundings? As I ran back near the bleachers, Gabriel got up.

"I heard you were looking for me." He had no emotion in his voice.

I stopped running, caught my breath, and walked over to him. "Gabriel, I'm deeply sorry about my behavior. I really don't want to be enemies with you. Some subjects are very touchy ones for me," I said, avoiding eye contact.

"Please look at me when you are talking to me," Gabriel said in a soft and gentle voice this time. "I could never classify you as an enemy. For one, I do not even really know you, and for two, I feel connected to you in some strange way. It's like I have known you forever, yet we just met. I am sorry that our conversation was a little bit unconventional and not how I would have liked it to have gone on Saturday night. I really want to be your friend."

"That's what I want too." I felt a little smile come from the corner of my mouth. "Let's start over." I stuck my hand out and said, "Hi, I'm Angel, and I'm incredibly pleased to meet you! Probably not the best time to do this; my hands are sweaty, and I look like crap right now."

Gabriel reached out to shake my hand back. "Hi, I am Gabriel; I am also pleased to meet you! Oh! Is it okay if I call you Evangeline? I really love that name. It's beautiful, just like you."

"Sure, Evangeline is fine coming from you, but beautiful? Mediocre in comparison to all the girls you hang with. Sorry, that wasn't called for," I added.

"Beauty is more than one's looks; true beauty is the multiple layers that one's heart contains. If I were to make a bet, it would be that you have many complex layers in your heart." Gabriel shook his head. "I like your strength, feistiness, and strong moral beliefs. I hope that I run into you more often. I could get used to having conversations with someone who isn't throwing themselves at me! I've got to be getting home for supper, though. Maybe I will see you tomorrow."

"Gabriel, thanks for not reacting like you could have towards my bad behavior. I will be here around five every day; that's usually when I run. You are welcome to come over and talk to me and perhaps run with me." I gave him a full smile.

Gabriel left in his awesome car. I was glad he'd come to find me in the amazing Camaro. I'd thought I'd seen him in it: hot guy with a hot car. It was a weight off my shoulders; I didn't want to make an enemy of him. I finished my run and went home. I was too preoccupied with the Gabriel subject to work out, so I had a shower and ate.

Amy came in late from school. Her friend was with her, so I went upstairs to get out of their way. She came up after Wesley left.

"You look a lot better tonight! You must have talked to Gabriel," Amy said as she entered my room. I had left my door open; I had a feeling she would want to talk to me.

"Yes, he actually came and found me at the track. I was so surprised to see him. I feared his reaction and was anxious as well. We worked things out and agreed to start over. I'm relieved. I'm still unsure of my feelings for Gabriel."

"Give it time and you'll figure it out. The worst part has been solved; just get to know each other and things will sort themselves," Amy exclaimed.

I thanked her for being there to listen to my problems; she was proving to be a great roommate. I never said more than hello to the other two. I went to bed and tried to figure out why Gabriel got to me so much. I thought I had fallen for him, but I wouldn't let him know my true feelings. I thought he might wear Dolce & Gabbana as his cologne; he smelled awesome. It had always been one of my favorite colognes. I hoped I got to see him more often now that he knew where I was. Perhaps his feelings towards me would grow, and he would have the same feelings I had for him.

The next couple of days, I kept an eye out for him, but I didn't see him, and he didn't come to the track. I had less time to worry about Gabriel, as the classes were in full throttle now and all assignments had been given. English was straightforward. We started to read *Gone with the Wind* and would discuss the thoughts of the characters and the structure of the book. I might have read the story before, but I really didn't remember much. It would be much easier if the first book had been *Twilight*. I had watched the movie over seventy-five times—not an exaggerated figure. And I watched *New Moon* about twenty times. I loved the storyline and loved everything to do with vampires. I couldn't wait for the next movie.

Mrs. Mathews seemed nice; she left me alone, for the most part. My English assignment was due before Christmas break. It was a fiction or non-fiction story on any topic I chose and must be at least five thousand words. I chose vampires as my subject; vampire stories and films gave a positive twist to a subject that was always portrayed as negative. As a child, young adult, and adult, I'd never changed my ideals about Vampires. I always said that, if there was ever a fictional way to go, I would choose to go as a vampire. Of course, they didn't exist, but if they did, it would be awesome, maybe even romantic. I know. I'm crazy. I have heard it many times before, but those are my feelings.

Mr. Vladimir seemed relaxed by nature, but you got the feeling that he liked things on the straight and narrow, never straying too far from the given path. Perhaps he might get a little ruffled under his feathers if things didn't stay in line. My assignment, due by the end of the year, was to create a poem, play, or really any piece of literature and then break it down, showing all the different things we'd learned throughout the semester. This assignment would be more of an ongoing creation, as we must learn the different styles used in literature to create the emotion and the point of view we wanted to get across to our readers. This could be the toughest of my assignments.

Art history was learning about different art periods and artists and the techniques, structure, and composition of their art pieces. My drawing classes continued to be about motion till the model started to have some complications and was put to bed rest and we were awaiting a new model. In the meantime, we drew some still lives, which was nice—no motion involved, so we could draw the subject with detail and definition. I loved to draw inanimate objects. I guess that's why we were drawing people, because they were harder to do, well, at least for me. I could draw almost any object, but people I needed help with.

Typography was intense. Who would have known that letter setting was so strict? Mrs. Reilly wanted everything exact, and she didn't accept anything other than perfection. I think art history and my typography class were going to be my biggest challenges. Photography was by far my favorite class. Mrs. Reilly gave us projects, and we would take pictures of the subjects and come up with a creative way to tell a story or depict the subject. Who would have thought that the same strict typography teacher could teach such a fun and creative class like photography? Goes to show that you can never judge a book by its cover.

Time went by, about a week or so, and I still thought about Gabriel, but he was probably just as busy as I was, and our paths didn't seem to cross. Every time I walked between both building through the beautiful gardens, I had a relaxing feeling come over me. I often took extra time walking through that area, feeling as though Gabriel was around, but I didn't see him. I even thought I smelled him, that sweet smell, quite often too. It was probably just me fantasizing about wanting to run into him, which I tended to do all the time.

I spent time, usually after my run, at the library doing research on vampires, and on the Monday before Halloween weekend, Gabriel just appeared in the empty chair beside me. Weird how he could sneak around so quietly like that. I could usually hear a pin drop, but I couldn't seem to hear or see him coming.

"Hey! Long time no talk," he said. "Sorry. I have been very busy with school. Are you going to Charlize and Caleb's Halloween party?"

"I just about forgot about the party. Charlize mentioned it to me a while back, but I haven't really talked to her lately. Just hello passing by, but I will probably be there. So, I have been wondering, do you take classes at the college or just model in the nude from time to time?" I had a huge grin on my face.

"When did you see me modeling? Have you been watching me?" Gabriel grinned back with a cute head nod.

"Maybe I have been looking a little, but I haven't seen you for a while," I answered with an *"I like what I see"* look on my face.

"What are you going to dress up as if you go?" Gabriel asked.

"I'm not telling; it will be a surprise!" I answered, quite excited. "What about you? What are you dressing up as?"

"I am not telling if you're not telling," Gabriel answered. "Do you have a little time to talk, or do you have work that is urgent to get finished right away?"

"I'm just researching for my English final assignment; it's not pressing, and I have just a little more information to collect. We can talk. I would like that." I smiled.

"Do you mind if I ask what subject you chose for your final assignment?" Gabriel seemed very interested in what I was working on.

"Vampires," I said, looking to see his reaction.

"Vampires," he repeated, and looked at me inquisitively. "You like vampires?"

"Yeah! You don't like the subject of vampires? Well, you wouldn't be the first to think the topic is a crazy one, but I have liked vampires ever since I watched my first movie as a child. I know they are totally a fictional character, but it seems kind of romantic to know one can choose an individual for an eternity and live forever. I have always thought of them as good, even though they have always been portrayed as evil. I was happy when they came out with the *Twilight* series. This was always the way I saw them, ever since I could remember. I hope that doesn't make you think any less of me," I said, a little wary of the reaction he would give me. "And yes, I know I tend to ramble on and on about nothing at times, but it's a nervous reaction."

"Nervous? Why nervous?" Gabriel looked surprised. "I make you nervous. A good nervous or bad nervous?"

When I didn't answer, he continued. "Well, I also enjoy watching vampire movies. I cannot say I think of them in a romantic fashion, but eternity with the one you love does sound great." Gabriel spoke sincerely. "Now back to this nervousness you feel around me. Don't avoid my question, is it good or bad?"

"Good nervous," I said and tried to avoid the topic. I hoped my outside didn't present itself like my insides felt. I was a mess inside—my body was experiencing the weirdest of feelings, and I wasn't even sure I could explain it if I tried. They were feelings I'd had never felt before. *Pull it together*, I told myself. *He's a guy like another, just a little bit hotter. Snap out of this funk you're in and just enjoy the conversation. Don't worry about later; live in the now.*

"I guess I'm a hopeless romantic," I said. "I'm not surprised to hear you say I feel different when we speak. Let me phrase that better: I'm not trying to offend you, but most guys couldn't find a romantic bone if it literally was placed in front of them. I'm very happy that you stopped to talk to me. I was beginning to think you hadn't forgiven me. I'm quite excited to learn more about you, like why and when you chose goth? What does your family think of your choice and how many are in your family? Where do they live? Where were you born and raised? I also know most of these things are none of my business, as we just recently met, and you don't have to answer." I felt a little lightheaded by pretty much saying I was really interested in him without saying it directly.

"Well, I am just as interested in those things about you! I do want to talk to you, but I must go for now, till tomorrow night," Gabriel said, dodging all the questions for now. "Oh! By the way, I do take courses at the college, third-year art and literature major. I do a little modelling for extra money."

"Gabriel, one more thing: Just in case I don't see you the rest of the week, how will we know each other Friday night if we don't know each other's costumes?"

"Don't worry. I will find you … or cheat and ask Charlize." He smiled and left. "I will see you before then, unless something happens."

I was very happy to have had him come talk to me and truly accept my apologies for Saturday's behavior. I couldn't continue my research after Gabriel left, so I packed up my stuff and went home. I had already grabbed a piece of pizza from the school cafeteria, so I went home and just decided to relax and watch some television. No one came to my room to talk; Amy must have been busy herself. I found myself thinking of what Gabriel might dress up as. I was unsure; I didn't know his likes and dislikes. I was going to dress up as a vampire—how appropriate, don't you think? Since I was also doing a report on them and had fantasized all my life of being one. I had everything I needed, as I had worn a vampire costume for other Halloween gatherings, even trick or treating when I was younger.

My mother had made me a cape in the fifth grade when I started to watch vampire movies, and of course, I wanted to be a vampire for Halloween. That year was the start of my vampire fantasies and desires. I had told Tom, Jim, Jenn, and Kelsie the past weekend about the party, and they'd agreed to come. Tom and Jim weren't fond of the dressing up, you know most guys, but I told them that, if they wanted to come, no one without a costume would be let in. Tom and Jim decided to be hobos, with torn and dirty clothes, dirty hands and faces, and sticks with packages on the end of them. Jenn would wear a mime costume, which she has worn many times over the years, and of course, Kelsie decided she would be a bar wench—Kelsie had to wear a costume that would show off her great body.

They were going to come over for supper and get dressed at my place; I asked my roommates if they were okay with this, as I didn't want to rock the boat this early in the year. They were all okay with it, as they were going to their own parties anyway. I was a little worried about finding Gabriel at the party. I fell asleep quite quickly, as I must have been worn out from all the study nights I had been having lately.

The rest of the week passed quickly, and I had seen Gabriel in the passing, but we hadn't talked, and finally, I woke up and it was Friday. Halloween. I decided to dress up as a mime for school, maybe trick some into thinking I would be a mime for the party also. I chose a mime because it was an extremely easy costume to pull off, and then I also could get away with not talking for the day. I put on a pair of black leggings, a black turtleneck shirt, black socks, and shoes. I pulled my hair up in a ponytail when it was still wet, so it would look darker, and put on white face paint and blood-red lips. I also painted two tears coming down from my eyes, and of course, my eyes were lightly done so they did not drown out in the white face paint. It took me fifteen more minutes to put my costume on than it usually took me to get ready. My roommates were impressed that I was dressed up for school.

I went to my photography class, and some people talked and snickered as they saw me, and others were impressed that someone had worn a costume to school. There were a few others that I saw wearing costumes also. No one recognized me until the teacher called out my name, as I'd sat in a different spot too. After class, I decided to return to the main building and see if others had dressed up and if anyone would recognize me. I ran into Mr. Vladimir.

"Nice costume. Are you good at miming? Oh! I forgot, you cannot answer that, just shake your head yes or no," Mr. Vladimir corrected himself.

I shook my head no and started to walk away.

"It's nice that some choose to part take in holidays still, Angel. Have a nice day!" Mr. Vladimir added at the last minute.

I didn't give any sign that he was right; I just walked away. Wow! I was overwhelmed that he knew who I was. I headed home to shower before everyone got there. We were going to grab a bite to eat before getting ready to go to the party. Kelsie showed up at five and the guys shortly thereafter. Steaks were on the menu tonight; it was a unanimous decision. The steak house was the choice for supper. I told everyone I had been a mime for school and that my literature teacher had guessed who I was.

Kelsie was interested in a guy we went to high school with, and he had left and apparently moved back. Nothing was going on, but there was potential there. Tom and Jim said they had seen a few hotties, but nothing more than conversation had taken place yet. I told them about how Gabriel had been there at the kegger on Saturday and how I'd made a fool of myself, but that I'd fixed everything. I told them about the track, the library, and said that hopefully I would see him tonight.

We got back to my place at about seven, and we took over the main mirror in the upstairs hallway. The party was a kegger again; Charlize and Caleb must always have keggers. This time there were tickets to be purchased at the door, for the beer, which made sense. If they paid for the beer all the time, I'm sure they would start to feel it in the pocketbook, and then there was also more control over the beer drinking. The first kegger was pretty much friends and family, whereas this one was a free-for-all invite, if tickets were purchased. There were even flyers given out around campus for the Halloween party.

It made me wonder how many people would show up. It could end up being more of a zoo, with everyone being dressed up and probably all wasted too! The tickets were two dollars per beer, so they didn't charge to make money off the keg, just to cover the cost of the beer, or to maintain some control on the drinking levels. I wasn't drinking, but I still bought a few tickets in case others needed some or in case I changed my mind.

A voice whispered from behind me, "Hi, Angel." It was Charlize. She and had guessed it was me because I'd walked in with four others and hummed and hawed about purchasing tickets. Charlize knew I was bringing the bunch with me. I didn't say anything. I just smiled.

"You two must be made for each other; you wore matching costumes. I would never have thought that he would have taken a serious interest in anyone, but lately I've overheard Caleb and him talking about you," Charlize expressed with uncertainty.

I pulled her to the side and whispered, "What are you talking about?"

"I'm talking about Gabriel. He's been talking to my brother about you lately, and he's dressed as a vampire also," Charlize said. "Go see for yourself; he's at the keg right now pouring himself a beer. Well, he was waiting in line for a beer a few minutes ago. Should still be there."

I went outside towards the gazebo, where the keg had been at the previous party. I saw a guy dressed up as a vampire, and he looked even hotter than usual, if that was possible. It could also just be because I was infatuated with vampires and him, and now, they were both together as one. I just stood there and watched him; he had a swarm of girls around him again, and I could feel the jealousy burning inside me. There must have been someone in his life he was interested in that even Caleb might not know about. That was an awfully large swarm of girls, most of whom were very pretty. I shouldn't have even bothered with my feelings for Gabriel and just settled with being his friend. Where did I get off thinking he would ever think of me as more than a friend? Average little me.

I must have talked to someone too long because I turned to look in his direction and he was gone. I started to look around for the vampire, and a voice said. "Are you looking for me, perhaps?" It was Gabriel's voice.

I turned around. "How did you know it was me? Did Charlize tell you, my costume?"

"No, I just saw a beautiful vampire standing across the way, not moving, and watching me. So, I took my chance it was you!" Gabriel replied. "I am not surprised that you chose to dress up as a vampire after the library conversation we had."

"Charlize told me your costume and where you were, so I made my way in the direction of the keg and found the vampire I was looking for. This isn't my first time wearing a vampire costume. I've dressed up as one often. My very first time wearing a vampire costume was when I was in grade five. I had begun watching movies with vampires in them, and yes, everyone I watched them with were scared. The movies portrayed the vampires as bad, but if they didn't kill people, would everyone still be frightened of them? I didn't see them as bad, just misunderstood and portrayed as the enemy. It was only a fictional character, so why couldn't it be good, or somewhat good or controlled? I fell in love with the thought of living forever, and I found the entire vampire/human relationship romantic. There is something very erotic, mysterious, and alluring about choosing to live forever. Forever is a very long time. What could, or would, you learn and how brave would you become? You could choose to live a great single life or find your soul mate for eternity. This is when you can interrupt and tell me that I'm very strange ..." I gently nudged Gabriel, trying to get him to follow me off to the side a little so we could talk. I hoped I didn't seem too aggressive, but it worked, and we moved off to the side without him reacting negatively to my gesture.

"Well, let me tell you that there was a reason I was attracted to you. You are hugely different than other girls, and no, I do not think you are strange, and I respect your opinion and deepest thoughts on the subject. I cannot pass any ill judgement on your feelings about vampires. I also have a fascination for them. I probably became part of the goth group because of that; it's like being a vampire, like they are portrayed in the movies, dressed in black. Goth people are also depicted as being bad or different, just like vampires in most movies. I am also an artist, so goth goes with the persona. I am glad we can talk like this. I feel I can trust you and that we have some sort of connection." Gabriel went quiet.

"I hope we can just build on the friendship we've started ... is it too soon to say we have crossed the line and are friends?" I asked. "I also feel like we've known each other in past lives perhaps. Sorry, there are many theories and opinions I have on life and past lives. I'm used to having individuals tell me they are not comfortable with my thoughts and beliefs. If you ever don't want me to continue with a direction of conversation, please just let me know."

"There is no topic I am not interested in hearing your opinion on. If anything, I have never met a more interesting individual. I think it is very alluring that you have strong opinions and ideals. I find you very fascinating and cannot wait to know as much as I can about you! I do have to go check on Mrs. Reese; would you like to come with me?" Gabriel had the biggest grin on his face.

"Sure," I replied.

Gabriel put his hand on the small of my back and led me towards the house; we went into the living room where Mrs. Reese was.

"Well, I can always count on you to hold up your promises, now can't I, Gabriel? Where are my children?" Mrs. Reese asked.

"Do not worry about them. I have recruited my own help. I am sure that this lovely young lady is very willing to help her fellow students." Gabriel looked at me with one eyebrow up and turned towards Mrs. Reese to give her assurance. He put his hand on my lower back once again and guided me into the kitchen.

"I am sorry to have involved you without asking your feelings first. Mrs. Reese made Caleb, Charlize, and I promise that, at midnight, we would start up the BBQ and make some snacks to sober up the drunken ones." Gabriel looked me in the eyes to get a reaction.

Charlize and Caleb were clearing off the tables outside and bringing the stuff into the kitchen. This must have been Charlize's directive to give Gabriel and I time alone together. We were the only ones in the kitchen, and we put things away and got ready to do some dishes.

"I'm always willing to help, especially when Mr. and Mrs. Reese are so nice to let us party at their beautiful home. I'm also happy to assist you in keeping a promise. You're like a son to Mrs. Reese, aren't you?" I asked.

"Well, I hope so. I have no mother of my own, and Mr. Vladimir is my adoptive parent. Don't get me wrong; I would never ask for a better father than him. I was lucky he saved me when he did. I lost both my parents in a car crash when

I was very young. Mr. Vladimir saw the accident happen, called an ambulance, took care of me until it arrived, and then followed it to the hospital. When he overheard the nurses say that, if I made it through surgery, I had no family to go to, he enquired with social services about taking me in till decisions were made. It just worked out that he decided to adopt me; therefore, I am eternally grateful. Anyway, I am probably boring you with my personal life."

Charlize and Caleb had stopped bringing stuff in and out of the kitchen, as they must have cleared everything. Gabriel and I were still alone. I was washing, and he was drying and putting things away.

"No, I'm very happy that you trust me to know this kind of personal stuff about you. I hope we get to know each other very well. I would like to know whatever you feel you want to share with me. I'm very intrigued by you; I don't think I have ever been as interested in anyone's personal life as I am in yours. I feel closeness between us, like I have known you for a long time; we are kindred spirits perhaps. What are we making on the BBQ?"

"I will make hot dogs and hamburgers," he said, "and if you want to start by making rounds with the veggie plate and the cheese and crackers, that would be great. While you are talking to everyone, make sure to tell them about the burgers and hot dogs, and can you get a feel of who is totally sloshed? Because we need to know if they have a ride. If you do not feel comfortable approaching anyone you think may have had too much, just let me know when you come back to the BBQ." Gabriel seemed to feel like he was imposing on me.

"Hey! I'm sure I can handle the situation, so don't worry about it," I replied.

I made my way around with the trays, and I made sure to let everyone know about the other food. I asked every individual if they had a ride or were staying over. There were a few that said they were driving that I thought had had a little too much to drink, and I asked them for their keys and that they come and see me later after they ate to get them back. There were a few that asked me who I was and what gave me the right to judge if they were sober enough to drive. I just stood my ground and told them that it didn't matter who I was and that I was checking everyone's conditions on behalf of Mrs. Reese, and if they chose not to comply, they wouldn't be allowed to the Reese parties again. They agreed after that, as who would want to be excluded from a great party like this? I ran into Charlize on my rounds, and she apologized for not checking the time more closely. I told her the rounds were done and the burgers and hot dogs were probably ready for eating.

"Hey! Any problems while you were out there? Your platters are pretty empty. Everyone's hungry?" Gabriel asked and pointed at his empty grill.

"Well, looks like they cleaned you out too!" I started to laugh.

"I like your laugh," Gabriel said, "and your smile is nice too."

We finished cooking and serving. Charlize and Caleb helped clean up, and Mrs. Reese was impressed with Gabriel and me. By the time we had finished cleaning up, there were about a dozen people left, half of whom were waiting for cabs. The others were crashing at the Reese's'. Tom and Jim had come to see me when we were starting the cooking and told me they were heading out. Tom was sober. Kelsie and Jenn were staying at my place, so they were waiting on me. I looked at the time. It was about two a.m.

I looked up at Charlize. "Well, I must thank you all for yet another wonderful party. We must be heading out." I smiled at Kelsie and Jenn.

The girls replied that they were quite ready to leave.

"How are you getting home?" Gabriel asked.

"We are walking back to the dorms. We will be okay. It's only three blocks away," I assured him.

"I will drive you in my car!" Gabriel insisted.

"No, Gabriel, we could use the exercise, and I think these two have alcohol to burn out of their systems," I replied.

"If you are insisting on walking, then I am insisting that I walk with you, and I am not talking no for an answer." Gabriel's eyes were profoundly serious, almost scary.

"Well, if you are insisting, then we thank you for being gentlemanly," I replied, a little puzzled by old-fashioned he was. The hand on the small of my back had thrown me for a loop and now he was walking us home—don't get me wrong, I liked it; it was just rare nowadays to have someone treat women that way.

On the walk back to the dorms, Kelsie asked, "Hey Gabriel, are you wearing contacts or are your eyes really that blue?"

This was a question I was going to ask myself in time, but obviously Kelsie needed to know now.

"Well, they are contacts … do my eye freak you out or look bad?" Gabriel asked with a worried tone.

"No, dude! Your eyes are totally cool," Kelsie replied, stumbling and slurring.

"You have the most alluring eyes." Jenn had had enough to drink to find the words without cowering.

"Well, what's your opinion, Evangeline?" Gabriel looked directly into my eyes.

At this point, we arrived at the dorms, and I let the girls in.

"We will go in and give you two some time alone," Kelsie said, grinning.

"Well, are you avoiding the question?" Gabriel asked.

I said, "Listen, I don't want to scare you away with my thoughts on you, so let's not go down this road. We are taking everything very slow in this new friendship, and I don't want to cause any situations that may end it."

"I really think you are just dodging the question; I want to know what you think of my eyes *and* your feelings. Please tell me," Gabriel insisted.

"I really hope you can handle what I have to say! First and foremost, I think you have the most incredible eyes I have ever seen. The night that you bumped into me, I had spotted you from afar. I was people-watching that night, trying not to be too obvious, and my eyes ran into you. I wasn't sure if I was seeing what I thought I was seeing; I couldn't just stare, and chance being caught. Then when you ran into me at the bar … that's why I seemed like a bitch, because it wasn't my imagination—you were as hot as I thought you were. So, I quickly turned away, as fast as I could, so you couldn't see me drooling or see my feelings through my eyes. You're the hottest thing I have ever seen, and I don't even know if you have a great body. Sorry, let me phrase that again… I have seen you with almost no clothes on—your back side that is, when you were modelling. You are hot, but you're also incredibly old-fashioned and your eyes speak to me as though I know you from somewhere." I stopped talking and took a deep breath.

"Well, I am glad that you are attracted to me, as I had seen you the moment you sat at the bar. Just for the record, no one pushed me into you; I bumped into you on purpose. I had seen you from the corner of my eye and needed to see you up close. I hope I am not scaring you now! I have enquired about you ever sense. I probably know where you have been every day since that run in. We are old souls, and there is an extraordinarily strong connection between us." Gabriel spoke in a very alluring voice.

"Why would you be looking at me? There are so many better-looking and more intelligent girls out there. You could have anyone you want. Why waste your time looking in my direction? If I could only have one guy, I would have wished to meet someone as beautiful as you, and it's more than that. It's the feeling I get from you! I can't even begin to break apart the emotions I have towards you. How can these feelings be? I have only just met you, and my feelings for you seem very real. I have had dreams and even daydreams … wide awake, yet in some sort of trance, just thinking of you!" I said, holding back tears.

"I understand … because I feel the same for you! The soul wants whom it wants. It has nothing to do with looks, and by the way, you are very beautiful in a very natural way. I would like to see half the girls you think are hot after they chisel the makeup off their faces. It must be scary to wake up next to them with no makeup; there are no worries with you. You are who you are, and you also express your feelings, which I also admire," Gabriel said, pulling me in close.

I wanted to kiss him so bad, and I thought he was leaning in for one, but I didn't want to make the first move just in case I'd misread the situation. We were looking into each other's eyes. If I were a piece of ice, I would no longer exist as a solid; I would merely be a puddle of water waiting to be molded. I was sure that my eyes were saying *"kiss me,"* and then it happened. It was a sweet kiss on my cheek, and then we both said goodnight.

I had been sure we would have a romantic kiss since we'd both just finished expressing our feelings to one another.

But Gabriel has proven to be very old-fashioned so far with his approach to many things, so the kiss on the check wasn't surprising. I went into the house and up to my room. The girls were sleeping; they had brought their sleeping bags and crashed on the floor in my room. I was happy that they'd fallen asleep, as the last thing I wanted to do at this time was explain the great conversation we'd had that should have ended with a real kiss but hadn't.

I woke up in the morning, and the girls were still sleeping. I lay there thinking, *why did he not kiss me, if what he said was true?* Maybe … no, he wouldn't have made up that story; it seemed too genuine. Gabriel's eyes also seemed very emotional when he'd told me how he felt; I was positive he was speaking from the heart. The girls woke up and just stared at me; they could tell something was bothering me.

"What's wrong, Angel? Did your conversation not go as you wanted it to? I'm sorry I fell asleep before you came in. Were you out there for a long time?" Jenn asked in a concerned tone.

"I'm very sorry I fell asleep too. I guess I shouldn't ask if there was any bodily contact." Kelsie still looked very inquisitive.

"Well, the conversation was great. If it were about the conversation, I would be very happy about the feelings he said he had for me. Gabriel seems sensitive and real. He is the most wonderful guy I could have ever asked to meet. I just don't know why he chose to pull me in for a hug and a kiss on the cheek. I was waiting for the romantic kiss after the words we spoke to each other."

"Angel, he kept putting his hand on the small of your back, opening all your doors, and asking you if you were alright the whole night. He's clearly old-fashioned in his ways. I'm positive that his feelings for you are very true, but maybe Gabriel believes in taking things slow. If that is the case, then be very happy, because those guys are few and far between, based on the ones we've met or dated," Jenn said in a serious tone.

We got up and went downstairs. It was ten a.m., and no one was around. I made some eggs, bacon, and toast for breakfast and the girls left shortly thereafter. They told me not to worry, that everything would work itself out. After they left, I had the hottest shower ever and went back to lie in my bed and watch television. I couldn't stop thinking of the conversation, the feelings expressed, and the question that kept coming up. Had he wanted to kiss me and just held back because he was old-fashioned, or did he just not really want to? I fell asleep again. I must have really been stressing over the whole situation and getting really exhausted, because I crashed a lot.

Amy knocked at my door and woke me up. I told her to come in.

"Are you okay? How was your Halloween party? Did Gabriel show up?" she asked.

"Yes, Gabriel was there, and he also wore a vampire costume. We spent most of the night together and did a lot of talking. He told me that he had feelings for me, and I also told him mine, but in the end, the kiss was not there. Gabriel kissed me on the cheek," I said in a depressed tone.

"Angel, Gabriel seems like a sensitive and genuine kind of guy; he's talking his time, probably wants everything to be perfect between you. Don't worry; if he told you that he had feelings for you, I am sure he does. Give it time. You only met a few months ago, right?" Amy said, trying to comfort me.

I fell asleep again and imagined what it might have been like if Gabriel would have kissed me on the lips. I was sure Gabriel had moist and juicy lips, but very firm and intense. His lips are very full, but not big. I hoped he chose to kiss me soon. I didn't know how I could take the intensity I felt inside of me.

If Gabriel were there at that very second, I would have to jump into his arms and hope he would catch me. Push him down on my bed and rip his shirt off. At this point, with the feelings I had for him, I would love him in any way, shape, or form, but I had a feeling it would be nice. Fantasizing was always great, but reality can be just as good too. I just really liked him.

Chapter Eight

The days passed, then weeks, and I started to worry about our conversation and if Gabriel had meant it or if he was like most other guys—full of crap and just trying to get into girls' pants. Though, I supposed, since he didn't even kiss me, that couldn't be. I thought he was around a few times, as I felt or sensed him as I walked through the gardens to classes. Maybe I just wanted to see him so bad that I thought I sensed him, because even I thought that was a little weird. I thought I smelled him again as well, like I'd walked in his path, and there was a moving aura or shimmering of heat waves moving around me. Weird, right? I know. I can't really explain it.

I asked Charlize probably every day if she heard anything about Gabriel liking me from her brother. She told me Gabriel did like me and that he would appear when I least expected it. Charlize sounded a little sick of my questions but seemed to also know how I felt. I ran into Caleb every so often and asked him the same questions; he was not as nice as his sister. He told me that Gabriel was not like any other guy I had ever met, that he did like me, and not to push the situation. He also stated that Gabriel knew everything I was doing and asked, even though I had not physically seen him myself. I decided to let it go and concentrate on school.

I had a meeting with Gabriel's father, Mr. Vladimir. It was the middle of November, and I had to let him know the subject I'd chosen for the assignment and show how the research was going. He seemed quite interested in the whole vampire topic; Mr. Vladimir asked me why vampires, and I explained the fascination I'd had since I was a young girl. He also seemed to notice I was a little distracted and asked if I needed any help with anything.

"Actually, you can help me! I need to know where Gabriel is. I haven't seen him since the Reese's Halloween party!" I asked, quite anxiously.

"Listen, it's probably better that you stay away from my son and concentrate on school. He's a good kid, but his relationships with young ladies do not seem to have very good outcomes. I would hate to see you ruin your school year because Gabriel cannot sort through his feelings."

"Are we done with this topic?" I asked. I really had such a hard time controlling my emotions. I felt like crying, I felt like hitting something or screaming at the top of my lungs. Now what? Did I take what Mr. Vladimir had just said to heart or did I continue as though he hadn't said it?

"No," he said, gently. "I am sorry about Gabriel, but I am looking out for you. Anyways, how is your research going? Will you be finished on time?" Mr. Vladimir asked.

"All my research is done; I just have to sort out the information and then write the report, and I should be done in about a week," I said firmly.

"Take your time, the report is not due till the day before Christmas break starts, and even then, it can be extended till the beginning of January if need be! I was also wondering, are your vampires good or the traditionally bad ones when you think of them?" Mr. Vladimir questioned.

"I have a different outlook on vampires in general. I think of them as being misunderstood and very romantic." I smiled and walked away. "See you later."

I went home that day and reflected on what Mr. Vladimir had said about Gabriel being emotionally screwed up. He made Gabriel out to be a very confused young man. Well, I thought, he was young. I didn't know how many classes he took, but he seemed to have a few majors on the go. I wasn't sure how all the traveling they had done had affected his studies. Maybe it was an ongoing challenge, and he was older than he seemed. Worst-case scenario, Gabriel was in his mid-twenties, and I was eighteen. I was legal. I didn't know where he lived or anything about him really, except that he supposedly liked me, if that was even true.

Whatever. I needed to stop with the over-dramatization of everything, and maybe do up a list of questions to ask him the next time I ran into him. I needed to stop worrying and thinking the worst. After all, I was here to get an education, not find a man, though both would be great.

I went to my drawing class and investigated the classroom before mine like I always did; Gabriel hadn't been there for a couple of weeks at least. I felt the sadness go through my body. I sat down in my desk, and Mrs. Tanner came in and asked everyone to be seated.

"I have a new model to introduce. He has done modelling before in some of the other classes, and you may have seen him in the halls or maybe even in your classes, as he is also a student. Let me introduce Gabriel Vladimir." Mrs. Tanner smiled as he walked to the center of the room.

My jaw dropped. I couldn't believe that I was going to draw—never mind that—*see* Gabriel almost naked. I was probably red in the face; I tried to calm myself down. Gabriel looked so calm, like it was nothing to get up in the middle of a room as Mrs. Tanner introduced him. I'm sure I could never do it myself. After being introduced, he went behind his wardrobe wall and came back out with a pair of Calvin

Klein's boxer briefs—the short shorts, not the long ones. The underwear was very tight, sat low on the hip area instead of on the waist, and everything looked very good, if you know what I mean. All the girls were making comments about him being cute or hot or that they knew him or had seen him around. I even heard a few of the girls say they had been with him or would be with him.

I was too full of jealous rage to really know what I was hearing. I would have to confront Gabriel on his prior engagements, if there was any truth of him being with some of the girls in my class, and how recent it was. I needed to know where I stood, but if I said the wrong thing, I might not even get a chance and might even lose his friendship.

You know how girls can be: just like guys, exaggerating about the actual goings on. It was probably just talk to make themselves look better in front of the others. Getting the hot guy…

Gabriel got up on platform and looked at me, winked, and had a little smirk on his face. All the girls then looked at me, almost a little resentfully. I didn't do anything, just sat there.

For the entire class, I drooled as I drew him; every inch of his body was muscular. Gabriel had the thighs of a hockey player and the definition of a runner, lean and slender, but still looked like he did or had done some weight training, and he even had well-developed calves. In my experience, as most of my boyfriends and guy friends were hockey players, they have the best thighs—inner thighs, to be exact. Gabriel's legs were legs to drool over, incredible, and his butt looked just perfect in the underwear, nice and firm like the rest of him. The upper body was just as beautiful to look at; he was very well-proportioned. He had some hair on his chest, light in color like his hair, well dispersed, with a slight trail leading down from his belly button into his underwear. I was in my own little world the entire class. I dreamed of laying my head on him and running my fingers along his chest.

The class went by fast. I woke up from daydreaming when Mrs. Tanner thanked Gabriel for being our model. Gabriel went behind the room divider to change; I tried to gather my things quickly to leave without him seeing me leave. I headed out the main doors and was crossing to the main schoolyard when I felt a hand graze my shoulder. I turned around, expecting to find Gabriel, but no one was there. I turned around again to continue walking, and he was right in front of me.

"How did you get in front of me? Were you the one who touched my shoulder?"

"I didn't see anyone around you, and I left out another door to be able to run into you," Gabriel replied. "Why did you leave so fast? Did you not like what you saw? You seemed in a daze all class. Listen, I am deeply sorry that I have kept my distance, but I had to gather my thoughts and feelings for you! It is true, I meant what I told you, but after I realized what I had said to you, I needed to reflect on my feelings. I have never felt like this before about a girl. My father told me that you had asked where I was and if I was alright. I am glad you asked him; it lets me know you are still thinking of me."

I nodded. "I know I left quickly. I was embarrassed, and I know I was in a daze. Ever since I met you or you ran into me, I have been in a daze. I just seem to get lost deep in my thoughts. I'm always daydreaming of you; I can't help it," I said, very disorientated. "As for our past conversation Halloween night, I just about wrote off everything that you had regurgitated that night to me. If you care for me at all, never leave me up in the air again, because if there is a next time, it will be the last. I can't deal without expressing my feelings to you and seeing if the feelings are reciprocated. I'm probably being harsh right now, but I'm very angry with the way that you've acted. I have no right, as I'm not your girlfriend and barely your friend, but I'm very possessive of you for some reason. For that I apologize, but not for being angry with you for ignoring me for such a long time."

"I am deeply sorry too! Really. I know that I have not acted like I care, but I would rather be always by your side. Can I please give you a hug? I need to be close to you and have your forgiveness," Gabriel pleaded with me.

"I don't . . ." was all I had time to say before Gabriel grabbed me and gave me the best hug I had ever received in my life. There was so much feeling and energy that I couldn't help but reciprocate, expressing the feelings I truly felt for him.

"Thank you for hugging me back," Gabriel said ever so softly in my ear. "I do need you in my life. I feel a void when I am not near, or when you are not in my sights."

"Gabriel, I never see you, so how can you be near me or around me?" I asked, quite puzzled. A part of me wanted to tell him of my jealous rage towards the girls always swarming around him and things I had heard them say, but I didn't even remember what was really said, as I'd let my frustration get the better of me in drawing class. If I tried to explain my feelings, perhaps he wouldn't want to be around me as much, and maybe I just needed to keep my crazy thoughts and jealous reactions to myself, at least for now.

"I am always around and always will be, no matter what. That I promise you," Gabriel said as he looked into my eyes and smiled. "I do have to go, though. My father and I have a supper to go to, but I will see you very soon, and we will talk. How about tomorrow night? Will you be in the library?"

"I will be there only because I have to, not because I think you'll even show up," I replied and gave the two-eyebrow lift, like I did not believe a word he was saying.

I went back to my dorm, and everyone was in the kitchen. I smiled and said hello and quickly ran upstairs to my room. I got changed and went to the track for a run. I needed to think and blow off some steam. There was one good thing about Gabriel making me angry, confused, or whatever I was: I seemed to know nothing lately, so I spend a lot of time running and lifting weights and doing homework to try and sort things out or occupy my brain and try to not think of him.

Gabriel was everywhere and nowhere. I really thought I had to let him know how I really felt, how this was all affecting me, and that the situation was not good for me. I had lost all the weight I had wanted to lose, and I had a four-pack, but I couldn't afford to lose weight this quickly. If our relationship continued the way it had being going, I would have a six pack by spring for sure. My food intake hadn't been there, as all I did was think of Gabriel, Gabriel, and more Gabriel. I was not eating and sleeping well; I seemed to be feeling more rundown lately.

After my run, I had a sugar craving, so I walked to the convenience store down the road. I got to the store, bought some jujubes and a Diet Coke— sometimes it needs to be done—and some beef jerky. I walked out of the store and in front of the restaurant in the plaza, and I saw Gabriel in the restaurant with his father and a few other people I didn't know. I just kept walking; I didn't want to make it obvious that I had seen him. I got a few stores down when I felt his presence, and I turned around and there he was. Gabriel came towards me, and my heart started to pound again. I had truly forgiven him for his previous behavior. Gabriel walked towards me, and I was probably smiling back without realizing it.

"Hello, Evangeline, twice in one day; it must be my lucky day!" Gabriel had a smile from ear to ear.

"Yeah! I go almost a month without seeing you, and I see you twice the same day," I said and shook my head. "Listen, we seriously need to talk. I'm all screwed up; I have lost too much weight these past few months thinking and wondering about you and me. I know we just met, but, well … I won't keep you today, but we do need to talk. Please, soon."

Gabriel hugged me again, and this time I relaxed a little and sank a bit into his body. He was so beautiful, and we could be so good together. I was almost certain of it. I was still scared that any time could very well be the last time I saw him, and that would be devastating.

"I just came out to quickly see you and get another hug from you, but I need to get back." Gabriel kissed me on the cheek again. "I will see you tomorrow in the library!"

"Thanks, Gabriel, you made my day and confused me again all at the same time," I said, a bit sad that he had to leave me.

I went back to the dorms, and the kitchen was empty, and the house was quiet. I wasn't hungry after the candy and the Coke, but I grabbed a boiled potato I had left in the fridge, and my beef jerky and a piece of cheese, just to say I had put some sort of nutrition in my body. It was lots of protein. I should have been eating tons of carbs right now, with this lack of energy I had, instead of straight sugar. I had to get it together. I had a shower, and as I was walking by Amy's room, she asked me in to talk.

"Hello, Angel, how is everything going? We have not talked for a few days." Amy looked inquisitive.

"It's been rough lately. I hadn't seen 'him' since the Halloween party and today he shows up in my drawing class. You would not believe what he was doing there; Gabriel is taking over the modelling! His body is even better than I would have ever expected it to be. Gabriel has the looks, the personality, and the body to boot; I just hope I can meet his standards if ever given the chance to be with him." I smiled ear to ear but was in a worried daze at the same time. I must have been floating … I sure felt like it, anyway. I continued. "I went for a run and to the corner store and ran into him again, and I got two hugs and two kisses from him in one day. I just hope I see him again tomorrow in the library!"

"Wow, I'm very happy for you, Angel. I hope that things keep looking up for you. He sounds like quite the guy." Amy smiled. "Sorry I wasn't there when you were going through the rough times. I have been busy with school, and I also miss my boyfriend. I think I'll take the bus and go see him this weekend. I was going to wait till Christmas, but I need to see him sooner than later."

"Yeah! I don't know how you do it; you must not be the jealous kind! I don't think I could have a long-distance relationship; I have a hard time trusting my significant others. Anyways, if you ever need to talk, I'm always here to listen; it doesn't have to be you listening to me all the time, Amy. I will talk to you later. I need to finish some homework before tomorrow's class. Have a good sleep," I said with a deep breath.

The next day went by slow; it was Thursday, and I had typography in the afternoon. It felt like Mrs. Reilly was gazing in my direction the entire class. I was working on my project, but I was daydreaming. What's new? I'm sure I had a smile the entire class as I was remembering the previous day in my drawing class. The image of the tiny briefs and the muscular form that stood before me seemed so vivid, like I could reach out and give it a quick squeeze. Oh, it would have been nice to feel those wonderful thighs, or caress Gabriel at that time, this time, all the time.

After class, I went home for a quick workout. I decided to skip the run today, and even shortened my workout in hopes of getting to the library as soon as possible to get some work done before Gabriel came. *If* Gabriel came, I should say! I put on very form-fitting jeans and a snug turtleneck and let my hair down. Amy asked me if she could come to the library with me.

"Sure," I replied. We got there, and Amy's friends had a table at the far end, kind of secluded, but it was full. So, I sat at the next table, which was also off on its own and had one other person sitting there. I hoped they would leave. I wanted to be able to finish my research and be done with the library for a while, and I wanted to have privacy if Gabriel showed up. I went to the section on mythical creatures, where I seemed to spend most of my time. I was looking to see if there had been any books returned that I had not grazed through. Suddenly, I felt what seemed to be hands gently grazing my back, as though someone were tickling me. I turned around and no one was there. I looked at the table I was sitting at, and Gabriel was sitting there, talking to Amy at the table beside mine. I was very happy to see that he'd kept his word. I returned to the table, put my books down, and put my hand on his shoulder.

"So," I said, "you've met Amy, my roommate."

"Gabriel is everything you said he would be," she said, smiling. "I will leave you two to talk, and don't be a stranger. Stop by the house sometime." With that, she turned back to her friends.

"So, you talk about me, eh?" Gabriel smiled as he got up from Amy's table and sat in the chair next to mine, which the other person had just left. He sat very close to me; any closer and we could have been snuggling. I really liked that idea but tried not to show it too much.

"Don't flatter yourself; I'm always furious with you when I mention you to anyone!" I replied hastily. I wasn't sure why, it just came out—a defense mechanism, perhaps, but without bad intent.

"Well, any talk, good or bad, means that you are thinking of me." Gabriel smiled.

"I just don't get you. Half the time I see a sensitive and genuine guy, but other times I think maybe it's just an act and that you are arrogant and conceited and think that your God's gift to women. I want to think the best of you, but you say things and then I don't see you for the longest time. You confuse me," I said, shaking my head.

"I am sorry for confusing you; it is not my intent. I am sensitive and genuine, but I am so used to acting like the other guys, because no one likes the nice guy. Most girls like the good-looking bad boy, and I just play on that role. It is hard to let down my guard and show my true self, even though you have seen the real guy, the mama's boy, if I had a mother. Other than Caleb, Charlize, and their family, no one knows the true me, except you now! It scares me to have the true me come out more and more." Gabriel put his head into his hands. "I find myself a little less self-confident around you. Weird. So that could be part of the behavioral changes from time to time."

"You're worried? About what? I like the sensitive Gabriel and not the one everyone seems to know. He is the one I want to continue spending time with and getting to know better. It would be nice to have more quality time to get to know one another, don't you think?" I looked into Gabriel's eyes as I spoke.

"I have kept my distance because I did not know how to deal with our situation," Gabriel added.

"What situation are you talking about?" I asked.

"I am not used to being around such a down-to-earth, smart, and straight-to-the-point young lady." Gabriel stared directly back into my eyes.

"That still doesn't explain why you keep a distance from me; if anything, it should make you want to spend more time, not less, getting to know me, should it not?" I gave Gabriel an inquisitive grin.

"I am just afraid of liking you too much; in the past, my record with young ladies is not good, and emotionally, I get too involved. It takes its toll on me. I am sure the young ladies may have also gotten involved and disappointed with the relationship. I just do not ever want to hurt you; you are very special to me, and if being friends is all we are meant to be, then I will have to deal with it, but I need you in my life," Gabriel said sincerely.

"Let's stop playing games. Do you like me, and do you want to be more than just friends?" I asked directly. "Since we are on the topic, or dancing around it, let me get something off my chest. I know I said I wanted to take time to get to know each other, but I can't do this anymore."

"Do what?" Gabriel sounded worried and shook his head. "No, don't answer. Please just let me talk for a bit. I do want to get to know you better and you me, and then you can determine whether you want to continue and grow into a more-than-just-friends relationship," Gabriel replied.

"I still didn't get a true answer to my question," I stated.

"Yes, I like you a lot, but I am scared for the both of us. I do not want to put my heart and soul into this relationship to just get it torn, and I do not wish you ill will ever." Gabriel brushed my cheek gently as he spoke.

"Let's start by actually spending time together—that would be a nice start!" I said a little sarcastically.

"I was going to ask you if you would like to join my friends and me for a little bowling, next Saturday—not this weekend but the next—and you are welcome to invite your friends to come also," Gabriel said.

"I will see my friend's tomorrow night for supper and a movie, and I can ask if they would like to come," I replied with a little excitement in my voice. "Will I see you next week to give you an answer? Because finding you is very hard to do."

"I promise that I will make time to see you, and you may even get sick of seeing me. Let's talk about general things to get to know each other better!" Gabriel seemed eager to ask me some questions.

We had been in the library for a while now, and it had cleared out pretty good. Amy and her friends had left the table next to us and the next tables over were at least ten feet away from us or more. It was a big library, and we were pretty much alone in our little corner.

"Okay," I said. "I'll start. What is your favorite color? What is your favorite movie? What is your favorite subject? And do you have ex-girlfriends at the college?"

"Well, my favorite color is red, and my favorite subjects are history and French. I am in the third year, and I take history, literature, French, Spanish, and German. As you can see, I like learning other languages. Never know when you can use them. I model to make extra money for spending, so I need not ask for more money than I need to from my father, as he does so much for me already. I did get some scholarship money, but I still try to help where I can. No, I have no girlfriend currently college or otherwise. I moved here three years ago, and I have not had any since I have been here. I am twenty-one. I graduated high school when I had just turned sixteen; I had some tutoring along the way. I have done lots of travelling throughout the years, as my father wanted me to be cultured, and he gets bored easily, so he chose for us to move around every year. Sometimes we stayed two, but this is the longest in one place; this is our third school year here in little town of Old's. My father says we moved to keep things interesting, and I have lived in England, France, Paris, Australia, Montana, British Columbia, the Northwest Territories, Newfoundland, and of course, Alberta. I may have missed a few. I was born in England and have never been back since. My parents died, and I was taken in by Mr. Vladimir. Mr. Vladimir was not from England; he just saved my life there and I had no family to go back to, so he was my legal guardian and later adopted me. I do not know anything about my parents, except that we were in a car crash. A wild animal was standing in the road, and my birth father swerved to miss it, and my birth parents did not survive. The nurse told me that my father, died quickly and did not suffer. Later, Mr. Vladimir told me he had went through the front window and died on impact, it was quick. My mother was brought to emergency, but only lasted a few hours from internal bleeding and too many injured organs to be saved. I barely made it myself.

"Fortunately, Mr. Vladimir found himself at the accident and pulled me out of the car. The right place and the right time, lucky for me... He followed the ambulance to the hospital, and apparently took care of everything for me, including giving me a home. I had a collapsed lung as I was being brought into the hospital. When I woke up, I had amnesia, and still till this day I have not gotten much of my memory back. I can't remember my birth parents at all really, I was twelve so I should, right? Maybe one of my repressed memories. I remember images of people in a car, no faces, and a big black shadow over me, and that's about all. I asked the doctors what they knew, and asked Mr. Vladimir if he had seen anything. All I got was the reason the police gave the doctors, which was that they must had swerved, perhaps to avoid an animal in the road. There were apparently lots of wild animal on the hillside there, and they often caused accidents.

"The entire experience was life changing. Mr. Vladimir said he didn't see anything near the car when he approached, and he called emergency. The doctors also said I was lucky he found me when he did and that there was a hospital nearby. It was like starting my life over again, with new experiences and a new family. Well, I think that it is your turn to share with me now!" Gabriel smiled.

"Wow, I am so very sorry to hear about your parents. I didn't mean to have you stir up such tragic memories when I said I wanted to get to know you better. I wasn't expecting you to tell me all of this. This is private stuff; don't get me wrong, I am very glad you trust me with such a traumatic experience. I am glad you were willing to tell me more than just the questions I asked. I don't have anything as interesting to tell you."

"I don't know what to say. I grew up in a small town, where everyone knew everyone. The town grew to be a city, which my mother used to work for. My father works for an oil company as an accountant and financial advisor, and ever since he started working there, my mother has been taking care of the house, filling in part time here and there for the city still and doing some charity and volunteer work, keeping herself busy. I have worked since I was fifteen years old for the city also, thanks to my mom and her connections. I am in my first year at the college, and I have not chosen my major yet. I am taking a year of general courses. I will either be majoring in literature or in the arts. I have a brother and a sister and both parents. I have only been in Canada, and even then, only in the provinces of Québec, Ontario, and British Columbia and have passed through the middle provinces on my way west to the east of Canada. I wish I could have visited the many places that you have. I grew up in Alberta and have been here all my life.

"I like to hike, go camping, fishing, rollerblading, and swimming, and I play street hockey, and occasionally go biking. I'm fairly easy going when it comes to sports; I have always played on school teams, and am usually the goon on the team, nowhere near good enough for a scholarship in anything. I swam on a team when I was younger but lacked the discipline to go all the way. I run almost every day and work out to stay in shape; I would like to grow old gently. I like all types of music and love to dance." I thought I should stop talking. "I can ramble on for hours; it's your turn."

"Well, you may think you are rambling, but if you do not ramble, as you say, how will I learn everything about you? You are well rounded, and maybe you will travel later in life. You are still young. I do not want to seem like I am not enjoying this conversation, because I am, but I should be heading home. I will make sure I find you on Monday, okay?" Gabriel put his hand on my face and kissed my lips ever so lightly.

"Bye." I couldn't find any other words; I was shocked that he'd kissed me on the lips and not on the cheek as per usual. The kiss was just a friendly peck, not the passionate, loving kiss I would have liked, and Gabriel left right after. I packed up my stuff and left also. It was about 9:45 p.m. and the library was closing at 10:00, so our conversation would have ended soon anyway, if he had not excused himself politely.

I got home and everyone was either still out or in bed because there was no movement throughout the house. I got ready for bed and lay down, re-hashing my day. It had been good. I imagined what a passionate kiss would be like, as Gabriel had been very gentle; therefore, I assumed a passionate kiss from him would probably not be aggressive or demanding. It probably would be intense, earth-shattering, warm, and thigh clenching.

On Saturday, Kelsie came by at four, as we were going to the big city to have a steak supper and watch a movie. The best steak in the city was at The Keg, and that's where we were going. Kelsie and I met Tom, Jim, and Jenn at Tom's dorm, and we all went for steak and a few beers before heading to the movie of choice: *Eclipse*, from the third book in the Twilight Saga.

Tom and Jim were not quite excited as Jenn, Kelsie, and I; we loved the romantic possibilities of mortals with vampires. The movie was great, and we decided to head to a dorm party. Apparently, the floor below Tom and Jim's was having a party. Before we got there, I remembered about the bowling invitation, and I asked everyone if they wanted to come down my way to go bowling next Saturday, but only Kelsie agreed to come. The others had major assignments due the following Monday, so homework and studying was on their schedules. I could always count on Kelsie to join me; she was always up for meeting new guys. Kelsie and I stayed for a while, and we got back to my place at eleven thirty. She decided to get in her car and go, as she was tired and had to get up early the next morning for a family thing.

I said goodbye and turned to open my house door when I stopped in my tracks and looked around quickly. I felt like I was being watched. This wasn't the first time I'd felt this way, but usually it was earlier and there were people out. I didn't see anyone, but I felt like there was someone there. I quickly opened my door and went in, locking the door behind me. I had never done that before, but it felt right now. I went to the kitchen window, where I could see the front door and the parking lot in front of my dorm. There didn't seem to be anyone there, but then thought I saw a shadow to the right in my peripheral vision. I turned to look, but nothing was there.

Maybe the movie had made me a little paranoid; I had been working on my vampire project lots lately. Though I know vampires and werewolves were mystical creatures, not real, perhaps I wished they were real a little too much. I quickly got ready for bed. Everyone was in their bedrooms already as per usual, maybe sleeping, so I wasn't sure if I should ask someone to come and double check on things with me or ask if they had seen anything strange around the building that evening. I decided to stop being a chicken and went to the kitchen and took another look outside. I didn't see anything or feel that there was anything there.

I went up to sleep, but I couldn't help but think of Monday. Was I going to see Gabriel, or would it be back to normal, with me having to wait maybe a week to see him?

Sunday, I just stayed in my dorm and worked on my assignments and watched television, cancelled on family afternoon planned. I didn't work out; I didn't even get dressed. I went downstairs three times for food and snacks. I ran into Kim and her friend, who was in some of my classes, said hello, and went about my business. I really didn't talk to anyone except Charlize or Gabriel's group or Amy, unless I was spoken to. I wasn't rude to anyone; I just had nothing to say. Amy got back late, and I was already in bed. She probably thought I was sleeping and didn't knock on my door, and I was too lazy and warm to get out of bed to ask her about her weekend.

CHAPTER NINE

I woke up wondering how this week would be. It could be another lonely week again unless Gabriel was going to keep his word. Don't get me wrong, I tended to keep to myself, so I had no one to blame for my loneliness or finding my days long but myself. Perhaps I needed to put myself out there more. Monday went by fast and there was no sign of Gabriel; as per usual, he seemed non-existent. I knew I was going to see him twice this week for sure for drawing class, unless he didn't show up to model, but I didn't count on anything outside of that. I wanted alone time or quality time with him.

I grabbed a sandwich to eat on the way back to the school for drawing class, and I was going to go to the cafeteria to grab a Coke. I should have just bought some Coke for the dorm and saved some money, since I seemed to buy one almost every day. Well, recently, I had only really gone to the school early to see if I could find Gabriel, not for the pop.

"Sorry, Evangeline." I got grabbed and spun around by Gabriel. "I am running late. I will see you after class in the gardens, between buildings for sure. Please meet me there." He gave me a big hug and kissed me on the cheek, then took off to class to get ready, I was guessing. I took my time. I had ten minutes, and maybe he had to talk with Mrs. Tanner before each class to know what her itinerary was for that day.

I was just people watching after being accosted by Gabriel in the cafeteria when I saw Charlize come in the front doors. She came up to me. It had been a while since we'd talked.

"Hey! Angel, how was your weekend? Did you talk to Gabriel last week or on the weekend? Sorry I didn't touch basis with you last week. Was busy with things. My parents have me helping them with a fundraiser they are doing. Are you coming bowling on Saturday?" Charlize asked.

"Hello," I replied. "I talked to Gabriel at the library on Thursday evening, and he did mention the bowling this Saturday. He said it was okay to invite my friends. Are you good with that too? Hey, by the way, if you or your parents ever need any help, feel free to ask. I always have time or can make time."

"Yes, of course," Charlize said, a little puzzled. "We are all friends now; they can come hang out anytime. About the fundraiser, thanks, we're all done with setting up, but if we need help the day of or with the next one, I will let you know and you can help. It would be great to have another set of hands; there are always lots of things to do. My parents never do anything simple or small."

"Oh!" I said, "I forgot, I also went to the city to catch a movie with my friends, *Eclipse*, the new twilight movie, and it was good. Then we went back to a Rez party, but we left early … we weren't in the mood for drinking. You should come into the city sometime with us; they have good keg parties at the Rez too. I laid low on Sunday, didn't even get dressed. How was your weekend?"

"For sure, I'll come with you guys, I am always up for a good party. Hey, listen," Charlize said as she placed her hand on my shoulder in a reassuring way. "I know that Gabriel isn't around like most guys, but I know for a fact that he does like you! My brother tells me that he talks about how you're great and not like any other girl he has ever met before. Why don't you come and hang out at my place in the evenings to study, or even pretend to? He is pretty much at my place every night, and you guys can hang out a little more, get a little more acquainted."

We did have homework we could do together, as we had some of the same classes together. I could go after my workout and maybe then I would be able to see more of Gabriel. I told Charlize I would take advantage of her generosity and that I would be there around seven o'clock.

I quickly made my way to my drawing class, excited to see Gabriel again so soon … and nearly naked. As I was entering the arts building from the beautiful gardens, I checked my watch; I had two minutes to get to class. I got there and found the door was already closed. I knocked, and Mrs. Tanner said to come in.

"Evangeline, is it?" Mrs. Tanner questioned.

"Yes, sorry I am late!" I replied, "It will never happen again."

"I don't care, but you may if you keep being late. I can assure you it will affect your marks," she said.

I went to my desk and got my sketchbook and pencils out; I was a little embarrassed, as Gabriel was there. I really didn't want the teacher, let alone Gabriel, to think I was irresponsible and unable to get to class on time. I kept my nose down and sketched Gabriel; we were concentrating on motion again. Mrs. Tanner asked us to go back to oval, circular motions to show the movement. I wasn't sure what Gabriel thought of me being late, so I didn't look at him in the eyes at all.

In keeping my head down all class in embarrassment, I could hear the same girls as before commenting on how great Gabriel's underwear looked today, and I could feel my jealousy acting up again. I took a deep breath. I had no right to be jealous; Gabriel was not mine and might never be, and I had to stop overthinking and reacting like this.

After class, I quickly gathered my stuff and headed out. I wasn't sure if I would wait for Gabriel in the gardens.

"Evangeline." I heard a whisper in my ear as I was just about to open the main school doors, after passing through the gardens very quickly. "Were you not going to wait for me? I thought we were going to spend some time together."

"Sorry, I just didn't want to face you after being late for class; I didn't want you to think I was irresponsible; it's embarrassing," I said, looking down at the ground.

Gabriel grabbed my chin ever so slightly and guided my face upward till our eyes met, and he spoke so genuinely. "Listen, Evangeline, it happens. I think no less of you for being late, and who am I to judge? Why were you late? If you don't mind me asking?"

We moved over to the left a little, by the busy picnic table, and we kept walking until we found ourselves near the waterfall. It was quieter and we were able to hear each other.

"Well, I ran into Charlize, and we started talking; time went by and before I knew it, I was late. It wasn't my intention; I was just going to grab a pop and head over and then I ended up late."

"See? There had to be a simple explanation. I cannot see you ever being irresponsible. You are too organized and detailed, from what I have seen so far, to ever be intentionally late." Gabriel gave me a little smirk. "So, what would you like to do? Do you have somewhere you need to be or go?"

"I was going to go for a run, but if you aren't busy, we can take a walk if you'd like." I was looking directly into his eyes as I talked to him this time.

Gabriel came around behind me. He pulled me near and whispered in my ear, "I cleared my schedule today to spend time with you; I have been looking forward to the school day being over all day long."

As he held me in his arms, I could feel the intensity in his body, yet he was still so gentle. He ran his fingers down the side of my cheek; it sent shivers down my spine and gave me goosebumps. I could feel my body temperature rising—my God, was I ever turned on! His body was close to mine for what seemed like a long time but wasn't; it was causing my body to have a weird reaction. I was shivering and sweating at the same time. Was that even possible?

"You like that,'" Gabriel said as he noticed the goosebumps. "You have such soft, perfect skin, so healthy and so white. You are so beautiful, so natural."

"I am so far from being beautiful; you're the one that's so beautiful. Usually that word wouldn't work for a guy, but it does when it comes to you. I am going to say something. I hope it'll come out right. I need to tell you about my feelings towards you. Hopefully you still want to talk to me after. You are … perfect. Every part of you speaks to me. Your eyes say how you're feeling, and I can tell when you are being genuine with me. I knew you were amazing the first time I saw you … or the second time at least. The first time doesn't count. I thought you were a figment of my imagination. I saw the breathtaking, perfect flawless porcelain skin you have, your gorgeous hair, and the outline of your perfect body."

He started to speak. I turned around and put my finger to his mouth to signal to him that I had more to say.

"Please let me finish. I have lots to say," I continued. "Then I got to see you practically naked, and there are no words to describe what I saw but perfection. I have studied and admired many forms of art; I tend to be fixated on the human body. I'm very opinionated about the beauty of a body. You appeal to me in every way. Without putting my hands on you and touching you, I know how you must feel by the texture and definition I see. Your muscles are very well defined, and your skin looks so soft, and pardon me for saying, but the thought of it just turns me on. Just now when you brushed my face, you may have seen the shivers, but I was also starting to sweat. My heart was beating faster, and my body was getting aroused with a mere touch of your hand on my cheek. I day-dream about you at least a half dozen times a day … what it would be like to be able to touch you whenever I wanted and be with you all the time. Sorry if I'm scaring you. I don't mean to. I know it may sound crazy, but it is ridiculously hard not to be around you. Something about you calls out to me. Perhaps that's why I get a little angry when I don't see you very often. Pent-up emotions. I think that's enough off my chest for now. You can send me away now or tell me that I have issues and need to get help if you would like." I finally stopped talking.

"I do not have a problem now or probably ever with you telling me how you feel or what you're thinking at any given time," Gabriel replied. "This is one of many reasons I find you so alluring. You are so different; you say what's on your mind, always trying to take everyone else's feelings into consideration."

"I never potentially set out to hurt anyone, so I tend to speak and then apologize for my behavior immediately after to try and undo any damage I may have created." I was trying to justify myself briefly.

"Listen, if the person you are talking to knows you, they would not take offense at your opinions," Gabriel took a deep breath. "Now back to you and I as the subject of conversation. The feelings you have for me make me feel a little overwhelmed. Before I tell you how I feel, I need to say that we need to take things slow, no matter what. Okay?" Gabriel looked to me for a response.

We were still standing between both buildings in the school gardens, but we were alone now. Everyone had gone to their classes or home I am guessing, and we were so into our conversation that we didn't even notice. Gabriel noticed me looking around at the empty courtyard, so he gently put his hand on my lower back like the perfect gentleman he was and guided us out of the gardens. We obviously didn't want to be seen, as we were supposed to be in class, so instead of going through the building as we normally would, we went out and around, continuing our conversation.

"I agree, but it will be hard …" I answered, and he placed his finger over my mouth.

"In saying that, I do want to spend as much time together as we can. So, let me tell you a little about my feelings for you. You already know I think you are beautiful, opinionated, and smart. I want to tell you how you make me feel. You make me feel hopeful—hopeful that someone could potentially accept me for me and not what everyone wants me to be. People put expectations on me, being a professor's kid. They expect me to be smart, good at sports, attractive, have a swollen head, and be a jerk. Sometimes I play on the jerk one a little, as it gives me more personal space. I have had a really hard time growing up. Moving around has been good in many ways, and yet when it comes to personal and meaningful relationships, maybe not so much. I have not had any real friends till I came here; all the others were more acquaintances, and I never let them get to know me. I have been here three years, and Caleb is truly my friend. He knows everything about me, even my deepest, darkest secrets. When I am with you, you make me feel worthy, like I can be and do whatever I want. I am not sure how to explain it … I feel calmer and less agitated when I am around you. Just knowing you are in my life helps ease my tension, knowing you are around or just catching a glimpse of you."

I tried to get a word in as Gabriel went on. "I think you are being hard on yourself and have given me too much credit . . ." He gave me an *"I am the one talking look now"* look.

I put my hands up to signal that I was sorry for interrupting.

"It's extremely hard for me to explain my feelings. I never open up to anyone. See, I trust you—just another reason you are so good for me. I want you in my life, but forever," Gabriel said with sensitivity and warmth in his eyes. He pulled me in close.

I thought he needed another hug, but as I was reciprocating, Gabriel stopped me and went in for a kiss. I was a little surprised, so the first contact of our lips wasn't where it should have been. We readdressed our positioning. His lips were so soft and gentle; Gabriel started with a small kiss to my upper lip, while I kissed his lower one.

When we connected, it sent a surge of energy through me, leaving me with a very warm sensation throughout my body and giving me goosebumps. The second kiss was a passionate and very sensuous kiss. *My God ...* I was overwhelmed; the kiss was so perfectly synced, as though we had done this over a thousand times before. I had imagined us kissing being great, but this was even better. I never wanted it to stop.

"That was nice; well, for me it was. I could kiss you forever," Gabriel said. "Hope nothing, I said or did makes you feel any differently about me."

"We said we were going to take things slow . . . kissing like that isn't going to move things at a slow pace. I'm ready to rip your clothes off right now," I stated very calmly and casually. "I disagree about that kiss being nice."

Gabriel looked at me with worry.

"I mean, that was a fantastic kiss, not nice. Better than I imagined, and I thought I had imagined it pretty good."

Gabriel's worry came off his face, and he gave me a smile from ear to ear. "Let's continue our walk."

We walked about a kilometer to a kids' water park. The water had been drained in anticipation of early frost or snow. It had frosted a little a few days after Halloween, but after sunrise on those days, it was gone. A month had passed, and no snow had fallen yet; we would probably have a brown Christmas. I would have liked a little snow to fall on Christmas Day. A nice snowfall, big flakes, and the temperature just around zero helps Christmas feel like Christmas and makes everyone feel more festive.

We talked about things we enjoyed doing in different weather. We had a lot in common, like staying active, watching movies, art, and literature. We had both played school sports, neither of us were "true athletes" or professionals in any given area. I didn't receive any scholarships, but apparently Gabriel got a scholarship in English and used it to major in literature and languages. He spoke many languages: French, Spanish, Italian, German, and English, of course.

By the time we got back to my house it was around six thirty and dark outside. We had been out walking and talking for well over three hours. I was very hungry and wasn't sure if he was or what he liked to eat. Gabriel and I talked about everything, but not food, which was strange for me. I usually always talked about food. He said he liked to eat healthy, but he liked to eat a lot of meat, especially red meat. I liked red meat but preferred chicken.

"Gabriel, are you hungry? I can make us something to eat, or we can order in?" I asked as we were walking up my street.

"My father and I eat around seven, and I didn't tell him I was not coming home for supper; he probably has something made or being made as we speak." He smiled. "Thanks for inviting me. We can do supper some other time … soon, I hope. I am going to head home; my father doesn't like it when I'm late."

Gabriel walked me up my stairs and opened my door for me. He leaned in for a kiss; it was gentle and very nice. A bit more than a peck on the lips, but not quite the *"I want to tear off your clothes"* type. I grabbed him and gave him a great big hug too. I didn't want to let him go or let him leave me.

"Thanks for spending time with me. I really enjoyed it." I smiled. "I hope we get to spend more time like this soon. I get to see you for sure on drawing days."

"I really enjoy spending time with you too," Gabriel replied and gave me another small kiss on the check.

I watched him leave till I couldn't see him anymore and then went in. Amy was coming down the stairs as I closed the door. I don't think she heard or saw Gabriel, as she never mentioned anything about it.

"Hey, Angel, have you eaten? Wesley is not joining me today; can I make my rice mixture and give you some?"

"Sure! I haven't eaten, and I'm starved. I will make you and Wesley supper soon, a thank you dinner for always feeding me," I said as I put my hand on her shoulder. "Thanks for being a great roommate. I will just go upstairs and change, and we can eat together down here."

"I will make it and bring it upstairs; we can eat it in my room and watch TV, if that's okay with you?" Amy asked.

"Sure." I shrugged. "Works for me."

I went upstairs and changed, got my homework ready for later, and cleaned up my room. Amy and I watched TV while we ate, and we really didn't talk about much. I mentioned things seemed to be getting better with Gabriel and I, and that we had talked and spent a little time together. She mentioned that her boyfriend had been calling her every night and that he wanted her to go to Edmonton over the Christmas holidays to spend time with him. Apparently, he was missing her lots; they were planning on getting married after they were done their schooling. Amy had about three years. Her boyfriend was studying to be a lawyer.

I didn't know how they did a long-distance relationship; I hoped it all worked out for them. I brought the dishes downstairs, washed everything up, and went to my room to do homework. I went to bed at around nine and fell asleep right away.

When I woke up in the morning, I remembered the dream I'd had. About Gabriel, of course. It was much like the walk we'd had the previous evening, except in my dream I couldn't help myself and had ripped his shirt right open and popped the buttons off. After the shirt came off, we were inside my room—you know how dreams are, they don't ever really make sense. I ran the palm of my hands over his well-developed chest muscles and down the front of his chest, down along his wonderful abs to the snap to open his jeans. Just as I was going to start undoing his jeans, I'd woken up. Well, what a dream! I hoped in real life Gabriel felt as good as he did in my dreams.

Just to clear things up a little, I'm not a virgin, but I have only been with two people. One was the guy who broke my heart; we were together for a year and only slept together maybe a handful of times. I think he cheated on me because I didn't sleep with him enough, but I was young and very inexperienced. Bottom line, it hurt too much, as he wasn't small. He wasn't my first. My first was something I'd had to do when the opportunity presented itself—it was wrong, but he was a dream. Everybody's dream, and he was mine, at least from time to time for about three years. We remained friends, and he was even there for me after my boyfriend, and I had a falling out when he cheated. We were special friends for a while; he was a really nice guy but had problems that he couldn't seem to shake. I hadn't been with anyone else, and it had been almost two years. I hadn't found anyone I felt I could trust with my heart again, and there was no need to add any more notches for nothing. I hadn't felt the need to rush into anything, as nothing seemed very promising.

I went the entire day without seeing Gabriel—no drawing class today. I was not really surprised, as we had spent the entire afternoon together yesterday, which was nice. Perhaps he'd had a large enough dose of me for a few days, but hopefully that was not the case, and he was just busy. I just wanted to spend more time with him and hoped the feeling was mutual.

I hadn't worked out the night before because I had gone for a walk with Gabriel, so today I had to make it a good workout. I ran my ten kilometers, and in between every two kilometers, I did two sets of fifty sit-ups and two sets of thirty push-ups. When I got to my last set after finishing my run, I was exhausted. I decided to stretch out a little. I hated stretching and never really did it, and I was not very flexible. As I got up from stretching, a car pulled up into the parking lot, and guess what car it was?

Oh, how I wished I wasn't soaking wet; I was drenched from head to toe, probably stinky too. I quickly made my way to his car instead of him having to get out. I didn't want him to see me all sweaty and stinky, but I had told him to stop by anytime. I always ran with a headset on and listened to country music; it soothed me. I was making my way to the parking lot, cleaning my pants off, as they'd gotten a little bit dirty when I sat on the ground to do my stretching, but when I looked up, Gabriel wasn't in his car. I felt like he was right next to me, and I thought I felt a hand on my shoulder. I got the same energy flow through my system as all the previous times we'd touched. I must have been making myself feel like he was around. It wasn't crazy enough that I thought of him all the time, now I was thinking he was touching me, but I clearly couldn't see him. He was here somewhere, just not touching my shoulder. I bent down to tie my shoelace, and as I stood back up, Gabriel was standing right in front of me.

"I saw you pulling up, and then I couldn't see you in your car, and I thought I felt you touch my shoulder, but you were nowhere to be seen, so clearly you couldn't have been touching me. I think I am starting to go crazy; I think of you all the time. I think I feel you touching me or feel your presence and smell you, but you aren't around," I said, very worried.

"Let me start by saying hello, Evangeline, and I do not think you are going crazy; you are maybe just crushing for me very hard." Gabriel gestured with his hand flowing top to bottom, signifying that he was all that, with a big smile on his face to boot. "By the way, you look even sexier when you are sweaty, and your hair is all over the place. I do not think you could ever look anything but good; naturally beautiful girls always look great. I hope it is okay that I came to see you at the track?"

Gabriel knew I would comment on his *"look at me, I'm all that"* gesture, so he didn't let me get a word in or comment right away; he'd kept talking instead. When he seemed done, I finally stated, "I knew I was making a mistake telling you how I feel; now your head is all swollen." I was wearing a huge ear-to-ear smile.

I really couldn't hold anything against him. I'd thrown my feelings out there knowing it may not be the right thing to do. You know if you got it or not, and some are just hotter than hot. Gabriel was very hot, and I knew for a fact that there were many others that thought so too. That's why I thought I was incredibly lucky to have him as my friend … maybe with benefits, or whatever this may be, but I wanted more; I wanted it all. He'd kissed me. I would take it and smile and hope I lucked out and got many more kisses.

Still smiling, I said, "I'm glad to see you too, but I wish I wasn't all soaking wet, and I probably smell very bad too. I thought I wasn't going to see you today. It's nearing the end of the day, but I am glad you decided to come and see me."

"You really don't believe what I said? I want to spend as much time as I can with you. I will try my best to see you every day, even if it's just to say hi and get a kiss from you. Do you at least believe that?" Gabriel asked.

"I don't know what I believe at this point! Only time will tell if I believe what you say. I forgot to tell you, when I talked to Charlize yesterday, she asked me about Saturday. I said that Kelsie and I will be there, but I forgot to double check the time. What time is everyone going to be there? Are there plans for after bowling? Oh! I guess most importantly, are you still going, or do you have other engagements to attend to?"

"There's that uncertainty question, with the underlying untrusting remark I was waiting for. Yes, I am going to be there. I made sure my schedule was cleared to be able to spend time with you and our friends. I am glad you have decided to come on Saturday. I will get you to realize that I meant what I said. I want to spend more time with you and get to know you even better. I want you in my life, Evangeline! Are you planning on going to the library in the evening this week? Oh, I was going to ask, do you even like bowling?" Gabriel looked at me inquisitively.

I was thinking of letting him know I was planning on studying at Charlize's house instead of at the library. No, Caleb always said that Gabriel always knew where I was, so I would see if he really did and just tell him I had other study plans and leave it at that.

"No, I have other plans after my work out this week, for a few days, anyways. I have finished all my research on my vampires and just must put it together. If you want to spend some time together, just let me know when it works for you, and I will make the time. In terms of bowling, I like bowling, I can either be exceptionally good or unbelievably bad; it depends on the day. What plans do you have after school this week, or do you not have any?"

"There will be an evening that I have an appointment with my father; I still do not know what day that is yet, probably Thursday. Other than that, some homework and studying or hanging out at my second home, perhaps some alone time with you." Gabriel looked at me to get a response.

"Your second home?" I questioned, knowing very well it was the Reese's.

"I spend probably more time at Caleb's than I do at my place, unless I have a scheduled date with my father," Gabriel replied.

"You make it seem like it's an unpleasant time when you have plans with your father. Do you not get along?" I asked, a little puzzled by the relationship Gabriel seemed to have with the man.

"Don't get me wrong, I love spending time with my father, but it would be better under different circumstances." Gabriel stared at the ground.

"Would you rather not talk about this topic?" I looked into his eyes when he looked up, and it seemed like I had hit a nerve.

"Yes, I do not like to speak about my relationship with my father; just know that I do appreciate that he took me into his care when he did. Speaking of my father, I should probably let you get back to your running and I should get home. I will try to see you tomorrow; I may even come for a run with you, if that's okay."

I really didn't want him to run with me, but any time with Gabriel was better than none. "Sure, I will be here about four, if you want to join me."

Gabriel leaned over to give me a kiss, and it was a gentle and sweet kiss like before, but he stayed long enough for me to participate a little. I couldn't wait for us to have a real romantic and passionate kiss again, though I was a little worried about the dream scenario coming true. Don't get me wrong, I looked forward to it, but it was too soon. I watched him walk to the parking lot and get into his car. I was done running and decided to skip the weights and grab a bite to eat, shower, and head over to Charlize's. I waited till Gabriel was out of sight, then grabbed my stuff and headed home, thinking about what to wear and if I should wear my hair down or not.

Amy and Wesley were in the kitchen cooking dinner. It was a little earlier than usual, but I didn't mind.

"Hi, Angel, I know it is a little bit early. Are we in your way?" Amy asked.

"It's okay. I am just going to grab some cheese and crackers and an apple to go. I got to eat, shower, and head out."

"Our supper will be ready in ten minutes; you can have some before you leave, if you would like," Amy offered and quickly added as I was heading upstairs, "Are you seeing Gabriel? Have you seen him lately?"

"Yes, he came to the track to see me as I was running. I really felt uncomfortable; I was sweaty and probably smelly too. I was happy and unhappy at the same time if that makes any sense. I can't seem to win. I either don't get to see him, or he appears when I'm not at my best. Gabriel has only ever seen me look somewhat good, well what I consider good at the university kegger when we briefly ran into each other. I hope Gabriel will show up at Charlize's house this evening; that was the point of going there to 'study.' Apparently, he goes there all the time to study and hang out with Caleb, his best friend. I know I am rambling on—"

"Angel, Angel..." Amy was trying to make me stop talking. "What are you talking about? You don't have to look at your best, because you are beautiful even with a pony and no make-up on. I don't want you to put yourself down, and Gabriel would be lucky to have an honest and smart young lady such as yourself."

"Are you sure I have nothing to worry about? Gabriel is hot and I'm not," I said.

"Once again, Gabriel would be very lucky to have someone like you, whether it's what you consider a 'good day' or not. What is your opinion, Wesley?" Amy replied and turned to Wesley.

"Well ..." Wesley paused and then said, "For a Canadian, I think you are very good looking. I prefer Asians myself because of the shared culture, but I find that you are very sensitive, honest, and friendly; these are very good qualities to have."

"Wesley means that he usually looks at Asian girls; most Asian guys won't even attempt to look at, let alone like, a Canadian girl. We tend to stay with our own and are looked down upon if one does cross that line, so Wesley meant no harm with what he said," Amy was quick to say.

"Did I say anything wrong? I didn't mean to; it's just a hard question," Wesley said apologetically.

"I know that you both mean well and that I carry on about myself and my problems too much. I should return the courtesy by asking you both about yourselves more often, and I promise to try more in the future." I smiled and walked up the stairs. I felt so pathetic, always thinking of myself instead of paying attention to those around me. I grabbed my clothes and headed downstairs to the shower, thinking about how I had let Gabriel consume my being.

If my parents only knew what I was getting myself into, they would disapprove. They wanted me to concentrate on school and have fun, not let a guy consume all my thoughts and time. They knew the hard time and torment I'd gone through after my boyfriend cheated on me. Thank goodness I hadn't let my grades drop; I was maintaining a 3.50 grade point average and needed to get to a 3.75 or higher to guarantee that I could get into whatever school and major I was going to choose.

I decided to wear a pair of tight, form-fitting jeans and a form-fitting jacket. It was still warm outside, considering that it was now nearly December. There was no snow on the ground yet, well any that stayed anyway. I went downstairs and no one was in the kitchen as I went out the front door. I was going to walk to Charlize's house since I had not finished my run, and the walk would do me good. It was only four blocks away, and the scenery was quite nice. I got to the Reese's' house at 6:45, rang the doorbell, and Caleb answered the door.

"It's not enough that I must see you and get questioned by you at school? Now you're coming over. What? Are you going to come over every day till Gabriel shows up?" Caleb pulled attitude on me.

Thank God Charlize came when she did and told him to shut his piehole and that I was welcome here any time I wanted. I smiled at Caleb and Charlize and went into the kitchen where the rest of the family was. Apparently, they had just finished eating.

"I'm sorry if I'm a little early. I didn't mean to interrupt your supper!" I felt uncomfortable.

"No, no, Angel, you are welcome here at any time. Have you eaten?" Mrs. Reese asked.

"I'm fine, thank you!" I smiled.

"What are you ladies up to tonight?" Mr. and Mrs. Reese asked together.

"We are working on our literature assignment; the one due before the final exam on a topic of our choice, ten thousand words. Remember? I told you about it at the beginning of the school year," Charlize said.

"I am sure you tell me a lot of things that I may not fully remember," Mrs. Reese said. "I am getting older, you know, and my memory isn't what it used to be, though the choice on a fictional paper does sound familiar. Will you ladies be working on this assignment tomorrow also? Angel, you could come over for supper if you would like."

"I'm pretty sure we will be working on our projects for a few more days," Charlize replied and gave me a mischievous grin.

It seemed that Charlize and her mom had their own silent way of conversing through facial gestures. I was sure she knew I was there for other reasons; she was a very smart one.

"I thank you for the invitation, but I have plenty of food that needs to be eaten at home and I don't want to overstay my welcome as I will be here studying for the next couple of days for sure." I smiled.

"Well then, I insist you come over tomorrow for pizza and wings, and any other Wednesday you like." She put her hand on my shoulder and gave me a look that seemed to give me no choice but to accept.

"Thanks, Mrs. Reese, I'll check all my Wednesday's, and I love pizza. Would you like me to bring anything?" I asked.

"Please, you are the student, and I am the parent, let us help you; it is our pleasure to have you over!" Mr. Reese smiled.

"Well, we'd better go downstairs and start on our projects, but first I will grab a bowl of Skittles and chocolate-covered almonds." Charlize scrambled through the cupboards for two smaller bowls.

I looked up as we were grabbing a couple pops, our snacks, and our books. Gabriel was walking in the French doors off the deck. My heart stopped momentarily, and my throat felt swollen shut. Everyone said hello, and of course, Mrs. Reese asked him if he had eaten.

"Hello, Evangeline, this is a surprise!" Gabriel smiled broadly.

"Yeah right, like this wasn't a planned situation or anything," Caleb said, not too impressed with me being there.

"Caleb, what is your problem?" Mrs. Reese asked, clearly unimpressed. "This is not the first inappropriate remark coming from your mouth today. You need to apologize and change your attitude; you are living under our roof, and you will act respectfully."

"Sorry, it was my inside voice; it won't happen again." Caleb put his head down and walked into the other room.

Charlize and I went downstairs to let the situation upstairs cool down; I wouldn't ever want to be on that women's bad side—that could be scary. She seemed serious, and she seemed to wear the pants, so to speak, in that family. If looks could kill, Caleb would have been near death after the comment he'd made to me.

"Hey, sorry about yesterday," I said, hoping we were good. "I was intending to come over and study, but Gabriel found me after school, and we spent some time together. We went for a nice long walk and did lots of talking, or at least I did. I think it went okay."

"It's all cool!" Charlize replied. "The invitation is open, and we didn't set things in stone. All this 'studying' is for you and Gabriel to spend time together anyway. Bowling on Saturday is an invitation though, so I do expect you to show up!"

"You're awesome. I'm glad we met and are friends." I smiled.

Charlize and I went about doing our own thing, as there really wasn't much, we could do together, and our topics were totally different. Charlize's was on Don Juan, some guy who was supposed to be a ladies' man—he was a gigolo or a womanizer of some sort. She knew my topic and the fascination I had with vampires; it's not like I keep it a secret.

I was going through my pages of notes and movie references. There were very few movies that showed vampires as being good entities. There was the Twilight saga and a couple of TV shows, but even then, there were a few killings that still occurred. In some of the references, the vampires were killed by having holy water thrown on them, others by having stakes driven through their hearts and then burned, their heads chopped off, and of course, the sunlight turning them into ashes. The newer, good version of vampires seemed to be able to be killed by having their heads removed and burned, they could be staked, and they could also seek to be put to their death by peers.

There were vampires who could walk in the sun, due to chemicals put into their system, wearing a cream for protection, and even those that just appeared different in the sunlight, even some wear a talisman like a ring or necklace and then the most common ones that burn to a crisp if in the direct path of the sun. There were many choices in the qualities I could give my vampires; it was a fictional story and a fictional character.

Just as I was going to start writing, Gabriel walked into Charlize's room. He was wearing actual blue jeans and a black-and-white sweatshirt that had a band logo of some sort on it. I wasn't sure who they were; it must have been one of the punk bands the goths listened to. Anyway, I couldn't believe that he had some sort of color on, and no long black jacket. His hair was perfect as usual, and his bright-blue eyes seemed to be exaggerated more against the white of his sweatshirt. He smelled so good; Gabriel always smelled so good. I lost my focus for a few seconds because Charlize was trying to snap me out of it after he asked me if I could take a short break.

"Sorry, I seemed to be lost in my thoughts, a break, sure, what did you have in mind?" I asked.

"I thought perhaps we could go into the back yard and take a stroll." Gabriel smiled.

"Sure, that sounds nice. Do you mind if I take a break with Gabriel? You are welcome to join us if you would like." I looked at Charlize.

"Sure, a break sounds good, but you two go ahead. I have a couple of things I need to do anyway."

"So, where are we going?" I smiled.

"Let's go walk around the garden as I suggested. Is that alright with you?"

"I'll follow you; just lead the way!"

CHAPTER TEN

Gabriel went upstairs, and we headed towards the sliding door, which led out back. Mrs. Reese asked where we were going, and we replied that we were taking a quick study break in the gardens. We didn't stop to get a reaction from her; we just kept walking. When we stepped outside, Caleb was on the deck, and he didn't seem pleased to see us together.

"Does Caleb have a problem with me being around you?" I asked uncertainly.

"I think he just worries about me; I do not have a great dating record," Gabriel stated.

"I have a confession to make. Caleb approached me when I got here and accused me of being here only because I knew that you would be here. I didn't respond, and Charlize stepped in before I could say anything. The fact is that Charlize invited me over to study, but we both knew I really didn't have anything to study for. I just have to gather my facts and rewrite the assignment. Charlize told me you were like her other brother and that you practically lived at her place and that I should come over to 'wink wink' study, and I probably would run into you! So, of course, I didn't disagree. I love running into you and having our short encounters, preferably when I'm not all sweaty, that is. I did have an ulterior motive. I want to spend as much time as possible with you, and it's the only way to get to know you better. I hope you aren't angry with me and that you can smooth things over with Caleb for me. I don't want him to hate me. That would make things awkward for me." I rambled a little there, but I still got nervous around him.

"Evangeline, I like spending time with you too. It does not matter how, why, or when we do. I am simply happy to spend the time together. I have told you that you are especially important to me and that we share some sort of connection. Perhaps we knew each other in our past lives. Soulmates. What do you believe in? What are your thoughts on destiny, reincarnation, God, the devil, and perhaps other mystical creatures?" Gabriel asked.

"Well, are you sure you want to hear my opinions? I have a lot of them."

"I would not have asked if I really did not want to know your opinions." Gabriel lifted his eyebrows.

"Okay, but make sure you stop me if I'm boring you or rambling on too much … Where should I start? … I believe in a higher power; to some, God is used to represent that power. I think of the almighty power as a force guiding us rather than a being and using the term 'God' represents the image of a person. How does one person create all that is, was, and will be created? I probably need to add that, if there is good, then there must also be evil. Though I think that the evil, like God, is not a person, so there mustn't be a 'devil,' just a mere evil power. Maybe evil power is too much of a descriptive term, but let's go with this: We all have it in us to be evil or do wrong, so that is a choice we have. There are those who may argue with that statement and say that one may have a chemical imbalance in their brain which prevents them from choosing right from wrong or good from evil …" I took a deep breath. "Are you tired of me rambling on yet?" I asked Gabriel, who seemed to be interested in what I was saying.

"I have never known anyone to be as passionate as you when they are explaining their beliefs." Gabriel had a large smile on his face. "Please continue. I have not really given as much thought to a higher power or good and evil, as you obviously have."

"Okay," I said, "but let me know when you have heard enough or need to go."

"I still have about another hour before I need to head home, so please continue." Gabriel brushed his hand on my cheek and gave me a little kiss.

We had been strolling for a while now. The Reese's' yard was quite big. There were pathways throughout made of small pea gravel, benches to rest at or from which to admire the beautiful surroundings. Gabriel and I came to a little bridge, where we stopped. There was a little pond with a water fountain in it. It didn't spray water everywhere; it was a statue of a little boy and girls with buckets, which was how the water was filtering through back to the pond. I quite liked this statue, and we stood there for a while as we talked.

"So where was I? Well, I do believe that everyone is good, or should I say, starts off good, and could surrender to perhaps a darker side of their being. I feel that one must learn to keep the darker side of them buried within and hope it stays contained forever. Destiny, well, you may think that I'm a little crazy after I explain my beliefs to you. Let's talk about freedom of choice first, as it will run into my thoughts on destiny. They say that you can choose to do what you will with your life, but why is it then that no two people have the same exact talents or abilities? I believe that the 'Higher Power' lets you believe that you have a choice in jobs, careers, and education. But how can this be? Let's give an example.

If person A is handy with tools, good with math, and good with their hands, then perhaps they can be a doctor, a nurse, a veterinarian, an accountant, a chemist, an architect, a carpenter, and a cabinet maker. Then Person B can draw, has the abilities to envision color schemes without seeing them on paper, to be extremely fit, to want to save and help others, to want to help keep the peace. Person B then can strive to be an artist, a designer, in advertising, a firefighter, policemen, a paramedic, and a lawyer. Should I stop? I said it would be a long explanation."

"No, continue; the explanation you are giving actually makes some sort of sense. I've never thought of it this way," Gabriel exclaimed.

"Okay, where was I?" I asked. "The two may have a few abilities the same, such as being a doctor, a nurse, and perhaps a paramedic, but the abilities may be stronger in one than the other. So, taking this into consideration, the 'Higher Power' gives the power of suggestion, the thought of having choice, but really everyone may only be given ten talents or abilities. In the ten chosen paths given out, there may only be five of the ten that you excel at. The 'Higher Power' knows that the path you take will be one of the five and throws in another curve ball. Perhaps you are emotionally scarred by a death or someone's behavior towards you, and it leaves only three choices. You thought you had all the choices in the world, but you are good at only certain things. Does this mean that you are in control of your destiny, or is it merely a form of manipulation, used as a sense of control and perhaps stability in humanity?"

I sighed. "Sorry, I sometimes get caught up in certain topics. You should stop me from embarrassing myself." I looked into his eyes to get some sort of reaction. His eyes were so kind, the kind that just made you melt. It would be like having him give me a big hug, and even better, having him hold me while lying on my bed … or even better, lying in the back of a truck, curled up in a sleeping bag, looking up at the stars. I could see any of these scenarios as though they could happen.

"Evangeline, are you okay? I kind of lost you for a second there." Gabriel was waving his hands before my eyes as I came to from my momentary lapse into my daydream.

"Yeah! Sure. I sometimes get lost deep into my thoughts." I gave my head a shake. "Who is kidding who? I always go to my little world. Maybe I'm a little different than most. My imagination gets the best of me quite often … I wonder what that means."

"I think it's great that you have a creative imagination; that's one of the many things that attracts me to you. You are different than most, and I mean that in the best way. You allow me to perhaps search within and find my own beliefs. I think having you around me will help me find myself; discover things I have buried from my past. I am sure I could remember things about my parents and well before Mr. Vla̓dimir took me in if I were open to it. I think I have shut myself down and have been living day by day. I feel more open to discovering things since we have met, and you have shared your views with me. So, I never think you are rambling about anything; I think you are helping me out with your openness regarding your ideas and opinions. I enjoy spending the time we do together. I admire you for having independent views and opinions on things." Gabriel seemed very sincere as he spoke.

I hoped that if Gabriel remembered things from his past, it wouldn't affect him in a bad way. Sometimes repressed memories could come out and bite you in the ass, so to speak, and it would be my fault. I would hate to have stirred up things that changed Gabriel in any way.

"So, do you believe that everything happens for a reason, and do you believe in fate? What about reincarnation and the feeling of déjà vu?" Gabriel seemed to really want to see what I had to say about these topics.

"Well, I think I have said enough for today and should leave the rest for another day. I believe it's your turn to tell me something, an opinion, a thought, or perhaps a theory on anything, just to learn more about you as an individual," I replied.

"Alright, well … I don't think that I believe in God … Perhaps there is a higher power, but if there is such a thing, then why do certain individuals have to go through hardship, pain, and loss for what seems like no apparent reason? If all of humanity is to be a happy family, then why does this 'God' let us destroy each other in one way or another? I can tell you that through all the uncertainties I have about many things, I do believe in fate and that there is perhaps someone created for each of us out there, a soulmate. I do think that destiny is what you make of it, though after hearing your opinion, I am left with lots of food for thought. We should head in. We have been out here for quite a long time, and Charlize is probably wondering if we got lost." Gabriel smiled as we made our way back to the house.

He and I were probably outside for over two hours, though it didn't seem like that long. I could spend every waking moment with him, though he might not feel the same way with all my ramblings. *Gabriel may need earplugs.* I wondered if Charlize was okay with that. She should be, as she knew I was taking her up on the study offer only so I could see more of Gabriel. I would still make sure Charlize was okay with the situation and clear my conscience. I wouldn't want to ruin our friendship, as it was still very new. She was so cool and easygoing though, so I was sure it was all good.

Gabriel and I parted ways, and I was left quite surprised that he wasn't bored and didn't think strangely of me and my ideas and theories on destiny and the whole God thing. I got inside and went quickly downstairs. Charlize was watching the television, not studying in her bedroom. I hoped she wouldn't be angry with me.

"Did you have a good walk? Did you have a chance to get some answers to the questions you had?" Charlize asked curiously.

"Thanks, Charlize, for being so great with all this; it's very nice of you to help me out with the whole Gabriel thing. Yes, Gabriel and I had a good conversation, but I ended up telling him more about myself than getting to understand him better. He seems to always get me on topics that interest me, or I maybe bring them up and then tend to do all the talking. I hope you aren't angry because I was out there for such a long time."

"Come on, we know this entire studying story was for you to spend more quality time with Gabriel. I'm just happy that he came over today and that you did get a chance for some alone time." Charlize smiled.

"Is it okay if we study tomorrow?" I winked at her.

"You're welcome to come over all week if you like!" I got a "*wink, wink*" back from her.

I went into the upstairs living room to say goodbye to Mr. and Mrs. Reese and to thank them for having me in their home, letting them know I would probably be back the next night if that was alright.

"Of course," Mrs. Reese said, "joining us for supper is still an offer, and remember you can come over anytime; you're always welcome. Never mind Caleb. Sometimes we don't understand what and why certain things come out of his mouth. I hope you got some studying done or whatever you were working on."

I smiled and headed out the door. I knew the Reese's weren't stupid, and that Mrs. Reese had seen Gabriel and I waking outside together. I got outside and saw that Gabriel was there with Caleb.

"I can give you a ride home or walk you home, if you prefer, Evangeline," Gabriel offered.

I sure would like a ride in that great car of his, but there would be plenty of time for that in the future, I hoped.

"No, it's alright; you look busy. Thanks for spending time with me in the gardens. I enjoyed our conversation." I smiled and kept walking. I didn't want Caleb to be even madder with me for sticking around. I was not sure if his issue was me or me taking interest in Gabriel. I put my Beats on and had the music up fairly loud. I got down about a block when I could hear the rumbling of a muscle car getting louder, or vibrations it must have been. I turned to have a look in hopes that it was Gabriel, and it was.

"Hey, I hope you don't mind, but I am headed this way anyways." Gabriel smiled.

"Of course, I don't mind; if I had my way, I would spend whatever time you could free up for me together. I like being around you." I went around his car and got in. It was nice to be sitting beside him in his beautiful car. Oh, how I had many a dream of us in his car, and in his bedroom or mine. Come to think of it, me, and Gabriel anywhere. The dream always started with him giving me kiss on the cheek, then the nose, and then a little teaser kiss on the lips. Whispering in my ear that he wanted me so bad, kissing my neck and nibbling or breathing in my ear, with a slight tongue action. Sending shivers up and down my spine, creating triple-decker goosebumps all over my body. I wasn't stupid. I knew there was a possibility that it may be all about looks. That's why I wanted to spend more time getting to know him. I wanted to see if there was more than the physical attraction.

"Is it all right if I hold your hand?" Gabriel asked quietly, grabbing my hand before getting an answer.

"Sure," I replied. Inside, my heart was racing, and I started to think of what this could mean. I had to stop myself, as I could be making more of this than was intended. The entire way home, we were quiet. I didn't want to say anything to make him change his mind about holding hands, so I waited for him to say something first. We didn't speak till we got near my dorm, and then Gabriel asked, "Are you alright? Were you okay with us holding hands? I'm not used to you being so quiet. If I have done something to offend you, please let me know."

"You probably could never do something to offend me; I told you before that I enjoy spending time with you, whatever that may be." We got back to my dorm, and I asked him if he wanted to come in, but he said he needed to get home. Gabriel pulled my hand in close to him, bringing my entire body into his, and leaned in for a kiss. I leaned in also, not trying to guide the situation, just following his lead. The kiss was tender, not a peck, per say, but not the long juicy kiss I longed for.

"Bye, I hope you know how much I like spending time with you," Gabriel added.

"Gabriel, any girl would have to be crazy not to want to be by your side. You're the most incredible guy I have ever met; there is something so mysterious yet extremely sexy about you! I could keep telling you how I feel, but really, I haven't been able to sort through all the feels to make any sense of it all. I don't want to scare you away—just know that I really want you to be in my life." I was looking into his eyes as I spoke to him.

My entire being wanted to give in to the situation, the want, the urge, the desire, the hope that Gabriel was "the one," my knight in shining armor. Every girl's dream of that perfect guy … but does he really exist? That is the question.

"I am glad we have feelings for each other," Gabriel said. "I knew I wanted to spend all my spare time with you, but in the past, my feelings were not often shared with the other person involved. Unfortunately, my feelings get the better of me and sometimes get me into trouble. I usually have a hard time communicating with the opposite sex, but I seem to be more comfortable with you! We have some sort of connection between us, like a magnetic force pulling us."

Gabriel barely had time to finish his sentence before I grabbed his arms with both hands and pulled his body towards mine. There was no struggle from his end, and this time, I was taking charge of the kiss being planted. I made sure he felt the intensity and passion, and he didn't seem to mind my lead; he reciprocated. It was quite the kiss, for our first passionate one; perhaps the next time it would be even better, as we would both hopefully go in with the same intention from the start. Our kiss came to an end, and I let go of his arms and said, "Now, that was much better than the previous kisses, I would definitely have to say."

"Well, any kiss from you, big or small, is great, but I definitely have to go agree with you on this. I quite enjoyed that one!" Gabriel had a grin from ear to ear.

"I think it was a good start to what is yet to come." I smirked.

"I wish we could continue this evening, as it is going very well, but I do need to be getting home. My father does get quite concerned if I come in late on a school night." Gabriel leaned in for another kiss, just a gentle and sweet kiss on the lips.

He left and I went to the kitchen, where Amy was standing there in the dark in awe. "I'm sorry," she said. "I just did not want to mess up your moment by turning on the light just to get a drink of water. I'm going to assume that was Gabriel! Wow! Now I know why you were in la-la land over him; he is a very good-looking guy. I have seen him around in the cafeteria, I think. I take it after that kiss it's safe to assume he has the same feelings for you?"

"I think he and I am on the same page about the feelings we have for one another. I hope we can spend more quality time together now. Shoot! I forgot to ask him about tomorrow! Anyway, I hate to cut this conversation short, but I am quite tired and have an early class in the morning." I smiled and went upstairs.

"No problem, I need to hit the sack myself. I haven't been able to sleep well. It must be the excitement of going home!" Amy replied.

I went into my room to process the day. A lot had happened, and I did not want to forget any of it. I was happy to have finally told Gabriel some of my feelings without being too careful. The kiss was good, but the next time it would be better. I started to daydream—or should I say, night dream—about us going to the river, finding a part that hadn't yet frozen over, and cuddling and kissing while watching and listening to the river flow. I always loved to watch flowing water, even more so with the ice forming around the edges. The temperature had been in the low minuses the past couple of days, enough to cause some ice formations, but still no "real" snow, the kind that stays.

Oh! Damn! I should have asked Amy about this weekend! I was all wrapped up in my little world and non-issues, forgetting to think of others. I had to start taking more interest in Amy's life; she was nice enough to ask about mine. I was a terrible friend and roommate.

CHAPTER ELEVEN

I woke up that morning with a gigantic smile. Yesterday was incredible. I just hoped today, and the rest of the week would bring me just as much hope and happiness. I was looking forward to perhaps taking another walk through the Reese's' garden, maybe walking further back on the property down by the river today too. I had noticed the river at the Halloween kegger, from afar, of course, as I was quite busy that night helping Gabriel keeps things under control.

I decided to wear some dress clothes and do my hair down; Gabriel had only seen me this way a few times. My roomies looked at me strangely as I walked into the kitchen all dressed up. Who knew that the one time I got dressed up for school, everyone would still be in the dorm?

"Let me guess." Amy grinned. "You must have drawing class today!"

"No, yesterday, and I saw Gabriel last night too!" I replied. "Hoping to run into him in the cafeteria and maybe go for lunch. We can catch up later, got lots to fill you in on. I'm kind of running late, sorry." I grabbed some toast and headed out. I felt a little weird having all eyes on me—not that I cared, but I was sure the others asked Amy what that was all about. I got to school and went to the cafeteria to grab a coffee, and there was Gabriel getting one too. He saw me approach and signaled me to join him in line.

"Wow! You look smoking this morning! What's the occasion? It would not be for me, would it? Because you know I like you with a ponytail and sweats just as much as this look. I know how beautiful you are inside and out; the clothes are nice but do not change my opinion of you." Gabriel looked pleased as he spoke, even though he did say that he preferred the sweats.

By the look in his eyes, I knew Gabriel preferred this look, even though he may not want to admit it.

I smiled. "I can see you are pleased with the change. I think the whole liking the sweats things and not caring for the done-up look is a little bit of a lie. I see the way you looked at me when you saw me coming! Now, if I were to say that to you, it would be the truth, as you are gorgeous no matter what. Oh! And no one says I got dressed up for you. I may have an appointment or something to go to today!" I just couldn't let his little comment slide. I really needed to work on not having the last word all the time or making snide comments when other opinions varied from mine.

Gabriel looked at me with a smile after that comment. I didn't think he was surprised at my comebacks anymore, or he just chose not to bite back. "I think some may disagree and perhaps even call you a little crazy with that remark you made of me," he said modestly.

"Dude! Sorry, that just came out. Gabriel, I don't think there would be one girl that would disagree with my statement, and there may even be some guys that would agree with me too. Do you happen to look at yourself in the mirror? Or maybe you don't have one! I know hot when I see it, and I still can't believe that you associate with me and that I have had the pleasure of hugging and kissing you!" I had to stop. I was getting carried away and getting a little bit warm around the edges if you catch my drift.

"Are you okay if I want to just hug and kiss you right here?" Gabriel looked unsure.

"Why would I mind? A hot guy wanting everyone to see him kissing a little mediocre girl like me. It would look good on me but perhaps ruin you." I gave a little snicker.

"Well, you do not give yourself enough credit, and it would only be my pleasure to have others see that we are together. If, of course, that is what we are?" Gabriel's eyebrows went up.

"I would love to be exclusively yours, if you are sure I'm who you want to spend time with—you can have any girl you want."

Gabriel grabbed my hand and pulled me towards him and gave me a soft and gentle kiss. It was just as I thought it would be. We turned to go to class and everyone in the cafeteria was looking at us, or it felt like that. There weren't that many students in the cafeteria at the time.

"I told you!" I smiled.

Gabriel walked me to my English class as the door was just about to close, gave me another small kiss, and we went our separate ways. The entire class, I thought of the walk, which might continue tonight after class. I didn't see him, and I'd forgotten to ask him about lunch, but it was probably a good thing, as I had drawing class after lunch. It would have had to have been a short lunch, and I didn't want anything cut short when it came to Gabriel and me. He must have been busy, because I didn't see him again till I was leaving to go home for lunch.

I was grabbing a pop again, thinking about not eating anything for lunch, when Gabriel came up from behind and gave me a hug and whispered in my ear. "Sorry I didn't see you again this morning; I got held back with Mrs. Tanner. She wants to take a different approach in my modelling for the next classes. Were you headed home for lunch?" Gabriel turned me around and planted one on me. "Do you want to go to lunch in town?" He gave me an inquisitive look.

"I was just hoping that you would be free for lunch. Do you feel like eating a nice juicy steak?" I asked.

"Sure, I can always eat a big juicy steak!" Gabriel answered. "Sometimes I try new things, but very rarely. I have eaten some meat-lovers pizza before, and it's okay."

"I guess I may have to start eating red meat more often then." I kind of went quiet.

"I'm glad you picked steak for lunch. I'll take you to a great steakhouse, but it doesn't always have to be steak; let's just make a point to always go somewhere where they serve red meat, and then you can order anything else you may want at that time." Gabriel tried to get eye contact with me.

I smiled. We went to the same steakhouse where I went with my parents and friends when I first got to town, where I had seen Gabriel having supper with his father and his friends that night, I'd had my sugar craving. The steak was good there, and there was no better cut of meat than a top sirloin or a filet minion.

Gabriel seemed to enjoy his steak but didn't touch the rest; he just said he wasn't as hungry as he had thought. He did order a sixteen-ounce cut of meat and ate it all, and I found it very strange that he ate it blue rare, not even Chicago, just blue rare. That was like fifty seconds on each side or something crazy like that … it was still mooing! I didn't comment on it; after all, it was his steak. My meal was great. I had a little six-ounce steak with a stuffed potato and tossed salad. During dinner we talked about everything and anything, but we both commented about the wonderful walk we'd taken in the Reese's' back yard the night before. I asked him if he was going to be there tonight for pizza night.

"Are you going there to study?" he asked.

"I was angry with Caleb the last time because he was right. I had planned to come over and make it seem like we had to study, but it was really Charlize's way to have us bump into each other and help us to spend time together, kind of a matchmaker of sorts. I guess she is getting tired of all the whining and questions that I continuously ask her. So, yes, I was planning to be there to see you and maybe get some studying done if you can't make it."

"So, should we get you back to school? You are a little late for your class. What do you think about just spending the rest of the afternoon together?" Gabriel had a really big smile on his face. "I have nothing planned this afternoon, and my dad isn't expecting me home; he has a conference today in the city, and I think he is planning on staying overnight."

I usually never missed any classes; even through high school I missed only two or three in total. I answered immediately, "Sure, this one time, but I won't make a habit out of this. Do you not have to model for the other drawing class next door today? What do you want to do?"

I was extremely excited inside and tried my best not to explode on the outside. Gabriel wanted to spend more time with me, but somewhere in all of this I had to remain with my head intact, remembering school was more important than guys. I wasn't sure what I wanted to spend the afternoon doing with Gabriel. Should we go to the gym together? I wasn't sure if Gabriel liked to work out. He was ripped, so he had to. Maybe Gabriel and Caleb worked out together. We could just go to the recreation center in Airdrie and figure it out. Or perhaps just go for a walk and talk; we seemed to be doing well at that so far.

"Mrs. Tanner said she wanted to use a still life with the class and practice shading and wondered if I was okay with taking the day off. I told her I was good with that! I was thinking we could go back to my father's house, since he is not home, and I can show you some of the things he has collected through our travels over the years. I am not bringing you there with any intentions of any funny business; I pride myself on being a gentleman." Gabriel seemed so sincere and worried that I would take the invitation the wrong way.

"I would love to see your place. Do you live in town?" I asked.

"No, we live just west of town; just a few minutes heading towards Sundrie on an acreage. Mr. Vladimir likes his privacy and having nature right outside his door. He likes hunting!" Gabriel was waiting on a reaction from me.

"Cool, let's go," I replied. "I keep wanting to ask you something, but I always seem to get sidetracked. It's about Mr. Vladimir, your father and It's a personal question, so of course if you don't want that's okay."

"Okay, ask away." Gabriel answered.

"Why do you refer to him as Mr. Vladimir and not father or dad?"

"He introduced himself to me that way and told me that I could call him that and that he didn't expect me to call him by any other name, like father unless I wanted to. I feel like it's the proper way he should be addressed, don't you? His presents demand respect, he's cultured, well-mannered and respected by everyone I know, shouldn't I respect him back, especially since he has and still does lots for me?" Gabriel looked me.

"Well, that makes sense, but do you think of him as your father?" I added.

"Yes, of course he has been in my life for a very long time." Gabriel seemed puzzled.

"Does he know you think of him in that manner? Perhaps telling him how you feel would show him just how much you do appreciate him. Just a thought!" I thought I would drop the subject now. "Anyways, should we go back to my place and change into more regular clothing?"

Gabriel was quiet, in thought, I had hoped that I hadn't overstepped, but I was curious.

"Sure, your place," was all he said.

Gabriel and I went back to my place, and no one was there; they were all in classes. I was being the bad girl, skipping school—if my high school friends could see me now! I quickly went up to change, and Gabriel stayed in his car listening to music, typical guy. I threw on a pair of my not-so-tight jeans and a dark T-shirt, which was better for riding horses. I grabbed us a couple of drinks for the ride. The drive to Gabriel's house was short and sweet. We took the road out of town, headed towards Sundrie, and a couple of kilometers away, we turned left at a graveyard. Most people would probably cringe at the thought of going to or living near a graveyard. I really didn't think it was that bad. I believed spirits lived amongst us, and I also believed that if I left them alone, they wouldn't bother me.

Gabriel didn't say much on the way to his place, still in deep thought, I guess.

"I can take you to the stables, and we can maybe ride. Have you ridden horses before?" Gabriel lifted an eyebrow inquisitively.

"I love horses and have ridden a few times; I would love to ride again," I said with a big smile.

When we turned left, we drove a few kilometers and then took a sharp bend in the road and came to a densely wooded area. The atmosphere was kind of eerie, like out of a scary novel. The trees were incredibly old and formed a tunnel around us as we passed through. I was sure it would look even scarier the darker it got. After we passed the trees, we got to a huge cast-iron gate that Gabriel had a remote for. As the gate opened, it made a heavy, creaky sound, almost like a movie scene, which I thought was so cool.

"Sorry about the gate; the maintenance guy was supposed to fix it. It has not been working its best lately; it's an old property. Mr. Vladimir has had lots of restoration work done on the house, and on the property, and it is a work in progress, he says. He also wasn't sure how long we would be staying here, so that plays a key part in it. I think he likes this town, the school, the people, and the area." Gabriel seemed worried about my thoughts on the place.

The house was very old and looked like a small castle, with one old creepy tree in the middle of the front lawn, cool but eerie, awesome, very vampire movie like I thought. On one side, there was an attached three-car garage, and the main body of the house had a large faded-burgundy double door with side lights. The house was very symmetrical, and looked like a two-story, with two huge windows about eight feet wide by twenty feet tall on either side of the door. There was a smaller window above the door, showing what seemed to be a vaulted ceiling in the entry way, and I could make out what seemed to be staircase. I could vaguely see what looked to be a grand chandelier as well. There were two pillars on either side of each window and the covered area heading to the door had smaller pillars. I had seen newer houses with this look, but this was an older style and had a stone facade.

"I can give you a tour of the house a bit later if you would like, or depending on the time, it might have to be another day." Gabriel smiled; we were supposed to go to the Reese's' for pizza tonight.

"Sure," I replied. I was simply happy to be with Gabriel. It was probably easier not to go into the house, with less temptation to get into trouble, if you know what I mean. We turned and headed towards the barn. I followed without saying anything—probably a first.

"Are you okay, Evangeline? I have never seen you so quiet." Gabriel looked concerned.

"Yeah, just happy to be with you; nothing on my brain at this moment, I guess. It's a surprise for me too." I smiled.

"I thought you would appreciate some of the things I want to show you first." Gabriel paused and opened the barn door. "The horses."

Wow! On the other side of the door was the most beautiful, majestic horse. It was a light brindle color, and it had an almost platinum-blonde mane and tail, though it had highlights. It seemed to glow, as though it was heavenly. I know it sounds crazy, but that's how it looked to me; almost like it should have had a horn on its head like a unicorn. Oh, I probably should tell you I'd had a fascination with unicorns as a child and had many unicorn items.

Anyways, this horse was the only one out of its stall, but there were a few other horses in the barn. As Gabriel opened the door, the horse came towards us, which was very unusual to me, as most horses were shy with strangers. This beautiful horse came right between Gabriel and me and put her head on Gabriel's shoulder. He gave her a rub on the side of her head. Then she gently moved her head to my shoulder; I slowly rubbed it too. Horses were supposed to be a good judge of character, and she sure liked Gabriel, which was a good sign, and she obviously approved of me.

"This is Maleficent, my horse. I would like you to ride her, but first I want to show you something else. The rest are for guests to ride. Mr. Vladimir has a stable guy who takes care of them. I guess he's a ranch hand, and he takes care of the rest of the property too. Come this way," Gabriel said, putting his hand across my lower back to direct me. "Let's go through this set of doors in front of us, but I will ask you to close your eyes and let me guide you to my next surprise. Do you trust me?"

"Yes, I trust you," I said as I closed my eyes.

We went through the doors and seemed to turn right and walk a few minutes before we stopped. I could hear another gate open and then close; we must have gone through another gate or door. Every time there was a change in elevation or something that could interfere with my walking, Gabriel would grab my waist with both hands to steer me or even hold me from falling. He was such a gentleman. I really was falling hard for him, perhaps even … well, you know.

After we went through the gate, I started to smell new scents in the air and hear water getting closer. I was getting anxious to see what Gabriel was going to show me. After a few more minutes, I could hear water running or flowing rapidly—a great, relaxing sound. Gabriel grabbed my waist to stop me.

"Before you open your eyes, I thought, knowing what I do know about you, that you would appreciate what I am going to show you. Not everyone feels and thinks the way you do, which is one of the very many things I cherish about you. That's why I know you must be the one I have been waiting for," Gabriel said. "Now, open your eyes."

CHAPTER TWELVE

My god! I was standing in the middle of the most magnificent garden I had ever seen. Gabriel and I had walked through several trees and bushes that enclosed it, acting like its own fence. There were what looked to be some oaks and poplar trees, then some willow trees descending to bushes; some had colorful leaves, and some had flowers on them, even this late in the fall. Then there were sections separated with brick and blocks, and one had a different assortment of flowers and pathways to walk in and around to enjoy them. I know it sounds crazy, but this garden must have been the size of a neighborhood block. We were on an acreage, with lots of room for a big garden, but it was just strange. Usually such a place was built in public parks for everyone to enjoy, like a government or provincial park, not closed off. Places like these cost a fortune to build and maintain.

I took in all the beauty around me. I had heard water since we'd first gone through the fence, and in the distant right side of the garden was the source: a waterfall.

"Gabriel, I have been trying to take in all this wonder since you asked me to open my eyes. I'm speechless, which you know in my case is highly unlikely to happen. I really am in awe of this magnificent garden. Can we go to the water, please?" I said, baffled and amazed.

"Of course," Gabriel said as we walked towards the water. "I am glad you like it; I spend a lot of time in here, and it's definitely one of my favorite places."

"So, tell me about it. I want to just listen to you talk for a while; tell me everything about this garden." I could feel my smile struggling to reach my ears.

"Well, I didn't see the garden before we moved here, but Mr. Vladimir said there was one. He said he'd hired a groundskeeper and given him designs, items he wanted in it and the flowers he didn't want, as that was a lot easier since there were only a few. Mr. Vladimir gave the groundskeeper a timeline and a budget and told him to 'have at 'er and impress me, and remember, I have been all over the world.' So, when we got here, I had no idea what was in the backyard beyond the fence line; all I could see was trees. I was asked to not go looking past the fenced area till the surprise was finished. It looked like a forest from my bedroom window. About a month after we got here, Mr. Vladimir said the surprise was complete, and I was to go explore. He wanted me to be the first to see and report back to him how it was before he went to look. I was amazed; there were a few things I asked to be added, like extra benches and a picnic table close to the waterfall, but all in all, I do not think it could have been much better designed."

"Well, I think it's spectacular!" I exclaimed.

Words can't begin to describe the waterfall, pond, and stream that were created in the far-right side of the garden. The waterfall looked like the one in the school yard, but twice as tall and wide. It was made to look like it was coming from a small rocky mountain source. It looked like when you were driving in the Kootenay area of the BC mountains after the spring melting of the snow, when all the water was descending the rocky hillside along the road.

The waterfall fell from about eight feet above and hit a few protruding boulders to slow it down before it hit the bottom, forming a small stream that flowed about fifteen feet and then formed a large pond. In the pond there were some large koi fish and lily pads. It was fabulous. I loved the sounds the waterfall made as it hit the different stages of its flow. At times the water would hit the boulders on the way down and make a huge splatter that could hit you if you were standing too close.

"So, what do you think, Evangeline?" Gabriel asked curiously.

"Words can't describe the feelings this place brings. I'm without words. I have literally been awed or overwhelmed with utter sensation," I managed to get out.

"That's why I brought you here; I thought you might enjoy it as much as I do." Gabriel grabbed me from behind and held me as we watched the waterfall, and we just stood there for about fifteen minutes. Then I turned around and looked deeply into his eyes. I knew that my eyes said, *"I love you"* and that I didn't have to say it. I was so happy. I didn't think I could ever be happier. I had found my true love, my white knight, my happily ever after. I went in for a kiss, and it was very sensuous; I had goosebumps from head to toe.

"I hate to ruin the moment, but we do need to get going it you want to go for a horse ride; it will be getting dark soon," Gabriel said.

"Well, are there lights out here in the garden?"

"Yes, the waterfall area is very well lit up. It looks even better in the night lights if you can believe it," Gabriel added.

"Would it just be okay to stay here till it gets dark and go horseback riding another time?" I smiled.

"Sure," Gabriel replied. "It's up to you. I am good with anything you want to do. I will go and grab you a warmer jacket and be right back."

I didn't even have time to say anything; he was gone. I went over to a bench a few feet away. I was glad Gabriel had gone to grab me a jacket, as it was getting colder by the minute as the sun was going down. There was a fire pit in front of the bench, and it didn't look like it had ever been used. Hopefully it worked, as our stay outside might be short lived if it kept cooling off.

As I started to see some of the lights come on, I felt a jacket go over my shoulders. It hadn't taken Gabriel more than ten minutes to go grab me a jacket, and he'd brought me a hot chocolate too. He came around the bench, sat down, and put his arm around my waist, pulling me towards him for a sideways hug and kissing me on my forehead.

"Thanks for the jacket and the hot chocolate. Didn't you want some?" I asked. "Do you want some of mine?"

"No, I'm good. Are you warmer now?" Gabriel smiled.

Then the fire pit in front of us turned on, making things even more perfect than they already were. We were quiet for a few minutes as we watched the fire and listened to the waterfall. It was dark outside now, and all the lights had come on. It was an amazing sight to see. I could pitch a tent and stay here forever.

"Silly me," Gabriel said out of nowhere. "You must be hungry. It's probably after five, and I should get some food into you. I will give the Reese's a call and let them know we won't make it for pizza night and that we lost track of time at my place. That way they will not order too much."

"Well, making the call is the right thing to do. I feel bad we lost track of time. I was a little hungry before the hot chocolate, but now I'm okay for a bit longer, but soon. I just don't want to wreck this wonderful evening. It's so beautiful here; I could just stay here forever, watching and listening," I said, very content sitting snuggled in Gabriel's arms.

We sat quietly for a few more minutes, and I felt calm, which was rare for me. I was always anxious, it seemed, but I was changing more the more I spent time with Gabriel.

"I hate to cut this short, but we still need to walk back and give the horses a treat before I take you back into town and feed you. I hope you enjoyed coming out here. I would like to have you over more often." Gabriel looked at me.

I'm sure my face spoke a million words, but I leaned in for a kiss. Then out of the blue, I stopped and jumped on his lap, facing him. Then I kissed him. It wasn't a gentle, passionate kiss, it was an *"I want you now and I'm extremely horny"* aggressive kiss. I don't know why or where it came from, but I just did it; it was getting harder for me to control myself. Gabriel didn't push me away. He seemed to enjoy it.

Then I stopped and looked at him. "Sorry. You bring out this side of me that I knew was there but kept hidden away inside. It's hard to explain. It's like a wild animal urge, the same crazy feeling that I get when I'm watching people being passionate in a movie or on TV. Sorry, rambling my inner thoughts outside again; probably shouldn't have said that. That's another thing; I'm not sure why I can just seem to say whatever, whenever when I'm with you," I said, puzzled.

"I am glad you feel open with me, and you can tell me and do whatever you want. I doubt there would be anything I would disapprove of." Gabriel smiled. "You are too nice to really do anything wrong."

I got off his lap, stood up, and gave him my hand. He grabbed it, and I gestured that we should probably head back. Gabriel stood and turned the fire pit off, and we started to walk back. The main path we walked down earlier was very well lit up; it was equally beautiful at night as it was in the day, just in a different way. There were enough solar lights amongst the plants to see them and get the idea of the beauty there was during the day.

We got back to the barn and were greeted by Maleficent again, who was such a beautiful horse. There was a little bar fridge in the barn, and Gabriel went to it and got some cut-up apples and carrots. He handed them to me and said, "You can give each horse two carrot pieces and two apple pieces."

I started with Maleficent, as she was standing right next to me. I gave her an apple slice and then another, then went to each stall and gave the other horses theirs. Gabriel had four other horses besides Maleficent. Then I gave the horses the carrots and gave Maleficent hers last. She was such a gentle and nice horse.

"Well, how experienced are you with riding horses?" Gabriel asked.

"I have ridden them about half a dozen times. I wouldn't classify myself as a good rider, but I'm not scared, and I hold my own, I think." I gave Gabriel a reassuring look.

"I think I would first put you on Coke, which is the horse in stall number two. She has been used for training new horse riders for most of her life. Mr. Vladimir got her from equine rehab place where the horses are trained to deal with all sorts of children's issues, so they are very calm and tolerant of different situation. So, by having you go on Coke, I can see how well you ride." Gabriel smiled.

"How is Maleficent to ride?" I asked.

"She is pretty calm, for the most part, but she does have a wild side to her; kind of like you, I guess." Gabriel had a devilish smile on his face, and he was waiting to see my reaction. "You will ride her, just maybe not your first ride; we'll see how you do on Coke, and when you have spent a little more time with Maleficent, you'll ride her."

I just kept stroking Maleficent. A few minutes later, Gabriel said we should go and feed me. We drove back into town, which was as a little bit spooky. As we approached the graveyard, I could see it was lit up in certain areas, but not enough, which gave me an eerie feeling. I didn't think I would want to walk in that graveyard—not that I went to graveyards, but this one was in the middle of nowhere.

"What would you like to eat, Evangeline?" Gabriel asked as we got into town.

"Wendy's drive thru works for me; can you get me two JBCs and a medium Diet Coke?" I asked and handed him a ten-dollar bill.

Gabriel handed me back my money. "Feeding you is the least I can do since I am the reason you are hungry and haven't eaten yet."

"Thanks. Can you grab me a three-piece chicken strip too? I'm quite hungry. You got to let me pay for my food eventually." I looked at him with a serious stern tone in my face.

"We will see about that. If you are my girl, I will always treat you right, and if that means feeding you all the time, then so be it." Gabriel looked serious.

We got to my place and Gabriel came around the car, opened the door, gave me a huge hug, and then gave me a passionate kiss. Then he gently pushed me away to see my face as he talked to me. "I had the most wonderful day today. I know I keep saying this, but each time we spend quality time together gets even better. I am so glad to have you in my life; you make my life full of happiness. I felt kind of empty before, now that I can compare how I feel now with how I felt before. I believe there is a person made for each one of us and you are my soul mate. I honestly believe this." Gabriel kissed me again.

"I'm glad I decided to go to college here, or I may have never met someone like you. I believe we were meant to meet also; I don't want too ever be without you. I feel much better when I'm with you too." I gave him three quick kisses, one on each cheek and one on the tip of his nose.

Gabriel left. I still couldn't believe that this was real; my feelings for him were deep now. That was scary for me. I'd had my heart broken before, and it had taken this long to let someone else in this way. If something were to happen between Gabriel and me, I might not recover.

I entered the house, and no one was in the kitchen, so I went up to my room. I think it was about nine thirty when I called it a night. I did a bit of schoolwork, organizing my assignments mostly, and I didn't feel like doing anything more. No one came to see me; Amy was probably too busy and stressed arranging her family trip, studying for her tests, and getting her assignments completed.

I fell asleep fairly quickly I assume, thinking of the wonderful garden and how Gabriel had looked even more beautiful in the evening lights. The waterfall was definitely my favorite part of the evening, besides just spending time with Gabriel. The entire evening was great, and I loved every part of it. I loved kissing Gabriel, but the best thing was Gabriel stating how happy he was with us being together.

CHAPTER THIRTEEN

My eyes shot open; it was going to be another great morning!

I got ready quick and headed out. I walked towards the cafeteria, and just before entering, I decided to skip the pop and go sit in the garden. The hallways were empty. I looked at my watch. It was seven thirty, so others were probably just waking up, as most classes started at nine, except for the unlucky few that had English class at eight.

I pushed the door heading into the garden area, and it opened easily. I almost lost my footing and fell into the person approaching from the other side. It was Charlize.

"Sorry, Angel!" she said, like she wasn't expecting anyone on the other side of the door. "Doesn't the school feel emptier than usual today?"

"It is quite empty this morning, but most mornings are like this at seven-thirty," I replied. I had never seen Charlize here so early. "Sorry about missing pizza night. Gabriel and I lost track of time; we were at his place and there was just so much to see and do. Hope you're not disappointed and your mom's not angry with us."

"It's an open invitation for every Wednesday, and Gabriel called just in time, so we hadn't ordered pizza yet. I'm here because I just woke up and figured it would be quiet here and I could use this time to catch up on research for one of my classes, but I 'm feeling a little off today, can't explain it, sure it will pass. No real rush on the research though, just didn't want to be at home, probably would have stayed in bed if I hadn't gotten up. So, enough about me; tell me about yesterday! So, you were with Gabriel? We had no alone time for me to get all the ins and outs of what has been going on the past few days with you and Gabriel. Sorry if I am being too nosey; just tell me to bud out if you don't want me to know."

"The least I can do is let you know how things are going because a lot of what Gabriel and I have has been made possible by your kind generosity of our 'studying.'" I winked. "Everything seems to be great, long walks, talks about anything and everything, and Gabriel even brought me to his house yesterday after our lunch at the steakhouse. I will fill you in on the rest after class if you want, or tonight. I will try to spend some time with you too, but we got to get to class. It must be close to eight now, as there are a few more people filling up the halls."

Charlize and I got to the classroom just on time, which seemed to be a pattern for me lately—a pattern I must change. I'd never had this problem in high school and had always been early. Class was good, I think ... I was in la-la land for most of it. I keep daydreaming about Gabriel naked. I guess it was from seeing him almost naked every other day ... well, that was an exaggeration. More like wanting to see him naked every day was causing me to think of him all the time. I was yearning for him. How pathetic, right? I was not sure what was going on with my feelings for Gabriel. I must have been really needing or wanting some physical connection with him other than hugs and kisses.

The morning went fine, but I didn't see Gabriel! I went to the gardens before heading home for lunch, hoping he would be there hanging with his goth buds. He was nowhere to be seen. I felt his presence, as I often did, and I swear I could smell him too. Maybe I was losing it, wanting to see Gabriel so bad that I created these senses or feelings in hopes of contenting myself. Though Gabriel's smell was quite distinct. I had never smelled anything like it before, not that I was a cologne expert of any sort. I swore I could feel him grazing my cheek or his hand on my lower back when I smelled him, but he was nowhere to be seen. I even caught a glimpse of a shimmer or heat wave, not sure how to explain it, when I sensed Gabriel around. Wow! Listening to myself say this is really making me believe I might be crazy.

Lunch was boring, as I really liked lunches with Gabriel. I had to get a handle on things; he wasn't my be all and end all of things. I walked back to the college in a daze. I felt a little bit like Charlize did this morning, out of sorts. Oh! I hoped nothing was going around; I would hate to get sick. I didn't get sick very often, as I was told by my doctor that I had a great immune system.

I went to the cafeteria and no, not for a pop this time, surprise, surprise. I know, right? I'd left the house without checking the time. See? Weird. Something was up. There was a huge clock about twenty feet up, straight ahead when you entered the cafeteria. The cafeteria was an open space, kind of cathedral-like, with extremely high ceilings and full of light. There was a second level in some areas of the college, but I had never been up there, where all those who were taking science classes spent their time. Amy told me there was extra ventilation up there for their chemical experiments. Sounds like it could be interesting, but I wasn't ever good at science.

I got to class with no time to spare, and the door was almost closed. Gabriel was nowhere to be seen, but then he came out, literally from a box on the platform: his stage. The "stage" had a black-and-white box big enough for him to sit inside it without anyone noticing. As Gabriel emerged from the box, Mrs. Tanner explained that we were not drawing motion anymore. She said this would be the first official drawing class where we put pencil to body, so to speak.

Mrs. Tanner told us she wanted us to sketch along Gabriel's outline as precisely as possible, allowing our perception of what we were seeing to flow through our minds, into our hands, and onto the paper, without looking at what we were doing. This would allow us to see how our sight works in conjunction to our hands, getting the precise lengths to create the right proportions. If we had time, we were to start on the muscles and the detailing. Though not to worry, she said, this was not a race, and she wanted us to do our best to see how our drawing skills were. Mrs. Tanner said we would have at least a few more classes till it was to be handed in. This would be one of our project marks for the year, and if we thought we could finish it without the model, then we could feel free to do so.

As I drew him, my pencil was following all the curvatures of his body. I was getting such a sensuous feeling that I could have sworn my hands were touching his body as my pencil was drawing and as my eyes were seeing all the detailed marvels of his body. Gabriel had great muscle definition; all I could think about was feeling his body.

I could not wait for class to be over.

I heard Mrs. Tanner saying, "Okay, guys, wrap it up for today. As I said, you will have a few more classes before this assignment's to be handed in. If anyone has any questions, or if you need extended time with Gabriel, we can discuss perhaps having him stay later or you can come in for extra help."

I was there, but I don't recall much talking or discussion in class. I'd been fixated on Gabriel's hot body and lost in my own little world. That had to have been the fastest class ever. Seemed like it, anyways. I packed my stuff up and looked at my drawing. It wasn't bad, considering I wasn't paying attention.

"Are you waiting for *Moi, madame?*" Gabriel said, with a bit of a French accent to boot.

"Why yes, monsieur!" I replied. "But of course! I hope that's all right with you."

"What are your plans for today? Or this afternoon and evening, I should say. Are you up for a walk? Are you planning on 'studying' at the Reese's' later?" Gabriel asked with an inquisitive smirk.

I replied with my eyebrow up and a *"What are you up to?"* look on my face. "Well, I do have to go for a run at least; all this eating and not working out will make me fat. I should think of doing some weight training too; I don't want to have flabby arms."

"Ha ha!" Gabriel said. "I think you're a long way from fat with flabby arms, but I'm up for a run. I am not sure how good I will be though. It's been a while."

"Sure, a run would be good," I replied, a little uncertainty in my voice.

"Are you sure? Your response didn't seem as convincing. I can just see you later if that works better for you," Gabriel said.

I was a bit worried about Gabriel running with me, as I didn't want to embarrass myself or him. I wasn't sure what my problem was; it was just a run! I wanted to spend more time with him, and then I gave him what seemed to be an uncertain answer. I had to get it together.

"No, a run would be good." Certainty flowed through my words this time. "Sorry, sometimes I'm so used to doing things myself that my first reaction to change comes out as uncertainty as I process the situation. I really want to spend as much time together as we can, and I need to get over being worried I will do something wrong around you or embarrass myself."

Gabriel grabbed me and pulled me in for a hug. He whispered in my ear, "I'm sure you could do no wrong; you're so calculating with everything you do. Even if something did happen, it would be okay. I'm not a judgmental person. I like you for you all your perfections and imperfections, Evangeline."

I liked it when he used my full name, even though the only other time I heard it was from my parents; it seemed right for him to do so. "Do you have something to change into or do we need to go to your place first?" I asked.

"I have my gym bag in my car. I always bring extra clothes just in case something comes up like this," Gabriel answered.

"I'm not surprised. Let's go back to my place and get changed," I replied.

We got into his car and drove over to my house. It was a five-minute walk, which we could have just done. We went in, and it seemed like no one was home; maybe they were in their rooms. Gabriel used the downstairs washroom to change, and I quickly went upstairs to get ready. I threw on a pair of shorts and one of my running shirts and a sweatshirt and headed back downstairs. Gabriel was sitting at the kitchen, looking out the window. He was so beautiful just sitting there, and in my kitchen to boot. Who would have thought? I could only have dreamed of such an amazing creature in my life liking a nobody like me.

"Ready?" I asked.

"Yes, I am," Gabriel answered. "Are we just running around the track?"

"Sure, unless you want to run somewhere else?" I questioned.

"I was just asking; the track is fine." Gabriel smiled.

He left his car at my place, and we walked over to the college track. I stretched a little, and Gabriel decided to stretch too. There was no one around; the parking lot had only a few cars in it. It was a very nice day for a run—the sun was shining, and there was no snow on the ground yet.

Gabriel and I ran around the college track. We didn't do much talking or stopping during. I run at a medium speed, and Gabriel just kept pace with me. I wasn't sure if that was fast or slow for him, but it seemed like he barely broke a sweat. We ran about seven kilometers; that was enough for me, maybe because I had company; my enthusiasm for running was not as it usually was. I was soaked, anyway; my emphasis on exercise had dwindled to a bare minimum. My mind was on Gabriel and spending as much time with him as possible.

I slowed down to walk a lap to signify that I was done running. Gabriel passed me as I stopped and then slowed down and came to a walk. He turned around to see what I was up to. I caught up to him, and we walked a lap as a cool-down.

"I cut it short today, not really into running for some reason, hope that's okay." I smiled as sweat ran from my forehead down my cheek.

"I'm good with whatever you like. I do not usually run around a track. I am here so I can be with you as much as possible." Gabriel wiped my sweat from my cheek too.

"I'm soaked, and you are barely sweating. How is that possible? Have I gotten that out of shape in the past month or so?"

"Do not be so hard on yourself," he said. "I don't sweat much no matter how much I run. I never have, not sure why. Maybe there's something wrong with me."

There was a pause as we walked towards my house, as though neither of us knew what was going to come next. Were we going our separate ways to shower and see each other later? We were still very new at spending unscheduled time together. In time, perhaps we would get a better feel for one another and just know what came next instead of asking.

Gabriel broke the silence "Well, you don't need to go to the Reese's' any more to see me; we can make our own plans now. I am not telling you what to do, of course, but I don't want to hide us anymore. I want everyone to know that we are together if that's alright with you."

"Are you sure you want me to be your girlfriend?" I asked. "I will become very possessive of you if you give me that title."

"I could not be more certain of anything else; this is what my entire being is telling me. I have never felt such overwhelming feelings before for anyone. I cannot even begin to explain the things I am feeling at this point, only that I don't think I can be without you." Gabriel had a little tremble in his voice.

"Then that's that. I guess we are officially a couple then," I said with big grin on my face. "Well, once we tell at least one person, that is." I couldn't have asked for anything else. This was what I had wanted since the first time I had laid my eyes on this beautiful creature. I couldn't explain my feelings for him either; they were so strong, as though I was being pulled by a magnet towards him. The closer I was to him, the more relaxed my body felt.

"Well, I did say I would be there for pizza yesterday," I said, "so I think we should go today and apologize for not making it there last night. If you can't make it, I will let them know you are sorry as well."

"Oh, I am not leaving you alone to apologize. I was supposed to go hunting tonight, but I talked to Mr. Vladimir at noon and asked if we could leave in the early evening, and he was okay with that. I will quickly run home, shower, change, chat with my father if he is there, and I will be back to pick you up. How does that sound?" Gabriel asked.

"Fantastic," I said with my big grin on my face. "I will be ready when you get back."

Gabriel left and I went up to shower and get ready. He said he would call or leave Caleb a message, letting him know we would be there in about an hour and a half, which would be around 5:30, for a brief visit.

I got ready, put jeans and a T-shirt on, and braided my hair. I went downstairs, and Amy was in the kitchen prepping food, waiting for Wesley to start cooking supper. I sat at the kitchen table, thinking maybe I should spend some time with her; I had been so busy and wrapped up in my own things that I had not said much to her in the past few weeks.

"Are you hungry?" Amy asked.

"No, I'm going to Charlize's house to apologize for missing pizza night last night, thanks anyways. Gabriel and I were out at his acreage last night and lost track of time." I smiled. "Always trying to feed me, such a kind person. So, Amy, how are things going?" I asked.

"Well, school is school; I think my grades are fine. I have done well on everything so far. I am going to go see my boyfriend in Edmonton over the Christmas holidays. I really miss John. After seeing him Thanksgiving weekend, I realized it is harder than I thought being away from him. I think next year I will enroll at his college. I am looking into courses I might want to take there," Amy said, quite bummed out.

"I can only imagine how you're feeling being away from John for long periods of time! I get antsy not just being able to catch a glimpse of Gabriel every day, and we haven't even been together really till now," I replied.

Amy's eyes were really big now as she asked, "Are you and Gabriel officially together now? An item?"

"Yes, I'm officially his girlfriend as of about an hour ago. Gabriel literally told me he didn't want to be without me and that he didn't want to hide his feelings from anyone anymore. Awesome, right?" I exclaimed.

"I'm so happy for you; even though I don't know Gabriel that well, he seems perfect for you. I know how much you have gone through these last months, figuring out how you feel and where you stand with him. I am glad you have found someone you feel you can trust. I know, in the past, relationships have been hard on you. Gabriel could be the one; your soulmate," Amy said with a big smile.

"Ever since he literally ran into me, I have felt something; I really think we are connected somehow. Speak of the devil. Gabriel is back. We are going to Charlize's together, and they will be the first … now second … people to know that Gabriel and I are officially together now!" I said, relief in my smile.

"I am glad things are good and that we had a chance to talk. Have a good evening; we will talk soon, okay?" Amy said.

"Yes, I will make sure I spend some time with you. Maybe now that Gabriel and I are 'together,' I will be able to focus on other things than just wanting to be with him. Thanks for the talk, Amy; you're a great roommate," I said as I walked out the door.

Chapter Fourteen

Gabriel had gotten out of his car as he saw me coming out, and he came around the car and opened my door for me. He made sure to guide me with the small of my back, to make sure I didn't slip, I guess. This was not normal behavior these days, but there was times Gabriel said or did things that were old-fashioned. I think Mr. Vladimir might have brought up old school or travelled to so many countries that he decided to instill those qualities in Gabriel. I just said thanks and took it with a grain of salt. I counted myself lucky; there were very few gentlemen around anymore.

As Gabriel got back into his car and started to drive, he said, "I am sorry tonight will be cut short, but I did get to spend some time with you today, and I normally would not have on a Thursday, it being hunting day. It's very important for Mr. Vladimir and I … together time. It's our family tradition, and we have done it since, well, for a while now, not sure how long it's been. I will be back some time tomorrow. I will see you at lunch or after school."

"Sure, not a problem. What do you hunt?" I asked.

"Mostly large game," Gabriel answered.

"What's large game? Like deer?" I asked inquisitively.

"Well, yes and larger than that too. Cougars, bears, and sometimes moose if we cannot find the others," Gabriel stated.

"Are you not afraid? That's kind of crazy. Sorry. I just have never heard of anyone or known anyone who hunts such dangerous animals. You must have permits for killing such an animal," I stated, a bit confused.

"I know it may seem strange; you are not the only one who has said so. Mr. Vladimir has permits and certain areas where he can hunt at certain times, not sure how it really works. The animals are sent somewhere to be taken care of, and I'm not sure of the details. Mr. Vladimir says it's not my concern, and that everything is done legally. Sometimes, it's very rare, though, we must fly out of town for the hunt." Gabriel seemed confident about what they were doing.

I decided to change the subject. "Hey, I briefly talked to Charlize this morning! So, she knows I am coming over to 'study.'"

"I talked to Caleb and told him we were both coming over together," Gabriel said with a big smile on his face.

"Really, you told Caleb we were coming over together. He must be pissed. I don't think he likes me or wants us to be together at all," I replied.

"Caleb has nothing against you. He is just protective of me, and he is like my brother. His family is my family; yes, Mr. Vladimir is there, but he is more of a parental or guardian figure, not a family. Is that wrong for me to think that way?" Gabriel asked.

"No, it makes sense. I just want Caleb to accept me around you and his family, that's all," I added.

"Everything will work itself out. Caleb will see that we are good together and that I am incredibly happy, and things will ease up. I promise!" Gabriel seemed very sure.

"I hope you're right!" I said, a bit worried.

We pulled into the Reese's' driveway, and Mrs. Reese waved with a big smile on her face. She was in the garage doing something, and the garage door was open as we got out of the car.

"This is nice. I am glad you are both here … missed you last night for pizza night, but thanks for letting us know you were not going to make it." Mrs. Reese didn't seem angry.

"So sorry, lost track of time. Didn't mean to miss out on pizza. I do love pizza. Thanks for understanding," I said.

"Pizza night every Wednesday, and you're always welcome, and thanks for calling. We already consider you part of the family!" Mrs. Reese said as she grabbed me and gave me a big hug. Gabriel and I went with her through the garage, which ended up just off the kitchen in a boot room. Mr. Reese was in the kitchen and was not surprised to see us walk in together.

"Hello, kids, nice to see you here. Missed you yesterday. Hope everything is okay." He smiled inquisitively.

"We lost track or time. Sorry," I answered.

"Yes, we came by to apologize for not being here. I brought her to the acreage yesterday, and we got caught up with the horses and stuff," Gabriel said.

Just then Caleb came into the kitchen. "Gabriel, Angel," he said, addressing us. "You did come together."

"I thought I heard voices." Charlize peered in the kitchen. "Well, all the important people are now here! Hopefully next week no one misses the best night of the week, pizza night, right? I expect this will be every Wednesday going forward from now on, right?"

"Okay!" Gabriel said, "I have something I need to get off my chest. Evangeline and I are officially together now. We have kind of been spending a lot of time together, and well, it's not enough, so we are now a couple."

Everyone kind of looked at each other and then everyone looked at us.

"I for one am not surprised," Charlize's mom said. "From the first time I met Angel, I thought she would be good for our Gabriel. "I think it's time we see Gabriel with a girl, and a nice one at that, and Angel fits my expectations for Gabriel perfectly."

Mr. Reese spoke next. "Well, I am a little surprised, but since Gabriel is like a son and Angel is becoming like a daughter, why not? But keep your squabbles to yourselves; I will never play favorites. I don't do it with my kids, nor will I do it with you two."

I had never seen Mr. Reese so serious before. I just didn't want to do anything wrong. I think the disappointment on his face would be devastating. I was worried for Caleb's reaction, but Charlize spoke up before he could.

"Well, I wasn't surprised today, but if you would have asked me at the beginning of the school year when Angel first let on that she liked Gabriel, I would have not predicted this outcome. After seeing and hearing of Gabriel's reaction with Evangeline, I knew there could be a chance. Gabriel is always nice with all the girls, but he nicely gets rid of them too. Angel came along and Gabriel wasn't pushing her away; I could see he wanted to spend time and be around her. So, that's why I suggested Angel come over to study, so they could run into each and perhaps spend more time together. Angel was all for this idea. What girl would not try to have Gabriel if he is also willing?" Charlize said with a mischievous smile.

I really had nothing to say. I was still awaiting Caleb's reaction to the news. I grabbed Gabriel close and wrapped my arms around his waist without even knowing that's what I did. I was happy and nervous and a million other feelings right now; I needed Gabriel close to give me a sense of comfort. He seemed happy I'd gone in for snuggle, and as I got in close, I seemed to relax or ease up a little. I wasn't sure how Gabriel could have had this effect on me; normally nothing could calm my anxiety, just running or solitude. I was glad I had Gabriel. Now if I could just keep him …

"I just don't want to hear the issues; keep them to yourselves," Caleb finally said. "I am glad if this all works out. Gabriel deserves to have someone nice in his life. Whether or not that is you, I am not truly sure yet. Just don't hurt my brother." He walked out of the kitchen, and Gabriel went to go talk to him.

I pulled Charlize to the side; I wanted to make sure we were okay. "Sorry, this all came out like this. I just want to know if we are good and how you feel about all this," I gently asked.

"Dude, I am so good with all this! Less sneaking around and lying. It works for me. Now we can all hang like friends and not have to tiptoe around the entire subject of you and Gabriel. I like the idea of you with him, my mom likes the idea, my dad thinks the more family the merrier, and well, Caleb will come around. Give him a little time; he is very protective of Gabriel. To be honest, I took a liking to you after the second time we talked. I feel like you are my sister and that I've known you for an awfully long time." Charlize pulled me in for a huge hug.

"Thanks for being there for me in every way. I think of you as a sister too! I wasn't just befriending you to get to Gabriel. I really wanted to get to know you. Your entire family is great … the bond you have and the generosity you all share. And to be able to let others into your family bond? It's fantastic. My family is great, but yours is even better," I exclaimed.

"I told you that Gabriel was a different type of guy. You would think that with those looks and that body that he would be conceited and arrogant, but he it so far from that. I am glad for the both of you; perhaps 'destiny' is a true thing," Charlize stated.

"Why did you not snatch him up?" I asked.

"Well, I find him to be quite incredible myself, but we went out a few times. We had one kiss, and we both agreed that we were more like brother and sister than anything else. Plus, he is my brother's best friend, after all. How crazy would that be to have to talk to your best friend about your sister or hear your sister talk about your best friend? There are no hard feelings between us, and I think that you make a great couple. Gabriel brushed me off as he does most females; that's why I had a feeling about you two—he seemed interested in you right from the start." Charlize smiled and we moved back with the others.

I nodded at Caleb. "Can I talk to you for a minute on the deck please?"

"Sure," he said and followed me out.

I could tell he wasn't very impressed with me nodding at him, but I felt the need to explain a few things to him. "Hey, Caleb! About the other day, you were right. I did come over to see Gabriel, not to study. I cleared things up with Gabriel today too. Sorry, I guess I wasn't ready to admit it, having it thrown in my face.

"I knew I was right! Chicks! Don't you know the truth is always better? No harm done, as long as my man is cool with it, then so am I. I meant what I said. I don't want to hear about your problems, and if your problems start to affect Gabriel and I, you will hear from me and very loudly. If you two are an item now, you take the good with the bad and don't ever hurt him," Caleb stated, and he was more serious than ever, if that was even possible.

"Thanks, Caleb." I gave him a little smirk and went in for a hug. He wasn't expecting it, and after a very brief hug, he pushed me away.

"Alright, let's back inside and you staying for supper?" Caleb nudged me back into the house.

"Oh! Caleb, we're not staying, Gabriel must go hunting with Mr. Vladimir, but you probably already know that, right?" I added before re-entering the kitchen.

"Well, well, I guess you two are officially an item now!" Caleb stated.

"Why do you say it like that?" I asked.

"Well, Gabriel never tells anyone but me about his hunting trips. What other things have you discussed? I am very curious as to how into you he really is," Caleb replied.

"We really didn't go into much detail on anything yet; we tend to talk more about my likes and dislike than his. Gabriel took me for lunch yesterday, and he expressed that he really likes to eat red meat, and I found it a little strange that he eats his meat so rare. Other than that, we discussed seeing each other tonight and making plans to see each other without involving the study coverup. Why do you care what we discuss, anyways? Is there something that I should know about him? Is he dangerous or something?" I said, laughing nervously with perhaps a little worry on my face.

I had to add that smart-ass comment in there, as his questioning me was starting to drive me crazy; it was as though he felt there were things that Gabriel would never open up to me about.

"I really don't care," he said. "I just think that Gabriel is a great guy, and maybe he has a few skeletons hidden away, but who doesn't? If he wants to talk about his issues, he can, or I'm sure they will come out. They always do. I wish you well. Hope it works out for you, but he has not had much luck in the past; well … since I've known him, anyway," Caleb added.

We stopped talking, as Charlize came towards us, Caleb gave me a sneering look and went into the kitchen.

"Don't worry, my brother is always a little bit stranger than usual when it comes to Gabriel. It's sometimes creepy, like he trusts him, but others shouldn't. Maybe he knows something about Gabriel that no one else does, and he just wants to protect everyone in his own peculiar way. I cannot help you understand Caleb; I do not get him at times myself. He used to be kind of normal come to think of it, Caleb changed shortly after Gabriel, and he started to hang out frequently."

"Do you find anything different about Gabriel? Has he ever shown another side than he has shown me? Should I question him on Caleb's strange conversation?" I asked, a bit worried.

"I have never experienced anything but a genuinely nice and polite guy. Gabriel seems pretty normal to me. I wish other guys were more like him, but not so much on the brotherly side. Don't worry about what my brother said. Caleb is Caleb. Just take what you want from his conversations and discard the rest; the rest of us do!" Charlize said, giving me a little squeeze on the shoulder before we headed into the kitchen with the others.

"So, Gabriel, isn't tonight your hunting night? I am surprised you're here," Mrs. Reese said.

"Well, you're right, but I felt I needed to come with Evangeline to apologize in person about missing pizza night last night," Gabriel answered, "but I do have to go. Mr. Vladimir said we could leave later, but we still must go. Evangeline, do you want a ride home or do you want to stay?"

"If you have time to drop me off that would be great; if not, I can walk home," I replied.

"Sure, I can drop you off; let's go."

"Hey, do you want to come with my mother and I to the food bank tonight, it would give you something to do since Gabriel will be gone. Only if you want, we could always use the help and you can stay for supper, I'm sure." Charlize questioned.

"Well, I will come with you, but I will have Gabriel take me home, if that's alright and you can pick me up on the way, does that work?"

"Yes, that works too, we will pick you up at seven, we're just having a quick sandwich, is Seven okay for you?" Charlize asked.

"Yes," I replied, "Seven is good, See you in a bit."

We left fairly quick; they were going to have supper soon, so it was good timing. They knew Gabriel had to get home as soon as possible since Mr. Vladimir was waiting to go hunting, and I just wanted to go home and have some me time.

"Gabriel! Gabriel," I said a few times to grab his attention. He was walking quite quickly. I caught up to him and put my hand on his shoulder to make him slow down so I could talk to him face to face. "Is there something wrong besides being late for hunting?"

We got to Gabriel's car, he opened the door, and I sat down as he quickly made his way around the car and got in.

"Listen, Evangeline, first, I am not as perfect as you seem to think I am. Please don't put me on a pedestal. I don't deserve that; you will see I'm just like everyone else. The fact that you say what you think and that you don't just agree with everyone else is one of the reasons I like being with you," Gabriel said. He placed his hands around my face as he pulled me in for a wonderful, moist, gentle, and passionate kiss. We were quiet on the drive back to my place, and Gabriel held my hand the entire way.

"Well," I said to try and break the quiet as we pulled into a parking space in front of my dorm. "Have we been quiet enough for your liking? Because I happen to like our regular conversations."

"I do enjoy our regular conversations, but I also enjoy just spending quiet time with you. I just do not think you understand what it means to have finally found the one," Gabriel said, looking into my eyes. I could see such intense emotion in them.

Gabriel got out of the car and came around and opened my door. I got out, and he looked into my eyes and kissed me. This kiss was different than the rest. The intensity I had seen in his eyes came through in his kiss as well. It's hard to really explain, but it made me feel safe, like I was in the right place and there couldn't ever be anywhere better than with him. If there was such a thing as a soul mate, it may have been this feeling that came over me— complete calmness throughout my body and mind. I felt at peace with everything, as though what happened in the past was the past and did not matter now or ever again. Perhaps this was true love, and the feeling that everyone who seemed extremely happy in their lives was experiencing.

Gabriel finally broke the silence. "I always feel so connected to you, as though we were one entity split into two beings. I am not sure if that makes sense and if you feel the same energy also. I could be wrong, but I truly believe that we were meant to be together and that we have finally found each other. If I am insane and there is no such thing as soul mates, then just let me believe that it is so."

"I'm glad that you spoke first. I was just wanting to tell you that I too feel energy from you entering me each time we touch. I, too, want to believe that there are those who were put on this earth to be soulmates. Now whether they always find each other, that is the question. I think I have found you, my better half. My soulmate." I looked in Gabriel's eyes to see his reaction.

"Well, I want to interrupt and say that you are definitely my better half, and I truly feel complete when I am with you." Gabriel had such a wonderful, genuine smile.

"You are the most incredible, thoughtful, and intelligent guy I have ever met. I hate to ruin this wonderful moment, but if you don't go meet Mr. Vladimir soon, he may never let you see me again." I smiled and gave him another quick kiss. "Now go … and be careful."

"See you some time tomorrow," he said.

Everyone seemed to be in the kitchen when I came home, which was unusual, so I said hi and quickly ran downstairs with my laundry, hoping no one else was using the washer. Lucky me, it was not being used. I threw a dark load in and went back upstairs. I got all my papers organized to hand in and then did a whitewash, stopping in the kitchen on my way upstairs to grab a glass of water and an apple and banana, something quick before Charlize and her mom got here. I let my roommates know I had a load in the washer and apologized in advance that I was leaving a wouldn't be back till later in case they needed the washer. I told them to just put my clothes in the drier if need be and the clothes on my work out bench if I wasn't home.

CHAPTER FIFTEEN

The doorbell rang, this was the first time I have heard the doorbell, I think. I came running down the stairs with my jacket in hand, Amy had already answered the door, it was Charlize here to pick me up. I quickly introduced Amy to Charlize, and we headed out the door. Mrs. Reese was driving, I got in the back seat and thanked them both for bringing me along.

I had volunteered at the food bank once before with my family, and I'd really enjoyed it. This was exactly what I needed to get my mind off Gabriel. "Sure, that would be great! I like helping at the food bank. What time should I be at your place?" I replied, probably a bit more excited than I should be.

When we got to the food bank, there were some people there already, and the counter was occupied, so we went to the sorting area.

There were only two areas where volunteers could help. One was in the back, where donated items were checked for damage and expiry and separated into packages for different size families. The second was up front, giving out the boxes and other essentials to those who came in for a little help to make ends meet. I liked up front a little better; it gave me a better sense of helping, being able to connect with the people that came in, and short bursts of perhaps-needed meaningful conversation. The process was very well organized and overseen.

The periods when it was slower, I found myself thinking of Gabriel, surprise, surprise. I was wondering what he could be doing right at that moment, had they already killed anything, was he being safe, and do they butcher the animal on sight, or do they have a special place they do that? I really have no clue when it comes to hunting, I probably could have asked Gabriel more details, topic for later conversation, I guess. I found myself worrying, I tried to stop thinking of Gabriel, I got busy again for a bit which helped. Then I went off in a daze, I thought back on how Caleb talked about everyone having some sort of skeletons in their closets. I was pretty much an open book with Gabriel, but perhaps there were some "skeletons in Gabriel's closet", who better to know than Caleb as they were best friends. *There's got to be something there, that's why Caleb keeps asking me if I think I really know Gabriel.*

Could there be something that Gabriel's keeping from me that would really affect the way I feel about him. I really don't think so, he's shared the death of his parents and how it affected him, how more personal and intimate of information could there be. That's one of the most private topics one could talk about, if he can tell me that then what couldn't he tell me, could there be anything worse.

We stayed to help clean up and take inventory, and it was shortly after 9:30 when we left. They dropped me off at home, and I thanked them both for bringing me along. I was so glad I had met Charlize and her family; they were so nice, like my other family. I would have to work on Caleb, but hopefully that would come with time.

The lights were still on in the kitchen at my place, as it was only nine. I opened the door and peeked in the kitchen;

it was Amy. I kind of knew it would be. She had just finished cleaning.

"Oh, hi, Angel! Are you hungry? I just put leftovers in the fridge. I can pull it out and heat it up for you." Amy smiled.

"I'm good," I said, "I had a sub sandwich at the food bank, thanks anyways! I'm kind of run off my feet, going to go up to bed. Talk to you tomorrow."

I went downstairs first to put my clothes in the dryer, someone must have done laundry because my clothes were on the work out bench and the had been laid out nicely, not all scrunched up in a pile getting wrinkled. It was probably Amy who set my clothes nicely to the side, I would have to thank her tomorrow. I went right upstairs to bed, and I even washed my face upstairs in the girls' washroom. I felt kind of bad not staying to talk to Amy, as she seemed to want to chat a little. I would try to catch her tomorrow.

I was very glad to spend time with Charlize and Mrs. Reese, as it took my mind off Gabriel for a bit. I was really missing him now, and I felt incomplete. I was happy that we had gone to the Reese's together to apologize and to let everyone know we were together, I was Gabriel's girlfriend. It took me a while to fall asleep; I lay there thinking of him. It had only been four to five hours since I was last with him, but it felt a lot longer. I pictured Gabriel and I at the college gardens admiring the waterfall and the sound of the water.

We were just standing there, Gabriel behind me, holding me cradled within his arms. I couldn't have imagined being happier than at this moment, till Gabriel also gave me a few nice kisses on my neck. He was so romantic; everything about him screamed perfect to me. Then I started to think of Gabriel and I alone at his house, how it made me feel when he was touching me and kissing me. Oh, how I so wanted to be with him every day, I loved how he looked at me and the way he made me feel wanted, I know that we could be great together and I wanted that so bad. I wanted him so bad, every part of my body wanted him, it's like at craved him.

I imagined us being together, making love and I think that would be the right term, as I don't see him being anything less than a passionate lover. He does everything smoothly, so I'm sure he would be nothing less than great at sex too. I was driving myself crazy thinking of he and I together, going all the way.

CHAPTER SIXTEEN

Morning seemed to come faster than usual, and I was tired. It felt like I had just fallen asleep and got woken up abruptly. I didn't even dream, or what I thought were my thoughts may have been in my dreams, nevertheless, thought or dream, it was a great moment. I took a deep breathe, and at that moment I felt lonely, but it had only been about fourteen hours since I'd seen Gabriel. I don't know how a guy could affect me so much. I often caught myself saying I wouldn't be that girl I saw in the movies, pining for my man, but there I was. I guess you just don't know till it happens to you … when you find that right guy.

I know you're thinking I'm just young, and I don't know anything yet, and that Gabriel is probably not "the one." But I wanted to believe that my feelings were telling me the truth, that Gabriel was my knight in shining armor and that he would ride in on his horse, and I would have my happily ever after, and the white picket fence too! I never said I was normal—not even once.

The house was quiet, as it usually was this early in the morning. I made my way downstairs, had my shower, and got ready. I was heading back upstairs when I saw the light on and heard some noise in the kitchen, Amy was fumbling around as I walked by.

"Good morning!" I said in a chipper voice, which was strange as I'd been bummed out just a few minutes earlier.

"I am glad to see you're in better spirits this morning—you were really tired last night. I was a little bit worried about you." Amy smiled.

"I extremely tired when I woke up, and now I seem okay … maybe it's you!" I replied.

"Sure! I have that effect on everyone," Amy said sarcastically.

"Did I wake you up? Your classes don't start till nine, right?" I enquired.

"I just found out last night that my family is taking a trip back home over the holidays. My father just got given the time off, and he wants me and John to come too! So, I must talk to all my professors about my time off and whether I have special assignments to be done or tests to write during that time. Then I need to check in with John on his schedule and if he can make the time to come with us. If John can't come, then I won't see him at all over the Christmas holidays." Amy became extremely frazzled.

"I'm sure it will all work out. Take a deep breath and try to relax." I couldn't believe I was saying that to Amy; she was usually the one that had to calm me down and talk me through the situations.

I gave her a big hug, and she seemed a little better after that; she could breathe at least.

"What about your Christmas? Any plans?" Amy asked.

"Well, my family usually does the same thing every year. My mom will have all the family, aunts, uncles, cousins, and some close friends over for Christmas Eve supper. We eat, catch up on things, play games, and open presents around nine so the little ones can play with their toys a bit before leaving. I will have to see what Gabriel and Mr. Vladimir do for Christmas; maybe they will join us!"

"Christmas sounds fun at your house! We have a family supper and exchange gifts, but that is usually the only time my family is all together. I don't see the rest of my family otherwise; they are too busy with their own lives. Sorry to cut this conversation short, but I have lots to do and plan. This was a much unexpected trip we are taking, and in only a few weeks' time," Amy said, stressed out.

"No problem but try to calm down! You will figure everything out, and everything will work out. Talk to you later," I said, and I headed out to walk to school. I opened the door and saw that there was snow on the ground. It was still warm enough out to wear a hoody and a fall jacket, and the sun was already shining, which cut the chill in the air. But it was not warm enough to melt the snow, so it might stay around for a bit. It was nice to see the snow; I liked it and it cleansed everything.

I had totally lost track of time … I hadn't been thinking of Christmas, was always lost in my thoughts. I wasn't sure what was going on with me. Ever since I'd started college, I had been out of sorts. I was always a very organized person, some would say anal at times, about having everything organized at least a month in advance and always being ready for anything different that may arise. I couldn't say that now; I didn't even know what date or season we were in, let alone if my shoes were even tied. How pathetic was I? I really needed to pull myself together.

I was almost at the school, and I was super early. The doors had probably just opened, and there were maybe two kitchen staff in the back. I went to see if the coffee was on yet, and they said they would bring me out a very large cup and some toast when it was ready, as I'd forgotten to eat at home.

I went and sat down in one of the love seats that were near the windows on the outside perimeter of the cafeteria. As I sat there waiting for my coffee and toast, I thought of my list and what Caleb had said. I pulled out my notepad; there had to be other things I knew about Gabriel that I just forgotten about when talking to Caleb. His favorite color is red, and he takes, History, French, Spanish and German classes, and he models on the side, almost in the nude. I also can't forget he told me about how Mr. Vladimir came into his life. Things that some may not feel comfortable taking about to someone they barely now. Gabriel was primarily a meat eater, liked hunting large game, and seemed to be quite cool in temperature all the time. Well, his hands, his face, and his lips, anyway; it could be bad circulation. He seemed to be very sneaky, like the day I thought I'd felt something touch my shoulder and turned around to find nothing yet turned to continue walking and Gabriel was there. He seemed to have great knowledge of history, as though he had seen the things himself, not from books. Mr. Vladimir was a history teacher, and they had travelled lots, so that could very well explain his smarts.

Gabriel and Mr. Vladimir both had very pale complexions, perhaps sensitive skin, and sometimes I thought I saw Gabriel's eyes change color, but perhaps he was just light sensitive, and maybe mood or the reflection of the color of clothing he wore could cause it; it wasn't uncommon. Gabriel was very old-fashioned, opened doors, directed me with a hand on the small of my back, and he loved to go for long walks. Let me ask you—when was the last time someone guided you by the small of your back and asked you if you wanted to go for a stroll in the gardens? Right, probably never! He also liked to listen, whereas most guys just wanted to talk about themselves. There had to be more that I knew about Gabriel …

I decided to turn off my brain so I could eat my toast. It didn't work; it was hard, and what Caleb had said was getting to me. What did I really know and what was I just presuming? I needed to finish my list and find out some answers during supper tonight at the Reese's', if Gabriel came over. I need to get answers soon, as this was starting to consume my thoughts.

This had all been brought on by Caleb. If he hadn't questioned me, I probably wouldn't have thought twice about what I already did or didn't know about Gabriel. Something seemed fishy, or Caleb was trying to get to me. I just knew it.

I went to my art history class, and it would have been nice to see Mr. Vladimir, signifying that Gabriel was back, but it was a substitute professor. I didn't catch his name, and I don't think I caught a word that he said except to make sure to read pages 475 to 500. He also passed out an outline of some sort for studying purposes.

I went back home for lunch, but I wasn't hungry. I went up to my room and lay on my bed. As I lay there, I got a bit of a chill, so I threw my blanket over me, and I could have sworn I saw some flickering light or distortion of some sort in my peripheral vision. I lay there thinking of Gabriel, of course, and with my eyes closed, I could vividly imagine him. I reached out in front of me to what would be his chest if he were over me; I ran my hands on top of his pec muscle, cupping and roughly squeezing. I was so turned on.

I must have fallen asleep. I opened my eyes and looked at the clock. I thought I had just closed my eyes for a second thinking of Gabriel, but the clock said 3:20 p.m. I'd missed my class, which was so not like me. I was a little down now; it just seemed like things were getting worse. I was losing track of myself and my morals and goals.

I thought I could get up and go for a run before heading over to Charlize's. I hadn't talked to her that day, so I was not sure if she was going to even be home tonight. I really didn't feel like doing anything; I was just very bummed out today.

My motivation was next to nothing at this point. I did want to go to the Reese's' and see if Gabriel was going to show up, but I didn't feel like getting myself up and getting ready.

I lay there and thought about Gabriel. It had only been a day since I had seen him, but I felt very lonely. Maybe I was depressed … I wasn't sure what was going on. It baffled me that I had always been so independent and now I was yearning for a guy I had met less than six months ago. I really didn't feel like getting ready, but time was ticking fast, and it was nearly four thirty.

I jumped out of bed, grabbed my clothes, and made my way downstairs to the shower. One of the other girls was in the kitchen, but she didn't hear me, so I quickly went to the bathroom to avoid a conversation. Once I was in the shower and the hot water was running on my head and into my face, I started to feel a bit better. The shower worked as it always seemed to. I was refreshed and awake now, ready to get ready and go.

I really hoped Gabriel showed up. I didn't want to get ready for nothing and not have him show. I knew I shouldn't think that—I was not really a good friend. I should have been going over there to see Charlize and the rest of the Reese family. I needed to stop thinking of me and think of others around me and in my life. The Reese's and Charlize had done lots for me in the past three months, so the least I could do was go spend some time with them.

I did my hair and make-up and put on dress clothes just for Gabriel. I checked the clock, and it was 5:20. I didn't want to be there too early, but I was also too antsy to just stick around home. I went downstairs and no one was around, which was good, as I wasn't in a talkative mood, even though I was going over to a friend's house and there would definitely be conversation there.

I was not making any sense lately—maybe I needed to go home to my parents and talk things through with my mother. She knew about Gabriel, but she didn't know all the craziness going on inside my head when it came to him. She had no idea how the whole Gabriel thing had affected my schooling and me in general. I was afraid to tell her because she would be a little disappointed in me; I hadn't ever let anyone pull me astray before. I had always been in control of everything until now. My mother was the only one that could help me. I would have to hear a bit of a disappointment speech, but in the end, it would be worth it if I could get myself sorted out.

As I headed out the door, Amy was coming up the walk, and she seemed in a hurry. "Hello, Amy, how was your day?" I asked.

"Crazy, stressed out with all this holiday planning, only a few weeks to go, if even that. I have many more calls to make and things to organize this weekend. I don't know why thing are always left till the last minute and thrown in my lap to take care of. Are you going out somewhere special, you're dressed up?" Amy added.

"Just going to Charlize's, thought I would wear something other than jeans. Gabriel might show up there later if he is back from hunting," I replied.

"Okay, sorry to cut the conversation short but I have lots to do. Hope Gabriel is back and that you have a great evening. I will catch up with you later or tomorrow," Amy said all in one breath.

Poor Amy. I had never seen her this way. Usually she was the calmest person, stress-free and always there to help others. Now she looked like she needed help, and there wasn't much I could do, as I didn't speak Cantonese. I started to walk to Charlize's, and it was past five thirty; maybe they would be done supper by the time I got there. I wondered again if Gabriel was going to show up. I had a weird, different feeling come over me, like he was near. I got a cold sensation right after, like I'd walked through a cold air pocket or something, and I could have sworn I smelled Gabriel. The smell was very vivid, like he was standing right by me.

See? I really was losing it! I was coming up to the alleyway before having to turn down the Reese's' street and I saw someone standing there in a very long trench coat. I couldn't recognize the person, as they were too far away, and it was too dark in the alley. The person looked too mysterious, kind of scary for my liking. The hood was big and covered their head and face. I decided to cross the street as to avoid the person, not wanting a bad encounter. I was very untrustworthy of others, especially if I couldn't see their faces. Most of the time the eyes or facial expressions would give it away if the person was friendly.

I got to the other side of the street and turned my head to check, and the person was gone. I took a quick look around, and I couldn't see him, but Gabriel's smell was there again, though there was no one around. I turned and headed back in the direction I was going when I heard a low voice say, "Are you looking for me?"

In that moment, I was both scared and excited. I could smell Gabriel, but I hadn't seen anyone a minute ago, and now I heard this voice and couldn't make it out. I took off very fast for a few steps and turned around to see who or what was behind me.

As I turned, I saw the guy from the alley, and he was reaching for his hood. I was about to turn around again and start running.

"Whoa, whoa! Relax, it's just me." The guy took his hood down, and it was Gabriel.

"Oh, my God! What the hell are you thinking? You scared the shit out of me! A hooded strange person appearing and disappearing, and I'm by myself? What the hell!" I said again and hit him pretty hard in the chest.

"I am sorry, I wanted to surprise you, not scare you! If you want to hit me again, if it will make you feel better and forgive me faster, then go ahead. I missed you, and I couldn't wait to get back home to you, or find you, I should say. Were you on your way to the Reese's'?" Gabriel didn't let me get a word in edgewise.

He seemed to really think I was angry with him. I had been angry in the moment, but I was happier to see him. I'd missed him too. "I was, in hopes that you would show up," I said with a smile.

"Well, here I am and so happy to see you." Gabriel had the biggest grin. He grabbed me and pulled me in right close and gave me the tightest, most comforting hug. Then he kissed my neck and went up towards my ears.

I stopped him. "If you continue that direction, we will have to jump in the bush and get naked," I said. Then I pulled him back in for a kiss to show him that I did want to be with him but that the ears were off limits. There were a few other places that would be off limits due to causing immediate clothes-removal if tampered with. Our lips touched, and the tempting sensation of clothes-removal was there, but bearable. Oh, how I missed his touch and his kiss. It was as if I hadn't seen him for days and weeks, and it had only been one day. We kissed like you see in the movies, slow, passionate, and with lots of tongue action.

I felt as though we were one, that we couldn't be pulled apart. I loved him. I knew in my heart that these feelings I had were the real thing.

"That was nice. I enjoy kissing you, Evangeline. I feel like we were made to kiss one another. I missed you so much, and I know we were only apart for a day, but it seemed like days or weeks. Even if I am not with you, I like to know that you are within reach, so to speak." Gabriel had a glow about him as he spoke.

Was I hearing correctly? Gabriel missed me as much as I missed him. I sometimes repeated myself about my feelings, but I had been burnt before and I was very careful now ... I wanted to make sure Gabriel felt for me as I did for him. I know he said he did, and I'm going to leave it at that. It doesn't matter, Gabriel has me heart and soul, and I would be devastated without him.

"So, do you really want to go to the Reese's? Or do you want to go for a walk or go back to your place?" Gabriel looked at me with a devious grin.

"We can go back to my place if you want ... Actually, how about your place? Is Mr. Vladimir home?" I asked.

"I think he is staying at my cousin's place for another day. I cut hunting and the visit short because I missed you," Gabriel said as he pulled me in for a short but sweet kiss. "Are you sure that is what you want?"

"Yes, let's go to your place!" I think I said that a little bit too anxiously.

"Okay, my car is just up the street. I saw you walking and pulled over to meet up with you," Gabriel said.

We walked to his car hand in hand, and he opened the door for me as he usually does, but before I could get in, he pulled me in for another passionate kiss. It was getting harder and harder for me to resist the temptation: My body wanted all his nakedness now!

CHAPTER SEVENTEEN

We didn't do much talking on the way to his place; I was experiencing many feelings. I was super horny, for one, and scared too. I had overwhelming desires running through my body. That last kiss had made me very wet, and my ovaries were just screaming. It had been a long time since I had had intercourse or had been tempted sexually in this way. I always got aroused when I daydreamed about the male body, but it was not like this form of physical arousal I was feeling now. Plus, I was in my hot time to boot; we women have crazy things that happen naturally with our bodies monthly without adding actual sexual arousal to the mix.

As we pulled into the driveway, I felt scared too. Could I be alone with Gabriel and stop myself went the time came? I really didn't want to go all the way today, but my body thought otherwise. Could I keep things under control? I was sure Gabriel could, as he had shown nothing but self-control so far. I was also afraid he wouldn't like what he saw. I had my faults, things I was vexed with about myself. Gabriel seemed so perfect; I just hoped I met his expectations.

Gabriel came around the car and opened my door, reached for my hand, and helped me out—such a gentleman. He put his hand on my lower back then and pulled me in for another kiss. My god, I loved kissing him. I had calmed down a little on the drive out, but now my body was in a frenzy once again. My lower woman areas were pulsating, yearning, and craving the sexual touch. I needed to get control of myself.

We entered the mansion that was like a small castle. It was somewhat normal on the inside, with themed rooms with special artefacts Mr. Vladimir must have collected on his travels throughout the years.

"Do you need anything? Are you hungry? Thirsty?" Gabriel asked.

"No, I am good. Thanks."

"Are you sure? Are you okay? You seem a little bit off, not yourself," Gabriel asked, worried.

"I'm a little nervous and scared," I said waiting, for a reaction.

"You are not afraid of me, are you? I can take you back to your place if you want. I will not do anything you do not want to do; I just want to spend time with you alone," Gabriel said, very concerned.

"It's me I'm worried about; my feelings for you are real, and I don't want to ruin anything. My body wants you so bad … when we kiss, I want to rip your clothes off, and it's too soon," I said, a little embarrassed.

Gabriel looked a little surprised. "You really want me that bad? I want you that bad too, but I can wait, and I will not let things move too fast. I will stop us, I promise." He sounded so sincere.

I got in close to Gabriel and went in for a kiss. "I do want you so bad; please try to keep the situation under control," I said.

This kiss was perfect, another movie kiss. I was hot—so hot at this point that my body was just screaming. I needed to be touched … to explode. I was so overdue for an explosion. It had been a long time, too long … so long that I couldn't remember. Gabriel unzipped my hoody and helped me take it off. He was standing behind me and started kissing my neck and slowly turned me around, and it felt so good. He gave me small kisses on my face and on my lips, and it was driving me crazy. He ran his hands down my sides and back up again, lifting my shirt up. I didn't stop him this time as he lifted my shirt. I even raised my arms up as if to say, *"take it off."*

As he was lifting my shirt, Gabriel brushed the sides of my breasts, sending my body into an even crazier frenzy. I was not even that sensitive in that area; my inner thighs and my ass were my most sensitive parts. Oh my god! I was so horny, I couldn't believe it, and this was driving me so crazy. This wasn't me usually; it normally took forever and a lot more to get me in this state.

My shirt was off! I was wearing my sexy bra, so I did feel good about that. Would he like my breasts? Were they too small? Not firm enough? I was so worried. Gabriel stepped back from me, and now I was really worried.

"Wow! You are amazing." He came back towards me and started to kiss my neck. He stayed away from my ears, as I had asked. His hands came up my waist, up my sides, and he cupped my breasts.

"Is this, okay?" he asked.

"Yes, perfect, my breasts want to be touched."

Gabriel gently massaged and rubbed my breasts as he slowly started to kiss down towards my chest. My god, I was ready to explode; I wanted the entire package right now. I didn't know if I could wait, as my lower insides were at their max—they needed more, craved more. This was torture, but good torture.

Gabriel was now cupping my breasts, lifting them up ever so slowly and kissing their tops, and it felt so good. My underwear was soaked at this point. He gently hooked his thumbs inside my bra, brushing my nipples slowly back and forth. His hands were a little cold, but he seemed cold all the time. My nipples were hard as rocks, and I had goosebumps on top of goosebumps.

"Can I remove your bra? We will not go any farther than that. I promise," Gabriel said.

"Sure," I answered. At this point I would probably go all the way; I was so past horny that I had no control of myself. I was in Gabriel's hands now.

I felt him unhook my bra and take my straps off. My breasts were perky, covered in goosebumps, my nipples hard. He stood back again, and I felt a little embarrassed.

"Incredible ... perfect, just like I thought they would be." Gabriel seemed to like what he saw.

I felt less self-conscious now, about my breasts, at least. Gabriel came close to me, grabbed my face with his hands, and gave me a few sweet kisses on my lips, running his hands down my chest gently, like a light tickle, stopping at my nipples and rubbing and circling around them once or twice and then continued down my stomach. He pulled me right against him, and we had another movie kiss—that's what I was going to call them from now on. I had always wanted someone to movie kiss with, and I'd found that person and he was hot to boot!

As we were kissing, Gabriel brought his hands up the small of my back and moved them to the front, gently cupping my breasts again and then started to descend with his kisses. He kissed my neck and then my shoulders and down to the top of my breasts. Then he relaxed his grip on my breasts, leaving my nipples exposed. Gabriel then went in for a gentle kiss on my right nipple. He was so gentle. Then he kissed the left one and proceeded to lick and suck my nipple so gently; it felt so good. I didn't know how much more I could take. It was so satisfying, but I needed more too. I craved more.

Gabriel was gently paying attention to the right breast as he was kissing the left one. After a few minutes, he switched breasts, and then came back up to my lips and gave me another movie kiss. He was now cupping my breasts a little bit tighter, and I liked it.

"I think we have gone far enough for today, don't you?" Gabriel asked.

"I don't know … I am really liking this … it feels so good," I replied.

"I know, you feel great … so great, but if I continue, I will not be able to control myself. You are so beautiful. I want to see and feel the rest, feel the rest of you, and would love to be inside you," Gabriel answered.

"So, what now?" I asked.

"We just stop; we can watch a movie if you want, or whatever," Gabriel said.

"You can stop just like that?" I asked with an inquisitive look on my face.

"Well, I should go have a cold shower. Do you need one?" Gabriel asked.

"You go have one. I will be alright … maybe …" I added.

Gabriel went to have a shower, and I thought about satisfying my own needs, but I managed to settle down faster than I thought I would. I would need to bring an extra pair of underwear next time; I'd soaked these ones pretty good.

Gabriel came back and found me curled up on the couch. I had almost fallen asleep lying there, thinking of him and me. Oh, how I wish it could have continued, but stopping was the right thing to do. It was too quick, too soon. I did want this to be a forever thing, not a "he gets what he wants and it's over thing," so this was the right way to go about things. I was just justifying our actions because I sure would have wanted it to go the other way. Good thing Gabriel was a gentleman, and he was in control of the situation.

"Are you tired, beautiful?" Gabriel asked.

"I'm a little tired after all that unfinished excitement," I replied.

"Sorry. Stopping was the right thing to do, though I was enjoying myself immensely and would have loved to continue. I just want you to know that I really enjoy being with you and want this to last, so I want to make sure we do not rush into things. The last thing I want is to do something to make you regret and make you think twice about being with me and it be over. I really want you in my life forever. I know you are the one I want and need; my energy feels complete when I am with you. I notice a feeling of emptiness when we are apart; even one day seems like forever. Crazy, I know, that's why I want to go slow. I want to show you that I am the one for you also." Gabriel was so sincere with his words. It made me very happy to know we seemed to feel the same about each other.

"I don't want to be without you either. I feel incomplete when I know I'm not able to see you," I replied. Gabriel was sitting by me on the coach, running his hands through my hair. He leaned over to give me a kiss on the forehead.

"Do you want me to drive you home? You can sleep here. Mr. Vladimir will not be home tonight, and I promise to continue being a gentleman," Gabriel said with a sweet smile.

"Sure, I can stay over. Can we sleep in your bed together?" I asked.

"Testing the waters, eh?" Gabriel smirked. "Yes, we can sleep in my bed together." We went up to his room, and he pulled the bed linens back and then went to his drawer. He pulled out what seemed to be a very large T-shirt and put it on the bed.

"I hope this will do for you to sleep in. I will be back in a few minutes," Gabriel said.

"Okay, thanks," I said as I picked up the shirt and headed to his washroom.

I hadn't been in his room before, but I figured that the door across the room was for a washroom or a very big closet. Well, it was a bathroom, and a large closet was at the end of that bathroom. It was a regular bathroom, with black and white décor, tiled in neutral colors. His room was the same, quite large, maybe sixteen feet by sixteen feet, if I were to guess, with a good size ensuite/closet, also in black and white. Gabriel also had black blinds on his windows; maybe he liked napping during the day or on summer evenings when it was light out till eleven-ish.

Gabriel came back into the room with a glass of water. I was just standing by his bed, as I didn't know which side he preferred sleeping on. I must have looked ridiculous just standing there, and he had a big smile on his face. "I am not fussy; pick whatever side you want to sleep on."

I liked that he seemed to already know what I was thinking instead of me asking and looking even sillier. Come to think of it, that seemed to happen quite frequently, with Gabriel answering my thoughts and questions before I even said them aloud. Were we already in sync with each that quickly? I know when couples are together for a very long time, they can finish each other's sentences and thoughts, but our relationship was just new. Strange!

Anyways, I was not just daydreaming all the time; now I was starting to overthink everything too. I really needed to go spend time with my mother. I chose the side of the bed closest to the washroom, as I sometimes needed to get up in the middle of the night to get water or go to the washroom. I know, if I didn't drink water before and during the night, I most likely wouldn't have to go … I have heard it many times before.

I got into bed and Gabriel took his clothes off right in front of me, which was not shocking, as he posed almost naked for many people every day … why would one person bother him at all? He was so perfect. Everything was proportioned, his skin texture looked and felt incredible, and he always smelled good too! Gabriel turned me on just thinking about him physically, and he was also smart and a gentleman. There weren't many full-package deals like him.

"Are you okay if I just sleep in my underwear? I could put a T-shirt on if you want?" Gabriel looked at me.

"I'm good with whatever you like. I don't think a shirt would change any of the feelings and thoughts going through me anyway," I answered with a big smile.

Gabriel got into bed and lay on his side, facing me with a big smile on his face. "So, how do you like to sleep? On your side, back, or stomach?"

"I am mostly a back sleeper and sometimes on the side, never a stomach sleeper," I replied. "I don't snore unless I am very sick and even then, it's deeper breathing rather than real snoring, or so I have been told."

"I don't snore either," Gabriel answered. "And I never get sick; not since I was a kid, anyway."

"Cool, do you take vitamins? Weird question for me to be asking, but that's why my mother says I don't get sick often; because I always have my vitamins." I heard myself say that after the fact and felt very dumb.

"I have a blood disorder. Nothing serious, but that's why I eat mostly red meat and fairly rare. My doctor says that if I eat lots of red meat and I take a few pills, my immunity should be very high, so I get sick much less than most." Gabriel looked at me for a response. "Is this too weird for you?"

"Why would it be weird? You got to do what the doctor says to stay healthy, so if that means eating rare red meat, so be it. I was going to ask you about that eventually; thanks for clearing up that question. I have a few more, but they can wait till tomorrow."

"Evangeline, you are so different than others. Most girls get very wigged out that I eat very little regular food and mostly red meat, and if I get the chance to explain why, they still feel weird about it. There are a few more things that may turn you off. I don't really want to talk about them right now if that's okay. I would rather not chance you not wanting to be with me at this moment." Gabriel seemed weird now.

"Listen, it's all good! I'm sure nothing you can tell me will change my mind about you. I really like you, and everyone has issues they must deal with; if you are okay and you're not dying, I'm good with probably whatever," I responded, "and yes, we can talk about the rest another day."

"See? I knew you were different. I really like you too. Let's stop this conversation and talk more about what you like," Gabriel quickly added.

"Sure," I replied. He really didn't like talking about himself. He just wanted to know things about me. I guess that was okay, but different; most guys wanted to brag about themselves and never really asked about others. I was going to humor Gabriel, but I needed to know more about him eventually.

"So, do you like to cuddle and be held when you sleep, or would you rather not be touched?" Gabriel asked.

"I definitely like to be cuddled before I go to sleep, but when it's time to actually go to sleep, I like my space, only because I tend to overheat if someone is holding me," I said and looked for a reaction. I had a feeling Gabriel liked to cuddle all the time, since he was usually on the cooler side.

"Okay, I just wanted to know. Can I cuddle with you now?" Gabriel asked anxiously.

"Yes, we can cuddle now." I smiled.

I turned around and Gabriel came to cuddle me. We didn't speak for a few minutes, and it was great. He wasn't the biggest guy, but he was bigger than me by enough to wrap nicely over me and still make me feel small and cared for. I liked it when someone could hold me and I felt smaller; it made me feel secure and wanted, I guess; maybe I had insecurities. I really didn't like being the same size or even bigger than the guy. It did nothing for me. Gabriel had one arm under the pillow and one arm wrapped around my waist, and there was no space between us at all. It felt good, it felt right, and I was starting to get turned on again.

Gabriel started to kiss my neck again and now my heart-rate was definitely elevated. It was very hard to just be there and not say screw it, let's do it. I had to learn self-control; I wasn't going to be able to have him naked and to myself all the time, though at this point that sounded good.

"Is it okay if I kiss your neck? I cannot help myself. You smell so good, and you are so beautiful, I have a hard time not touching you. I was incomplete till I met you and did not know how incomplete I was. I really do not want to be without you. I like the feeling of being complete too much. I feel lost even being away from you for one day," Gabriel whispered in my ear.

"I'm okay with whatever; I just like having you with me. I'm just not used to all this attention," I answered.

"I felt the need to meet you and get to know you the first time I bumped into you too! Something lured me to you … something told me that we needed to meet; I was not sure about the strong pull till recently. Mr. Vladimir strongly believes that there are those with strong connections that are meant to be together, but that they rarely find each other and most settle for second choice, so to speak. I thought he was a little crazy, as I do with some of his other stories and beliefs, but maybe there is truth in what he says after all. Now I think Mr. Vladimir is right … because I found you. You are strong and beautiful, inside, and out, and I cannot wait to know everything about you. I want to be with you forever, and I hope that me saying that doesn't scare you off." Gabriel had so much sincerity in his eyes as he spoke to me.

"I don't know what to say, but I'm not going anywhere. I feel complete with you too!"

No more words came to my mouth; this must have been a first. I always had something to say, to ask, but not this time. For once, someone had just as much to say as I did.

Gabriel was playing with my hair, rubbing my sides, and holding me. It felt good being cared for, being wanted, yet it still seemed surreal. This was all I'd wanted from the first time I saw him—to be with him. I thought it was only a dream, that I wasn't good enough for him. Look at me now. I was in his bed, and he was wrapped around me, touching me, and saying he wanted to be with me forever.

"Can I ask you something else?" Gabriel seemed unsure.

"Sure," I replied.

"Can I please feel your butt … with clothes on, of course?" Gabriel added quickly.

"Sure, you already saw my breasts, why not feel my butt too!" I said, smiling.

"You have great breasts, by the way. Perfect. I like them very much. Thanks for letting me feel your butt too!" I could feel Gabriel's smile even though I couldn't see it. He kissed my neck again and ran his hands down my sides and onto my butt, which was covered by my underwear and part of the shirt; I was practically naked. I guess the feel wasn't enough, so he grabbed my ass and firmly shook it.

"Sorry, I had to do it! It is what I suspected with all that running you do, very firm and grabbable," Gabriel said.

"It's all good; glad you like it." I smiled.

"Like? What is this 'like' word? I love your ass and your breasts. You are perfect. Is it okay if I keep touching you, or have you had enough?" Gabriel asked, a little concerned.

"I'm quite enjoying this. Sorry I'm not touching you back, but if I touch you, I will have no control over my actions. None. This is already hard to control. I feel you up against me already … are you sure you want to keep touching me? You may need another cold shower," I added.

"Yes, perhaps a cold shower will be needed again, but just not right now. If you do not want to touch me, I am okay with that. I am not here to force anything to happen that you do not want. I am just happy you are here with me," Gabriel said.

We were quiet for a bit. I was trying to keep control of myself. Gabriel was grabbing, rubbing, and massaging my ass, and it felt so good, and then he moved to my stomach and grabbed my breasts firmly.

"My god, woman, you are so hot and desirable, but that is quite enough for today because I am having trouble controlling myself now. I want you so bad, and I need to go have that cold shower right now. Do not go anywhere … I will be right back."

He got up quickly, and I could see he needed a cold shower; I had felt it against me too. I knew he was well aroused. My ass was very sensitive, and I'd felt it against me, making me even hornier.

He seemed to have gone to have a shower in another room, to leave me his bathroom. I got up and went to the washroom, decided to turn on his shower to cold and get in quickly to cool off. I was in for less than thirty seconds and got out; it was just to calm my hormones. I didn't even get my hair wet. I quickly dried off and put his shirt back on. I went to get back into bed and found that Gabriel was already back.

"I thought only I needed the cold shower; glad to see the feeling was mutual." Gabriel smiled.

"You have no idea. I never calmed down from our first arousal in the living room. I couldn't keep myself calm now, especially when you were aroused, and it was touching my butt. My butt is the most sensitive part of me … hard to control when the butt is involved," I added.

"Glad to know for next time." Gabriel giggled mysteriously. "I will let you sleep now; it's pretty late, sleep good."

"Goodnight. I'm glad we spent the night together. You have a good sleep too." I leaned over and gave Gabriel a kiss.

We looked at each other for a few minutes, and then he gave me another kiss. I turned on my side, grabbed his arm, and wrapped it around my waist. Gabriel got in closer, and before I knew it, I woke up to an alarm. I was lying on my back and Gabriel was nowhere to be seen.

A few minutes later, he came into his room with a coffee in hand. "Your breakfast will be ready in a few minutes. How do you like your eggs?"

CHAPTER EIGHTEEN

"I like my eggs any way you want to serve them, as long as the whites are fully cooked," I replied.

This was the beginning of another great day; I just knew it! I'd been woken up by the hottest guy after an incredible night. Today was going to be our first night out together, not including the previous night when we'd gone to the Reese's' together and given them the good news that we were together. I couldn't think of anything better. I didn't like spending any time away from him now. How pathetic was I, right? I'd never thought it would be me on this end of things. I made fun of others about being dependent and now I found myself in the same situation. I couldn't help myself. This must be love.

I got up and got dressed, washed my face, and saw that there was a toothbrush with a sticky note on it with my name on it: "Evangeline." He'd thought of everything. I caught sight of a clock on my way downstairs. It was eight thirty. I was a little surprised it was still that early. Breakfast smelled good, and Gabriel and I ate it quickly and then cleaned the kitchen.

"I really had an incredible time last night; I hope that's the first of many great nights to come. I know we didn't talk about it, but what are you up to today? Tonight, is bowling, but do you want to hang out today?" I asked.

"No, sorry, I must go grab Mr. Vladimir from the airport at one. I had a text this morning saying he was coming home today instead of Sunday; something urgent came up and he must get back and get some stuff here done and head back out tomorrow, first thing apparently," Gabriel said and didn't seem too impressed. "We can hang out for a bit if you want. Do you want to go see Maleficent and maybe go to the garden?"

"Sure, sounds good to me. I will spend as much time as I can with you." I must have had a smile from ear to ear.

"Do you want to have a shower? I can give you a T-shirt to wear if you'd like. Or you can wear no shirt and no pants, come to think of it," Gabriel added.

"You're pretty funny. I don't think so!" I replied.

"I am just kidding … Actually, I'm not, you would look great walking around in your underwear, or naked, I'm sure." Gabriel had the biggest smile and was giggling.

"I'm not going to comment, but I will take you up on the shower and T-shirt. Do you have a blow dryer?"

"Yes, let's go upstairs and you can pick a T-shirt you want to wear, and I will grab you the blow dryer." Gabriel guided me up the stairs with his hand at the small of my back to make sure I didn't fall … such a perfect gentleman.

Gabriel got me a towel, facecloth, and a blow dryer and left them on the counter for me.

"Okay, give me a minute." Gabriel left the bathroom and came back with three white T-shirts. "So, these are too tight on me, so they will probably fit you."

"I will take the T-shirt that has the red NIKE on it, thanks." I took it and closed the washroom door behind me. I had my shower, got dressed, and blow dried my hair in about fifteen minutes. I didn't shave … I'd have another shower later, before I got ready for bowling. I came out of the bathroom, and Gabriel was lying on his bed.

"Are you tired?" I asked.

"No, just thought I would just lay here and wait for you; that was fast."

"Ready to go?" I asked. I knee-dropped on the bed beside him and bounced back up to my feet.

Gabriel got up and gave me a big smile. "You seem to have a lot of energy."

We went down to the kitchen and Gabriel grabbed a few carrots. I was guessing they were for the horses. We headed out to the stable, and he opened the door. Maleficent was right there, like she knew we were coming. She was so beautiful and loving, and she snuggled her head into my neck. I gave her some nice pets. We fed each horse a couple of pieces of quartered apples and half a carrot; they seemed to really enjoy their treats.

"Would you like to brush Maleficent?" Gabriel asked.

"Sure!" I exclaimed.

Gabriel went to the first stall to the right, which contained all the horse gear. He handed me a brush, and I brushed Maleficent. She seemed to enjoy it.

"Shouldn't we brush the rest of them? They might be jealous that she got brushed and they didn't," I asked, concerned.

"No need to worry, they all get a good brushing almost every day. Mr. Vladimir's gardener is well versed with everything on an acreage or farm, including taking care of the horses. Do you want to go for a ride or go to the garden?" he asked.

"I think we could perhaps go for a ride another time. I would rather go to the garden; the waterfall is calling me right now."

"Sure, whatever you want to do," Gabriel answered.

We walked out through the gate we had gone through before, but now it was with my eyes open. It was simply beautiful; we entered the garden and it looked just as amazing in the daytime as it had in the evening. Gabriel came behind me and wrapped his arms around my waist, then grabbed my hand and spun me around. He pulled me in close and gave me a passionate kiss. I could feel the warmth of his feeling towards me come through in the kiss. Oh, how I loved to kiss Gabriel; I couldn't have imagined it any better. I had never been kissed so passionately and with so much feeling.

I was scared for a minute and thought, *what if this is just a thing and Gabriel won't be mine forever*? Would I be able to deal with losing him? Well, that was not going to happen, I hoped, not if I had anything to do with it. I pulled him into me again for another wonderful kiss.

"I can't believe how beautiful you are! You are very beautiful, a natural girl; most girls could only hope to have your beauty. I feel special to have you by my side, and wow, when you get dressed up, you are stunning, cannot wait to see you in a dress. I know you do not think of yourself as being hot, but sorry, you are a knockout! Some … a *lot* of beautiful girls have to work hard to reach their state of beauty, but it is just there for you; it's not pushed and never looks overdone. It's just naturally you, Evangeline." Gabriel always said the right thing.

"I think you are exaggerating a bit, but I'm happy that you feel this way about me."

"So, I have few questions to ask you. I hope that's all right?" I looked at Gabriel. I couldn't imagine things being any different, and I was a bit worried about asking him personal questions. Would it be that bad? Caleb made it seem like I would change my mind about Gabriel if I really knew him.

"Well, shall we start with the questions, or shall I just start telling you everything from start to finish, and then you can ask things that I may miss as we go?" Gabriel asked.

"I'm just happy you are willing to be open with me about yourself, and that you feel comfortable about telling me what happened to your parents." I gently swept his cheek with the back of my hand to signify that I appreciated him. "I want to ask you something, and I'm so sorry for asking such emotional questions, and you don't have to answer, because the past must bring up a lot of memories that hurt you." I felt so bad for asking, but I was so curious. "How did you cope with everything then, and how are you coping with things now? Does the accident still affect you, and did you receive help?"

"It's okay, I want to be able to tell you as much as I can. It's been a while now since the ordeal, and I have learned to deal with it as best as possible. I went home from the hospital to a strange place with a strange man that was now my "father," and my parents were both dead. I think I went through a few years of being quiet, repressed in my thoughts … I really wasn't thinking. I was more … numb. Mr. Vladimir was patient with me and my behavior. He sent me to see therapists, and after many, I started to come out of my shell a little. He tried to get me to speak about the accident and my parents more than once, but I really had nothing to say.

"I was and I am very thankful for everything Mr. Vladimir has done for me. I do love him, I guess. He is my father, and he has been there for me like a real father would through everything. I went through many phases and seemed to come out of each with his help and the help from therapists. I used to think how my life would have possibly been if my parents had not died, but I do not think of it anymore. I am thankful for how I am now, and especially now that I have met you, Evangeline. You are the answer to my prayers … if I prayed."

Gabriel paused and looked into my eyes. "I do want to change this topic, but I did want to say that I went through some very trying times, but my life changed for the better after I tried to take my life and nearly succeeded. I became a new man after that, and I am very thankful that Mr. Vladimir was there to save me."

"Sorry again for the question. I promise I will stop with the questions after one more, if it's alright?" I asked.

"I told you I would try to answer anything you wanted to know; I really do not want any secrets between us." Gabriel smiled.

"So, you know I think you are incredible, and so beautiful. You may not like that word as a description, but that's as a person and an art form. I just want to know why you're not in a relationship and why Mr. Vladimir told me that I should perhaps stay away from you." I looked at Gabriel sincerely.

"Well, having gone through the many phases I went through, it was very hard on the young ladies I did have in my life. I was emotional, all over the place, went through fits of rage and depression, and this took a toll on the girls I was with. I guess I was perhaps even emotionally abusive with them, though never physical. I stopped getting into relationships, as I needed to find myself and learn to control my feelings. When Mr. Vladimir saved me, I vowed to change, and it took me some time to deal with the new me I wanted to be. I have only had one girlfriend since, and it did not work out; she did not want to know about my past and me. She could not accept how I was in the past and what I was since I came back to life, so to speak." Gabriel paused, still looking into my eyes, and then kissed me.

"I promise I won't ask any more questions. I will wait for you to share things with me as you feel like it." I smiled and kissed him again.

"I do want to say, I am so glad you are in my life; you are the person I have been waiting for, for what seems to be a very long time." Gabriel grabbed me and hugged me and held me for a few minutes without saying anything. "I guess I should explain the incident a little bit, as you are probably wondering what it was that I claimed caused me to change, right?" Gabriel looked to me for a reaction.

"Yes, please, I said I wouldn't ask any more questions but there's so much more I want to know about you, so if you want to tell, I will listen." I was beside myself that he wanted to tell me more.

"Well, I had tried and never succeeded in taking my life a few times, but this time, I wanted my life to end once and for all. I drank so much and even injected myself with something. I'm not even sure what it was. I did not care. I don't remember how I ended up where I did; the last I remembered I was at some house with people I did not know. The next thing I knew I was walking in the woods like I usually did when I needed to think and be by myself. I had some pills in my pocket and a mickey in my hand. I took all the pills and chased them down with the mickey, and I was sure this would do it, finish me off for good.

"I was hearing animal noises, which I always did walking through the woods, and then I heard what sounded like something coming at me from behind, but I could not run ... the pills and alcohol had started to shut down my system. I went to turn around, and I woke up in my bed with my father over me and a terrible headache, and I was very hungry and thirsty. Mr. Vladimir told me I was lucky to live, that a wild animal or something, perhaps a bat, had bitten me, and the doctor gave me a rabies shot and some penicillin. I was out for twenty-four hours. He asked me how I felt, and I told him I needed to eat. After eating I was fine, even better than normal, I would say."

"I am interrupting again; can I see the bite marks? Would it not have been cool to have turned into a vampire like in the movies? Anyways, that's just my crazy mind talking." I was so excited suddenly.

"Well, I do have bite marks, but they are very faint, and yeah, it probably would be cool to be a vampire!" Gabriel answered.

"Yeah, continue, I would have never thought someone could be so interesting." I could feel my never-ending smile.

"Thanks. Never thought of myself that way … strange, maybe, or different, not interesting," Gabriel seemed to say this with relief in his tone.

I smiled and didn't say another word. He went on to say that it was like the bat, if that was what had bit him, or it was the mixture of pills and alcohol ingestion that had made him change a little. He didn't seem to need as much sleep as before and eat as much, which may have something to do with his stomach lining being burnt. He would eat lots when his body asked for it and said that certain foods didn't sit well in his stomach like they had before the attack. His hearing and sense of smell got better, and his tastebuds got worse. I found all of this very fascinating.

He explained that after waking up yet again with Mr. Vladimir at his side, it gave him respect for his new father, which in turn brought them closer together.

"Now, Evangeline, if I have missed out on anything you might want to know, please ask away and I will try to answer as best as I can," Gabriel said.

"Well, since you asked, I do have a few questions. Why are you and your father so pale? It cannot be hereditary, as you are not blood related. I also noticed that your eyes change color, I thought you wore contacts. Do Mr. Vladimir's change also? Oh! Also, you always seem a little on the cooler side,

I've noticed. I understand you being cool and pale, because of your blood disorder, but what about Mr. Vladimir?" I asked hesitantly.

"You are quite detailed in your questions. Does my blood disorder and how it affects my body bother you?" Gabriel asked with a worried tone.

"No, I just want to know everything about you. Now, don't change the topic on me, as you often do when I am trying to understand you better," I answered, trying to ease the worry he seemed to have.

"I am not trying to avoid your questions. I promised you would get the answers that you wanted, and I shall deliver. I do not think of myself as pale, though come to think of it, I guess the sunscreen I wear may make me appear paler than others. I am used to hanging out with the other goths, so I never really think of myself as pale. I began to be light sensitive after I got bitten, and I guess Mr. Vladimir is pale because he never goes outside unless necessary. I am not really sure why he tends to stay indoors more. As for my eyes changing color, I do not wear contacts, I just say that, so people do not keep questioning my eye color. I am light sensitive … maybe it has something to do with that. I am not sure. I personally never see my eyes change color!" Gabriel answered.

"I still have a problem believing that you, Gabriel, the hottest guy in college and perhaps all of Olds, wants to be with me." I gave him a *"you got to be crazy look"* and shook my head.

"Evangeline, I am not sure what I can say to make you believe how much you mean to me. Maybe time will be the only way that you can truly believe you are the only one for me. I have been waiting for you' there is chemistry between us, and I have never felt that sort of energy between me and any other before." Gabriel looked so sincere.

"Tonight, is bowling night," I said, "where all your other friends will officially meet me and Kelsie and know that we are a couple. I'm a little nervous, but they have all seen me around, so it probably won't be that much of a surprise." I smiled, then continued. "Will Mr. Vladimir cause us problems in the future? You know that he told me to be careful and that perhaps you were a path I didn't want to go down," I said, a little concerned.

"My father and I have an agreement; we do not get into each other's business, but we do question motives at times. I do not think there will be any problems if I do not interfere with your grades and emotions. When he sees how we are together and he feels how I feel about you, it will be okay," Gabriel reassured me.

"I don't want to ever lose you!" I said. "I really don't know what would happen if you decided not to be with me any longer. My heart, my brain, and all my being says that you are the one for me. You consume me already; I wake up, think of you throughout the entire day, and even go to sleep with you on my mind. I know that I am pushing the "us" pretty far, as we are new in our relationship, but I think my feelings go beyond just getting to know each other slowly. I am starting to ramble; I do that when I feel uncomfortable or scared. I am going to stop before I embarrass myself." I looked down as I spoke.

"Evangeline, I will tell you once again that I will not ever get upset with what you say or ask of me. Now, if you do not have any more questions for me, I have a few for you!" Gabriel smiled.

"I think I'm good for now. Ask away," I said.

"How sexually experienced are you? Or is that too personal of a question?" Gabriel asked with one eyebrow up.

"It wouldn't be fair if I didn't wish to answer your questions when I asked so many of you, right? That would be a little one-sided," I answered.

"Yes, but I do not really need to know. I want to be with you no matter what," Gabriel added.

"I have always had a boyfriend, but till I was fifteen there had only been kissing and no fondling of any nature. When I was fifteen, I met a guy through a friend at a party, and he was hot. I had seen the guy around before; he played sports, so our schools competed against each other. His name was Austin, and he had a girlfriend at the time, but what I didn't know was that I knew her. The girl was in my English class and sat behind me. I helped her with her homework from time to time, and even let her cheat off my exams ... she was quite a nice girl. I couldn't believe they were together, not because she wasn't his type, but because I didn't know him enough to think that. I pictured him with a ... well, with me! Anyways, a few months went by, and I had seen him at parties, and he even came into the arcade once with Dean, a guy I was seeing at the end of the previous year and through the summer.

"He and I stayed good friends, and there was no falling out after we broke up; it was a mutual decision. I went to speak to him the next time we ran into each other, and he told me that Austin and the girl were no longer together. Dean asked me if I was interested, and I said hell yeah! Dean introduced us at the next party, and we were together for almost a year. Then Austin figured I wasn't enough or what he wanted; I don't think I put out enough for him, so he decided to pursue my best friend.

"That friendship came to a quick end, as she fell directly into his bed the weekend after he broke it off with me. Anyway, he broke my heart, and I was devastated for a long time. It still hurts to talk about it. I had a few boyfriends after that, but he tore my heart so deep I didn't think I could possibly want another like that again till I saw you! I'm not just saying that I really need you. I have thought of you every day and night and even in my dreams since my eyes caught sight of you at the other end of the bar! I hope me being so open with you doesn't scare you. I just need to let you know how deep my feelings run for you," I said, noticing how long a story this was.

"I am not scared. I want to be with you and only you forever, or as long as you want. I am so sorry about your broken heart, and I hope that I can help mend it for you." Gabriel smiled.

There was silence, and Gabriel pulled me in for a nice passionate kiss. I got goosebumps. I couldn't wait for the next time we could be together like we'd been last night. I didn't think I would hold back with anything next time. I was ready, and I wanted to be with Gabriel so bad. My loins ached just thinking about it.

"I am really enjoying our time together as I always do, but I should get you home. I need to get to the airport on time to pick up Mr. Vladimir; he does not do well with tardiness," Gabriel stated, but you could see he really didn't want to go.

"Okay, I certainly don't want you to be late or ever have me be the reason that Mr. Vladimir is unhappy with you." I gave Gabriel a little smirk.

We made our way back to the stable, and I gave Maleficent a quick rub and snuggle and told her I would see her soon.

Gabriel was quiet on the drive back to my place. "Are you alright?" I asked.

"Yes, of course, sorry. I just really do not want to leave you. I know I will see you later at the bowling alley, but I wish you could come with me to the airport. I miss you already, and I have not even left you yet." Gabriel grabbed my hand and kissed it as we drove up to my dorm.

He leaned over and gave me another kiss, and I left his car and went into my house. Gabriel always seemed tense, or his mood changed, any time Mr. Vladimir was mentioned or if he had something he had to do with him. Strange to be that way with a father figure; you would think they would be closer than they were, and that Gabriel would like to spend time with him. Perhaps Gabriel would answer some of my other questions in time.

I walked into my house and the living-room light was on, which was strange. I had never actually seen anyone use the living room before. We were usually out in the kitchen or in our rooms. I made my way to the living room and saw Amy sitting there on her computer.

"Hello, Amy!" I said quietly as to not startle her. "What's up? I have never seen you down here on your computer before."

"Hello, Angel, I'm working on my list, double checking everything. I only have a few days left to make sure all is ready for the family trip. I have everything booked, and I have only a few more gifts to buy for the relatives. I must get them bought and sent by priority mail on Monday, so they get there in time for Christmas." Amy looked very exhausted.

"Why do you have to do all this? Can't anyone else help you?" I asked.

"Everyone is very busy with work, so they always seem to think I'm the best candidate for setting up things. I'm the most organized of the bunch." Amy smirked.

"Well, I hope they appreciate all that you are doing; you are busy enough with school, let alone setting up everything and buying gifts for everyone. Don't take this wrong, but you look very tired. You need rest," I stated as nicely as I could.

"I know. After Monday, I will have a week or so to get back to concentrating on school and getting some rest. Thanks for caring, Angel!" Amy added.

"I need to go for a quick run." I smiled. "I will talk to you when I get back if you are still around. Sorry."

CHAPTER NINETEEN

Today was the day that Gabriel and I would make our first public appearance, where all our friends would be in one location and finally see us together! It was Saturday, and the last weekend before having to buckle down on schoolwork. All major assignments were due at the beginning of next month, so you would think I would have lots to worry about, but I didn't. I always got on my assignments when they were given to me. I didn't wait till the last minute. The pressure of doing that, like most others did, gave me anxiety attacks, and I avoided it.

Since it was still early enough and Gabriel was busy, I decided to still have my "me" day. I'd been planning on doing an extensive workout, but I would have to settle for just a run. I would still get a manicure/pedicure and then get my hair cut and done for this evening. My mani/pedi appointment was booked for one p.m. and my haircut at three. Everything worked out well. I'd had a great night and morning with Gabriel and would still be able to make my "me" appointments.

I stretched out a little before starting to run. Something just told me to, or I might pay for it later, plus I had to bowl this evening. I didn't want to overdo anything and not be able to. I ran about eight kilometers. I kept looking around during my run. I could have sworn that Gabriel was around, but I didn't see him. Sometimes when I thought of him, he just appeared, which was maybe why I thought of him so much—because I thought he would appear, just like that.

It was almost suspicious, like something from a book or a movie, where one's wishes seem to come true and there's some sort of telepathic connection somehow. Never mind. I'm just rambling again; I think I'm maybe too much of a romantic.

I often thought things I watched or read could come true, that there could be a happily ever after. Ha ha! Like that could ever be true. Well, there was no harm in wishing or being optimistic that someone writing those stories had reached that happily ever after at some point in their lives. Maybe that was why I hadn't been able to trust; I had been burnt before and didn't want it to happen again. Therefore, I'd put my life on hold, fearing moving forward, in fear of not finding that perfect relationship. I just thought it would be different with Gabriel with that connection we shared, and I hoped it was the happily ever after.

I finished my run, and believe it or not, I even stretched after. I went home shortly before noon—I was cutting it tight with time. Amy was in the kitchen making herself lunch.

"Hi Amy, wow, twice in one day! How is everything going?" I asked.

"Oh, I forgot to tell you earlier that I was at the school till the doors closed at eleven last night, but I was working on school assignments, trying to catch up this morning too. I got lots done. I am just grabbing some coffee and toast and heading back to the school to work and finish some other assignments. I am hoping that, by the time the weekend is over, I am almost caught up on things." Amy seemed exhausted, but better than before.

"Well, I am glad you are less stressed than when we spoke earlier. I was worried about you," I said.

"Thanks for being a great friend! I must get to the school. Have fun bowling tonight, and maybe we can talk later. I will probably be home later too! I noticed you didn't come home last night; I want to know everything next time we talk." And then Amy left.

She was great, and I didn't know how she did it—she even remembered that I had bowling that night. I didn't remember when we'd talked about me going bowling. I sure hoped Amy was all caught up by the end of this weekend so she could have a little down time before her "Christmas holidays," which wouldn't be a holiday at all for her, with taking care of her family.

I had a large bowl of cereal and headed upstairs to grab some clothes. Then I showered and get ready to go get my nails done. I brushed my hair and tied it up; I didn't wash it since it would get washed later. Then I went straight out the door—I had less than twenty minutes to get to my nail appointment.

I was cutting it close on time, but I lucked out with the bus; it was just getting to the bus stop as I got here. It made a few stops along the way, and by the time I got to my appointment, I was five minutes late. I was usually early for everything, never late, but there was always a first for everything, and this would be a first for me.

The lady was very nice, and the place was empty. She brought me back to her pedicure chair with a compartment in the front where they put nice warm water to moisten the skin on your feet. I was also having a spa manicure too, so she wrapped my hands in baggies with warm wax to help moisten and soften my very rough hands. It's very relaxing. I had a tea, and I picked a sparkly dark purple for my nail color, as I was going to wear a new T-shirt with a black, purple, and blue design on it.

It seemed to go quickly. I decided to head over to the hair salon, which was in a small plaza near my house where Gabriel and I had gone out for supper a few times now. The steakhouse was next door to the salon. I got there just before three, and the lady, Janice, took me right back to the washing station and sat me down. She washed my hair and told me I could use a deep conditioner if I wanted it and had time. They put the conditioner on my hair, wrapped it up with a plastic bag and then stuck me under the big blow dryer for ten minutes or so. Janice rinsed my hair after and brought me to a cutting station.

I thought she was my hair stylist, but apparently, she wasn't. "Hello, miss, what can I do for you today?" asked the stylist, whose name was Cherry.

"Can you cut my bangs and trim the rest, please, and put in some highlights?" I replied. We discussed what I wanted and decided on a tapered cut with thin highlights using very light blonde, a medium strawberry blonde, and a light brown and a darker blonde.

"Would you mind layers in your hair? Long layers, of course. You won't lose your length, and it will add volume to your hair," Cherry added.

"Normally I don't like my hair being changed, but something says do it today. So, yes, long layers it is." I smiled.

When she was done, she said, "Would you like me to style it for you? Can you see the highlights, okay? Do you like them?"

"The highlights are great, awesome color choices. No styling, but can you blow dry it and perhaps put it into a French braid? I have to go bowling later and I don't want my hair in the way. I know, it defeats the purpose of coming to get my hair done, right?" I asked.

"Whatever you want. I can definitely braid your hair. Probably better to have it out of the way," she replied. She finished my hair, and it looked great with all the highlights. The light blonde was almost perfectly centered in each cross of the braid.

By the time I left the hair salon, it was four thirty. This gave me enough time to stop at my place and quickly change and head over to Charlize's house. I was supposed to be there at five thirty at the latest to head over to the bowling alley for six.

I got home, changed, and brushed my teeth, and got to Charlize's house at 5:35 p.m., almost on time. I apologized for being late, but Charlize was still finishing getting herself ready when I got there, so I really wasn't late. We left her place at 5:50 and got to the bowling alley just before six. It was not too far away, and no one was there yet, so we went and got our lanes and ordered pizza.

This was going to be the first time that Jim, Tom, and Jenn would meet the mystery guy I had often talked their ears off about. Of course, Kelsie had met Gabriel several times at the Reese's' parties, and she was the only reason the others even believed Gabriel existed and wasn't one of my crazy dreams. Gabriel's friends had seen me around school, usually with Charlize, but on occasion talking to Gabriel. I was not sure how he referred to me, if at all, when talking to them. The entire way back to the dorm, not that it's far from the plaza, I thought about how I create a lot of my worries for nothing. I tended to overthink each situation. I needed to stop and take things as they came.

"Hey! Where are your brother and Gabriel?" I asked, a little concerned.

"Caleb said something about having to go pick Gabriel up, that he needed to help out his father before he came out," Charlize answered.

"Okay, then! Everything is alright, though?" I asked.

"Let's just get everyone settled in, registered, and shoed. I'm sure both Caleb and Gabriel will be here soon enough. You need to calm down, take a deep breath in, and release." Charlize seemed a little annoyed with my questioning.

I looked over at the entrance doors and Jim, Tom, Jenn, and Kelsie were walking in. I waved them down. We were at the counter organizing things. "Did you all come here together?" I asked.

"I drove in with Jim and Tom," Jenn said. "I met them at their dorm. I figured I could drive the guys back if they wanted to have a few drinks. I had a few too many last night; there was little party next door to me yesterday and I dropped in for a bit … a long bit.

"And I drove myself in, coming from the other direction and all, but we got here at the same time, met up in the parking lot," Kelsie added.

"You all look good this evening, fresh or pretty fresh haircuts I see, boys! Special occasion? Couldn't be just for bowling," I remarked with a snicker.

"Well, of course we did it for bowling," Jim said sarcastically. "No, we had a hot double date last weekend. We needed haircuts no matter what anyway, date or no date; we were starting to look like bums."

"Well, talk for yourself," Tom said. "I quite liked the shaggy hair. It was easy to do. Wash, towel dry, shake, and go. Maybe run a brush through it."

"Really, Tom, you with your hair not neatly done? And what date? No one is keeping me in the loop! Why?" I questioned.

"I sent you a text a couple weeks back but didn't hear back from you," Tom said. "I told you I was interested in this girl in one of my classes; we had lunch a few times at the cafeteria, and we decided to try a date. We invited our best friends and made it a double date; we just went to the movies and a quick snack and drink after."

"So, Jim, how was the friend?" I asked.

"Excellent, we have gone out a few times. I think we may proceed with a relationship. We have many things in common. Her name is Nancy, and she is quite cute. You would like her, Evangeline; she reminds me of you in a lot of ways." Jim smiled.

"I will have to meet this 'Nancy' girl. And how do you know I would get along with her?"

"You'll see," Jim said.

"What about you, Tom? Like this girl you have gone out with a few times?" I asked with an inquisitive eyebrow up.

"Well, Janice and I have been out many times; we even stay at each other's places at times. So, I think it's safe to say we are together, or an 'item,' as you like to put it!" Tom had a grin from ear to ear.

"Cool, and when do I get the pleasure of meeting this, Janice?" I asked.

"Actually, we invited them here, if that's okay, but they had a prior family thing at Nancy's parents' place not far from here. They said they may drop by later!" Tom smiled.

"Sure, the more the merrier. Charlize and I booked the party area for pizza and beers later." I smiled back.

"Where's Gabriel?" Kelsie asked.

"Not sure, family emergency or something! Should be here soon, I hope." I probably looked worried when I said that.

The entire time we were all catching up I kept staring at the door, waiting for Gabriel and Caleb to walk in, but they still weren't here. It was about 6:10 when Gabriel's goth gang started to make their way in. I was not surprised, as they were quite laid back. Gabriel and Caleb were both still missing at 6:15, but I was not worried till 6:30. Then I started to ask crazy questions.

"Charlize, do you think we should call them? It's not like Gabriel to be late. Well, he has never been late when we went out, anyways!" Panic started to come out in my voice.

"Don't worry; if they are not here by seven, then we will track them down. I know Caleb said Gabriel had something pressing to do before he could leave. Maybe that something is taking longer than expected." Charlize was trying to stay calm with me, but she was clearly annoyed at my unneeded panic.

Just then Caleb walked in, and I waited for Gabriel to come strolling in after him, but no one came. Caleb walked straight towards me and handed me a note and Charlize looked at me.

"Sorry, and I sure wish you had been right instead of me this time," Charlize said sincerely.

Everyone was staring at me, and I did not know what to say or do. *Should I just leave and read the letter myself or read it now, so everyone knew what was going on?* I turned around and asked Caleb, "What is this? Is Gabriel not coming? Should I read it here?" I was definitely in a state of panic now.

"I suggest that you read it somewhere else. Whatever you choose to do. Please, Charlize, go with her … Angel will need you! Gabriel is not coming, Evangeline, and again, I am truly sorry." Caleb looked sincere.

I stood there in awe, and Charlize took one arm and Kelsie took the other and they dragged me out of the bowling alley. I was crying so hard I started to have panic attacks. Kelsie told me to take deep breaths and calm down, and that I really did not know what the note said anyway.

"Read it, Kelsie or Charlize or someone!" I sat down and put my hands on either side of my face and kept crying.

Charlize took it out of my hand and gave it to Kelsie while she ran into the bowling alley to get me a drink of water. Kelsie read it to herself while Tom, Jim, and Jenn tended to me.

"What does it say? Don't hide anything from me; tell me exactly what it says! It's not good, is it?" I was a mess.

"Listen." Kelsie said calmly to me. "Gabriel said that there was a family issue and he needed to go help his family. He says he does not know when he will be back, but he will be in touch in a few days, when he knows how bad the situation is. He apologizes for ruining this night for you and that it wasn't his intention. He hopes you can forgive him, and he will talk to you soon."

"That's it? There's nothing else in the letter?"

"That's it, Evangeline; it's not so bad, right?" Kelsie replied.

I was quiet for what seemed to be quite a while. Charlize came back with water and offered for everyone to go back to her place. Jim, Tom, and Jenn said they would head home, that I probably needed a little time and space and that they would call tomorrow to see how I was doing tomorrow. They left straight from the bowling alley, and I kind of felt bad; they had come from Calgary, and everything was ruined for the evening. Kelsie came back to Charlize's with me. I walked in and Mr. and Mrs. Reese were there, and they saw that I was sobbing.

"What's wrong?" they asked. "What can we do or how can we help?"

"Mom, Dad," Charlize replied, "I mean this in the nicest way, but not now! Evangeline needs a little time and then she or I will let you in on the situation at hand."

Charlize, Kelsie, and I went downstairs, and I started to freak out even more than before. "I need both of you to re-read the letter before I do. I want to make sure that I or we didn't misinterpret any part of the letter or skip over more information. It seems quite vague, don't you think?" I said, not acting completely rationally.

The girls each took their turn reading the letter, and they both said that it still sounded like Gabriel couldn't make it because he had to go take care of a family emergency and that his father insisted, he go. It didn't say anything bad; it did not state that Gabriel didn't show because he didn't want to be with me or want anyone to know that we were an item. He seemed sincere with his apology and wishes that he could have been there with me.

"Evangeline," Charlize said, comforting me by rubbing my back, "Gabriel really cares for you; I see it when you are in a room together and his attention is totally on you! I see the things you do together, like the walks in the garden and the supper dates you go on. I would have to say that I think he truly loves you. Those feelings aren't mine to express though; I am just telling you what I see."

"Come on, Evangeline, it's going to be okay; let's just take the letter at face value, nothing more or nothing less." Kelsie smiled.

"All right, I guess I can wait to hear from Gabriel and hope that I am thinking the worst of the situation!" I shook my head.

It was only eight o'clock, but I had exhausted myself so much with the no-show and the letter that I was too tired to get up and go home. I don't remember even falling asleep, but I woke up the next morning and no one was around. I had slept on the couch, and my neck was a little sore from having my head on the arm. I got up to check if Charlize was in her room, and no one was to be found, so I made my way upstairs. I could hear noise from the kitchen. I walked in there and Charlize and her parents were making breakfast.

"Good morning, sleepyhead, breakfast is almost ready," Mrs. Reese said.

"I don't know if I can eat anything. I still don't feel good!" I answered.

"Charlize let us in on what happened last night; I hope you're okay with that? There is nothing to worry about. Gabriel really cares about you, and I'm sure he would have rather been with you than with his relatives fixing or dealing with family problems," Mrs. Reese added.

"Men know when one is serious about a girl, and I know that Gabriel is smitten with you," Mr. Reese said with a smile and a wink.

I nodded. "I certainly hope that we're alright, and that the situation isn't what I'm making it out to be." I felt empty.

"Now, you must eat a little!" Mrs. Reese smiled.

I ate a pancake, and even though I wasn't very hungry, it was the most delicious blueberry pancake I had ever tasted. I even had a second pancake and a few pieces of bacon. No one really spoke after that; I think they were waiting to see if I was going to say anything else about the whole ordeal.

"Well, breakfast was excellent. I really didn't feel like eating, but those blueberry pancakes were amazing! I feel better now. I will let things be till I hear from Gabriel and find out if I was reading things into his letter." I tried to smile.

"Good," they all said at the same time.

"By the way, where did Kelsie go?" I asked.

"She crashed here but had somewhere to be early this morning. She left at about eight and said she couldn't stay for breakfast and to tell you that she will call you later in the afternoon." Charlize gave me a quick shoulder rub to signify I should relax a little and smiled.

I helped clean up the kitchen, thanked them for breakfast, and headed home. Charlize asked me if I was going to be okay, and I told her I would wait for word from Gabriel before I made more of this than I already had. I lied, as I wanted to sit and drown in my sorrows. Charlize drove me home. I don't think I could have walked; I didn't even remember turning onto my street. She told me to get some rest and call her later. I got in the door, and Amy came running towards me. She was excited till she seen how puffy my eyes were and then her voice turned to concern.

"Evangeline, what's wrong, your evening did not go well?" Amy asked.

"Let's go upstairs," I said.

I didn't want anyone else to know what a terrible evening I'd had, and the kitchen was full of people, which was rare, so now they all knew something was not right. We went upstairs and I started to cry, and the crying didn't stop. Amy couldn't get a word in; she just rubbed my back and asked me to tell her what happened.

"Gabriel was late and then didn't show, and then Caleb, Charlize's brother, arrived without Gabriel and handed me a letter. I got Kelsie to read it and it said that Gabriel had a family emergency and couldn't make it. I made Charlize and Kelsie re-read the letter and make sure we were all clear on its contents, and they told me there was nothing negative to worry about in the letter and to wait for more news from Gabriel." I was picking and scratching at my face.

"Well, are you going to be, okay? If there is nothing that states that there is a problem, then just take the letter for what it is: an apology for not being able to make it because of a family emergency. Wait, like everyone else has suggested, for more news from Gabriel. Are you really upset from the letter or because you could not have the evening as planned? I know this was an evening you had been waiting for a long time," Amy said.

"I guess I'm more upset that everyone couldn't see how Gabriel and I are together and that I'm not making him up as being mine. My guy friends seem to think that he can't be all that and a cup of tea too! I just wanted to prove them wrong and have all his friends know he is truly taken," I stated.

"I knew it was not the letter, and he did apologize for not being able to be there, but when family calls, family calls. That only makes him an even better person for leaving the most important night for you and probably for him on the line," Amy added.

"I guess I'm blowing this out of proportion for nothing, and I should think of the situation he is in instead of just thinking of how my night was ruined. I guess I must seem very selfish to you now. I hope you don't think any less of me after this ordeal?" I looked up at Amy.

"No, Evangeline, I know how long you wanted Gabriel and you to get together, and it is very understandable that you want the world to know he is yours and you are his. You love Gabriel, and I think the feeling is mutual; just give him time to sort out his family issues and then you can find out if you are reading more into this." Amy was being very supportive.

"Thanks, Amy. I'm going to have a nap. I'm still very tired." I smiled.

Amy left and I put my pajamas on and curled up in a little ball. I was selfish; I wanted everyone to see Gabriel and me together, to know that Gabriel was mine and that I was his. I gave my head a shake. I sounded like all the girls I made fun of as "high maintenance," the girls on sappy romance movies and crazy sitcoms. I couldn't believe it; I had to get a grip on reality. This wasn't me, and I swore I wouldn't ever be this way, yet I was. How sad was I now?

I just stayed in my room the entire day, and Amy dropped off some soup and crackers to make sure I ate something. She just smiled and let me know that if I needed anything I should just let her know. I ended up going to sleep early, still wishing the evening would have worked out as planned.

I woke up in the late afternoon and went downstairs to get a drink of water. No one was around. I felt very weak, too weak to even take a shower. I went back to my room, and Amy opened her door.

"Are you feeling any better?" she asked.

"No, I'm very weak and tired; I think I'm going to go back to bed," I replied.

"Did you eat anything since I brought you the soup?" Amy asked.

"No, I just woke up, and I have no energy to do anything." I couldn't even bring myself to smile.

"Well, I will come and check in on you after I make supper. I want you to eat something, okay?" Amy seemed very insistent.

"You don't have to cater to me. I'm not hungry, and I just want to sleep," I answered.

"You can sleep all you want after you eat something." Amy sounded like my mother.

"Okay! Thanks for being there for me; you're a great roommate and friend." I think I pulled off a smirk that time.

Amy headed downstairs. I was happy Amy was so nice, and she was probably right; a little food was probably going to make me feel better and sleep better. I watched some TV, and then I heard a knock at the door.

"Come in," I replied.

"I'm back. Are you asleep yet?" Amy peered into my room.

"No, but I do feel it coming on quick," I answered, all snuggled up in my blankets.

"Well, I had leftover chicken from last night's supper, so I made you a chicken salad sandwich, and I brought you some apple pie with vanilla ice-cream. Dessert always helps when one is feeling down, don't you think?" Amy had a very convincing smile on her face.

"A little dessert never hurt; thanks again for being there for me. I needed this. I will repay you later," I said with a smile.

"Whatever, you do not owe me anything. I am just happy to help! Now eat up and rest," Amy ordered.

"Yes, ma'am!" I said. "Thanks again."

Amy left, and I ate and went right to sleep. I woke up the next morning, got myself out of bed, and decided to go have a shower. The shower was a bad idea, as I had a chance to think too much, and I was as down as ever. I wanted to hear from Gabriel, to find out if there was anything to worry about, to see if it was really about his family. I wasn't going to be any better until I found out.

I spent all day in bed, and I called Charlize to see if Caleb had heard from Gabriel, but as far as she knew there was no word yet. She told me not to worry, and she would ask Caleb to try and get a hold of him. I didn't hear back from Charlize, so I assumed Caleb hadn't talked to Gabriel yet, and he hadn't called me either. I did take the time to leave my room a few times to eat a little something. Amy had left me another chicken sandwich in the fridge with my name on it, telling me to it eat. So, I couldn't let it go to waste. I was pretty picky about sandwiches, but hers were very good. I took another shower and it happened again; I started to think too much. I was down again. I went to my room and called Charlize, and she told me Caleb couldn't get a hold of him, and that the minute he did, he would let her know to call me.

My phone rang, and I really didn't want to pick it up, but it might be Gabriel. I reached over to see who it was, and it was the school calling. Oh no, it was Monday and I had already missed two classes that morning. I didn't feel like getting dressed and going to school.

I answered the phone and let them know I was all right but had personal issues and would be back tomorrow and that I was sorry. It was short and sweet, as I didn't feel like having a conversation with anyone unless it was about Gabriel and when and if he was back.

I went to sleep without knowing what was going on, and I woke up on Tuesday morning to the sun shining brightly in my room. I must have slept through everything and forgotten to close the blinds the night before. I had woken up for a few minutes sometime last night to get a glass of water and was staring at the sky, waiting to see a falling star to wish Gabriel back into my arms or me in his arms I should say. I feel scared not knowing what was really going on, and there was a part of me that felt something just was not right.

I looked at my phone, and I was late for my first-period class again. I threw on some jeans, a T-shirt, and a hoody, and quickly washed my face and brushed my teeth. I ran across to the school. I looked like crap, so they would believe I was under the weather. I made my way to my second and third period classes, and I spoke to both professors. They said they hoped to see me tomorrow and to get some rest. I stopped by my English class as it was getting out, and I kept my head down. When everyone had emptied the classroom, I went in.

"Hello, Mrs. Mathews, sorry I missed yesterday and today's classes. I'm not feeling well. I will try to be here tomorrow morning. I hope I feel better … if not, I will be here Thursday, no matter how I feel," I was a little worried about her response; she could be tough at times, depending on her mood.

"Well, Evangeline, you need to get yourself better. Here are the reading assignments for this week. Have them done for Monday for sure, even if it's just to hand them in and go. Please be here for your last exam before Christmas break and make sure your final assignment is done and handed in. One more week to have that done, and it's worth thirty percent of your term mark, remember?" Mrs. Mathews gave me that concerned frown face. "I am sure your other classes work the same. Go talk to your other teachers; if you hand in your assignments next Monday, I am sure it will be okay. Get yourself better; get some rest."

"My assignment is almost finished; I just must put it together and re-write it. I will make sure I'm caught up with my reading for Friday's test, and I will try to be here tomorrow," I answered, not feeling any better about missing classes.

I stopped in to see my other teachers briefly, and they gave me my week's assignments or agenda and reminded me to hand assignments in on Monday or Tuesday and make sure my final projects were handed in before Christmas break. They all told me to get some rest and get better.

I kept my head down and headed back home. No one saw me because they were all in their second classes now. I got home and the house was empty and quiet. I just couldn't find it in me to leave my room. I was waiting for the phone to ring, and it just wouldn't ring. I waited till after supper to call Charlize.

"Hi, I guess your brother hasn't heard anything since my phone didn't ring yet," I said.

"No, sorry, I know that this must be killing you, but I'm sure that everything will be okay! Perhaps there is no phone or reception where Gabriel is. I know that he has relatives that live in the middle of nowhere and some that live overseas. I will see if any of the teachers know where Mr. Vladimir went. Please try to get some rest for school tomorrow; final projects are due this week and next. You must hand them in." Charlize sounded very concerned. Her tone also meant to pull it together and quickly.

"I know. I will try to get it together for class tomorrow. All my projects are almost ready to hand in; I may need the weekend, but I will have them ready to hand deliver to the teachers on Monday for sure. How are we supposed to work on our final drawing projects if the model isn't around for us to draw? I hope Caleb hears from him soon; the more time goes by, the more worried I'm becoming, if that is at all possible." I was feeling drained again.

"Please just concentrate on the things that need to get done. I'm sure we will get some news as to what is going on. I will see you at school tomorrow. Get some rest, please."

"Yes, but that's all I have been doing is sleeping. Thanks for caring and being there for me. I will see you tomorrow. Bye." I probably sounded a little frustrated, but I was tired of not being able to reason with my feelings.

I got off the phone with Charlize, and there was a knock at my door. "Come in!"

"Hi." Amy opened the door. "How are you today? And did you eat?" Amy inquired with one eyebrow up. "I knocked on your door last night and you didn't answer, so I know you didn't eat supper. Though I see you must have found the sandwich I left you."

"Yes, I did get up to get the essential things done like shower and eat, went to talk to my teachers, but not much more than that." I smirked with a little "*yes, Mom*" undertone. "Thanks for the sandwich. I will be fine not eating one meal."

"Any word from anyone yet?" Amy asked.

"No, Gabriel isn't returning any of Caleb's calls. I'm getting more and more worried by the minute. I feel like something just isn't right." I was starting to feel worse now.

"What do you mean?" Amy seemed worried

"Just a gut feeling that there is more to this than the letter let on," I replied. I was starting to really worry about Gabriel, not just about "Gabriel and me."

"I'm sure things will get resolved soon. There is probably nothing majorly wrong," Amy added.

"I sure hope all of you are right and that my gut isn't, because I don't know how I will take more bad news." I pulled up my blankets, getting myself snuggled in for another nap.

"I came to see if you were hungry. I made some soup. Would you like some?" Amy asked.

"No thanks, I just ate a couple pieces of pizzas, and I am just getting ready to settle into bed for the night," I said as I was snuggling myself in.

"Okay, if you need anything, just knock on the wall and I will come and see you. Try to get a good night's rest, and I will make sure to see you in the morning. I have an early class as well." Amy smiled.

"Amy, thanks again for being a great friend. I hope that wherever you may go, we will still stay friends. Goodnight!" I said with the utmost sincerity.

"I would like that, Evangeline, goodnight." Amy smiled.

I was so happy to be so lucky to find what I would consider another lifelong friend. I never got out of my pajamas, so I didn't have to get in them. I was going to watch a little TV before going to sleep. I tried, but I kept seeing Gabriel's beautiful face, his smile, and remembering his smell that always seemed to linger. I felt him from time to time, and something just did not seem right. I had grown close to the feelings Gabriel gave off, and even though I didn't know where and what he was doing, I could swear there was something wrong.

The rest of the week was about the same as Monday and Tuesday. I didn't go to school, and I barely showered. Each day flowed into the other. I took the odd shower and changed my PJs, once I think. I just slept and ate when I had the energy to walk down the stairs, which wasn't much. Thanks to Amy, I was well fed. She brought me food whenever she was around, so I ate at least twice a day, which was plenty, as all I was doing was sleeping anyway.

It was the weekend then, one week since the worst weekend of my life. I had to find the time to finish all my weekly assignments and to make sure my final projects or assignments were ready to hand in the next week. I had been working on last week's homework when I wasn't sleeping. I found time to get most of the stuff done, and there was just a bit more to do.

CHAPTER TWENTY

It was Monday morning, the day after the worst-possible week ever; well, the weekend before was just as bad. Forget about getting a decent night's rest—I'd dreamt that Gabriel wasn't coming back, that he had to take care of the children left behind from some uncle he had. I don't know where that dream came from, but I sure hoped it didn't come true. I just wanted him to come home to me.

If it weren't for the fact that all my assignments needed to be handed in or finished in class that day, I don't think I would have dragged my butt out of bed. I walked down the stairs, and everyone was staring at me … Did they know or hear what had happened? I felt a little awkward, but I just kept walking. When I looked in the mirror, I noticed the bags under my eyes and how puffy and swollen they were, never mind how bloodshot my eyes themselves were. No wonder everyone was staring at me. I would stare at me too. After a very long shower, I got ready and came out. I didn't look so bad now, but I was still not myself. No one was in the kitchen now; they all must have left for classes. I went upstairs to gather my books, projects, and my thoughts.

Amy came to my door. "Hey, are you okay? Sorry about the stares, we are just not used to seeing you so under the weather. I did not say anything to the others. I figured if they asked you, maybe you would share the goings on if you wanted to. You look better now if that helps you out any."

"Yeah, I guess this is as good as it gets, or going to get, till I find out what is going on and when Gabriel is coming back. I just wish I could have Saturday night back and that it had worked out the way I had it planned. Who am I kidding? It never works out for me. Something's got to fail somewhere. My dreams couldn't possibly ever come true! Perhaps I am meant to drown in my sorrows, forever chasing those who can never be mine."

"Stop all this nonsense. Everything will turn out okay. Gabriel will call and will return, and you can have another tell-all evening. Evangeline, you must get a grip on reality; sometimes emergencies take place that could not have been prevented. Your need to rationalize the situation. Go to your classes; they are the most important thing at this time. Please just take a deep breath and go out that door!" Amy was quite insistent.

If it had been anyone else, I probably would have made a stink, but she had been there for me from the very day we moved in together, so I know she had my back. Amy was not one to say something just to say it; her intentions were pure, and I hoped she was right about Gabriel.

I got to school, and I had a few minutes to spare. Instead of waiting for my classes to hand in my assignments, I decided to see if any of my teachers were in their classrooms. I was able to drop off all my assignments, giving the teachers my "I'm sick and need to go back to bed" story. They bought it, and why not? I had never missed classes and always had my assignments in on time. The only project not finished and handed in was my drawing assignment, and that was only because it had to be done in class tomorrow. I would have to go in tomorrow, even if I didn't want to. But what good would it do? The subject of the assignment was missing in action.

As I was leaving the school, I sensed eyes on me. I was right … Caleb and a few friends were in their usual area and had shot me a glance. As I looked in their direction, Caleb gave me a glare that meant *I do not know where Gabriel is,* followed by a shrug. I was sure Caleb was sick of me by now, and my calling and asking Charlize if he had heard from Gabriel yet! So, I took the shrug for what it was worth and kept walking.

I got back home and didn't feel Gabriel around at all. I just felt empty inside. I went in and no one was home, so up the stairs I went and back into my bed. Nothing came out. No emotions: I just had a blank expression even though I was so upset, worried, and empty.

Amy came in after knocking and not getting a response. "Did you go to your classes?"

"I did. All my assignments are handed in except for one due tomorrow, and the teachers accepted them. I told them I was not feeling well and needed to go back to bed."

"Well at least this ordeal will not wreck your marks! Now what, Evangeline? Are you going to lock yourself in your room for the rest of the week?" Amy was not pleased with my actions.

"I will go to class tomorrow and will then go home earlier than planned for Christmas. Now, thanks for your concern, but I want to be alone."

Later, Amy knocked on my door and walked in and placed food on my desk and just left. No words had been exchanged, but her concern for my wellbeing was appreciated, nevertheless. I did eat the sandwich she had made for me; I needed it and she knew I would.

I didn't hear from anyone else that night. I had hoped my phone would ring and that Charlize would have the ins and outs on what was going on with Gabriel. It was a quiet night and there were no good dreams, just a nightmare about Gabriel not wanting anyone to know about the two of us.

I woke up and I felt the same: Numb. No emotions. I went downstairs to get ready. No one was in the kitchen this morning. I didn't look as bad as the previous day. Don't get me wrong, I still didn't look up to par, and I had an emotionless face staring back at me. I got to school and didn't see Caleb, nor did I feel Gabriel's presence. I turned right back around and went back home. I decided that, since I'd told the teachers I might not be in today; they probably wouldn't be surprised not having me in class today, though I knew I'd have to come back in later for the drawing class.

I went back up to my room and lay down for a nap. I think all the girls were up, but they were in their rooms. I set my alarm for eleven thirty a.m. just in case I slept that long. It was only eight thirty, so I should get up on my own by then, you would think.

I fell asleep very fast. I was surprised when my eyes shot open, and I felt rested. I looked at the clock and saw that it was ten thirty. No one had woken me up or knocked on my door to see if I was okay. Surprise! I got up and went downstairs to the washroom, and I did look a bit better than I had earlier this morning. The bags under my eyes were very minimal. I went to the kitchen and made myself some scrambled eggs and toast and then I got ready to go to class.

Amy walked in the door. "Good morning, sleepyhead, you didn't feel well enough for your earlier classes this morning?"

"I went and came back and decided to get more rest. The only real class I needed to go to today is my drawing class to finish my assignment. The model probably won't show up," I said sarcastically.

Amy could sense I wasn't in a talking mood, so she went upstairs. I quickly ate and cleaned up. I wanted to get out of the house before I ran into anyone else. I wasn't very sociable today; I just wanted to get to class and get the day over with.

I was quite early, and everyone was on lunch, so the schoolyard was busy. I didn't see Caleb and saw very few of his little clan. I went to my class and sat down. I didn't care if I had to wait a half hour for class to start. I wanted to be alone. When the class started, the teacher let us know that our model would not be in and that there was a change in the assignment. We were to use what we had and finish by composing an abstract figure with what we had and what we could remember of the model.

It sure was a long class, but I did manage to finish and hand in my assignment. I'd had most of mine done previously, so I just added some crazy shapes. I still had no expression on my face. Some people asked if I was okay and even my teacher showed concern, but I just responded that I must be coming down with something and that I just needed to sleep it off. I let my teacher know I would see her in the new year and told her to have a great Christmas and New Year's.

On my way out of the school, I stopped by my classrooms to see if there were any teachers that weren't busy, but they were all preoccupied. Some students had exams the next couple of days, like Amy, who was taking more sciences and academic courses.

I got back to the dorm and texted my parents that I would be home later in the afternoon and asked Kelsie to meet me at my parents' house when she could. I told her it was urgent. I packed up what I needed and wrote Amy a thank-you note, saying not to worry about me, that I would be fine, and to have a good Christmas and that I would see her in the New Year. I was really a terrible friend. I was wrapped up in all my emotions and problems. Amy had been there for me, and I wasn't there for her. She was having a rough time too with all her stuff, and she could have used the support too, but she was there for me. Amy was a great friend; I would have to get her something special for all her kindness.

I tried to call Charlize, but there was no answer; she was either sick of the whole Gabriel subject or was just still at school. I didn't have any lengthy conversations with her; I was too engulfed with the Gabriel situation to even know that I wasn't being a good friend to anyone! I left Charlize a text saying that I would call her and to keep me informed if any news did come along. I wished her and her family a very Merry Christmas and a Happy New Year, in case I didn't see her and said that I was sorry for my crazed behavior.

I left my dorm and went home to my parents' place. When I pulled up to the driveway, Kelsie was waiting for me on the front steps. She must have estimated the time it would take me to get there from when I texted.

"Hey, got your text, what's up? You sounded like the world was coming to an end! Look around; everything still looks fine!" Kelsie said.

"Well, I still haven't heard from Gabriel; no one has, and I am worried about everything. I haven't really gone to classes, though I did hand in all my assignments and projects. I have been in my room crying or emotionless since that weekend. I just didn't know what to do, so I decided to come home. Do you think I'm blowing this way out of proportion?" I stared at Kelsie.

"Well, you should have heard something by now. I don't know what to say … maybe there is something going on and he can't get to the phone. All I know right now is that you are jumping to conclusions, most likely for nothing." Kelsie gave me a hug.

"Should I just stop waiting around for a call? I have a bad feeling about the entire situation. I just think there's more going on than the note he gave me said." I started to cry again as she was hugging me.

"When was the last time you ate something? Let's eat and do whatever will get your mind off Gabriel for a while." She tried to get a look at my face.

"I guess I should eat, as I just had a cookie or two all day. I don't think anything can possibly take my mind of the situation." I sniffled as I lifted my face from her shoulder.

"Alright, what do you want me to make? Forget that. We are going out for pizza, my treat. Perhaps a mani/pedi. What do you think of that?" She tried to get some sort of reaction from me.

"I need a drink. I also want to talk to my parents first before we go anywhere." I sniffed again.

"Whatever, I am yours for the rest of the day!" Kelsie stated. "I cleared my schedule for you, baby!"

We went into the house, and no one was home. I quickly texted both of my parents telling them I was home earlier than they expected and asked when they would be home. My mother responded first, saying she would be home for supper around four unless I needed her there before. She told me that my father had to fly out of town this morning and would be back hopefully Friday morning, if everything went well. I told her not to hurry, that I was going out with Kelsie anyway and that I would see her later.

"My mother will be home around four and my father flew out of town this morning to deal with an emergency. So, let's go do something," I answered.

"Pizza and a beer it is! Let's just head on over to Boston Pizza. Are you good with that?" Kelsie was rubbing my back, trying to soothe me.

"Oh yeah! I need a Schooner for sure, maybe even two." I smiled.

"Drinking will not solve anything, but it will relax you. Just don't get in the habit of dealing with this by drinking, alright!" Kelsie said, concerned.

"Yeah, I won't overdo it, MOM! Usually, it's me telling everyone the rights and wrongs!" I replied.

"You're usually the one who has their life figured out, and that just isn't the situation right now, is it?"

"You're right, thanks for looking out for me, Kelsie! So, let's drop the subject, shall we!" I tried to smile when saying it.

Kelsie and I had pizza, and I had my first Schooner drank in no time at all. There was no bad talk for the rest of the night. I drank my second Schooner and that was it, I was done. I woke up on the couch at my mom's and Kelsie was on the other couch. I got up and fell, and I got back up and noticed a large glass of water on the coffee table and drank it. I tried to walk to the bathroom, which was around the corner, but I fell again, so I decided to crawl to the bathroom. I got to the bathroom and pulled myself up using the counter. After washing my hands, there was a faint knock on the door.

"Are you okay, Angel?" Kelsie asked.

"Yes," I said as I opened the door. "I just had a hard time getting here, that's all." I giggled a little … I was probably still drunk.

"I heard you fall a few times and was worried that you hurt yourself!" Kelsie was holding herself back from laughing.

"I'm good; sorry for the noise. I'm just going to go back to the couch now. What happened last night?" I asked.

"You know, just don't worry about it, and we will talk about it in the morning, okay? Do you need anything while I'm here, perhaps another glass of water?" Kelsie asked.

"Well, if you don't mind. A glass of water would probably help the state that I'll be in come morning," I said.

Kelsie got me a glass of water, and I fell asleep just like that. When I woke up again the sun was shining brightly in the window, and I could smell bacon and eggs cooking in the kitchen. I wasn't sure if I really wanted to get up just yet; my body was not feeling so hot. I waited for what seemed to be a good ten minutes but was probably just a few. I had a splitting headache and needed something to get rid of it. I headed to the kitchen where the great smell was coming from, and my mother was hard at work while Kelsie read the paper and drank her coffee.

"Good morning!" Kelsie said. "Do you need something for your head?" She smirked.

"Yes! Hah ha ha! How did you know?" I managed to get a smirk out.

"Would you like a cup of coffee with your pills?" Kelsie just couldn't seem to wipe that ear-to-ear grin from her face.

My mom didn't say anything. I could see that she was worried, probably because I'd drank too much and that wasn't normal for me now.

"Yes, and a large glass of water, thanks. So how bad was I last night?" I asked.

"Well, you were very drunk, but you behaved yourself considering the amount of beer you consumed," Kelsie said, still grinning.

"I guess that's one good thing. I only had two schooners, right?"

"Well, actually, you almost finished three. You guzzled the first one and drank the second quite fast too, so by the time it all hit you, the third was half done and so were you! Are you ready to eat? Do you want more water?" Kelsie was being a good hostess.

"Yes please. Thanks, Kelsie, but I can get things for myself. What are your plans for today?" I asked.

"It's all good; you're a little rough this morning. As for today, well, it's Wednesday, a school day for me. I have a project to finish this afternoon, so I must go. Are you going to be, okay?"

"Yeah, I should probably go and get unpacked and maybe sleep some more." I felt hungover and probably looked it too.

I finished eating and thanked my mom for breakfast. She didn't mention anything, just told me to get some rest and that we would talk later. I think Kelsie must have told her a bit of what was going on. I hadn't talked to my parents since Saturday morning, when I'd been very excited about the bowling evening. My mom didn't know that the evening didn't go well, as I hadn't talked to her, and I wasn't in the right state of mind to do so now.

Weird how being in college makes you feel like you really don't belong anywhere. You're no longer a resident where you grew up, nor are you really a true resident at the school you are attending; you just float from one place to the next. I took some pills for my splitting headache and went to have a bath. I didn't make it to my bed; I passed out in the bathtub and woke up to a knock on the door.

"Hey! It's Mom. How long have you been in there? Do you have any skin left?" she asked.

I didn't answer at first, as I was kind of in a daze. She knocked again, this time more aggressively.

"Yes, Mom, I must have fallen asleep. What time is it?"

"It's about one o'clock in the afternoon! I decided to come have lunch here and check on you. I was worried; it's very unusual that you would be in this kind of state. You were still in a very rough state when I left for work this morning. I will make you a grilled cheese sandwich." I could hear the worry in her voice.

"I'm okay. It's been a terrible week. I barely went to classes but did manage to hand in all my assignments before I left. I'm getting out of the bath now and will be down after I get dressed," I answered quietly, so as to not annoy my aching head any more than necessary.

I, Evangeline, didn't attend my classes this week; I had never missed a school day since the day I'd started kindergarten. School had always been the most important aspect of my life. All my friends were there, and my life was there. How could I let myself down? Especially when I had no idea what was wrong, or if anything even was. I was probably making a mountain out of a hill. I had no real proof that there was anything wrong between Gabriel and I, or any reason to think something had happened to him. No one had heard from him, and they say that no news is good news, right?

"Evangeline, please finish getting ready and meet me downstairs. We can figure things out." My mother sounded very worried.

"Yes, Mom, I will be right out!" I answered as loud as I could. I needed to take more pills for the crazy headache I had.

I tried to get up slowly, but I was still a little dizzy. I guess I had been in the bath too long. I sat back down in the tub and let the bath water run out so my body temperature would cool down. I stood up a second time, and I was okay this time. I got dressed as quick as I could in the state I was in, brushed my hair, and left it wet. I went downstairs to talk to my mother; she was waiting for me patiently in the living room.

"Are you okay? You look a little flushed," she asked.

"I was a little lightheaded; that's why it took me so long to get down here. I think my blood sugar being low and the heat of the bath was a little too much. Let alone my mental state. I'm surprised I'm functioning at all." I had a sulky tone in my voice.

"Alright, let me have it. What has been going on with you? Missing school? That is not you!"

"Mom, I know, I know. I have been running everything through my head. I just have been having personal issues … well, that is the problem, I really don't know if I have personal problems or not." I heard myself as I answered my mom, and it didn't resonate well.

"Hold on, hold on. Evangeline, you are not making sense. Start from the top."

I told her about the bowling night and the letter, and then said, "Well, I still haven't heard from him, and I'm worried that something may be wrong! I really don't know what is really going on, but I'm going crazy. I'm head over heels for this guy, and it's messed up my school and my mind in general." I was crying at this point.

"Evangeline, I understand that you care for this guy, but you do not know, good or bad, what is going on. You just said it yourself. You need to calm down and get things back into perspective. Wait to hear back from Gabriel, and then you can figure it out from there. A guy is a guy, and if it doesn't work, there will be another. The right one will come, but this may or may not be the one. Don't let this event affect the rest of your life! Take this Christmas break to get yourself together, please." My mom's face told it all. I knew she was asking herself who this guy must be to have shaken me down this way. I was usually the one with the "who cares" attitude, and now I was on the other side, the one sobbing about a guy with no reasoning behind it.

"I know, and I will. I know myself that this behavior is very unbecoming of me, but for some reason, it's got the best of me. I hope you aren't too disappointed in me!" I looked to my mom for reassurance.

"Your father and I will always love you and be there for you. You'll come out of this just fine; you're a strong and wise young lady." She rubbed my back with concern.

I thanked my mother and gave her a great big hug and a kiss on the cheek. I knew I needed to get it together. I had two weeks to figure things out before getting back to school. There were a few times when I thought I had smelled Gabriel and sensed him around, but that was crazy, as he was clearly not around my family without me seeing him. If I took too much time to myself, alone, I did daydream about him a little too. How could I not?

Christmas came and went, and all the family events took my mind off the situation. I did briefly think of him throughout the days, but there was always something going on to take my mind off it. I spent a lot of time cooking and eating!

CHAPTER TWENTY-ONE

Well, New Year's Eve was tomorrow, and I really hadn't talked to anyone. I talked to Kelsie a couple of times, but we'd had no time to hang out, with all the family stuff going on. I did call Jenn, Tom, and Jim on Boxing Day to see how Christmas and the holidays were going. Everyone was still planning to go to the Reese's', because no one could possibly plan a better party, let alone on New Year's Eve! My parents were giving a New Year's Day supper and invited the Reese family to attend. There were usually fifty people at this supper, but it was a buffet style, so it wasn't that big a deal. My parents had it catered, plates and all, so there was no cleaning up after. I was very curious to see what the Reese's had planned for their big night.

I decided to call Charlize. I was wondering if Caleb had heard from Gabriel. "Hey! Charlize. How was your Christmas? Was Santa good to you?" I asked in a cheerful voice.

The Reese's had gone up to the mountains for Christmas, as a couple of their family members lived in Banff. It was a family tradition for the entire family to go there for Christmas. They apparently did some ice fishing and horseback riding, and they even took a sleigh ride pulled by the horses while nibbling on baked goods and drinking spiked coffee and/or hot chocolate. Maybe one Christmas I might be able to spend it in Banff with Charlize. I was sure it would be a great time.

"Hello, Evangeline. How was your Christmas? Mine is always fun. I got a new computer and iPhone. We also played a fun game," Charlize answered, quite cheerful also.

"Cool, what kind of game?" I asked.

"Well, it's a gift-exchange thing. Each person had to bring an extra gift to put into a pile. It had to be under ten dollars and should be a gag gift. Each person gets a turn, picks a present from the pile or can take one away from some else. No one could open their gift till everyone had a turn. At the end of the game, you end up with what you end with; some gifts were nice, and some were gag gifts. It was a great game and took up quite a bit of an evening to play. Anyways, it was fun, and maybe next time you can come play too," Charlize said. "You are still coming tomorrow? And are your parents coming? My parents are very anxious to meet yours," Charlize added.

"I don't think they will actually come. They usually have New Year's Eve plans made the year before, like dinner theater, but I forgot to ask, with being wrapped up in this whole Gabriel thing and it being Christmas and all. I will ask, though; maybe they don't have plans. I'm pretty sure I told them about it, but who knows? Sometimes I think I have said something, and it was only me saying it in my mind," I commented.

"Well, either way, we will be at your parents' place New Year's Day. Cocktails are at five and for supper, right? We will all be there with bells on, and our parents can meet there for sure," Charlize said with excitement in her voice.

"You bet they will!" I replied. "Hey, you know I have to ask … Has Caleb heard from Gabriel?"

"I knew it was coming, and it's okay. I totally understand you do not have any answers to go on. I am sorry to say that Caleb still has not heard from Gabriel. I asked him yesterday because I knew you were going to ask," Charlize stated.

"I knew it was a long shot. What are the rest of your plans for today?" I asked.

"Just hanging out, helping my parents with odds and ends. Other than that, not much. What about you?" she asked.

"Well, I need to find something to do because just sitting around makes me dwell on Gabriel, and I need to focus on relaxing and putting things into perspective. I may see if my parents need help too, but they are getting everything catered, so there probably is not much left to do," I answered. I paused. "Let me know if you need me for anything," I said, knowing there were too many hours in a day to try in occupy myself and not think of Gabriel.

"Well, I hope your evening will be relaxing, and I will see you tomorrow for the New Year's Eve party. Not sure how we are all going to feel New Year's Day for supper at your house; things could get crazy tomorrow. Some of my parents' friends, or work associates, I should say, tend to get carried away, and kids will be kids right!" I could sense the ear-to-ear grin on her face as she spoke.

"Okay! If you do need my help tomorrow, don't hesitate to ask. I can come over earlier, if need be," I said.

"I will call if we need extra help. Bye," Charlize said.

"Okay, bye." I hung up the phone. I really had to stop with the Gabriel thing with Charlize. I didn't want to annoy her too bad, if I hadn't already, and lose her as my friend.

Charlize was right: It could be a crazy New Year's Eve party. It would be a kegger as per usual with the Reese's, but they were also having a couple of separate stations, one for shots and one for cocktails. I was sure there must be some sort of restriction put on the types of drinks you could get at each station; there were way too many types of shots and cocktails for one party. All free of course, but donations could be given to charity.

I hoped I was not annoying anyone too much about the Gabriel subject, but I wished I would hear something, so I would know what was going on and whether I was just jumping to conclusions. Maybe it had nothing to do with our relationship. I just wanted to know something new; it had been over two weeks since the "family emergency" note.

I still hadn't eaten yet, though it was early afternoon, so I made my way to the kitchen. I didn't hear anyone in the house. My mom did say she had a few last-minute errands to run today, and maybe my dad went with her. I went to the fridge and opened it up, but nothing tempted me. My mom must have been worried, as there was a triple-decker club sandwich in the fridge for me with a note on it saying, "Eat me, Evangeline." She had mentioned a few times in the past few weeks that I needed to eat more and asked if I had lost weight. I wasn't sure. Perhaps I had though, as come to think of it, some of my clothing was looser on me. Not by much though as I hadn't really noticed. It wasn't like they fell off; they just weren't as tight as usual.

My sandwich was fantastic! My mother made the best sandwiches—so good, but not calorie friendly. I love me a good sandwich. I ate and went upstairs to shower. I paused in front of the mirror, naked, and thought, *It does look like I have lost a little weight.* All my body issues were still there, would always be there, but I'm not going to talk about my likes and dislikes about my body. After my shower, I decided to jump on the scale. Taking into consideration the large sandwich I'd just eaten; I could guesstimate that I'd lost between five to ten pounds in the past couple of months. Well, that would probably explain my mom's comment on the note left for me. If things didn't change soon, I would need to get help, but I needed to try and pull myself out of this funk by myself first. I was going through a depression, and I was just admitting it now. I would give myself some time to try and let go or get a handle on this Gabriel thing or to hear back for him, and then I needed to let it go or get serious help.

I got dressed and was blow drying my hair when the phone rang.

"Hey, whatcha doing?" Charlize asked.

"Just blow drying my hair, why?"

"I figured after I talked to you earlier that I should find out what I need to get done and then fit you into my schedule. I need to keep you busy; help get your mind kind off the situation. So, get ready, I will pick you up in a half hour, and I am not taking no for an answer," Charlize insisted and hung up.

I finished blow drying my hair. I had put sweats and a hoodie on, but now changed into jeans and a T-shirt, and went downstairs. There was no sign of my parents. I pulled the curtain back. No car. I wrote them a note, letting them know I was going to be with Charlize and if they needed me for anything to call me or shoot me a text.

Charlize showed up exactly a half hour after she called.

"What are we doing?" I asked.

"I got some more accessories to go grab for the New Year's party, and we can go grab some supper." She smiled. "I also wanted to keep you busy. I figure I haven't done my part keeping your mind off the goings on very well, like a friend should. What do you say about having a movie marathon tonight?" Charlize looked at me inquisitively.

"Sure, but we're going to be up late tomorrow too! I need to go back upstairs to see get some PJs to wear tonight if I am staying at your place."

"Come on, let's finish this year with a bang. We have all next year to sleep if we want. We could go out for supper, but we could go run my mom's errands and then order pizza and start our movie night earlier too, if you want?" Charlize was very persistent. "We can even watch whatever movies you want. What kind do you like? I guess I really don't know you that well, but you like vampires, so those are probably on your list, right?" Charlize smiled.

"Wow! How much coffee did you have this morning?" I asked, eyebrows up. This was totally out of character for Charlize; she was usually the cool, calm, and collected one and I was the one running my mouth a hundred miles per hour. She was right though; we did spend time together, but it was never quality friend time. It was always me worrying about getting to know Gabriel or me worrying about where he was. I was self-absorbed, and it seemed to be always about me and my problems. I was a terrible friend.

"Come on!" Charlize jumped in front of me, swung me around, put her arm around my shoulders, and dragged me towards her car.

"Okay, sounds good," I answered.

We got in her car. "I going to give my mom a call before I commit to this all-night plan and make sure my parents don't need me for anything first."

"Good idea!" Charlize smiled.

I called my mom and asked if they needed help and told her I was going to Charlize's for the night.

"Thanks for checking," she said, "but I think your father and I are all right. We don't have much to get, as the caterers do most of it. We are just grabbing extra plates and cutlery and stopping at the liquor store. We are good with you spending the day and evening with Charlize. It's up to you, honey. We are fine. Thanks for calling and asking though. Have fun and enjoy your night."

I turned and looked at Charlize. "Sorry, I know I haven't been a good friend. I will try to do better in the New Year but starting now too. Pizza and movies sound great, and my parents are good, so let's do this. What errands are we doing?"

"Well, we need to go to the party rental place; there are a few decorations like banners, streamers, and balloons to pick up that my mom picked out online. There are tables and chairs too, but they are getting delivered tomorrow morning. Then we need to go to the bakery and pick up an assortment of buns and I think some muffins and a cake. I think we will go there first; seems like the better choice as there are probably more and larger items there." Charlize was kind of mumbling to herself at this point, I think trying to figure out if everything was going to fit in her car.

I was just along for the ride and to help out where I could. Charlize didn't decide to go to the bakery first; we ended up next door at the butcher shop first. We pick up the order placed under "Reese," and it was a good thing Charlize had stopped here first, as there was platter after platter of assorted meats. There were six large trays of cold cuts, which was so much food, and we were just starting our pickups. Good thing those trays could be stacked well. Then we got back into the car and headed to the grocery store to get three trays of mixed veggies and two trays of mixed fruit. We added this to the piles in the car, and then went back to the bakery and got bags of buns and two trays of assorted cut-up breads.

"My God," I said. "Good thing you have very large parties, because you would have food for a month for just the four of you, and even then, you may still need help."

"I think this is a bit more than the usual. My parents are anticipating a few more people this year, with my father's expansion of his company. One more stop: the party store. I think there are just a few banners and streamer things to pick up … my mom and her online shopping." Charlize looked like she was getting tired.

"Everything okay?" I asked.

"Yeah. Glad we're almost done. Hopefully Caleb is home to help us take this stuff out of the car. I just want to order pizza, watch movies, and veg." Charlize looked at me with a smirk on her face.

We walked in and out of the party store in a matter of minutes, as there wasn't much to pick up there. When we got back into the car, Charlize grabbed her phone and texted Caleb. We got back to her house and her brother came out the door. We had the car emptied quite fast, just a few trips each. We ran the trays downstairs to a cold room they had under the stairs. The storage room looked like a little store of its own after we'd filled it.

Then we went to the living room we used to "study" in when I was trying to get to know Gabriel. Charlize grabbed my hand and pulled me towards a shelving unit with some books and a few old classic movies on it. It seemed strange, but then she went to grab a movie and the shelving unit slid open about three feet.

I think my mouth dropped … it was like being in an old movie where they have hidden rooms. It was so cool. We walked through the shelving unit into a small space, like a corridor, which went about eight feet in either direction and lit up as we entered, and guess what? It was filled with shelves and shelves of movies. I was like being in a video store, and across from us was another door. Charlize opened it, and I couldn't believe my eyes. It was a theater. A very cool theater.

"I always thought your basement was a little bit small in comparison to the size of the upstairs, but sometimes people don't have the basement as large, so I thought this was the case in your house. Your house is quite big anyways, but now I know why the basement seemed lacking in size. This is so cool." I smiled.

"This is my dad's room, and we tend to only use it on special occasions, but my dad uses it all the time. He is a movie freak. He probably has every movie, or close to it. I rarely come in here without him. I am sure he will be okay with you and I and maybe Caleb having a movie marathon tonight though. And who knows? He may even come down here with us."

The door opened and there was a room about twenty feet by twenty feet by twenty-four feet with two rows of recliners. The second row was raised, and the screen must have been twelve feet wide by six feet high. There were wall units at each end, with more movies, and the entire opposing twenty-foot wall behind the recliners was also full of movies. To the right of the recliners was a counter with cupboards below and a bar fridge.

I was in awe of this room; only millionaires would have this in their houses. I knew the Reese's were very well off, but I didn't think they were millionaires. The eight recliners were in two rows, with about two feet between them.

"So, you're a little quiet … great room, right?" Charlize asked.

"Yeah! Just a little … it's amazing, can't believe you have you have such a great theatre room in your house. No one would know. It's totally hidden … a secret room," I said in awe.

"So, you're probably looking forward to movie night more now, right?" Charlize had a huge smile on her face.

"I was looking forward to it before, but this is going to be a fantastic movie night, and I can't wait to see things on such a big screen. I'm probably going to jump out of my chair a few times."

"Oh, yeah you will!" Charlize said. "There are movies I had watched on a regular TV that I watch in here and I jumped or even got scared, whereas before it hadn't fazed me. Just wait! It's an experience to be had."

"So, can I ask you something? You don't have to answer if it's none of my business. I know your family is very well off, but how well off are you?" I asked, not sure if Charlize was going to answer the question or not.

"Well, my dad is a CEO of a quite large oil company, which you know, right?" Charlize looked at me for confirmation.

"Right," I replied.

"Well, you don't know this, and very few do, so what I am going to tell you has to stay between us, right?" Charlize gave me the same look again.

"Right," I replied again, nodding my head.

"My father may be the CEO of the company, but he owns the company too. He and my Uncle John are partners, but the company name is under their stepfather's name. My grandma remarried a very wealthy and amazingly smart businessman who hired my dad and uncle in his business right out of high school. He put them through school, one as a business manager and one as a chartered account. They both took extended courses like their stepfather wanted, not arguing at all, accepting that this was the best thing they could do for their future. So, my father and his brother own the company and have a figure that represents the ownership, and they dictate the goings on silently, you could say. My grandfather passed of health issues and left the company to them, and it runs itself pretty much. They are just there to make sure everything follows the flow put in place. So, to answer your question, my father has no issues with money and probably never will." Charlize looked to me for a comment.

"Cool, I don't know what to say. I won't say anything. You know that right?"

"Yes, I know, that's why I told you. I think I have only ever told one other person in my life, and she is like a sister to me, as are you. Weird how I have only known you for a short while, but it seems like I have known you my entire life." Charlize grabbed me and stole a hug. "So, what kind of movie night do you want it to be? Scary, action-packed, mystical, or full of romance?"

I'm not sure how long I thought for … it seemed like a long time but was probably only a few minutes. I really felt like watching vampire movies for some reason, maybe because of the research I had been doing at school this semester. Besides thinking, fantasizing, and worrying about Gabriel, I had been thinking about how I wanted a happily ever after. I wanted the romance and to be truly loved.

I snapped out of my trance. "Sorry, got lost in my thoughts there for a second. I'm not sure what I want to watch. Too many choices."

"Well, if we watch action or scary, my father and Caleb may come and watch with us. Romance and mystical, my father may come and watch depending on the mood he is in, but I doubt Caleb wants to watch those types of movies."

I was quiet for a few minutes, as there are so many movies we could watch. I loved all kinds of movies. You could probably call me a little obsessive when it comes to watching movies. I even made a habit of watching some entire series every year. There were probably some movies I had seen over fifty or even seventy-five time. Pretty pathetic, come to think of it…

"Hello, earth to Angel," Charlize said, snapping her fingers in front of my face, trying to get my attention. "Everything okay?"

"Yeah! It's too hard for me to choose … just not scary movies today; let's keep those for around Halloween, okay?" I gave her a kooky smile.

"Do you like the movie *Footloose*?" Charlize asked.

"That's one of my favorite childhood movies. I first watched that when I was around ten years old with my best friend. I'm sure we watched it over thirty times till we were in our early teens, and then she moved away. I have watched it at least another twenty times since. So, yeah! Let's do it. Will your father and Caleb watch it with us?" I asked, super excited to watch it on such a big screen.

"No, I doubt Caleb would watch it. My father likes that movie for the music, but he probably will not be home till later, and I think we should watch it right away. I called for pizza, and it should be here momentarily. We can watch *Footloose* and maybe watch a movie everyone wants to watch after. What do you think?"

"Sure, I'm good with anything and everything. I'm the guest here. Just happy to be invited and honestly to be your friend." I smiled.

"You're more than a friend. Even my parents think of you as family, and you are the sister I never had. We may have just recently met, but there is some sort of bond or connection we have that makes all the new, unknown things about each other not matter. I just feel that I will get to discover what I may not know in time and if needed. Anyways, enough babble, I just heard the doorbell, must be the pizza. Let's go get it and watch the movie." Charlize headed out of the theater room.

I followed her upstairs and waited in the kitchen. I remembered where the plates were and grabbed a few and put them on the island. As Charlize brought the pizza in the kitchen, Caleb walked in … surprise, surprise. He must have heard the doorbell or smelled the pizza from the living room.

"We're watching a movie in the theater room; would you like to join us?" Charlize asked him.

"What are you watching? Probably some girly movie, right?" Caleb snickered.

"Not a girly movie, but a movie with a little romance and dancing in it. How about it, bro?" Charlize smiled.

"No thanks, let me know if you watch something better or worth watching," Caleb said with a smart-aleck attitude.

Charlize shook her head. "Whatever." We grabbed our food and a pop from the wine cooler and headed back downstairs. We got into the theater room and Charlize grabbed a remote and pushed a button. The front row of reclining chairs went into the floor about halfway to improve our view of the screen. I wondered if her father had come up with that idea or if it was the designer.

"Great idea, right? The back row of chairs is a little bit more comfortable. Wait till we start watching the movie!" Charlize had the biggest grin on her face. She went over to the second shelf on the back wall and didn't even have to look for the movie; she knew where it was.

"*Footloose* is one of my favorite movies too. I don't think I have watched it quite as much as you have, though."

We sat down in the two middle seats and the lights went down and the screen lit up. It was brilliant. Charlize tilted the screen, so the top came down a little, and told me to recline my seat and see if I liked the screen where it was or if it needed to be tilted a little bit more. So, I reclined my chair, and the screen was perfect. I could see the entire thing. This was another incredible idea.

"Did your dad come up with the seat thing and the tilting of the screen?"

"Yes, everything in the house that is over and above the norm is my father's doing. He has a very creative imagination and especially when it comes to his theater room or his extracurricular activities, and he does have the money."

"Awesome!" I was awed by everything. "The screen is great. Everything is great!"

The movie started, and there was plenty of pizza and the smell of freshly popped popcorn in the old-style popcorn maker in the left side of the room, where the candy and drinks were too! Mr. Reese had thought of everything. I could live down here if there were replenishments of pizza … and clothes and a shower. Oh, and Gabriel too!

I ate three pieces of pizza, and then grabbed a small bag from beside the popcorn maker and filled it up. I sat back down. We were still at the beginning of the movie, the part where Renn was in the school hallway and sees Ariel walking past him with Rusty and says, "Ariel, Renn," reminding her of his name, and Ariel responds, "Very good; you know your name" and turns around and keeps walking. That was the last thing I remember, then I snapped out of my daydream when Chuck, Ariel's so-called boyfriend, smacks her hard by the bleachers after she took a crowbar to his truck.

I had started thinking about Gabriel, who watching movies was supposed to keep my mind off of … it obviously didn't work. When Renn addressed Ariel, I thought of Gabriel and when we first talked, and I remembered him bumping into me and how rude I was not fully addressing his apology and turning away from him. Gabriel said he had no ill will against my reaction to his apology. I just continued going through our entire relationship if that's what it was called.

He'd said he wanted to be with me, but where was he now? Gabriel could have at least called someone and let us know what was going on. Anyways, by the time I snapped out of my daydream, half of the movie was over. Charlize noticed I had not been really paying attention, and she asked me if I was okay and still wanted to watch this movie.

"I just must go to the washroom. I do still want to watch the movie. I got a little sidetracked thinking of Gabriel. I'm going to try and just watch the movie; I must let go of this Gabriel thing. I think that, even if I do see him again, I need to tell him we can't be anything more than friends, because I drive myself insane worrying about us and our relationship. Perhaps even us being friends may have to come to an end. Maybe I can't handle that either. What is my problem? How can I have let a guy get the best of me? I told myself at a young age that I would never let myself be one of those girls that dwell over a guy and look at me now. Pretty pathetic. I seriously need to snap out of it."

I went to the washroom, which was just across from the theater room. I had told Charlize to just keep playing the movie, since I already knew what was going to happen, and that I would be right back. I didn't miss much, and I finished watching it without thinking of you-know-who. After *Footloose*, we went upstairs to see if her dad was home. Caleb was in the kitchen grabbing a snack and Mrs. Reese walked in shortly after.

"Hello, kids, how are we all doing? Were you downstairs or upstairs?" she asked.

"Hi, Mom, just watching TV," Caleb answered.

"Angel and I were watching *Footloose* in the theater room, and we came up to see if dad was home and if anyone else wanted to come watch movies with us. Do you want to, Mom?" Charlize asked.

"What are you going to watch?"

"Well, there's too much to decide from," I said. "Anything you would like to watch?"

"How about *Dracula*? That new movie that just came out recently. Dad brought it home last week, I think it's not even unwrapped yet," Caleb added before his mom could answer.

"Well, I really don't think we should be touching something your father hasn't even watched yet," Mrs. Reese said as Mr. Reese walked into the kitchen. "I didn't hear you come in, my dear."

"I think that's a good idea, if everyone is good with that," he said. "We can watch it all together, and it's not a new movie; it's been out for a while. I just missed this one for some reason and overheard someone talking about it, so I went out and bought it." Mr. Reese looked around the room to get a reaction to the idea.

We all said sure at the same time.

"Just give me a few minutes to get changed. Everyone, grab what you need and meet me downstairs," Mr. Reese said.

We all grabbed snacks and headed down to the theater to watch the movie. It was a good Dracula movie, but nothing like *Twilight*, and I had seen it before. I would be very surprised if there were any vampire movie I hadn't seen.

We took a short break and Caleb came by me and asked, "Did you like that movie? Did it scare you at all? How are you with vampires? The blood and the killing and other stuff?"

I wasn't sure how to respond. Truthfully? Caleb could really think of me as crazy if he knew where I sat on the whole vampire thing. I just said, "I like everything vampire," and I walked away.

"So, what do we watch next?" Caleb asked. "Let's stay with the same theme, how about *Interview with a Vampire* or *Underworld*?

"I'm good with either, any other vampire movie," I replied.

"Well, I am not. If you want to stick with vampires," Charlize quickly replied, "I will watch *Underworld*, but I have no interest in the other one."

Mr. and Mrs. Reese said they were going to their room; apparently Mr. Reese had to go into work early for a few hours.

"So, *Underworld* it is," Caleb said and went to grab it from the shelf.

Caleb seemed like a vampire enthusiast also. We sat down and settled in, and I watched contentedly. It was amazing how watching a movie on a very large screen changed how you saw a movie. With every movie we had watched, no matter how many times I had seen it, it was a new experience today.

I must have fallen asleep while watching the movie, as Charlize woke me up and it was over. "Let's go upstairs to bed."

"Sorry for ruining the movie night." I looked at Charlize as I lay in her bed.

"You didn't ruin anything; this movie night was just getting your mind off things, and it somewhat worked, right? You get some sleep; the next two days are going to be busy ones." Charlize gave me a smirk.

"Goodnight, and thanks for inviting me over. I really like spending time with you and your family." I gave her a hug. I must have fallen asleep again as soon as my head hit her pillow, as I don't remember anything after that.

CHAPTER TWENTY-TWO

I woke up in the morning and almost forgot where I was. I'd had such a good sleep, much better than normal. Well, lately anyways. So much for the all-night movie marathon. Bad, eh? I'd made it through maybe two and a half movies before I passed out. Charlize was still sleeping, so I just lay there for a bit, and of course, thought of Gabriel. I could smell him, and I thought I felt his hand brush my hair off my face as I lay there with my eyes closed. I was clearly losing my mind. I opened my eyes, and I was still lying there beside Charlize.

A few minutes passed and Charlize's eyes opened. I must have woken her up looking at her. You know how sometimes when someone looks at you and your eyes are closed, you just have a feeling that they are looking at you and must open your eyes?

"Sorry if I woke you," I said. "I'm kind of happy, though. I really have to go to the washroom and didn't want to wake you, and now I can."

"How long have you been up?" Charlize asked.

"About an hour, I think," I replied.

I got up and went to the washroom; I had to pee so bad that I'd almost peed the bed. When I got back to the room, Charlize was up and brushing her hair.

"Are you ready to go downstairs or are you still tired?" she asked.

"I'm good to go downstairs." I brushed my hair too, and we headed down. I could smell bacon. I thought I was hungry before and now I knew I was. It was ten, and everyone was gathered in the kitchen when we got in there.

"Would you like some coffee, Angel?" Mrs. Reese asked.

"Coffee would be great, thanks." I grabbed the cup from Mrs. Reese as she handed it to me.

"Cream, milk, sugar, and sweetener are already on the island; help yourself. I am not sure what you take in your coffee." She smiled. "Breakfast will be ready shortly. There's bacon, scrambled eggs, hash browns, pancakes, and toast. Help yourself to whatever you want."

It was like being at a buffet, and it was incredibly good. My tastebuds were very satisfied. We finished eating and Charlize and I cleaned up the kitchen.

"Mrs. Reese, do you need me to help with anything for tonight's occasion?" I asked.

"All right, Angel, please call me Gloria or Mom, because Mrs. Reese is getting old," Mrs. Reese exclaimed.

"Okay, Gloria is probably better, just in case you and my mom happen to be in the same room together sometime in the near future." I smiled.

"So, if I can get all of you to help with the tables and chairs, that would be great. I just saw the truck pull up. Thanks," Mrs. Reese said.

We helped the gentlemen set up the tables and chairs; they even had all the tablecloths and settings. By the time we finished setting everything up, it was about two, and I told Charlize I was going to head home, work out, and have a shower.

"I will be back later. What time you would like me to be here?"

"You can come back anytime you want. You could even have a shower here and we can clean your clothes, or I am sure Charlize has something you could wear," Mrs. Reese quickly answered.

"That's true, Angel. Do you want to do that? Because you can, you know." Charlize smiled.

"I'm good with borrowing some clothes, because I wouldn't have to put you out having to drive me back home. Let's start with me calling my mom to see if she needs me for anything today, and then we can talk about the rest," I said, feeling bad thinking Charlize might need to drive me back home, even though she had chosen to come get me.

I called my mom and left her a voice message. She sent me a text back stating that she was busy and couldn't talk, but that all was good. She said I could just stay at Charlize's if I wanted and that my parents would make an appearance at the party at the Reese's' in the early evening. I texted back, asking if she could bring my car for me this evening, so I didn't have to bother Charlize to drive me home tomorrow. She could be hungover tomorrow, and I wouldn't want to put her out by her having to drive me home. My mom said she would bring my car. I had an extra key on the key hook in the kitchen just in case something happened; you just never knew. I'd locked my keys in my car once, and there was no extra key, so I'd had to call a tow truck to help me out. To be honest, I would rather have gone home today, but I would let Charlize decide what she would rather do.

"Well, it's totally up to you! I'm good whatever," I answered.

"Okay, then let's go to my room and pick you out something to wear. I will wash your jeans, and there's a pair of shorts for you to wear." We got to her room, and she threw a black pair of running shorts at me and a white T-shirt that said "Girl's Rule" on it in hot pink.

"Okay, get changed, give me your jeans, and I will wash them right now along with my jeans." She went to her closet and pulled out a turquoise sweater and a magenta sweater. "Which one would you rather wear? Both colors look great on you," she said, and she passed me a nice white lace camisole to wear under it. The sweaters were both a little too low cut to wear without a camisole.

"Thanks, I like both. I will see once my jeans are done." I smiled. "What are we going to do the next couple hours while we wait for our clothes to be ready?" I asked.

"How about we go for a dip in the hot tub?" Charlize offered.

"Okay. Where is your hot tub? I thought I saw your entire back yard the couple times I'd been back there before, even the beautiful garden," I said. "I didn't see the hot tub … and where is the pool?

"First, here's a swimsuit for you; the pool is around the side. It's emptied now though. I'll show you another time." She handed it to me. "Get changed and meet me downstairs in the kitchen; I will grab us some drinks."

I got changed and went downstairs, and Charlize was in the kitchen grabbing us some ice teas. We met as she came out of the kitchen, and we headed to the deck. Mrs. Reese was already sitting at the table. We sat and talked with her for a bit.

"Hello, Mrs. Reese, or I mean Gloria. How long have you been outside?" I asked.

"I have been outside most of the morning working on the garden, cleaning up, helping Reggie, the gardener. I just got myself cleaned and changed about an hour ago once it warmed up. The temperature is good outside now. "You girls slept in pretty late this morning; did you go to bed late?"

"Angel was tired; she fell asleep during the second movie. So, when it was done, I woke her, and we went to bed. We chit-chatted in bed this morning." Charlize seemed to feel like she had to address the sleeping-in question.

I wasn't sure why Charlize threw that into the conversation, and I didn't respond. There was something going on under the surface that I was unaware of. I just let it go and smiled. "So do you need any help with anything?"

"No, you guys helped quite a bit already. We'll see a little later when everyone gets here. I may need your help bringing the food and snacks out. I will let you know if everything is good around suppertime. Thanks for asking, though, Evangeline."

"I'm just curious, when do people start arriving?" I asked.

"Well, they are supposed to come in the early evening, after they have supper. They start with drinks, and we bring out the food and snacks around eight or nine, depending on how everyone is doing. If people are starting to get too carried away with the alcohol, we will bring the food out earlier. We will have activities for those that want to play, like beanbag toss and horseshoes in the lower garden area, since there's no snow. Reggie was able to rake what there was out of the way. Card games will be set up in the house and on the deck. The empty swimming pool and hot tub will be gated off, as alcohol and water don't mix well. I need to have things as safe as possible; I don't want anything bad happening to anyone and be responsible if an accident happens." Mrs. Reese seemed serious.

I dropped the conversation, looked at Charlize, and she signaled me to follow her. I grabbed my iced tea and followed her to another deck level hidden around the side of the house. The gardens were spectacular. I'd thought I had seen the entire yard till I went through a gate that was hidden in an eight-foot hedge. There was an entire other yard on the other side of the house. The pool was a lap pool, not kidding;

only two lanes wide, but probably about twenty feet long. I couldn't believe it; I was in awe. The Reese's had the best of the best and were not flaunting any of it. They never mentioned anything, and you had to be family or a close family friend to even know that they had some of these things.

When I was growing up, my rich friends made sure they told everyone what they had and were getting; they were always flaunting the money their families had. My parents had a good house and a sufficient pool, but nothing fancy. We never went without, but we never overdid anything. I think my parents could have afforded more, as they both made good money, but I never asked for much. I had all I needed. I think the way I was raised kept me well grounded. I was surprised Charlize and Caleb were both grounded, and they never flaunted the money they had, though I had only known them for a short time. Come to think of it, Gabriel had a lot too and had never mentioned it.

"In the summer, you can come swim laps if you want," Charlize stated.

"Yeah, perhaps I will take you up on that when the weather warms up." I smiled.

We didn't do much talking, and Mrs. Reese came out and asked if we were hungry. We both said we could eat. We'd had pancakes, hashbrowns, and bacon around ten thirty, and I wasn't quite sure what time it was now, but it seemed like it might be mid-afternoon.

Mrs. Reese called us in. She had made a triple-decker club for each of us. It was amazing, mouth-watering just looking at it, and let me tell you, it tasted even better than it looked. It was almost as good as my mom's.

I was stuffed, and I asked what time it was.

"No worries, but your jeans are ready, and we should probably shower and get ready, because it's just after four and there will probably be some last-minute things that need doing before guests start showing," Charlize said calmly. I was panicking inside, not being used to big events, as my mother got her smaller events catered.

CHAPTER TWENTY-THREE

I had an amazing shower, and Charlize showed me how to use the other showerheads to give myself a full body massage and wash. I dried off and got dressed and blow dried my hair. I wasn't sure if I was going to put it up or leave it down. Then I suddenly felt sad; I had done a pretty good job not thinking about Gabriel, but now I could smell him and even imagined that I could see him in the mirror.

He was so beautiful, with wonderful soft hair, gorgeous eyes, and an amazing body … the perfect guy for me. I remembered when we were together, alone at his house … him gently moving my hair and kissing my neck, my cheeks, my nose, and my lips. The kiss was juicy … sensuous. It was an amazing kiss that sent chills through my body and made me so wet. I remembered him touching my sides and feeling my breasts. If he had chosen to take me right then and there, I wouldn't have denied him. I was so taken by him at that moment. I remembered his hand on my body and me having to take a cold shower. Gabriel was a perfect gentleman. I wasn't sure if we were together or not. I knew nothing and just want this question answered so I could move forward.

"Hey, earth to Angel, snap out of it." Charlize was literally snapping her fingers. "You were thinking of him again, right?"

"Yeah! I just thought he was the one. I still hope I can see him, get some sort of explanation. Closure. If Gabriel doesn't want me in his life, he doesn't need to stay away; he just needs to come clean with everything. I also need to know that he is okay." I was a bit bummed.

"I'm sure there is an answer to all your questions, and the reason he isn't around most likely has nothing to do with you and him. I believe Gabriel truly loves you." Charlize came over to me and gave me a hug.

I was so happy that I'd met Charlize and her family, and I hoped our parents hit it off too. We went up to the kitchen to find out what needed to be done before the guests started arriving. There was no one to be seen in the house, but we heard noise outside in the backyard. Charlize and I went towards the deck and the doorbell rang, and then Mrs. Reese came into the house and almost ran into us. I think something was wrong, or she was waiting for something or someone, as she ran to the door. I had never seen her that way before. The door opened, and there were a guy standing there with platters with cold cuts and cheese.

"Thank goodness," she said.

The guy came back and forth a few times. I wasn't sure why there was so much food, as Charlize and I had already gotten trays. Mr. Reese came into the kitchen when the delivery guy left.

"Okay, ladies, the old trays are in the living room, salvage what you can. I think all the veggies are good. Everything needs to look good and be good; we don't want anyone to get food poisoning," Mrs. Reese exclaimed, frazzled. "I haven't lost my mind. The downstairs fridge stopped working, so I ordered more platters, because I didn't know how much was going to still be good. Now, I need you to sort through the platters, and the repair man should almost be done fixing the fridge. Please put the platters back downstairs when he leaves. It's too early to have the food out. Thanks. Other than that, I think everything is ready, oh, except for the punch.

Can you please make the punch after all the stuff is in the storage room and the ice is in the freezer?"

Caleb had come into the kitchen when Mrs. Reese was explaining what had happened and what needed to be done, and he offered to make the punch. Charlize and I went into the dining room, sorted through the trays, and smelled all the meat. A few trays of meat were suitable to serve, and all the veggies and the desserts were fine; we just had to throw away the ranch dip and get new ranch from the fridge. It may have been okay, but it was warm, and we didn't want to chance anyone getting sick. When we finished, Charlize went down to see if the repair man was done. He was already gone, and the fridge was cooling, so we put all the platters back down there. The fridge upstairs was now full too; there were trays on top of trays in both fridges.

We went back into the kitchen and Caleb was still there.

"Do you need help with the punch, Caleb?" Charlize asked.

"No, all done. I put it in the freezer downstairs. Is there enough room in the fridge downstairs for the punch?" Caleb asked.

"No not in the fridge, it's completely full, is it pretty strong?" Charlize smiled.

"Well, some might think so," Caleb answered.

"Then that will work. When the guests get here, we can add lots of ice and some more juice, and it should be good. I will go take it out of the freezer soon," Charlize replied.

"What are you working on now, Caleb?" I asked.

"I am working on making a Jell-O shooter mixture, just getting ready to pour the mixture into the molds." Caleb smiled. He made four ice trays of Jell-O shooters and stuck them in the kitchen freezer. I was looking forward to a few later.

"How long before those are ready?" I asked Caleb.

"They should be ready at around nine or ten, just in time to probably get the party started." Caleb seemed to be full of smiles tonight.

It was about six thirty. I think it was just before seven when the first guest arrived, a work friend of Mr. Reese's, I think. Charlize went downstairs and came back up with the punch. There was a table just inside the house as you are heading out towards the deck with the punch, pretzels, a few flavored popcorns, and chips.

People were starting to arrive in herds, and there were about thirty people when my parents arrived around eight. I was a little surprised that they'd come at all, as it was already late for them, and they'd said they would be here in the early evening. Early evening wasn't eight, was it? I went towards the door to introduce my parents to the Reese's.

"Hi, Mom and Dad, I thought maybe you weren't coming … it's a bit late for you to just arrive, isn't it?" I enquired, probably with a weird look on my face.

"Yeah, it is a little bit later than we had planned, but we ran into some acquaintances at dinner. So, we are here now. Is that okay?" she asked.

"Yes, of course, I'm sorry if I sounded ungrateful, just surprised, and happy that you are here." I gave my mom a big hug.

I introduced my parent to the Reese's, and the ladies went to the kitchen while the men got some drinks and headed outside. The Reese's' friends kept coming. Caleb's friends came, and a few of the girls I had seen Charlize hanging with. I was never really introduced to them, as I was always worrying about Gabriel and not paying attention to the goings on around me or others. Tom, Jim, Jenn, and Kelsie got there around eight thirty, as apparently, they had grabbed a bite to eat.

There were approximately seventy-five people at the party. All keys were handed in at the door and cabs were called for those who wanted to leave. The number one rule at the Reese's' house was no drinking and driving, and she even had a breathalyzer for those that argued about being able to drive. I was not sure how they had one, probably some sort of connection.

It was about nine thirty when Mrs. Reese asked if we could bring out all the trays, so we did. There was a lot of alcohol to be consumed and people had even brought their own, which was unnecessary as the Reese's had bought enough. I suggested that Charlize and I walk around with the trays, and my mom and Caleb volunteered too. Charlize led the gang with plates and napkins. I got about halfway through the people in the backyard and had to run and get a second meat and cheese platter. We finished our round in the back yard, and I made sure all the platters inside the patio door were refilled and took a short break. I grabbed myself a drink, as I had only had two drinks since seven. I was too busy helping to do any real drinking, which worked out for me as I shouldn't really be drinking anyways.

It was about eleven when I suggested we make another round with the snacks, but everyone seemed preoccupied. So, I just decided to go around with the meat and cheese platter in one hand and the veggie platter in the other and hope for the best. The girls must have seen me, so Jenn grabbed the veggie platter from me, and Kelsie went to the table and grabbed the fruit platter.

It took almost three trays of each, as everyone was drunk and hungry. By the time we got done our second round, it was getting close to that time, about twenty-five minutes till New Years. I grabbed the girls and brought them to the kitchen and hoped there were Jell-O shooters left. I opened the freezer door, and there was a tray left. Tom and Jim just happened to walk in to see how we were doing. We each had two Jell-O shots, and the girls and I grabbed the noisemakers and handed them out to everyone that wanted one.

There were five minutes till New Year's and Mr. Reese grabbed a microphone from somewhere and said loudly, "Attention everyone, can I have your attention, please? It's just about that time, and there should be noisemakers coming your way if you don't already have them. Countdown will commence at twenty seconds to midnight."

As the big moment approached, Mr. Reese picked the microphone back up, the music got turned down, and the countdown started: "Twenty, nineteen …" It went all the way down and everyone joined along, "Five, four, three, two, one, Happy New Year!"

Everyone hugged, some kissed, and then the music turned back up and everyone danced and partied on. Around half the people left at about twelve thirty, so there were about thirty people left: Charlize's friends, my friends from home, Caleb's friends, and a few of Mr. and Mrs. Reese's friends. My parents left after New Year's rolled in. I was surprised they'd stayed, as they were usually in bed early and up early.

I was a little hungry, as I hadn't really eaten much while serving everyone and making sure they were having fun. No one told me to help, but I was just like that; that's why parents always loved having me around. I went to the food table, and it was fairly empty. I checked the upstairs fridge, and it was empty, so I went downstairs. There were some trays left, so I brought them all upstairs and grabbed myself something to eat. There were others that needed to eat too. I thought there would be lots of food left over, considering that Mrs. Reese was worried about the fridge being down and had ordered extra platters. The night was still going though, so the food would probably be long gone by the time everyone left.

I tried to wave everyone down, but it was too hard, as the yard was too big, and everyone was spread out. So, I went to Mr. Reese and asked if I could use his microphone and said I wouldn't be too loud.

"Thanks." Mrs. Reese handed me the microphone and I clearly said, "Anyone who would like to join me for some Doctor Pepper shooters, please meet me at the kitchen island." I went into the kitchen, and Charlize had taken out everything needed for shooters. It was not a shooter that everyone liked, as it's a big drink to guzzle. All of us college kids were in the kitchen, and it was crowded.

"Does very one want a doctor pepper shooter?" I asked.

A few others said they didn't know what it was, and some said they just wanted to watch first. Charlize and I got the first set of shooter and beer mixture ready to go, and when we were ready, we started the countdown, and everyone was watching.

"Three, two, one, go!" I said. I watched everyone drop and guzzle. Caleb won the round, a few didn't finish it all, and all I could do was smile. "So, who's in for the second round? Only new people, the third round can be anyone that wants to go again."

Charlize and I took a count and came up with the same number and got the next set of shooters ready. This time Caleb was going to count down.

"Are we ready?" Caleb said and looked around the island. "Ready? Three, two, one, go!"

I dropped and guzzled and put down my mug. I was first, of course; I had never been beat before. I asked who was in for the next round. I think we all did a few more rounds, and then people started to drop out. I was done after four, as I didn't want to get out of hand. A few went to six rounds of Doctor Peppers and then a few people asked for some China white shooters. I wasn't sure what was in them, but I had had some before, and they were pretty good. Apparently, Charlize knew how to make them. I just made myself vodka slime, my favorite drink.

It was almost two, and everyone ate and made plans to get home. One of Charlize's friends hadn't had anything to drink since just after ringing in the New Year, so she was going to drive them home with one of Caleb's friends, her cousin, I think. So, that left one of Caleb's friends, but he was apparently staying over. Tom really didn't drink much throughout the night and ate his fair share, so he drove Jim and Jenn home, and Kelsie stayed over. My mom remembered to bring my car, so I could just bring Kelsie to my house, as she was invited to the New Year's Day dinner at my parent's house. Mr. and Mrs. Reese's friends lived down the street, so they just walked home.

The girls and I looked at each other and said simultaneously, "Bedtime." Morning comes fast, and our sleeping time was already half over. We made our way downstairs. Kelsie had gone and gotten her bag when the others left, so she was all prepared, leaving me to borrow Charlize's stuff once again. We all got ready for bed and called it a night. Kelsie and I pulled out the sofa bed in the downstairs living room, just outside Charlize's room. We said goodnight and were out.

I dreamt that Gabriel had showed up and that I'd gotten a great big hug and a passionate kiss. We hung out all night and he helped me and was by my side all night. I'm sure I slept with a big smile on my face.

CHAPTER TWENTY-FOUR

I woke up realizing that it had just been another Gabriel dream, in which Gabriel was lying beside me holding me and fondling my bum … oh, how I wished it were true. I had wished Gabriel and I would start the New Year together, but no surprise there. I still didn't know if he was okay, what had happened, and if we were still supposed to be "an item." I got up to go to the washroom. Kelsie was still sleeping, and when I got back, she was up.

"Did I wake you?" I asked.

"No, I have been in and out of sleep for a few hours, I think." Kelsie smiled. "I had a rough sleep; my stomach isn't very happy with me … maybe it's the mix of alcohol and/or too much eating last night too."

Just then, Charlize walked out of her room. "Hi guys, how was your sleep?"

"Both of us have upset stomachs. Maybe breakfast and coffee will help." We looked at Charlize's wide inquisitive eyes.

"Well, let's go upstairs, and I will get some coffee on and look into making breakfast."

As we walked up the stairs, we could smell the coffee and bacon. My stomach was growling, but come to think of it, I really hadn't each much last night, too busy taking care of things. I was just like that, a mother hen. I liked things to run smoothly, even if it was not my party … part of my OCD or control issues. The Reese's did so much for everyone, myself included, that the least I could do was help and make sure things ran as smoothly as possible.

Breakfast was great, just what the doctor ordered to help my stomach; I think the Doctor Pepper shooters hadn't gone down that well, and perhaps the lack of food hadn't help too much either. After breakfast, we just cleaned up and gathered all our stuff up, and by then it was almost noon and I needed to get back to my parents' house to get ready for the next party. Charlize offered to come early to help. I told her we would be good, but she was more than welcome. Kelsie and I thanked the Reese's for everything, and they said they would see us later for supper.

Kelsie and I got back to my parents, and it looked like they just finished cleaning up after having brunch. "Good morning, girls!" It sounded like my mother was standing right next to my ear and screaming in it.

"Hey, not so loud, some of us are still trying to get back to some sort of normalcy. This morning started off pretty rough, not so bad now, but I still have a lingering headache." I tried to give her a smile. "We're going to have showers and get ready for this afternoon. What do you need us to do?"

"You girls go upstairs and get cleaned up. You can have a nap if you want, as long as you are up and ready for three o'clock. I will need some help with a few things. The caterers should be here at around five, and we will be serving the food by six," my mom stated.

"Okay, not sure if we are going to nap, but might rest and take our time getting ready. We will make sure we are down here to help by three. Love you, Mom." I smiled, and this time it was a real smile, or at least it felt better than the previous one I gave her.

Kelsie and I went upstairs to my room, or my old room, I should say. She looked tired. I caught a glimpse of myself in the bathroom mirror as we were walking towards my room, and I looked rough too!

"So, Kelsie, are you down with a nap? I think we both look a little rough and could use an hour or so of sleep to get ready for tonight." I gave Kelsie a head nudge.

"Yeah, I think it definitely wouldn't hurt to get some additional rest; could be another rough one," Kelsie replied.

We jumped in my bed and went to sleep. I dreamt that the caterers came, and that Gabriel walked into my parent's house right after them and then he snuck up behind me and pulled my hair back away from my neck and kissed me. I turned around and smiled, and we kissed; it was a long passionate kiss. Then my eyes shot open. I knew I was dreaming, because if someone snuck up on me and kissed my neck, they would probably get a smack or a punch in their face, or worse, a kick in the nuts, depending on what the situation was. Also, Gabriel had no idea where my parents lived, so the probability of him finding the house would be very unlikely. I didn't know how I was going to deal with this situation—my grades were suffering and so was my mental state.

"Are you okay, Angel?" Kelsie asked, "I have been trying to get your attention for a few minutes now, and you were lost somewhere. Let me guess, you had a Gabriel dream again."

"Yeah! I don't know how to deal with all of this, it's been about four weeks or around there and no one's heard anything. Nothing makes sense; I just need to hear something, good or bad, at this point," I added. "You can jump in the shower first,"I said.

"Okay," she replied.

While Kelsie was in the shower, I chose a nice top and jeans to wear and went downstairs. She usually took a ten-minute shower or so. My mom was in the kitchen organizing the dessert platters; she got all the main food catered, but she made a few salads of her own and the dessert platters too. She had the best potato salad and pasta salad.

I heard the shower finish upstairs, so I headed upstairs to shower and get ready. I had a quick shower, and Kelsie and I were finished getting ready just before three, just on time.

We went back downstairs, and my mom was throwing her salads together. Kelsie and I had a little bit of both, just to make sure it was good, you know. Well, glad to report that they were just as good as they always were. Kelsie and I made a punch and put out the coolers with the beer, wine coolers, and other beverages in them.

The doorbell rang, and I looked at the clock. It was four thirty, a little too early for the caterers. I looked at my mom, who was in the kitchen still putting things together, and she gave me the *"Can you go get the door please?"* look. It was my uncle and his wife, but no children; they would probably show up a bit later. They were just a few years younger than I was, and you know teens, they walk to the beat of their own drum most of the time. Then others started to roll in slowly.

"Evangeline," my mother called. "Hun, can you go downstairs and grab the couple snack platters I have in the fridge? Thanks."

"Do you need my help, Angel?" Kelsie asked.

"Sure, I'm not sure what's down there, thanks," I said.

We did as we were asked and answered the door and got drinks for people as they arrived. Charlize and her parents got there just after five and Caleb came with them. I was a little surprised to see him, and I wished his best friend would have come with him as well.

I grabbed myself two Advil and a large glass of water, then grabbed a cooler. Might as well get the evening started; it might help me feel better, but I needed to go slow on the drinking. Jenn, Tom, and Jim arrived as the caterers were starting to set up; they seemed to always know when there was food being served. They looked well rested and ready to go. It probably wouldn't be as crazy of a party as last night was at the Reese's, but it would still be good.

The caterers were finished setting up all the food stations; they were lined up along the perimeter of the dining room on three tables. The first was the sushi station with platters on a bed of ice to keep everything cool. There were eight types of sushi rolls, including my two favorites, the dynamite roll, and the spider roll, which was giant and deep fried. Oh, I almost forgot the best thing, which was tempura shrimp. I loved the sauce and ate it with all my rolls. Most were to be kept chilled, but anything that was deep fried was kept under a warmer.

The second station had Chinese food. There were spring rolls, salt and pepper shrimp, beef and chicken satay, chicken fried rice, chicken balls, lemon soo gai (another chicken dish), and ginger beef.

The final table was a carving station with a roast beef and a maple ham under a heat lamp. The rest of the table had salads on it, with my mom's salad, a tossed salad, and a Caesar salad.

Everyone ate like pigs ... I know I did. I ate so much sushi, but I always overdid it when there was sushi; I couldn't help myself. After everyone finished, the caterers condensed what was left onto the large table and left. There was still quite a bit of food, on ice or on warming plates, covered up for later.

It was about eight now, and it was beautiful outside; the sky was clear and filled with stars and the moon was so bright. My mom came out and said, "Okay, who's up for a game of cards?" About half the people wanted to play, including my friends and me. My mom wrote all the names of those who wanted to play and put them into a hat. Jenn pulled the names out for my mom, and we created four teams. There ended up being six people per team, and it lasted for about an hour and a half. By the time we cleaned up and had a snack, it was just before ten. Most of the people had left right after the charades and some even during. There were about twenty people left, including my friends.

"Hey, how about we go to Hay City?" Kelsie said.

"Well, I will be DD if anyone wants to go. I did enough drinking over the holidays and my last drink was a few hours ago. I'm good to drive and wouldn't mind playing some pool," Tom stated.

"I'll drive too," I said. "I'm not into drinking tonight; still not feeling well after last night. I think the Doctor Pepper shooters did me in."

Tom and Jim took Caleb, and I took Kelsie, Jenn, and Charlize. We got to Hay City, but the twenty-five-minute drive seemed like it took an hour; guess I was even more tired than I thought. I probably shouldn't have driven, but the girls kept me occupied with their loud singing. The main parking lot was completely full, and the second parking lot across the street was almost full too. I guess there were many others with the same thought we had. Hay City was a pretty great cowboy bar. It was quite overcast, not snowing but it potentially could, and the moon was covered, making it even darker than usual. I got to the bar, and I noticed I had forgotten my bank card in the car. I told the girls I would be right back. Kelsie asked if I wanted her to come with me, and I told her I was good. They went inside, and I went back out to my car.

It was quite dark. I'd parked across the street near a big Ford 350 dually, and I think it was blue. I knew it was jacked up high with very large tires. I could hear a few guys somewhere in the first parking lot. They were very loud, and I tried to stay as far as possible from the loud group, trying to get to my car as fast as possible. After a few minutes, I heard a guy say, "Aren't you a pretty, young thing. I bet you have a nice tight ass and nice perky tits too."

I saw him coming around the corner from a pickup truck in front me and another guy was coming up behind me. "Yeah, I think you are right. Quite nice."

I was getting very scared. I turned left and tried to find the quickest route back to the bar or someone outside I could go to for help. Another guy came out from another truck. There were too many tall vehicles in a cowboy bar parking lot. These guys were not little guys; one was at least six feet tall and probably no less than 250 pounds. The others were almost as tall, but a bit slimmer. The big guy had a full bushy beard, and he was wearing a lumber jacket and a black cap.

He was still far enough away that I couldn't see distinct features. I took a quick glance at the guy coming from behind me, and he had dirty- blond hair. He wasn't wearing a hat, and he had longer shaggy hair, some sort of hair on his face, and was wearing a black jacket. My glance was quick, so that's all I caught. The guy that came out from the second truck, kind of cutting off my fastest route back to the bar, was very similar to the guy that was coming up behind me, but he had a clean-cut goatee.

I was scanning the next-quickest route away from these guys and back to the bar, and I heard some people screaming, having fun as they were coming out of the bar, I think. I screamed out for help, loud, and the guy from behind me ran up and grabbed my mouth with one hand and my waist with the other. He was trying very hard to find the bottom of my jacket, and then I felt him try to undo my pants for a moment, then lift my jacket to go up my shirt.

I could see the other guy coming at us. This wasn't good. I tried punching the guy that had me in the head, but he was tall and had me from behind. I twisted, tried to turn, tried to bend, tried to get out of the situation. I knew I was in trouble if I couldn't get out of this guy's grip, as the other one was coming. I stomped on his foot and kept trying to twist and turn and bend. It seemed like this was happening for a long time even though it must have only been seconds. I have always been able to weasel my way out of being held down when wrestling, I just had to keep my head straight, not panic, and get out of this situation too.

I got loose somewhat and felt his grip slipping on me. His hand came off my mouth a little, just enough for me to bite him, and I bit him so hard, like my life depended on it, because it probably did. I probably bit him so hard that I broke his finger, and I kept moving around, never stopping. I didn't want him to get a full grip on me. I was able to turn enough and swung my arm as hard as I could, hoping I would hit him enough to let go of me.

I hit him in the nuts. I wasn't dead on, but it was enough for him to let go for a split second, and then I slammed him with an upper cut. I was free, but the other guy was there, and he pushed me against a truck, trying to grab hold of me. I kept moving, never stopping, and screaming anytime my mouth wasn't covered. The guy that had me before grabbed a hold of my mouth again. Now I had two guys holding me, and one had my mouth covered and was using his body to hold my right shoulder, arm, and the side of my body to the truck, restraining me. The other guy had his arm across my chest and had his leg between mine, keeping me from being able to move around too much.

I felt the second guy unzip my jacket and start feeling me up over my clothes, then he untucked the rest of my shirt, and I felt his hands on my breasts. "So perky and firm, just how I thought they would be like on such a young thing like you."

I was struggling and trying to get loose. The guy went to my pants, let go of my chest, and I was kind of free. The other guy still had my one side, but some of me could still move. I was trying to get out of the situation; I wasn't ready to give up yet. The guy ripped my jeans open and was trying to get down my pants. The guy slammed me against the truck again, and I struggled and struggled, and the other guy lost his grip of my right side. I tried to grab the guy in front of me by the hair. I was hitting, punching, kicking, and doing whatever I could to try to get free of him too.

Finally, I was moving enough that his hands were out of my pants, but now the other guy wanted to get a feel too, I guess. He grabbed both sides of my jeans and pulled them down. They were just down to my thighs at this point, and if they got any lower or off, I could be in even more trouble. I decided to try and give it my all and not think of how much it might hurt if I broke something. These next seconds could be the last seconds of my life. This was do or die and maybe die anyways.

Okay, on the count of three, one ... two ... three, I counted in my head and then I unleashed every ounce of strength I possibly could. I moved my arms and legs as much as I could, closing my fists as I struggled. I tried to hit them, kick them, bite them, and scream all at the same time. The third guy was just about here, and there was no way I would be able to do anything then. I was surprised at this point that I hadn't been raped already or wasn't dead. I could feel the two guys losing their control or grip of me. Then the third guy came in like a tornado and pushed the other two off to the sides and rammed me into the truck, saying, "You're not going to get away from me. You're mine for the taking."

Then, one guy grabbed one arm and the other grabbed the other and the third guy that just slammed me into the truck told them to hold me tight, he was going in. The third guy grabbed my shirt and I heard it tear. At this point I knew I was done for, there was nothing else I could do, I had no more energy. Then, I felt the one guy get pulled off me and then the other and finally something happened, and I felt like I was free for a slip second.

All I remember after that was being slammed into the truck a few more times extremely hard, falling to the ground and hearing guys screaming and seeing blood everywhere. One of the guys had been slammed into the truck beside me, looked torn apart, and was bleeding profusely as he slid down beside me. I think I say an animal of some sort, big white teeth, and crazy blue eyes. Was Gabriel here, I think it was his eyes I had seen. And then I blacked out.

"Impossibilities X 3"
(Book two)

Printed in Canada